Thrilling praise for

TESS
GERRITSEN

'Tess Gerritsen is an automatic must-read in my house.
If you've never read Gerritsen, figure in the price
of electricity when you buy your first novel by her,
'cause, baby, you are going to be up all night. She is
better than Palmer, better than Cook… Yes, even
better than Crichton.'
—Stephen King

'[Gerritsen] has an imagination…so dark and
frightening that she makes Edgar Allan Poe…
seem like goody-two-shoes'
—*Chicago Tribune*

'Superior to Patricia Cornwell and
as good as James Patterson…'
—*Bookseller*

'It's scary just how good Tess Gerritsen is…'
—Harlan Coben

'Gerritsen has enough in the locker to seriously worry
Michael Connelly, Harlan Coben and even the great
Denis Lehane. Brilliant.'
—*Crimetime*

'Gerritsen is tops in her genre.'
—*USA TODAY*

'Tess Gerritsen writes some of the smartest, most
compelling thrillers around.'
—*Bookreporter*

TESS GERRITSEN

OMNIBUS

Keeper of the Bride

Whistleblower

HARLEQUIN®MIRA®

Published in Great Britain 2014.
Harlequin MIRA, an imprint of Harlequin (UK) Limited,
Eton House, 18-24 Paradise Road,
Richmond, Surrey, TW9 1SR.

Keeper of the Bride © 1996 Terry Gerritsen
Whistleblower © 1992 Terry Gerritsen

ISBN: 978-1-848-45279-4

60-1013

Harlequin (UK) Limited's policy is to use papers that are natural, renewable and recyclable products and made from wood grown in sustainable forests. The logging and manufacturing processes conform to the legal environmental regulations of the country of origin.

Printed and bound by
CPI Group (UK) Ltd, Croydon, CR0 4YY

Keeper
of the Bride

Chapter One

The wedding was off. Cancelled. Canned. Kaput.

Nina Cormier sat staring at herself in the church dressing room mirror and wondered why she couldn't seem to cry. She knew the pain was there, deep and terrible beneath the numbness, but she didn't feel it. Not yet. She could only sit dry-eyed, staring at her reflection. The picture-perfect image of a bride. Her veil floated in gossamer wisps about her face. The bodice of her ivory satin dress, embroidered with seed pearls, hung fetchingly off-shoulder. Her long black hair was gathered into a soft chignon. Everyone who'd seen her that morning in the dressing room—her mother, her sister, Wendy, her stepmother, Daniella—had declared her a beautiful bride.

And she *would* have been. Had the groom bothered to show up.

He didn't even have the courage to break the news to her in person. After six months of planning and dreaming, she'd received his note just twenty minutes before the ceremony. Via the best man, no less.

Nina,
I need time to think about this. I'm sorry, I really am. I'm leaving town for a few days. I'll call you.
Robert

She forced herself to read the note again.

I need time.... I need time....

How much time does a man need? she wondered.

A year ago, she'd moved in with Dr. Robert Bledsoe. It's the only way to know if we're compatible, he'd told her. Marriage was such a major commitment, a permanent commitment, and he didn't want to make a mistake. At 41, Robert had known his share of disastrous relationships. He was determined not to make any more mistakes. He wanted to be sure that Nina was the one he'd been waiting for all his life.

She'd been certain Robert was the man *she'd* been waiting for. So certain that, on the very day he'd suggested they live together, she'd gone straight home and packed her bags....

"Nina? Nina, open the door!" It was her sister, Wendy, rattling the knob. "Please let me in."

Nina dropped her head in her hands. "I don't want to see anyone right now."

"You need to be with someone."

"I just want to be alone."

"Look, the guests have all gone home. The church is empty. It's just me out here."

"I don't want to talk to anyone. Just go home, will you? Please, just go."

There was a long silence outside the door. Then Wendy said, "If I leave now, how're you going to get home? You'll need a ride."

"Then I'll call a cab. Or Reverend Sullivan can drive me. I need some time to think."

"You're sure you don't want to talk?"

"I'm sure. I'll call you later, okay?"

"If that's what you really want." Wendy paused, then

added, with a note of venom that penetrated even through the oak door, "Robert's a jerk, you know. I might as well tell you. I've always thought he was."

Nina didn't answer. She sat at the dressing table, her head in her hands, wanting to cry, but unable to squeeze out a single tear. She heard Wendy's footsteps fade away, then heard only the silence of the empty church. Still no tears would come. She couldn't think about Robert right now. Instead, her mind seemed to focus stubbornly on the practical aspects of a cancelled wedding. The catered reception and all that uneaten food. The gifts she had to return. The nonrefundable airline tickets to St. John Island. Maybe she should go on that honeymoon anyway and forget Dr. Robert Bledsoe. She'd go by herself, just her and her bikini. Out of this whole heartbreaking affair, at least she'd come out with a tan.

Slowly she raised her head and once again looked at her reflection in the mirror. Not such a beautiful bride after all, she thought. Her lipstick was smeared and her chignon was coming apart. She was turning into a wreck.

With sudden rage she reached up and yanked off the veil. Hairpins flew in every direction, releasing a rebellious tumble of black hair. To hell with the veil; she tossed it in the trash can. She snatched up her bouquet of white lilies and pink sweetheart roses and slam-dunked it into the trash can as well. That felt good. Her anger was like some new and potent fuel flooding her veins. It propelled her to her feet.

She walked out of the church dressing room, the train of her gown dragging behind her, and entered the nave.

The pews were deserted. Garlands of white carnations draped the aisles, and the altar was adorned with airy sprays of pink roses and baby's breath. The stage had been beautifully set for a wedding that would never take place. But the lovely results of the florist's hard work was scarcely noticed by Nina as she strode past the altar and started up the aisle. Her attention was focused straight ahead on the front door. On escape. Even the concerned voice of Reverend Sullivan calling to her didn't slow her down. She walked past all the floral reminders of the day's fiasco and pushed through the double doors.

There, on the church steps, she halted. The July sunshine glared in her eyes, and she was suddenly, painfully aware of how conspicuous she must be, a lone woman in a wedding gown, trying to wave down a taxi. Only then, as she stood trapped in the brightness of afternoon, did she feel the first sting of tears.

Oh, no. Lord, no. She was going to break down and cry right here on the steps. In full view of every damn car driving past on Forest Avenue.

"Nina? Nina, dear."

She turned. Reverend Sullivan was standing on the step above her, a look of worry on his kind face.

"Is there anything I can do? Anything at all?" he asked. "If you'd like, we could go inside and talk."

Miserably she shook her head. "I want to get away from here. Please, I just want to get away."

"Of course. Of course." Gently, he took her arm. "I'll drive you home."

Reverend Sullivan led her down the steps and around the side of the building, to the staff parking lot. She gathered up her train, which by now was soiled from all that dragging, and climbed into his car. There she sat with all the satin piled high on her lap.

Reverend Sullivan slid in behind the wheel. The heat

was stifling inside the car, but he didn't start the engine. Instead they sat for a moment in awkward silence.

"I know it's hard to understand what possible purpose the Lord may have for all this," he said quietly. "But surely there's a reason, Nina. It may not be apparent to you at the moment. In fact, it may seem to you that the Lord has turned His back."

"Robert's the one who turned his back," she said. Sniffling, she snatched up a clean corner of her train and wiped her face. "Turned his back and ran like hell."

"Ambivalence is common for bridegrooms. I'm sure Dr. Bledsoe felt this was a big step for him—"

"A big step for *him?* I suppose marriage is just a stroll in the park for me?"

"No, no, you misunderstand me."

"Oh, please." She gave a muffled sob. "Just take me home."

Shaking his head, he put the key in the ignition. "I only wanted to explain to you, dear, in my own clumsy way, that this isn't the end of the world. It's the nature of life. Fate is always throwing surprises at us, Nina. Crises we never expect. Things that seem to pop right out of the blue."

A deafening boom suddenly shook the church building. The explosion shattered the stained glass windows, and a hail of multicolored glass shards flew across the parking lot. Torn hymn books and fragments of church pews tumbled onto the blacktop.

As the white smoke slowly cleared, Nina saw a dusting of flower petals drift gently down from the sky and settle on the windshield right in front of Reverend Sullivan's shocked eyes.

"Right out of the blue," she murmured. "You couldn't have said it better."

"YOU TWO, WITHOUT a doubt, are the biggest screwups of the year."

Portland police detective Sam Navarro, sitting directly across the table from the obviously upset Norm Liddell, didn't bat an eyelash. There were five of them sitting in the station conference room, and Sam wasn't about to give this prima donna D.A. the satisfaction of watching him flinch in public. Nor was Sam going to refute the charges, because they *had* screwed up. He and Gillis had screwed up big time, and now a cop was dead. An idiot cop, but a cop all the same. One of their own.

"In our defense," spoke up Sam's partner, Gordon Gillis, "we never gave Marty Pickett permission to approach the site. We had no idea he'd crossed the police line—"

"You were in charge of the bomb scene," said Liddell. "That makes you responsible."

"Now, wait a minute," said Gillis. "Officer Pickett has to bear some of the blame."

"Pickett was just a rookie."

"He should've been following procedure. If he'd—"

"Shut up, Gillis," said Sam.

Gillis looked at his partner. "Sam, I'm only trying to defend our position."

"Won't do us a damn bit of good. Since we're obviously the designated fall guys." Sam leaned back in his chair and eyed Liddell across the conference table. "What do you want, Mr. D.A.? A public flogging? Our resignations?"

"No one's asking for your resignations," cut in Chief Abe Coopersmith. "And this discussion is getting us nowhere."

"*Some* disciplinary action is called for," said Liddell. "We have a dead police officer—"

"Don't you think I know that?" snapped Coopersmith.

"*I'm* the one who had to answer to the widow. Not to mention all those bloodsucking reporters. Don't give me this *us* and *we* crap, Mr. D.A. It was one of *ours* who fell. A cop. *Not* a lawyer."

Sam looked in surprise at his chief. This was a new experience, having Coopersmith on his side. The Abe Coopersmith he knew was a man of few words, few of them complimentary. It was because Liddell was rubbing them all the wrong way. When under fire, cops always stuck together.

"Let's get back to the business at hand, okay?" said Coopersmith. "We have a bomber in town. And our first fatality. What do we know so far?" He looked at Sam, who was head of the newly re-formed Bomb Task Force. "Navarro?"

"Not a hell of a lot," admitted Sam. He opened a file folder and took out a sheaf of papers. He distributed copies to the other four men around the table—Liddell, Chief Coopersmith, Gillis, and Ernie Takeda, the explosives expert from the Maine State Crime Lab. "The first blast occurred around 2:15 a.m. The second blast around 2:30 a.m. It was the second one that pretty much levelled the R. S. Hancock warehouse. It also caused minor damage to two adjoining buildings. The night watchman was the one who found the first device. He noticed signs of breaking and entering, so he searched the building. The bomb was left on a desk in one of the offices. He put in the call at 1:30 a.m. Gillis got there around 1:50, I was there at 2:00 a.m. We had the blast area cordoned off and the top-vent container truck had just arrived when the first one went off. Then, fifteen minutes later—before we could search the building—the second device exploded. Killing Officer Pickett." Sam glanced at Liddell, but this time the

D.A. chose to keep his mouth shut. "The dynamite was Dupont label."

There was a brief silence in the room. Then Coopersmith said, "Not the same Dupont lot number as those two bombs last year?"

"It's very likely," said Sam. "Since that missing lot number's the only reported large dynamite theft we've had up here in years."

"But the Spectre bombings were solved a year ago," said Liddell. "And we know Vincent Spectre's dead. So who's making *these* bombs?"

"We may be dealing with a Spectre apprentice. Someone who not only picked up the master's technique, but also has access to the master's dynamite supply. Which, I point out, we never located."

"You haven't confirmed the dynamite's from the same stolen lot number," said Liddell. "Maybe this has no connection at all with the Spectre bombings."

"I'm afraid we have other evidence," said Sam. "And you're not going to like it." He glanced at Ernie Takeda. "Go ahead, Ernie."

Takeda, never comfortable with public speaking, kept his gaze focused on the lab report in front of him. "Based on materials we gathered at the site," he said, "we can make a preliminary guess as to the makeup of the device. We believe the electrical action fuse was set off by an electronic delay circuit. This in turn ignited the dynamite via Prima detonating cord. The sticks were bundled together with two-inch-wide green electrical tape." Takeda cleared his throat and finally looked up. "It's the identical delay circuit that the late Vincent Spectre used in his bombings last year."

Liddell looked at Sam. "The same circuitry, the same dynamite lot? What the hell's going on?"

"Obviously," said Gillis, "Vincent Spectre passed on a few of his skills before he died. Now we've got a second generation bomber on our hands."

"What we still have to piece together," said Sam, "is the psychological profile of this newcomer. Spectre's bombings were coldbloodedly financial. He was hired to do the jobs and he did them, *bam, bam, bam.* Efficient. Effective. This new bomber has to set a pattern."

"What you're saying," said Liddell, "is that you expect him to hit again."

Sam nodded wearily. "Unfortunately, that's exactly what I'm saying."

There was a knock on the door. A patrolwoman stuck her head into the conference room. "Excuse me, but there's a call for Navarro and Gillis."

"I'll take it," said Gillis. He rose heavily to his feet and went to the conference wall phone.

Liddell was still focused on Sam. "So this is all that Portland's finest can come up with? We wait for *another* bombing so that we can establish a *pattern?* And then maybe, just *maybe,* we'll have an idea of what the hell we're doing?"

"A bombing, Mr. Liddell," said Sam calmly, "is an act of cowardice. It's violence in the absence of the perpetrator. I repeat the word—*absence.* We have no ID, no fingerprints, no witnesses to the planting, no—"

"Chief," cut in Gillis. He hung up the phone. "They've just reported another one."

"What?" said Coopersmith.

Sam had already shot to his feet and was moving for the door.

"What was it this time?" called Liddell. "Another ware-house?"

"No," said Gillis. "A church."

THE COPS ALREADY had the area cordoned off by the time Sam and Gillis arrived at the Good Shepherd Church. A crowd was gathered up and down the street. Three patrol cars, two fire trucks and an ambulance were parked hap-hazardly along Forest Avenue. The bomb disposal truck and its boiler-shaped carrier in the flatbed stood idly near the church's front entrance—or what was left of the front entrance. The door had been blown clear off its hinges and had come to rest at the bottom of the front steps. Broken glass was everywhere. The wind scattered torn pages of hymn books like dead leaves along the sidewalk. Gillis swore. "This was a big one."

As they approached the police line, the officer in charge turned to them with a look of relief. "Navarro! Glad you could make it to the party."

"Any casualties?" asked Sam.

"None, as far as we know. The church was unoccupied at the time. Pure luck. There was a wedding scheduled for two, but it was cancelled at the last minute."

"Whose wedding?"

"Some doctor's. The bride's sitting over there in the patrol car. She and the minister witnessed the blast from the parking lot."

"I'll talk to her later," said Sam. "Don't let her leave. Or the minister, either. I'm going to check the building for a second device."

"Better you than me."

Sam donned body armor, made of overlapping steel plates encased in nylon. He also carried a protective mask, to be worn in case a second bomb was identified. A bomb tech, similarly garbed, stood by the front door awaiting orders to enter the building. Gillis would wait outside near the truck; his role this time around was to fetch tools and get the bomb carrier ready.

"Okay," Sam said to the technician. "Let's go."

They stepped through the gaping front entrance.

The first thing Sam noticed was the smell—strong and faintly sweet. Dynamite, he thought. He recognized the odor of its aftermath. The force of the blast had caused the pews at the rear to topple backward. At the front, near the altar, the pews had been reduced to splinters. All the stained glass panels were broken, and where the windows faced south, hazy sunlight shone in through the empty frames.

Without a word between them, Sam and the tech automatically split up and moved along opposite sides of the nave. The site would be more thoroughly searched later; this time around, their focus was only on locating any second bombs. The death of Marty Pickett still weighed heavily on Sam's conscience, and he wasn't about to let any other officers enter this building until he had cleared it.

Moving in parallel, the two men paced the nave, their eyes alert for anything resembling an explosive device. All the debris made it a slow search. As they moved forward, the damage visibly worsened, and the odor of exploded dynamite grew stronger. Getting closer, he thought. The bomb was planted somewhere around here....

In front of the altar, at a spot where the first row of pews would have stood, they found the crater. It was about three feet across and shallow; the blast had ripped through the carpet and pad, but had barely chipped the concrete slab below. A shallow crater was characteristic of a low-velocity blast—again, compatible with dynamite.

They would take a closer look at it later. They continued their search. They finished with the nave and progressed to the hallways, the dressing rooms, the restrooms. No bombs. They went into the annex and surveyed the church offices, the meeting rooms, the Sunday school classroom. No bombs. They exited through a rear door and searched the entire outside wall. No bombs.

Satisfied at last, Sam returned to the police line, where Gillis was waiting. There he took off the body armor. "Building's clean," Sam said. "We got the searchers assembled?"

Gillis gestured to the six men waiting near the bomb carrier truck. There were two patrolmen and four crime lab techs, each one clutching empty evidence bags. "They're just waiting for the word."

"Let's get the photographer in there first, then send the team in. The crater's up front, around the first row of pews on the right."

"Dynamite?"

Sam nodded. "If I can trust my nose." He turned and eyed the crowd of gawkers. "I'm going to talk to the witnesses. Where's the minister?"

"They just took him off to the ER. Chest pains. All that stress."

Sam gave an exasperated sigh. "Did anyone talk to him?"

"Patrolman did. We have his statement."

"Okay," said Sam. "I guess that leaves me with the bride."

"She's still waiting in the patrol car. Her name's Nina Cormier."

"Cormier. Gotcha." Sam ducked under the yellow police line and worked his way through the gathering of onlookers. Scanning the official vehicles, he spotted a silhouette in the front passenger seat of one of the cars. The woman didn't move as he approached; she was staring straight ahead like some wedding store mannequin. He leaned forward and tapped on the window.

The woman turned. Wide dark eyes stared at him through the glass. Despite the smudged mascara, the softly rounded feminine face was undeniably pretty. Sam motioned to her to roll down the window. She complied.

"Miss Cormier? I'm Detective Sam Navarro, Portland police."

"I want to go home," she said. "I've talked to so many cops already. Please, can't I just go home?"

"First I have to ask you a few questions."

"A few?"

"All right," he admitted. "It's more like a lot of questions."

She gave a sigh. Only then did he see the weariness in her face. "If I answer all your questions, Detective," she said, "will you let me go home?"

"I promise."

"Do you keep your promises?"

He nodded soberly. "Always."

She looked down at her hands, clasped in her lap. "Right," she muttered. "Men and their promises."

"Excuse me?"

"Oh, never mind."

He circled around the car, opened the door, and slid in behind the wheel. The woman next to him said nothing; she just sat there in resigned silence. She seemed almost swallowed up by those frothy layers of white satin.

Her hairdo was coming undone and silky strands of black hair hung loose about her shoulders. Not at all the happy picture of a bride, he thought. She seemed stunned, and very much alone.

Where the hell was the groom?

Stifling an instinctive rush of sympathy, he reached for his notebook and flipped it open to a blank page. "Can I have your full name and address?"

The answer came out in a bare whisper. "Nina Margaret Cormier, 318 Ocean View Drive."

He wrote it down. Then he looked at her. She was still staring straight down at her lap. Not at him. "Okay, Miss Cormier," he said. "Why don't you tell me exactly what happened?"

SHE WANTED TO go home. She had been sitting in this patrol car for an hour and a half now, had talked to three different cops, had answered all their questions. Her wedding was a shambles, she'd barely escaped with her life, and those people out there on the street kept staring at her as though she were some sort of sideshow freak.

And this man, this cop with all the warmth of a codfish, expected her to go through it again?

"Miss Cormier," he sighed. "The sooner we get this over with, the sooner you can leave. What, exactly, happened?"

"It blew up," she said. "Can I go home?"

"What do you mean by blew up?"

"There was a loud boom. Lots of smoke and broken windows. I'd say it was your typical exploding building."

"You mentioned smoke. What color was the smoke?"

"What?"

"Was it black? White?"

"Does it matter?"

"Just answer the question, please."

She gave an exasperated sigh. "It was white, I think."

"You think?"

"All right. I'm sure." She turned to look at him. For the first time she really focused on his face. If he'd been smiling, if there'd been even a trace of warmth, it would have been a pleasant enough face to look at. He was in his late thirties. He had dark brown hair that was about two weeks overdue for a trim. His face was thin, his teeth were perfect, and his deep set green eyes had the penetrating gaze one expected of a romantic lead movie cop. Only this was no movie cop. This was an honest-to-goodness cop with a badge, and he wasn't in the least bit charming. He was studying her with a completely detached air, as though sizing up her reliability as a witness.

She gazed back at him, thinking, *Here I am, the rejected bride. He's probably wondering what's wrong with me. What terrible flaws I possess that led to my being stood up at the altar.*

She buried her fists in the white satin mounded on her lap. "I'm sure the smoke was white," she said tightly. "For whatever difference that makes."

"It makes a difference. It indicates a relative absence of carbon."

"Oh. I see." Whatever that told him.

"Were there any flames?"

"No. No flames."

"Did you smell anything?"

"You mean like gas?"

"Anything at all?"

She frowned. "Not that I remember. But I was outside the building."

"Where, exactly?"

"Reverend Sullivan and I were sitting in his car. In the parking lot around the side. So I wouldn't have smelled the gas. Anyway, natural gas is odorless. Isn't it?"

"It can be difficult to detect."

"So it doesn't mean anything. That I didn't smell it."

"Did you see anyone near the building prior to the explosion?"

"There was Reverend Sullivan. And some of my family. But they all left earlier."

"What about strangers? Anyone you don't know?"

"No one was inside when it happened."

"I'm referring to the time *prior* to the explosion, Miss Cormier."

"Prior?"

"Did you see anyone who shouldn't have been there?"

She stared at him. He gazed back at her, green eyes absolutely steady. "You mean—are you thinking—"

He didn't say anything.

"It wasn't a gas leak?" she said softly.

"No," he said. "It was a bomb."

She sank back, her breath escaping in a single shocked rush. Not an accident, she thought. Not an accident at all....

"Miss Cormier?"

Wordlessly she looked at him. Something about the way he was watching her, that flat, emotionless gaze of his, made her frightened.

"I'm sorry to have to ask you this next question," he said. "But you understand, it's something I have to pursue."

She swallowed. "What...what question?"

"Do you know of anyone who might want you dead?"

Chapter Two

"This is crazy," she said. "This is absolutely nuts."

"I have to explore the possibility."

"*What* possibility? That the bomb was meant for *me?*"

"Your wedding was scheduled for two o'clock. The bomb went off at 2:40. It exploded near the front row of pews. Near the altar. There's no doubt in my mind, judging by the obvious force of the blast, that you and your entire wedding party would have been killed. Or, at the very least, seriously maimed. This *is* a bomb we're talking about, Miss Cormier. Not a gas leak. Not an accident. A bomb. It was meant to kill someone. What I have to find out is, who was the target?"

She didn't answer. The possibilities were too horrible to even contemplate.

"Who was in your wedding party?" he asked.

She swallowed. "There was…there was…"

"You and Reverend Sullivan. Who else?"

"Robert—my fiancé. And my sister, Wendy. And Jeremy Wall, the best man…."

"Anyone else?"

"My father was going to give me away. And there was a flower girl and a ring bearer…"

"I'm only interested in the adults. Let's start with you."

Numbly she shook her head. "It—it wasn't me. It couldn't be me."

"Why couldn't it?"

"It's impossible."

"How can you be sure?"

"Because no one would want me dead!"

Her sharp cry seemed to take him by surprise. For a moment he was silent. Outside, on the street, a uniformed cop turned and glanced at them. Sam responded with an *everything's fine* wave of the hand, and the cop turned away again.

Nina sat clutching the rumpled hem of her gown. This man was horrid. Sam Spade without a trace of human warmth. Though it was getting hot in the car, she found herself shivering, chilled by the lack of obvious emotion displayed by the man sitting beside her.

"Can we explore this a little more?" he said.

She said nothing.

"Do you have any ex-boyfriends, Miss Cormier? Anyone who might be unhappy about your marriage?"

"No," she whispered.

"No ex-boyfriends at all?"

"Not—not in the last year."

"Is that how long you've been with your fiancé? A year?"

"Yes."

"His full name and address, please."

"Robert David Bledsoe, M.D., 318 Ocean View Drive."

"Same address?"

"We've been living together."

"Why was the wedding cancelled?"

"You'd have to ask Robert."

"So it was his decision? To call off the wedding?"

"As the expression goes, he left me at the altar."

"Do you know why?"

She gave a bitter laugh. "I've come to the earth-shattering conclusion, Detective, that the minds of men are a complete mystery to me."

"He gave you no warning at all?"

"It was just as unexpected as that..." She swallowed. "As that bomb. If that's what it was."

"What time was the wedding called off?"

"About one-thirty. I'd already arrived at the church, wedding gown and all. Then Jeremy—Robert's best man—showed up with the note. Robert didn't even have the nerve to tell me himself." She shook her head in disgust.

"What did the note say?"

"That he needed more time. And he was leaving town for a while. That's all."

"Is it possible Robert had any reason to—"

"No, it's *not* possible!" She looked him straight in the eye. "You're asking if Robert had something to do with it. Aren't you?"

"I keep an open mind, Miss Cormier."

"Robert's not capable of violence. For God's sake, he's a doctor!"

"All right. For the moment, we'll let that go. Let's look at other possibilities. I take it you're employed?"

"I'm a nurse at Maine Medical Center."

"Which department?"

"Emergency room."

"Any problems at work? Any conflicts with the rest of the staff?"

"No. We get along fine."

"Any threats? From your patients, for instance?"

She made a sound of exasperation. "Detective, wouldn't I know if I had enemies?"

"Not necessarily."

"You're trying your damn best to make me feel paranoid."

"I'm asking you to step back from yourself. Examine your personal life. Think of all the people who might not like you."

Nina sank back in the seat. *All the people who might not like me.* She thought of her family. Her older sister, Wendy, with whom she'd never been close. Her mother, Lydia, married to her wealthy snob of a husband. Her father, George, now on his fourth wife, a blond trophy bride who considered her husband's offspring a nuisance. It was one big, dysfunctional family, but there were certainly no murderers among them.

She shook her head. "No one, Detective. There's no one."

After a moment he sighed and closed his notebook. "All right, Miss Cormier. I guess that's all for now."

"For now?"

"I'll probably have other questions. After I talk to the rest of the wedding party." He opened the car door, got out, and pushed the door shut. Through the open window he said, "If you think of anything, anything at all, give me a call." He scribbled in his notebook and handed her the torn page with his name, Detective Samuel I. Navarro, and a phone number. "It's my direct line," he said. "I can also be reached twenty-four hours a day through the police switchboard."

"Then...I can go home now?"

"Yes." He started to walk away.

"Detective Navarro?"

He turned back to her. She had not realized how tall he was. Now, seeing his lean frame at its full height, she wondered how he'd ever fit in the seat beside her. "Is there something else, Miss Cormier?" he asked.

"You said I could leave."

"That's right."

"I don't have a ride." She nodded toward the bombed-out church. "Or a phone either. Do you think you could give my mother a call? To come get me?"

"Your mother?" He glanced around, obviously anxious to palm off this latest annoyance. Finally, with a look of resignation, he circled around to her side of the car and opened the door. "Come on. We can go in my car. I'll drive you."

"Look, I was only asking you to make a call."

"It's no trouble." He extended his hand to help her out. "I'd have to go by your mother's house anyway."

"My mother's house? Why?"

"She was at the wedding. I'll need to talk to her, too. Might as well kill two birds with one stone."

What a gallant way to put it, she thought.

He was still reaching out to her. She ignored his outstretched hand. It was a struggle getting out of the car, since her train had wrapped itself around her legs, and she had to kick herself free of the hem. By the time she'd finally extricated herself from the car, he was regarding her with a look of amusement. She snatched up her train and whisked past him in a noisy rustle of satin.

"Uh, Miss Cormier?"

"What?" she snapped over her shoulder.

"My car's in the other direction."

She halted, her cheeks flushing. Mr. Detective was actually smiling now, a full-blown ate-the-canary grin.

"It's the blue Taurus," he pointed out. "The door's unlocked. I'll be right with you." He turned and headed away, toward the gathering of cops.

Nina flounced over to the blue Taurus. There she peered in disgust through the window. She was supposed to ride in *this* car? With that mess? She opened the door. A paper cup tumbled out. On the passenger floor was a crumpled McDonald's bag, more coffee cups, and a two-day-old *Portland Press Herald.* The back seat was buried under more newspapers, file folders, a briefcase, a suit jacket, and—of all things—a baseball mitt.

She scooped up the debris from the passenger side, tossed it into the back, and climbed in. She only hoped the seat was clean.

Detective Cold Fish was walking toward the car. He looked hot and harassed. His shirtsleeves were rolled up now, his tie yanked loose. Even as he tried to leave the scene, cops were pulling him aside to ask questions.

At last he slid in behind the wheel and slammed the door. "Okay, where does your mother live?" he asked.

"Cape Elizabeth. Look, I can see you're busy—"

"My partner's holding the fort. I'll drop you off, talk to your mother, and swing by the hospital to see Reverend Sullivan."

"Great. That way you can kill *three* birds with one stone."

"I do believe in efficiency."

They drove in silence. She saw no point in trying to dredge up polite talk. Politeness would go right over this man's head. Instead, she looked out the window and thought morosely about the wedding reception and all those finger sandwiches waiting for guests who'd never arrive. She'd have to call and ask for the food to be delivered to a soup kitchen before it all spoiled. And then there were the gifts, dozens of them, piled up at home. Correction—*Robert's* home. It had never really been *her* home. She had only been living there, a tenant. It had been her idea to pay half the mortgage. Robert used to point out how much he respected her independence, her insistence on a separate identity. In any good relationship, he'd say, privilege as well as responsibility was a fifty-fifty split. That's how they'd worked it from the start. First he'd paid for a date, then she had. In fact, she'd insisted, to show him that she was her own woman.

Now it all seemed so stupid.

I was never my own woman, she thought. I was always dreaming, longing for the day I'd be Mrs. Robert Bledsoe. It's what her family had hoped for, what her mother had expected of her: to marry well. They'd never understood Nina's going to nursing school, except as a way to meet a potential mate. A doctor. She'd met one, all right.

And all it's gotten me is a bunch of gifts I have to return, a wedding gown I can't return, and a day I'll never, ever live down.

It was the humiliation that shook her the most. Not the fact that Robert had walked out. Not even the fact that she could have died in the wreckage of that church. The explosion itself seemed unreal to her, as remote as some TV melodramas. As remote as this man sitting beside her.

"You're handling this very well," he said.

Startled that Detective Cold Fish had spoken, she looked at him. "Excuse me?"

"You're taking this very calmly. Calmer than most."

"I don't know how else to take it."

"After a bombing, hysteria would not be out of line."

"I'm an ER nurse, Detective. I don't do hysteria."

"Still, this had to be a shock for you. There could well be an emotional aftermath."

"You're saying this is the calm before the storm?"

"Something like that." He glanced at her, his gaze meeting hers. Just as quickly, he looked back at the road and the connection was gone. "Why wasn't your family with you at the church?"

"I sent them all home."

"I would think you'd want them around for support, at least."

She looked out the window. "My family's not exactly the supportive type. And I guess I just...needed to be alone. When an animal gets hurt, Detective, it goes off by itself to lick its wounds. That's what I needed to do...." She blinked away an unexpected film of tears and fell silent.

"I know you don't feel much like talking right now," he said. "But maybe you can answer this question for me. Can you think of anyone else who might've been a target? Reverend Sullivan, for instance?"

She shook her head. "He's the last person anyone would hurt."

"It was his church building. He would've been near the blast center."

"Reverend Sullivan's the sweetest man in the world! Every winter, he's handing out blankets on the street. Or scrounging up beds at the shelter. In the ER, when we see patients who have no home to go to, he's the one we call."

"I'm not questioning his character. I'm just asking about enemies."

"He has no enemies," she said flatly.

"What about the rest of the wedding party? Could any of them have been targets?"

"I can't imagine—"

"The best man, Jeremy Wall. Tell me about him."

"Jeremy? There's not much to say. He went to medical school with Robert. He's a doctor at Maine Med. A radiologist."

"Married?"

"Single. A confirmed bachelor."

"What about your sister, Wendy? She was your maid of honor?"

"Matron of honor. She's a happy homemaker."

"Any enemies?"

"Not unless there's someone out there who resents perfection."

"Meaning?"

"Let's just say she's the dream daughter every parent hopes for."

"As opposed to you?"

Nina gave a shrug. "How'd you guess?"

"All right, so that leaves one major player. The one who, coincidentally, decided not to show up at all."

Nina stared straight ahead. *What can I tell him about Robert,* she thought, *when I myself am completely in the dark?*

To her relief, he didn't pursue that line of questioning. Perhaps he'd realized how far he'd pushed her. How close to the emotional edge she was already tottering. As they drove the winding road into Cape Elizabeth, she felt her calm facade at last begin to crumble. Hadn't he warned her about it? The emotional aftermath. The pain creeping through the numbness. She had held together well, had weathered two devastating shocks with little more than a few spilt tears. Now her hands were beginning to shake, and she found that every breath she took was a struggle not to sob.

When at last they pulled up in front of her mother's house, Nina was barely holding herself together. She didn't wait for Sam to circle around and open her door. She pushed it open herself and scrambled out in a sloppy tangle of wedding gown. By the time he walked up the front steps, she was already leaning desperately on the doorbell, silently begging her mother to let her in before she fell apart completely.

The door swung open. Lydia, still elegantly coiffed and gowned, stood staring at her dishevelled daughter. "Nina? Oh, my poor Nina." She opened her arms.

Automatically Nina fell into her mother's embrace. So hungry was she for a hug, she didn't immediately register the fact that Lydia had drawn back to avoid wrinkling her green silk dress. But she did register her mother's first question.

"Have you heard from Robert yet?"

Nina stiffened. *Oh please,* she thought. *Please don't do this to me.*

"I'm sure this can all be worked out," said Lydia. "If you'd just sit down with Robert and have an honest discussion about what's bothering him—"

Nina pulled away. "I'm not going to sit down with Robert," she said. "And as for an honest discussion, I'm not sure we ever had one."

"Now, darling, it's natural to be angry—"

"But aren't you angry, Mother? Can't you be angry *for* me?"

"Well, yes. But I can't see tossing Robert aside just because—"

The sudden clearing of a male throat made Lydia glance up at Sam, who was standing outside the doorway.

"I'm Detective Navarro, Portland Police," he said. "You're Mrs. Cormier?"

"The name's now Warrenton." Lydia frowned at him. "What is this all about? What do the police have to do with this?"

"There was an incident at the church, ma'am. We're investigating.

"An incident?"

"The church was bombed."

Lydia stared at him. "You're not serious."

"I'm very serious. It went off at 2:40 this afternoon. Luckily no one was hurt. But if the wedding had been held…"

Lydia paled to a sickly white. She took a step back, her voice failing her.

"Mrs. Warrenton," said Sam, "I need to ask you a few questions."

Nina didn't stay to listen. She had heard too many questions already. She climbed upstairs to the spare bedroom, where she had left her suitcase—the suitcase she'd packed for St. John Island. Inside were her bathing suits and sundresses and tanning lotion. Everything she'd thought she needed for a week in paradise.

She took off the wedding dress and carefully draped it over an armchair where it lay white and lifeless. Useless. She looked at the contents of her suitcase, at the broken dreams packed neatly between layers of tissue paper. That's when the last vestiges of control failed her. Dressed only in her underwear, she sat down on the bed. Alone, in silence, she finally allowed the grief to sweep over her.

And she wept.

LYDIA WARRENTON WAS nothing like her daughter. Sam had seen it the moment the older woman opened the front door.

Flawlessly made up, elegantly coiffed, her slender frame shown to full advantage by the green gown, Lydia looked like no mother of the bride he'd ever seen. There was a physical resemblance, of course. Both Lydia and Nina had the same black hair, the same dark, thickly lashed eyes. But while Nina had a softness about her, a vulnerability, Lydia was standoffish, as though surrounded by some protective force field that would zap anyone who ventured too close. She was definitely a looker, not only thin but also rich, judging by the room he was now standing in.

The house was a veritable museum of antiques. He had noticed a Mercedes parked in the driveway. And the living room, into which he'd just been ushered, had a spectacular ocean view. A million-dollar view. Lydia sat down primly on a brocade sofa and motioned him toward a wing chair. The needlepoint fabric was so pristine-looking he had the urge to inspect his clothes before sinking onto the cushion.

"A bomb," murmured Lydia, shaking her head. "I just can't believe it. Who would bomb a church?"

"It's not the first bombing we've had in town."

She looked at him, bewildered. "You mean the warehouse? The one last week? I read that had something to do with organized crime."

"That was the theory."

"This was a church. How can they possibly be connected?"

"We don't see the link either, Mrs. Warrenton. We're trying to find out if there is one. Maybe you can help us. Do you know of any reason someone would want to bomb the Good Shepherd Church?"

"I know nothing about that church. It's not one I attend. It was my daughter's choice to get married there."

"You sound as if you don't approve."

She shrugged. "Nina has her own odd way of doing things. I'd have chosen a more...established institution. And a longer guest list. But that's Nina. She wanted to keep it small and simple."

Simple was definitely not Lydia Warrenton's style, thought Sam, gazing around the room.

"So to answer your question, Detective, I can't think of any reason to bomb Good Shepherd."

"What time did you leave the church?"

"A little after two. When it became apparent there wasn't anything I could do for Nina."

"While you were waiting, did you happen to notice anyone who shouldn't have been there?"

"There were just the people you'd expect. The florists, the minister. The wedding party."

"Names?"

"There was me. My daughter Wendy. The best man—I don't remember his name. My ex-husband, George, and his latest wife."

"Latest."

She sniffed. "Daniella. His fourth so far."

"What about your husband?"

She paused. "Edward was delayed. His plane was two hours late leaving Chicago."

"So he hadn't even reached town yet?"

"No. But he planned to attend the reception."

Again, Sam glanced around the room, at the antiques. The view. "May I ask what your husband does for a living, Mrs. Warrenton?"

"He's president of Ridley-Warrenton."

"The logging company?"

"That's right."

That explained the house and the Mercedes, thought Sam. Ridley-Warrenton was one of the largest landowners in northern Maine. Their forest products, from raw lumber to fine paper, were shipped around the world.

His next question was unavoidable. "Mrs. Warrenton," he asked, "does your husband have any enemies?"

Her response surprised him. She laughed. "Anyone with money has enemies, Detective."

"Can you name anyone in particular?"

"You'd have to ask Edward."

"I will," said Sam, rising to his feet. "As soon as your husband's back in town, could you have him give me a call?"

"My husband's a busy man."

"So am I, ma'am," he answered. With a curt nod, he turned and left the house.

In the driveway, he sat in his Taurus for a moment, gazing up at the mansion. It was, without a doubt, one of the most impressive homes he'd ever been in. Not that he was all that familiar with mansions. Samuel Navarro was the son of a Boston cop who was himself the son of a Boston cop. At the age of twelve, he'd moved to Portland with his newly widowed mother. Nothing came easy for them, a fact of life which his mother resignedly accepted.

Sam had not been so accepting. His adolescence consisted of five long years of rebellion. Fistfights in the school yard. Sneaking cigarettes in the bathroom. Loitering with the rough-and-tumble crowd that hung out in Monument Square. There'd been no mansions in his childhood.

He started the car and drove away. The investigation was just beginning; he and Gillis had a long night ahead of them. There was still the minister to interview, as well as the florist, the best man, the matron of honor, and the groom.

Most of all, the groom.

Dr. Robert Bledsoe, after all, was the one who'd called off the wedding. His decision, by accident or design, had saved the lives of dozens of people. That struck Sam as just a little bit too fortunate. Had Bledsoe received some kind of warning? Had he been the intended target?

Was that the real reason he'd left his bride at the altar?

Nina Cormier's image came vividly back to mind. Hers wasn't a face he'd be likely to forget. It was more than just those big brown eyes, that kissable mouth. It was her pride that impressed him the most. The sort of pride that kept her chin up, her jaw squared, even as the tears were falling. For that he admired her. No whining, no self-pity. The woman had been humiliated, abandoned, and almost blown to smithereens. Yet she'd had enough spunk left to give Sam an occasional what-for. He found that both irritating and amusing. For a woman who'd probably grown up with everything handed to her on a silver platter, she was a tough little survivor.

Today she'd been handed a heaping dish of crow, and she'd eaten it just fine, thank you. Without a whimper.

Surprising, surprising woman.

He could hardly wait to hear what Dr. Robert Bledsoe had to say about her.

IT WAS AFTER five o'clock when Nina finally emerged from her mother's guest bedroom. Calm, composed, she was now wearing jeans and a T-shirt. She'd left her wedding dress hanging in the closet; she didn't even want to look at it again. Too many bad memories had attached themselves like burrs to the fabric.

Downstairs she found her mother sitting alone in the living room, nursing a highball. Detective Navarro was gone. Lydia raised the drink to her lips, and by the clinking of ice cubes in the glass, Nina could tell that Lydia's hands were shaking.

"Mother?" said Nina.

At the sound of her daughter's voice, Lydia's head jerked up. "You startled me."

"I think I'll be leaving now. Are you all right?"

"Yes. Yes, of course." Lydia gave a shudder. Then she added, almost as an afterthought, "How about you?"

"I'll be okay. I just need some time. Away from Robert."

Mother and daughter looked at each other for a moment, neither one speaking, neither one knowing what to say. This was the way things had always been between them. Nina had grown up hungry for affection. Her mother had always been too self-absorbed to grant it. And this was the result: the silence of two women who scarcely knew or understood each other. The distance between them couldn't be measured by years, but by universes.

Nina watched her mother take another deep swallow of her drink. "How did it go?" she asked. "With you and that detective?"

Lydia shrugged. "What's there to say? He asked questions, I answered them."

"Did he tell you anything? About who might have done it?"

"No. He was tight as a clam. Not much in the way of charm."

Nina couldn't disagree. She'd known ice cubes that were warmer than Sam Navarro. But then, the man was just doing his job. He wasn't paid to be charming.

"You can stay for dinner, if you'd like," said Lydia. "Why don't you? I'll have the cook—"

"That's all right, Mother. Thank you, anyway."

Lydia looked up at her. "It's because of Edward, isn't it?"

"No, Mother. Really."

"That's why you hardly ever visit. Because of him. I wish you *could* get to like him." Lydia sighed and looked down at her drink. "He's been very good to me, very generous. You have to grant him that much."

When Nina thought of her stepfather, *generous* was not the first adjective that came to mind. No, *ruthless* would be the word she'd choose. Ruthless and controlling. She didn't want to talk about Edward Warrenton.

She turned and started toward the door. "I have to get home and pack my things. Since it's obvious I'll be moving out."

"Couldn't you and Robert patch things up somehow?"

"After today?" Nina shook her head.

"If you just tried harder? Maybe it's something you could talk about. Something you could change."

"Mother. Please."

Lydia sank back. "Anyway," she said, "you *are* invited to dinner. For what it's worth."

"Maybe some other time," Nina said softly. "Bye, Mother."

She heard no answer as she walked out the front door.

Her Honda was parked at the side of the house, where she'd left it that morning. The morning of what should have been her wedding. How proudly Lydia had smiled at her as they'd sat together in the limousine! It was the way a mother *should* look at her daughter. The way Lydia never had before.

And probably never would again.

That ride to the church, the smiles, the laughter, seemed a lifetime away. She started the Honda and pulled out of her mother's driveway.

In a daze she drove south, toward Hunts Point. Toward Robert's house. What had been *their* house. The road was winding, and she was functioning on automatic pilot, steering without thought along the curves. What if Robert hadn't really left town? she thought. What if he's home? What would they say to each other?

Try: goodbye.

She gripped the steering wheel and thought of all the things she'd *like* to tell him. All the ways she felt used and betrayed. *A whole year* kept going through her head. *One whole bloody year of my life.*

Only as she swung past Smugglers Cove did she happen to glance in the rearview mirror. A black Ford was behind her. The same Ford that had been there a few miles back, near Delano Park. At any other time, she would have thought nothing of it. But today, after the possibilities Detective Navarro had raised...

She shook off a vague sense of uneasiness and kept driving. She turned onto Ocean House Drive.

The Ford did too. There was no reason for alarm. Ocean House Drive was, after all, a main road in the neighborhood. Another driver might very well have reason to turn onto it as well.

Just to ease her anxiety, she took the left turnoff, toward Peabbles Point. It was a lonely road, not heavily traveled. Here's where she and the Ford would surely part company.

The Ford took the same turnoff.

Now she was getting frightened.

She pressed the accelerator. The Honda gained speed. At fifty miles per hour, she knew she was taking the curves too fast, but she was determined to lose the Ford. Only she wasn't losing him. He had sped up, too. In fact, he was gaining on her.

With a sudden burst of speed, the Ford roared up right beside her. They were neck and neck, taking the curves in parallel.

He's trying to run me off the road! she thought.

She glanced sideways, but all she could see through the other car's tinted window was the driver's silhouette. *Why are you doing this?* she wanted to scream at him. *Why?*

The Ford suddenly swerved toward her. The thump of the other car's impact almost sent the Honda spinning out of control. Nina fought to keep her car on course.

Her fingers clamped more tightly around the wheel. Damn this lunatic! She had to shake him off.

She hit the brakes.

The Ford shot ahead—only momentarily. It quickly slowed as well and was back beside her, swerving, bumping.

She managed another sideways glance. To her surprise, the Ford's passenger window had been rolled down. She caught a glimpse of the driver—a male. Dark hair. Sunglasses.

In the next instant her gaze shot forward to the road, which crested fifty yards ahead.

Another car had just cleared the crest and was barreling straight toward the Ford.

Tires screeched. Nina felt one last violent thump, felt the sting of shattering glass against her face. Then suddenly she was soaring sideways.

She never lost consciousness. Even as the Honda flew

off the road. Even as it tumbled over and over across shrubbery and saplings.

It came to a rest, upright, against a maple tree.

Though fully awake, Nina could not move for a moment. She was too stunned to feel pain, or even fear. All she felt was amazement that she was still alive.

Then, gradually, an awareness of discomfort seeped through the layers of shock. Her chest hurt, and her shoulder. It was the seat belt. It had saved her life, but it had also bruised her ribs.

Groaning, she pressed the belt release and felt herself collapse forward, against the steering wheel.

"Hey! Hey, lady!"

Nina turned to see a face anxiously peering through the window. It was an elderly man. He yanked open her door. "Are you all right?" he asked.

"I'm—I think so."

"I'd better call an ambulance."

"No, I'm fine. Really, I am." She took a deep breath. Her chest was sore, but that seemed to be her only injury. With the old man's help, she climbed out of the car. Though a little unsteady, she was able to stand. She was shocked by the damage.

Her car was a mess. The driver's door had been bashed in, the window was shattered, and the front fender was peeled off entirely.

She turned and glanced toward the road. "There was another car," she said. "A black one—"

"You mean that damn fool who tried to pass you?"

"Where is it?"

"Took off. You oughta report that fella. Probably drunk as a skunk."

Drunk? Nina didn't think so. Shivering, she hugged

herself and stared at the road, but she saw no sign of another car.

The black Ford had vanished.

Chapter Three

Gordon Gillis looked up from his burger and fries. "Anything interesting?" he asked.

"Not a damn thing." Sam hung his jacket up on the coatrack and sank into a chair behind his desk, where he sat wearily rubbing his face.

"How's the minister doing?"

"Fine, so far. Doctors doubt it's a heart attack. But they'll keep him in for a day, just to be sure."

"He didn't have any ideas about the bombing?"

"Claims he has no enemies. And everyone I talked to seems to agree that Reverend Sullivan is a certifiable saint." Groaning, Sam leaned back. "How 'bout you?"

Gillis peeled off the hamburger wrapper and began to eat as he talked. "I interviewed the best man, the matron of honor and the florist. No one saw anything."

"What about the church janitor?"

"We're still trying to locate him. His wife says he usually gets home around six. I'll send Cooley over to talk to him."

"According to Reverend Sullivan, the janitor opens the front doors at 7:00 a.m. And the doors stay open all day. So anyone could've walked in and left a package."

"What about the night before?" asked Gillis. "What time did he lock the doors?"

"The church secretary usually locks up. She's a part-timer. Would've done it around 6:00 p.m. Unfortunately, she left for vacation this morning. Visiting family in Massachusetts. We're still trying to get hold of..." He paused.

Gillis's telephone was ringing. Gillis turned to answer it. "Yeah, what's up?"

Sam watched as his partner scribbled something on a notepad, then passed it across the desk. *Trundy Point Road* was written on the paper.

A moment later, Gillis said, "We'll be there," and hung up. He was frowning.

"What is it?" asked Sam.

"Report just came in from one of the mobile units. It's about the bride. The one at the church today."

"Nina Cormier?"

"Her car just went off the road near Trundy Point."

Sam sat up straight in alarm. "Is she all right?"

"She's fine. They wouldn't have called us at all, but she insisted they notify us."

"For an accident? Why?"

"She says it wasn't an accident. She says someone tried to run her off the road."

HER RIBS HURT, her shoulder was sore, and her face had a few cuts from flying glass. But at least her head was perfectly clear. Clear enough for her to recognize the man stepping out of that familiar blue Taurus that had just pulled up at the scene. It was that sullen detective, Sam Navarro. He didn't even glance in her direction.

Through the gathering dusk, Nina watched as he spoke to a patrolman. They conversed for a few moments. Then, together, the two men tramped through the underbrush to view the remains of her car. As Sam paced a slow circle around the battered Honda, Nina was reminded of a stalking cat. He moved with an easy, feline grace, his gaze focused in complete concentration. At one point he stopped and crouched to look at something on the ground. Then he rose to his feet and peered more closely at the driver's window. Or what was left of the window. He prodded the broken glass, then opened the door and climbed into the front seat. What on earth was he looking for? She could see his dark hair bobbing in and out of view. Now he seemed to be crawling all over the interior, and into the back seat. It was a good thing she had nothing to hide in there. She had no doubt that the sharp-eyed Detective Navarro could spot contraband a mile away.

At last he reemerged from her car, his hair tousled, his trousers wrinkled. He spoke again to the patrolman. Then he turned and looked in her direction.

And began to walk toward her.

At once she felt her pulse quickening. Something about this man both fascinated and frightened her. It was more than just his physical presence, which was impressive enough. It was also the way he looked at her, with a gaze that was completely neutral. That inscrutability unnerved her. Most men seemed to find Nina attractive, and they would at least make an attempt to be friendly.

This man seemed to regard her as just another homicide victim in the making. Worth his intellectual interest, but that was all.

She straightened her back and met his gaze without wavering as he approached.

"Are you all right?" he asked.

"A few bruises. A few cuts. That's all."

"You're sure you don't want to go to the ER? I can drive you."

"I'm fine. I'm a nurse, so I think I'd know."

"They say doctors and nurses make the worst patients. I'll drive you to the hospital. Just to be sure."

She gave a disbelieving laugh. "That sounds like an order."

"As a matter of fact, it is."

"Detective, I really think I'd know if I was..."

She was talking to his back. The man had actually turned his *back* to her. He was already walking away, toward his car. *"Detective!"* she called.

He glanced over his shoulder. "Yes?"

"I don't— This isn't—" She sighed. "Oh, never mind," she muttered, and followed him to his car. There was no point arguing with the man. He'd just turn his back on her again. As she slid into the passenger seat, she felt a sharp stab of pain in her chest. Maybe he was right after all. She knew it could take hours, or even days, for injuries to manifest themselves. She hated to admit it, but Mr. Personality was probably right about this trip to the ER.

She was too uncomfortable to say much as they drove to the hospital. It was Sam who finally broke the silence.

"So, can you tell me what happened?" he asked.

"I already gave a statement. It's all in the police report. Someone ran me off the road."

"Yes, a black Ford, male driver. Maine license plate."

"Then you've been told the details."

"The other witness said he thought it was a drunk driver trying to pass you on the hill. He didn't think it was deliberate."

She shook her head. "I don't know what to think anymore."

"When did you first see the Ford?"

"Somewhere around Smugglers Cove, I guess. I noticed that it seemed to be following me."

"Was it weaving? Show any signs of driver impairment?"

"No. It was just…following me."

"Could it have been behind you earlier?"

"I'm not sure."

"Is it possible it was there when you left your mother's house?"

She frowned at him. He wasn't looking at her, but was staring straight ahead. The tenor of his questions had taken a subtle change of course. He had started out sounding noncommittal. Maybe even skeptical. But this last question told her he was considering a possibility other than a drunk driver. A possibility that left her suddenly chilled.

"Are you suggesting he was waiting for me?"

"I'm just exploring the possibilities."

"The other policeman thought it was a drunk driver."

"He has his opinion."

"What's your opinion?"

He didn't answer. He just kept driving in that maddeningly calm way of his. Did the man ever show any emotion? Once, just once, she'd like to see something get under that thick skin of his.

"Detective Navarro," she said. "I pay taxes. I pay your salary. I think I deserve more than just a brush-off."

"Oh. The old civil servant line."

"I'll use whatever line it takes to get an answer out of you!"

"I'm not sure you want to hear my answer."

"Why wouldn't I?"

"I made a brief inspection of your car. What I found

there backs up quite a bit of what you just told me. There were black paint chips on the driver's side, indicating that the vehicle that rammed yours was, indeed, black."

"So I'm not color blind."

"I also noticed that the driver's window was shattered. And that the breakage was in a starburst pattern. Not what I'd expect for a rollover accident."

"That's because the window was already broken when I went off the road."

"How do you know?"

"I remember I felt flying glass. That's how I cut my face. When the glass hit me. That was *before* I rolled over."

"Are you sure?" He glanced at her. "Absolutely sure?"

"Yes. Does it make a difference?"

He let out a breath. "It makes a lot of difference," he said softly. "It also goes along with what I found in your car."

"*In* my car?" Perplexed, she shook her head. "What, exactly, did you find?"

"It was in the right passenger door—the door that was jammed against the tree. The metal was pretty crumpled; that's why the other cops didn't notice it. But I knew it was there somewhere. And I found it."

"Found what?"

"A bullet hole."

Nina felt the blood drain from her face. She couldn't speak; she could only sit in shocked silence, her world rocked by the impact of his words.

He continued talking, his tone matter-of-fact. Chillingly so. *He's not human,* she thought. *He's a machine. A robot.*

"The bullet must have hit your window," he said, "just to the rear of your head. That's why the glass shattered. Then the bullet passed at a slightly forward angle, missed you completely, and made a hole in the plastic molding of the opposite door, where it's probably still lodged. It'll be retrieved. By tonight, we'll know the caliber. And possibly the make of the gun. What I still don't know—what *you'll* have to tell me—is why someone's trying to kill you."

She shook her head. "It's a mistake."

"This guy's going to a lot of trouble. He's bombed a church. Tailed you. Shot at you. There's no mistake."

"There has to be!"

"Think of every possible person who might want to hurt you. Think, Nina."

"I told you, I don't have any enemies!"

"You must have."

"I don't! I don't...." She gave a sob and clutched her head in her hands. "I don't," she whispered.

After a long silence he said, gently, "I'm sorry. I know how hard it is to accept—"

"You *don't* know." She raised her head and looked at him. "You have no idea, Detective. I've always thought people liked me. Or—at least—they didn't *hate* me. I try so hard to get along with everyone. And now you're telling me there's someone out there—someone who wants to..." She swallowed and stared ahead, at the darkening road.

Sam let the silence stretch on between them. He knew she was in too fragile a state right now to press her with more questions. And he suspected she was hurting more, both physically and emotionally, than she was letting on. Judging by the condition of her car, her body had taken a brutal beating this afternoon.

In the ER, he paced the waiting room while Nina was examined by the doctor on duty. A few X rays later, she emerged looking even more pale than when she'd entered. It was reality sinking in, he thought. The danger was genuine, and she couldn't deny it any longer.

Back in his car, she sat in numb silence. He kept glancing sideways at her, waiting for her to burst into tears, into hysteria, but she remained unnervingly quiet. It concerned him. This wasn't healthy.

He said, "You shouldn't be alone tonight. Is there somewhere you can go?"

Her response was barely a shrug.

"Your mother's?" he suggested. "I'll take you home to pack a suitcase and—"

"No. Not my mother's," she murmured.

"Why not?"

"I…don't want to make things…uncomfortable for her."

"For *her?*" He frowned. "Pardon me for asking this, but isn't that what mothers are for? To pick us up and dust us off?"

"My mother's marriage isn't…the most supportive one around."

"She can't welcome her own daughter home?"

"It's not her home, Detective. It's her husband's. And he doesn't approve of me. To be honest, the feeling's mutual." She gazed straight ahead, and in that moment, she struck him as so very brave. And so very alone.

"Since the day they got married, Edward Warrenton has controlled every detail of my mother's life. He bullies her, and she takes it without a whimper. Because his money makes it all worthwhile for her. I just couldn't stand watching it any longer. So one day I told him off."

"Sounds like that's exactly what you should have done."

"It didn't do a thing for family harmony. I'm sure that's why he went on that business trip to Chicago. So he could conveniently skip my wedding." Sighing, she tilted her head back against the headrest. "I know I shouldn't be annoyed with my mother, but I am. I'm annoyed that she's never stood up to him."

"Okay. So I don't take you to your mother's house. What about dear old dad? Do you two get along?"

She gave a nod. A small one. "I suppose I could stay with him."

"Good. Because there's no way I'm going to let you be alone tonight." The sentence was scarcely out of his mouth when he realized he shouldn't have said it. It sounded too much as if he cared, as if feeling were getting mixed up with duty. He was too good a cop, too cautious a cop, to let that happen.

He could feel her surprised gaze through the darkness of the car.

In a tone colder than he'd intended, he said, "You may be my only link to this bombing. I need you alive and well for the investigation."

"Oh. Of course." She looked straight ahead again. And she didn't say another word until they'd reached her house on Ocean View Drive.

As soon as he'd parked, she started to get out of the car. He reached for her arm and pulled her back inside. "Wait."

"What is it?"

"Just sit for a minute." He glanced up and down the road, scanning for other cars, other people. Anything at all suspicious. The street was deserted.

"Okay," he said. He got out and circled around to open her door. "Pack one suitcase. That's all we have time for."

"I wasn't planning to bring along the furniture."

"I'm just trying to keep this short and sweet. If someone's really looking for you, this is where they'll come. So let's not hang around, all right?"

That remark, meant to emphasize the danger, had its

intended effect. She scooted out of the car and up the front walk in hyperspeed. He had to convince her to wait on the porch while he made a quick search of the house.

A moment later he poked his head out the door. "All clear."

While she packed a suitcase, Sam wandered about the living room. It was an old but spacious house, tastefully furnished, with a view of the sea. Just the sort of house one would expect a doctor to live in. He went over to the grand piano—a Steinway—and tapped out a few notes. "Who plays the piano?" he called out.

"Robert," came the answer from the bedroom. "Afraid I have a tin ear."

He focused on a framed photograph set on the piano. It was a shot of a couple, smiling. Nina and some blond, blue-eyed man. Undoubtedly Robert Bledsoe. The guy, it seemed, had everything: looks, money and a medical degree. And the woman. A woman he no longer wanted. Sam crossed the room to a display of diplomas, hanging on the wall. All of them Robert Bledsoe's. Groton prep. B.A. Dartmouth. M.D. Harvard. Dr. Bledsoe was Ivy League all the way. He was every mother's dream son-in-law. No wonder Lydia Warrenton had urged her daughter to patch things up.

The phone rang, the sound so abrupt and startling, Sam felt an instant rush of adrenaline.

"Should I get it?" Nina asked. She was standing in the doorway, her face drawn and tense.

He nodded. "Answer it."

She crossed to the telephone. After a second's hesitation, she picked up the receiver. He moved right beside her, listening, as she said, "Hello?"

No one answered.

"Hello?" Nina repeated. "Who is this? *Hello?*"

There was a click. Then, a moment later, the dial tone.

Nina looked up at Sam. She was standing so close to him, her hair, like black silk, brushed his face. He found himself staring straight into those wide eyes of hers, found himself reacting to her nearness with an unexpected surge of male longing.

This isn't supposed to happen. I can't let it happen.

He took a step back, just to put space between them. Even though they were now standing a good three feet apart, he could still feel the attraction. Not far enough apart, he thought. This woman was getting in the way of his thinking clearly, logically. And that was dangerous.

He looked down and suddenly noticed the telephone answering machine was blinking. He said, "You have messages."

"Pardon?"

"Your answering machine. It's recorded three messages."

Dazedly she looked down at the machine. Automatically she pressed the Play button.

There were three beeps, followed by three silences, and then dial tones.

Seemingly paralyzed, she stared at the machine. "Why?" she whispered. "Why do they call and hang up?"

"To see if you're home."

The implication of his statement at once struck her full force. She flinched away from the phone as if it had burned her. "I have to get out of here," she said, and hurried back into the bedroom.

He followed her. She was tossing clothes into a suitcase, not bothering to fold anything. Slacks and blouses and lingerie in one disorganized pile.

"Just the essentials," he said. "Let's leave."

"Yes. Yes, you're right." She whirled around and ran into the bathroom. He heard her rattling in the cabinets, collecting toiletries. A moment later she reemerged with a bulging makeup bag, which she tossed in the suitcase.

He closed and latched it for her. "Let's go."

In the car, she sat silent and huddled against the seat as he drove. He kept checking the rearview mirror, to see if they were being followed, but he saw no other headlights. No signs of pursuit.

"Relax, we're okay," he said. "I'll just get you to your dad's house, and you'll be fine."

"And then what?" she said softly. "How long do I hide there? For weeks, months?"

"As long as it takes for us to crack this case."

She shook her head, a sad gesture of bewilderment. "It doesn't make sense. None of this makes sense."

"Maybe it'll become clear when we talk to your fiancé. Do you have any idea where he might be?"

"It seems that I'm the last person Robert wanted to confide in…" Hugging herself, she stared out the window. "His note said he was leaving town for a while. I guess he just needed to get away. From me…"

"From you? Or from someone else?"

She shook her head. "There's so much I don't know. So much he never bothered to tell me. God, I wish I understood. I could handle this. I could handle anything. If only I understood."

What kind of man is Robert Bledsoe? Sam wondered. What kind of man would walk away from this woman? Leave her alone to face the danger left in his wake?

"Whoever made that hang-up call may pay a visit to

your house," he said. "I'd like to keep an eye on it. See who turns up."

She nodded. "Yes. Of course."

"May I have access?"

"You mean...get inside?"

"If our suspect shows up, he may try to break in. I'd like to be waiting for him."

She stared at him. "You could get yourself killed."

"Believe me, Miss Cormier, I'm not the heroic type. I don't take chances."

"But if he does show up—"

"I'll be ready." He flashed her a quick grin for reassurance. She didn't look reassured. If anything, she looked more frightened than ever.

For me? he wondered. And that, inexplicably, lifted his spirits. Terrific. Next thing he knew, he'd be putting his neck in a noose, and all because of a pair of big brown eyes. This was just the kind of situation cops were warned to avoid: assuming the role of hero to some fetching female. It got men killed.

It could get *him* killed.

"You shouldn't do this by yourself," she said.

"I won't be alone. I'll have backup."

"You're sure?"

"Yeah, I'm sure."

"You promise? You won't take any chances?"

"What are you, my mother?" he snapped in exasperation.

She took her keys out of her purse and slapped them on the dashboard. "No, I'm not your mother," she retorted. "But you're the cop in charge. And I need you alive and well to crack this case."

He deserved that. She'd been concerned about his

safety, and he'd responded with sarcasm. He didn't even know why. All he knew was, whenever he looked in her eyes, he had the overwhelming urge to turn tail and run. Before he was trapped.

Moments later, they drove past the wrought iron gates of her father's driveway. Nina didn't even wait for Sam to open her door. She got out of the car and started up the stone steps. Sam followed, carrying her suitcase. And ogling the house. It was huge—even more impressive than Lydia Warrenton's home, and it had the Rolls-Royce of security systems. Tonight, at least, Nina should be safe.

The doorbell chimed like a church bell; he could hear it echoing through what must be dozens of rooms. The door was opened by a blonde—and what a blonde! Not much older than thirty, she was wearing a shiny spandex leotard that hugged every taut curve. A healthy sweat sheened her face, and from some other room came the thumpy music of an exercise video.

"Hello, Daniella," Nina said quietly.

Daniella assumed a look of sympathy that struck Sam as too automatic to be genuine. "Oh Nina, I'm so *sorry* about what happened today! Wendy called and told us about the church. Was anyone hurt?"

"No. No, thank God." Nina paused, as though afraid to ask the next question. "Do you think I could spend the night with you?"

The expression of sympathy faded. Daniella looked askance at the suitcase Sam was carrying. "I, uh…let me talk to your Dad. He's in the hot tub right now and—"

"Nina has no choice. She has to stay the night," said Sam. He stepped past Daniella, into the house. "It's not safe for her to be alone."

Daniella's gaze shifted to Sam, and he saw the vague

spark of interest in those flat blue eyes. "I'm afraid I didn't catch your name," she said.

"This is Detective Navarro," said Nina. "He's with the Portland Bomb Squad. And this," she said to Sam, "is Daniella Cormier. My, uh...father's wife."

Stepmother was the appropriate term, but this stunning blonde didn't look like anybody's mother. And the look she was giving *him* was anything but maternal.

Daniella tilted her head, a gesture he recognized as both inquisitive and flirtatious. "So, you're a cop?"

"Yes, ma'am."

"Bomb Squad? Is that really what you think happened at the church? A bomb?"

"I'm not free to talk about it," he said. "Not while the investigation's underway." Smoothly he turned to Nina. "If you're okay for the night, I'll be leaving. Be sure to close those driveway gates. And activate the burglar alarm. I'll check back with you in the morning."

As he gave a nod of goodbye, his gaze locked with Nina's. It was only the briefest of looks, but once again he was taken by surprise at his instinctive response to this woman. It was an attraction so powerful he felt himself at once struggling to pull away.

He did. With a curt good-night, he walked out the front door.

Outside, in the darkness, he stood for a moment surveying the house. It seemed secure enough. With two other people inside, Nina should be safe. Still, he wondered whether those particular two people would be of much help in a crisis. A father soaking in a hot tub and a spandex-and-hormones stepmother didn't exactly inspire feelings of confidence. Nina, at least, was an intelligent woman; he knew she would be alert for signs of danger.

He drove back to Robert Bledsoe's house on Ocean View Drive and left the car on a side street around the corner.

With Nina's keys, he let himself in the front door and called Gillis to arrange for a surveillance team to patrol the area. Then he closed all the curtains and settled down to wait. It was nine o'clock.

At nine-thirty, he was already restless. He paced the living room, then roamed the kitchen, the dining room, the hallway. Any stalker watching the house would expect lights to go on and off in different rooms, at different times. Maybe their man was just waiting for the residents to go to bed.

Sam turned off the living room lights and went into the bedroom.

Nina had left the top dresser drawer hanging open. Sam, pacing the carpet, kept walking back and forth past that open drawer with its tempting glimpse of lingerie. Something black and silky lay on top, and one corner trailed partway out of the drawer. He couldn't resist the impulse. He halted by the dresser, picked up the item of lingerie, and held it up.

It was a short little spaghetti-strap thing, edged with lace, and designed to show a lot. An awful lot. He tossed it back in and slammed the drawer shut.

He was getting distracted again. This shouldn't be happening. Something about Nina Cormier, and his reaction to her, had him behaving like a damn rookie.

Before, in the line of duty, he'd brushed up against other women, including the occasional stunner. Women like that spandex bimbo, Daniella Cormier, Nina's stepmother. He'd managed to keep his trousers zipped up and his head firmly screwed on. It was both a matter of self-control as well as self-preservation. The women he met on the job were usually in some sort of trouble, and it was too easy for them to consider Sam their white knight, the masculine answer to all their problems.

It was a fantasy that never lasted. Sooner or later the knight gets stripped of his armor and they'd see him for what he really was: just a cop. Not rich, not brilliant. Not much of anything, in fact, to recommend him.

It had happened to him once. Just once. She'd been an aspiring actress trying to escape an abusive boyfriend; he'd been a rookie assigned to watch over her. The chemistry was right. The situation was right. But the girl was all wrong. For a few heady weeks, he'd been in love, had thought *she* was in love.

Then she'd dropped Sam like a hot potato.

He'd learned a hard but lasting lesson: romance and police work did not mix. He had never again crossed that line while on the job, and he wasn't about to do it with Nina Cormier, either.

He turned away from the dresser and was crossing to the opposite end of the room when he heard a thump.

It came from somewhere near the front of the house.

Instantly he killed the bedroom lights and reached for his gun. He eased into the hallway. At the doorway to the living room he halted, his gaze quickly sweeping the darkness.

The streetlight shone in dimly through the windows. He saw no movement in the room, no suspicious shadows.

There was a scraping sound, a soft jingle. It came from the front porch.

Sam shifted his aim to the front door. He was crouched and ready to fire as the door swung open. The silhouette of a man loomed against the backlight of the streetlamp.

"Police!" Sam yelled. *"Freeze!"*

Chapter Four

The silhouette froze.

"Hands up," ordered Sam. "Come on, *hands up!*"

Both hands shot up. "Don't hurt me!" came a terrified plea.

Sam edged over to the light switch and flipped it on. The sudden glare left both men blinking. Sam took one look at the man standing in front of him and cursed.

Footsteps pounded up the porch steps and two uniformed cops burst through the doorway, pistols drawn. "We got him covered, Navarro!" one of them yelled.

"You're right on time," muttered Sam in disgust. "Forget it. This isn't the guy." He holstered his gun and looked at the tall blond man, who was still wearing a look of terror on his face. "I'm Detective Sam Navarro, Portland Police. I presume you're Dr. Robert Bledsoe?"

Nervously Robert cleared his throat. "Yeah, that's me. What's going on? Why are you people in my house?"

"Where've you been all day, Dr. Bledsoe?"

"I've been—uh, may I put my hands down?"

"Of course."

Robert lowered his hands and glanced cautiously over his shoulder at the two cops standing behind him. "Do they, uh, really need to keep pointing those guns at me?"

"You two can leave," Sam said to the cops. "I'm all right here."

"What about the surveillance?" one of them asked. "Want to call it off?"

"I doubt anything's coming down tonight. But hang around the neighborhood. Just until morning."

The two cops left. Sam said, again, "Where've you been, Dr. Bledsoe?"

With two guns no longer pointed at his back, Robert's terror had given way to righteous anger. He glared at Sam. "First, you tell me why you're in my house! What is this, a police state? Cops breaking in and threatening home-owners? You have no authority to be trespassing on my property. I'll have your ass in a sling if you don't produce a search warrant right now!"

"I don't have a warrant."

"You don't?" Robert gave an unpleasantly triumphant laugh. "You entered my house without a warrant? You break in here and threaten me with your macho cop act?"

"I didn't break in," Sam told him calmly. "I let myself in the front door."

"Oh, sure."

Sam pulled out Nina's keys and held them up in front of Robert. "With these."

"Those—those keys belong to my fiancée! How did you get them?"

"She lent them to me."

"She *what?*" Robert's voice had risen to a yelp of anger. "Where is Nina? She had no right to hand over the keys to my house."

"Correction, Doctor. Nina Cormier was living here with you. That makes her a legal resident of this house. It gives her the right to authorize police entry, which she did." Sam eyed the man squarely. "Now, I'll ask the question a third time. Where have you been, Doctor?"

"Away," snapped Robert.

"Could you be more specific?"

"All right, I went to Boston. I needed to get out of town for a while."

"Why?"

"What is this, an interrogation? I don't have to talk to you! In fact I *shouldn't* talk to you until I call my lawyer." He turned to the telephone and picked up the receiver.

"You don't need a lawyer. Unless you've committed a crime."

"A crime?" Robert spun around and stared at him. "Are you accusing me of something?"

"I'm not accusing you of anything. But I do need answers. Are you aware of what happened in the church today?"

Robert replaced the receiver. Soberly he nodded. "I...I heard there was some sort of explosion. It was on the news. That's why I came back early. I was worried someone might've been hurt."

"Luckily, no one was. The church was empty at the time it happened."

Robert gave a sigh of relief. "Thank God," he said softly. He stood with his hand still on the phone, as though debating whether to pick it up again. "Do the police—do you—know what caused it?"

"Yes. It was a bomb."

Robert's chin jerked up. He stared at Sam. Slowly he sank into the nearest chair. "All I'd heard was—the radio said—it was an explosion. There was nothing about a bomb."

"We haven't made a public statement yet."

Robert looked up at him. "Why the hell would anyone bomb a church?"

"That's what we're trying to find out. If the wedding had taken place, dozens of people might be dead right now. Nina told me you're the one who called it off. Why did you?"

"I just couldn't go through with it." Robert dropped his head in his hands. "I wasn't ready to get married."

"So your reason was entirely personal?"

"What else would it be?" Robert suddenly looked up with an expression of stunned comprehension. "Oh, my God. You didn't think the bomb had something to do with *me?*"

"It did cross my mind. Consider the circumstances. You cancelled the wedding without warning. And then you skipped town. Of course we wondered about your motives. Whether you'd received some kind of threat and decided to run."

"No, that's not at all what happened. I called it off because I didn't want to get married."

"Mind telling me why?"

Robert's face tightened. "Yes, as a matter of fact," he answered. Abruptly he rose from the chair and strode over to the liquor cabinet. There he poured himself a shot of Scotch and stood gulping it, not looking at Sam.

"I've met your fiancée," stated Sam. "She seems like a nice woman. Bright, attractive." *I'm sure as hell attracted to her,* he couldn't help adding to himself.

"You're asking why I left her at the altar, aren't you?" said Robert.

"Why did you?"

Robert finished off his drink and poured himself another.

"Did you two have an argument?"

"No."

"What was it, Dr. Bledsoe? Cold feet? Boredom?" Sam paused. "Another woman?"

Robert turned and glared at him. "This is none of your damn business. Get out of my house."

"If you insist. But I'll be talking to you again." Sam crossed to the front door, then stopped and turned back. "Do you know anyone who'd want to hurt your fiancée?"

"No."

"Anyone who'd want her dead?"

"What a ridiculous question."

"Someone tried to run her car off the road this afternoon."

Robert jerked around and stared at him. He looked genuinely startled. "*Nina?* Who did?"

"That's what I'm trying to find out. It may or may not be connected to the bombing. Do you have any idea at all what's going on? Who might try to hurt her?"

There was a split second's hesitation before Robert answered. "No. No one I can think of. Where is she?"

"She's in a safe place for tonight. But she can't stay in hiding forever. So if you think of anything, give me a call. If you still care about her."

Robert didn't say anything.

Sam turned and left the house.

Driving home, he used his car phone to dial Gillis. His partner, predictably, was still at his desk. "The bridegroom's back in town," Sam told him. "He claims he has no idea why the church was bombed."

"Why am I not surprised?" Gillis drawled.

"Anything new turn up?"

"Yeah. We're missing a janitor."

"What?"

"The church janitor. The one who unlocked the building this morning. We've been trying to track him down all evening. He never got home tonight."

Sam felt his pulse give a little gallop of excitement. "Interesting."

"We've already got an APB out. The man's name is Jimmy Brogan. And he has a record. Petty theft four years ago and two OUI's, that kind of stuff. Nothing major. I sent Cooley out to talk to the wife and check the house."

"Does Brogan have any explosives experience?"

"Not that we can determine. The wife swears up and down that he's clean. And he's always home for dinner."

"GIVE ME MORE, Gillis. Give me more."

"That's all I have to give, unless you want me to slit open a vein. Right now I'm bushed and I'm going home."

"Okay, call it a day. I'll see you in the morning."

All the way home, Sam's mind was churning with facts. A cancelled wedding. A missing church janitor. An assassin in a black Ford.

And a bomb.

Where did Nina Cormier fit in this crazy thicket of events?

It was eleven-thirty when he finally arrived home. He let himself in the front door, stepped into the house, and turned on the lights. The familiar clutter greeted him. What a god-awful mess. One of these days he'd have to clean up the place. Or maybe he should just move; that'd be easier.

He walked through the living room, picking up dirty laundry and dishes as he went. He left the dishes in the kitchen sink, threw the laundry in the washing machine, and started the wash cycle. A Saturday night, and the swinging bachelor does his laundry. Wow. He stood in his kitchen, listening to the machine rumble, thinking about all the things he could do to make this house more of a home. Furniture, maybe? It was a good, sound little house, but he kept comparing it to Robert Bledsoe's house with its Steinway piano, the sort of house any woman would be delighted to call home.

Hell, Sam wouldn't know what to do with a woman even if one was crazy enough to move in with him. He'd been a bachelor too long, alone too long. There'd been the occasional woman, of course, but none of them had ever lasted. Too often, he had to admit, the fault lay with him. Or with his work. They couldn't understand why any man in his right mind would actually choose to stay with this insane job of bombs and bombers. They took it as a personal affront that he wouldn't quit the job and chose *them* instead.

Maybe he'd just never found a woman who made him *want* to quit.

And this is the result, he thought, gazing wearily at the basket of unfolded clothes. The swinging bachelor life.

He left the washing machine to finish its cycle and headed off to bed.

As usual, alone.

THE LIGHTS WERE on at 318 Ocean View Drive. Someone was home. The Cormier woman? Robert Bledsoe? Or both of them?

Driving slowly past the house in his green Jeep Cherokee, he took a good long look at the house. He noted the dense shrubbery near the windows, the shadow of pine and birch trees ringing both edges of the property. Plenty of cover. Plenty of concealment.

Then he noticed the unmarked car parked a block away. It was backlit by a streetlamp, and he could see the silhouettes of two men sitting inside. *Police,* he thought. They were watching the house.

Tonight was not the time to do it.

He rounded the corner and drove on.

This matter could wait. It was only a bit of cleanup, a loose end that he could attend to in his spare time.

He had other, more important work to complete, and only a week in which to do it.

He drove on, toward the city.

At 9:00 A.M., the guards came to escort Billy "The Snowman" Binford from his jail cell.

His attorney, Albert Darien, was waiting for him. Through the Plexiglas partition separating the two men, Billy could see Darien's grim expression and he knew that the news was not good. Billy sat down opposite his attorney. The guard wasn't standing close enough to catch their conversation, but Billy knew better than to speak freely. That stuff about attorney-client confidentiality was a bunch of bull. If the feds or the D.A. wanted you bad enough, they'd plant a bug on anyone, even your priest. It was outrageous, how they'd violate a citizen's rights.

"Hello, Billy," said Darien through the speaker phone. "How're they treating you?"

"Like a sultan. How the hell d'you *think* they're treating me? You gotta get me a few favors, Darien. A private TV. I'd like a private TV."

"Billy, we got problems."

Billy didn't like the tone of Darien's voice. "What problems?" he asked.

"Liddell's not even going to discuss a plea bargain. He's set on taking this to trial. Any other D.A.'d save himself the trouble, but I think Liddell's using you as a stepping stone to Blaine House."

"Liddell's running for governor?"

"He hasn't announced it. But if he puts you away, he'll be golden. And Billy, to be honest, he's got more than enough to put you away."

Billy leaned forward and glared through the Plexiglas at his attorney. "That's what I pay *you* for. So what the hell're you doing about the situation?"

"They've got too much. Hobart's turned state's witness."

"Hobart's a sleazeball. It'll be a piece of cake to discredit him."

"They've got your shipping records. It's all on paper, Billy."

"Okay, then let's try again with a plea bargain. Anything. Just keep my time in here short."

"I told you, Liddell's nixed a plea bargain."

Billy paused. Softly he said, "Liddell can be taken care of."

Darien stared at him. "What do you mean?"

"You just get me a deal. Don't worry about Liddell. I'm taking care of—"

"I don't want to know about it." Darien sat back, his hands suddenly shaking. "I don't want to know a damn thing, okay?"

"You don't have to. I got it covered."

"Just don't get me involved."

"All I want from you, Darien, is to keep this from going to trial. And get me out of here soon. You got that?"

"Yeah. Yeah." Darien glanced nervously at the guard, who wasn't paying the least bit of attention to their conversation. "I'll try."

"Just watch," said Billy. A cocky grin spread on his lips. "Next week, things'll be different. D.A.'s office will be happy to talk plea bargain."

"Why? What happens next week?"

"You don't want to know."

Darien exhaled a deep sigh and nodded. "You're right," he muttered. "I don't want to know."

NINA AWAKENED TO the bass thump of aerobics dance music. Downstairs, she found Daniella stretched out on the polished oak floor of the exercise room. This morning Daniella was garbed in a shiny pink leotard, and her sleek legs knifed effortlessly through the air with every beat of the music. Nina stood watching in fascination for a moment, mesmerized by that display of taut muscles. Daniella worked hard at her body. In fact, she did little else. Since her marriage to George Cormier, Daniella's only goal in life seemed to be physical perfection.

The music ended. Daniella sprang to her feet with an easy grace. As she turned to reach for a towel, she noticed Nina standing in the doorway. "Oh. Good morning."

"Morning," said Nina. "I guess I overslept. Has Dad already left for work?"

"You know how he is. Likes to get started at the crack of dawn." With the towel, Daniella whisked away a delicate sheen of perspiration. A discomforting silence stretched between them. It always did. It was more than just the awkwardness of their relationship, the bizarre reality that this golden goddess was technically Nina's stepmother. It was also the fact that, except for their connection through George Cormier, the two women had absolutely nothing in common.

And never had that seemed more apparent to Nina than at this moment, as she stood gazing at the perfect face of this perfect blonde.

Daniella climbed onto an exercise bike and began pedaling away. Over the whir of the wheel, she said, "George had some board meeting. He'll be home for dinner. Oh, and you got two phone calls this morning. One was from that policeman. You know, the cute one."

"Detective Navarro?"

"Yeah. He was checking up on you."

So he's worried about me, thought Nina, feeling an unexpected lifting of her spirits. He'd cared enough to make sure she was alive and well. Then again, maybe he was just checking to make sure he didn't have a new corpse on his hands.

Yes, that was the likely reason he'd called.

Feeling suddenly glum, Nina turned to leave the room, then stopped. "What about the second call?" she asked. "You said there were two."

"Oh, right." Daniella, still pumping away, looked serenely over the handlebars. "The other call was from Robert."

Nina stared at her in shocked silence. "Robert called?"

"He wanted to know if you were here."

"Where is *he?*"

"At home."

Nina shook her head in disbelief. "You might have told me earlier."

"You were sound asleep. I didn't see the point of waking you." Daniella leaned into the handlebars and began to pedal with singleminded concentration. "Besides, he'll call back later."

I'm not waiting till later, thought Nina. *I want answers now. And I want them face-to-face.*

Heart thudding, she left the house. She borrowed her father's Mercedes to drive to Ocean View Drive. He'd never miss it; after all, he kept a spare Jaguar and a BMW in the garage.

By the time she pulled into Robert's driveway, she was shaking from both anger and dread. What on earth was she going to say to him?

What was he going to say to *her?*

She climbed the porch steps and rang the doorbell. She didn't have her house keys. Sam Navarro did. Anyway, this wasn't her house any longer. It never had been.

The door swung open and Robert stood looking at her in surprise. He was wearing running shorts and a T-shirt, and his face had the healthy flush of recent exercise. Not exactly the picture of a man pining for his fiancée.

"Uh, Nina," he said. "I—I was worried about you."

"Somehow I have a hard time believing that."

"I even called your father's house—"

"What happened, Robert?" Her breath rushed out in a bewildered sigh. "Why did you walk out on me?"

He looked away. That alone told her how far apart they'd drifted. "It's not easy to explain."

"It wasn't easy for me, either. Telling everyone to go home. Not knowing why it fell apart. You could have told me. A week before. A *day* before. Instead you leave me there, holding the damn bouquet! Wondering if it was all *my* fault. Something *I* did wrong."

"It wasn't you, Nina."

"What was it, then?"

He didn't answer. He just kept looking away, unwilling to face her. Maybe afraid to face her.

"I lived with you for a whole year," she said with sad wonder. "And I don't have the faintest idea who you are." With a stifled sob, she pushed past him, into the house, and headed straight for the bedroom.

"What are you doing?" he yelled.

"Packing the rest of my things. And getting the hell out of your life."

"Nina, there's no need to be uncivilized about this. We tried to make it. It just didn't work out. Why can't we still be friends?"

"Is that what we are? Friends?"

"I like to think so. I don't see why we can't be."

She shook her head and laughed. A bitter sound. "*Friends* don't twist the knife after they stab you." She stalked into the bedroom and began yanking open drawers. She pulled out clothes and tossed them on the bed. She was beyond caring about neatness; all she wanted was to get out of this house and never see it again. Or him again. Up until a moment ago, she'd thought it still possible to salvage their relationship, to pick up the pieces and work toward some sort of life together. Now she knew there wasn't a chance of it. She didn't want *him*. She couldn't even recall what it was about Robert Bledsoe that had attracted her. His looks, his medical degree—those were things she'd considered nice but not that important. No, what she'd seen in Robert—or imagined she'd seen—was intelligence and wit and caring. He'd shown her all those things.

What an act.

Robert was watching her with a look of wounded nobility. As if this was all her fault. She ignored him and went to the closet, raked out an armful of dresses, and dumped them on the bed. The pile was so high it was starting to topple.

"Does it all have to be done right now?" he asked.

"Yes."

"There aren't enough suitcases."

"Then I'll use trash bags. And I need to take my books, too."

"Today? But you've got tons of them!"

"This week I've got tons of time. Since I skipped the honeymoon."

"You're being unreasonable. Look, I know you're angry. You have a right to be. But don't go flying off the damn handle."

"I'll fly off the handle if I *want* to!" she yelled.

The sound of a throat being cleared made them both turn in surprise. Sam Navarro stood in the bedroom doorway, looking at them with an expression of quiet bemusement.

"Don't you cops *ever* bother to knock?" snapped Robert.

"I did knock," said Sam. "No one answered. And you left the front door wide open."

"You're trespassing," said Robert. "*Again* without a warrant."

"He doesn't need a warrant," said Nina.

"The law says he does."

"Not if I invite him in!"

"You didn't invite him in. He *walked* in."

"The door was open," said Sam. "I was concerned." He looked at Nina. "That wasn't smart, Miss Cormier, driving here alone. You should have told me you were leaving your father's house."

"What am I, your prisoner?" she muttered and crossed back to the closet for another armload of clothes. "How did you track me down, anyway?"

"I called your stepmother right after you left the house. She thought you'd be here."

"Well, I am. And I happen to be busy."

"Yeah," muttered Robert. "She's really good at being busy."

Nina spun around to confront her ex-fiancé. "What's that supposed to mean?"

"I'm not the only one to blame in all this! It takes two people to screw up a relationship."

"I didn't leave *you* at the church!"

"No, but you left me. Every night, for months on end."

"What? *What?*"

"Every damn night, I was here on my own! I would have enjoyed coming home to a nice meal. But you were never here."

"They needed me on the evening shift. I couldn't change that!"

"You could've quit."

"Quit my *job?* To do what? Play happy homemaker to a man who couldn't even decide if he wanted to marry me?"

"If you loved me, you would have."

"Oh, my God. I can't believe you're turning this into my fault. I didn't *love* you enough."

Sam said, "Nina, I need to talk to you."

"Not now!" Nina and Robert both snapped at him.

Robert said to her, "I just think you should know I had my reasons for not going through with it. A guy has only so much patience. And then it's natural to start looking elsewhere."

"Elsewhere?" She stared at him with new comprehension. Softly she said, "So there was someone else."

"What do you think?"

"Do I know her?"

"It hardly makes a difference now."

"It does to *me*. When did you meet her?"

He looked away. "A while ago."

"How long?"

"Look, this is irrelevant—"

"For six months, we planned that wedding. Both of us. And you never bothered to tell me the minor detail that you were seeing another woman?"

"It's clear to me you're not rational at the moment. Until you are, I'm not discussing this." Robert turned and left the room.

"Not *rational?*" she yelled. "I'm more rational now than I was six months ago!"

She was answered by the thud of the front door as it slammed shut.

Another woman, she thought. *I never knew. I never even suspected.*

Suddenly feeling sick to her stomach, she sank down on the bed. The pile of clothes tumbled onto the floor, but she didn't even notice. Nor did she realize that she was crying, that the tears were dribbling down her cheeks and onto her shirt. She was both sick and numb at the same time, and oblivious to everything but her own pain.

She scarcely noticed that Sam had sat down beside her. "He's not worth it, Nina," he soothed quietly. "He's not worth grieving over."

Only when his hand closed warmly over hers did she look up. She found his gaze focused steadily on her face. "I'm not grieving," she said.

Gently he brushed his fingers across her cheek, which was wet with tears. "I think you are."

"I'm not. I'm *not*." She gave a sob and sagged against him, burying her face in his shirt. "I'm not," she whispered against his chest.

Only vaguely did she sense his arms folding around her back, gathering her against him. Suddenly those arms were holding her close, wrapping tightly around her. He didn't say a thing. As always, the laconic cop. But she felt his breath warming her hair, felt his lips brush the top of her head, and she heard the quickening of his heartbeat.

Just as she felt the quickening of her own.

It means nothing, she thought. He was being kind to her. Comforting her the way he would any hurt citizen. It was what she did every day in the ER. It was her job. It was his job.

Oh, but this felt so good.

It took a ruthless act of pure will to pull out of his arms. When she looked up, she found his expression calm, his green eyes unreadable. No passion, no desire. Just the public servant, in full control of his emotions.

Quickly she wiped away her tears. She felt stupid now, embarrassed by what he'd just witnessed between her and Robert. He knew it all, every humiliating detail, and she could scarcely bear to look him in the eye.

She stood up and began to gather the fallen clothes from the floor.

"You want to talk about it?" he asked.

"No."

"I think you need to. The man you loved leaves you for another woman. That must hurt pretty bad."

"Okay, I *do* need to talk about it!" She threw a handful of clothes on the bed and looked at him. "But not with some stone-faced cop who couldn't care less!"

There was a long silence. Though he looked at her without a flicker of emotion, she sensed that she'd just delivered a body blow. And he was too proud to show it.

She shook her head. "I'm sorry. Oh God, Navarro, I'm so sorry. You didn't deserve that."

"Actually," he said, "I think I did."

"You're just doing your job. And then I go and lash out at you." Thoroughly disgusted with herself, she sat down beside him on the bed. "I was just taking it out on you. I'm so—so angry at myself for letting him make me feel guilty."

"Why guilty?"

"That's the crazy part about it! I don't know why I should feel guilty! He makes it sound as if I neglected him. But I could never quit my job, even for him. I love my job."

"He's a doctor. He must've had long hours as well. Nights, weekends."

"He worked a lot of weekends."

"Did you complain?"

"Of course not. That's his job."

"Well?" He regarded her with a raised eyebrow.

"Oh." She sighed. "The old double standard."

"Exactly. I wouldn't expect my wife to quit a job she loved, just to make dinner and wait on me every night."

She stared down at her hands, clasped in her lap. "You wouldn't?"

"That's not love. That's possession."

"I think your wife's a very lucky woman," she said softly.

"I was only speaking theoretically."

She frowned at him. "You mean…it was just a theoretical wife?"

He nodded.

So he wasn't married. That piece of information made her flush with a strange and unexpected gladness. What on earth was the matter with her?

She looked away, afraid that he might see the confusion in her eyes. "You, uh, said you needed to talk to me."

"It's about the case."

"It must be pretty important if you went to all the trouble of tracking me down."

"I'm afraid we have a new development. Not a pleasant one."

She went very still. "Something's happened?"

"Tell me what you know about the church janitor."

She shook her head in bewilderment. "I don't know him at all. I don't even know his name."

"His name was Jimmy Brogan. We spent all yesterday evening trying to track Brogan down. We know he unlocked the church door yesterday. That he was in and out of the building all morning. But no one seems to know where he went after the explosion. We know he didn't turn up at the neighborhood bar where he usually goes every afternoon."

"You said *was*. That his name *was* Jimmy Brogan. Does that mean…"

Sam nodded. "We found his body this morning. He was in his car, parked in a field in Scarborough. He died from a gunshot wound to the head. The gun was in the car with him. It had his fingerprints on it."

"A suicide?" she asked softly.

"That's the way it looks."

She was silent, too shocked to say a thing.

"We're still waiting for the crime lab report. There are a number of details that bother me. It feels too neat, too packaged. It ties up every single loose end we've got."

"Including the bombing?"

"Including the bombing. There were several items in the car trunk that would seem to link Brogan to the bomb. Detonating cord. Green electrical tape. It's all pretty convincing evidence."

"You don't sound convinced."

"The problem is, Brogan had no explosives experience that we know of. Also, we can't come up with a motive for any bombing. Or for the attack on you. Can you help us out?"

She shook her head. "I don't know anything about the man."

"Are you familiar with the name Brogan?"

"No."

"He was familiar with *you.* There was a slip of paper with your address in his car."

She stared at him. His gaze was impenetrable. It frightened her, how little she could read in his eyes. How deeply the man was buried inside the cop. "Why would he have my address?" she asked.

"You must have some link to him."

"I don't know anyone named Brogan."

"Why would he try to kill you? Run you off the road?"

"How do you know *he* did it?"

"Because of his car. The one we found his body in."

She swallowed hard. "It was black?"

He nodded. "A black Ford."

Chapter Five

Sam drove her to the morgue. Neither one of them said much. He was being guarded about what information he told her, and she was too chilled to ask for the details. All the way there, she kept thinking, *Who was Jimmy Brogan and why did he want to kill me?*

In the morgue, Sam maintained a firm grip on her arm as they walked the corridor to the cold room. He was right beside her when the attendant led them to the bank of body drawers. As the drawer was pulled out she involuntarily flinched. Sam's arm came around her waist, a steady support against the terrible sight she was about to face.

"It ain't pretty," said the attendant. "Are you ready?"

Nina nodded.

He pulled aside the shroud and stepped back.

As an ER nurse, Nina had seen more than her share of grisly sights. This was by far the worst. She took one look at the man's face—what was left of it—and quickly turned away. "I don't know him," she whispered.

"Are you sure?" Sam asked.

She nodded and suddenly felt herself swaying. At once he was supporting her, his arm guiding her away from the drawers. Away from the cold room.

In the coroner's office she sat nursing a cup of hot tea while Sam talked on the phone to his partner. Only vaguely did she register his conversation. His tone was as matter-of-fact as always, betraying no hint of the horror he'd just witnessed.

"…doesn't recognize him. Or the name either. Are you sure we don't have an alias?" Sam was saying.

Nina cupped the tea in both hands but didn't sip. Her stomach was still too queasy. On the desk beside her was the file for Jimmy Brogan, open to the ID information sheet. Most of what she saw there didn't stir any memories. Not his address nor the name of his wife. Only the name of the employer was familiar: the Good Shepherd Church. She wondered if Father Sullivan had been told, wondered how he was faring in the hospital. It would be a double shock to the elderly man. First, the bombing of his church, and then the death of the janitor. She should visit him today and make sure he was doing all right…

"Thanks, Gillis. I'll be back at three. Yeah, set it up, will you?" Sam hung up and turned to her. Seeing her face, he frowned in concern. "You all right?"

"I'm fine." She shuddered and clutched the mug more tightly.

"You don't look fine. I think you need some recovery time. Come on." He offered his hand. "It's lunchtime. There's a café up the street."

"You can think about lunch?"

"I make it a point never to skip a chance at a meal. Or would you rather I take you home?"

"Anything," she said, rising from the chair. "Just get me out of this place."

NINA PICKED LISTLESSLY at a salad while Sam wolfed down a hamburger.

"I don't know how you do it," she said. "How you go straight from the morgue to a big lunch."

"Necessity." He shrugged. "In this job, a guy can get skinny real fast."

"You must see so many awful things as a cop."

"You're an ER nurse. I would think you've seen your share."

"Yes. But they usually come to us still alive."

He wiped his hands on a napkin and slid his empty plate aside. "True. If it's a bomb, by the time I get to the scene, we're lucky to find anyone alive. If we find much of them at all."

"How do you live with it? How do you stand a job like yours?"

"The challenge."

"Really, Navarro. How do you deal with the horror?"

"My name's Sam, okay? And as for how I deal with it, it's more a question of *why* I do it. The truth is, the challenge is a lot of it. People who make bombs are a unique breed of criminal. They're not like the guy who holds up your neighborhood liquor store. Bombers are craftier. A few of them are truly geniuses. But they're also cowards. Killers at a distance. It's that combination that makes those guys especially dangerous. And it makes my job all the more satisfying when I can nail them."

"So you actually enjoy it."

"*Enjoy* isn't the right word. It's more that I can't set the puzzle aside. I keep looking at the pieces and turning them around. Trying to understand the sort of mind that could do such a thing." He shook his head. "Maybe that makes me just as much a monster. That I find it so satisfying to match wits with these guys."

"Or maybe it means you're an outstanding cop."

He laughed. "Either that or I'm as screwy as the bombers are."

She gazed across the table at his smiling face and suddenly wondered why she'd ever considered those eyes of his so forbidding. One laugh and Sam Navarro transformed from a cop into an actual human being. And a very attractive man.

I'm not going to let this happen, she thought with sudden determination. *It would be such a mistake to rebound from Robert, straight into some crazy infatuation with a cop.*

She forced herself to look away, at anything but his face, and ended up focusing on his hands. At the long, tanned fingers. She said, "If Brogan was the bomber, then I guess I have nothing to worry about now."

"If he was the bomber."

"The evidence seems pretty strong. Why don't you sound convinced?"

"I can't explain it. It's just...a feeling. Instinct, I guess. That's why I still want you to be careful."

She lifted her gaze to meet his and found his smile was gone. The cop was back.

"You don't think it's over yet," she said.

"No. I don't."

SAM DROVE NINA back to Ocean View Drive, helped her load up the Mercedes with a few armloads of books and clothes, and made sure she was safely on her way back to her father's house.

Then he returned to the station.

At three o'clock, they held a catch-up meeting. Sam, Gillis, Tanaka from the crime lab, and a third detective on the Bomb Task Force, Francis Cooley, were in attendance. Everyone laid their puzzle pieces on the table.

Cooley spoke first. "I've checked and rechecked the

records on Jimmy Brogan. There's no alias for the guy.
That's his real name. Forty-five years old, born and raised
in South Portland, minor criminal record. Married ten
years, no kids. He was hired by Reverend Sullivan eight
years ago. Worked as a janitor and handyman around
the church. Never any problems, except for a few times
when he showed up late and hung over after falling off
the wagon. No military service, no education beyond the
eleventh grade. Wife says he was dyslexic. I just can't see
this guy putting together a bomb."

"Did Mrs. Brogan have any idea why Nina Cormier's
address was in his car?" Sam asked.

"Nope. She'd never heard the name before. And she
said the handwriting wasn't her husband's."

"Were they having any marital troubles?"

"Happy as clams, from what she told me. She's pretty
devastated."

"So we've got a happily married, uneducated, dyslexic
janitor as our prime suspect?"

"Afraid so, Navarro."

Sam shook his head. "This gets worse every minute."
He looked at Tanaka. "Eddie, give us some answers.
Please."

Tanaka, nervous as usual, cleared his throat. "You're
not going to like what I have."

"Hit me anyway."

"Okay. First, the gun in the car was reported stolen a
year ago from its registered owner in Miami. We don't
know how Brogan got the gun. His wife says he didn't
know the first thing about firearms. Second, Brogan's car
was the black Ford that forced Miss Cormier's Honda off
the road. Paint chips match, both ways. Third, the items
in the trunk are the same elements used in the church

bombing. Two-inch-wide green electrical tape. Identical detonator cord."

"That's Vincent Spectre's signature," said Gillis. "Green electrical tape."

"Which means we're probably dealing with an apprentice of Spectre's. Now here's something else you're not going to like. We just got back the preliminary report from the coroner. The corpse had no traces of gunpowder on his hand. Now, that's not necessarily conclusive, since powder can rub off, but it does argue against a self-inflicted wound. What clinches it, though, is the skull fracture."

"What?" Sam and Gillis said it simultaneously.

"A depressed skull fracture, right parietal bone. Because of all the tissue damage from the bullet wound, it wasn't immediately obvious. But it did show up on X ray. Jimmy Brogan was hit on the head. *Before* he was shot."

The silence in the room stretched for a good ten seconds. Then Gillis said, "And I almost bought it. Lock, stock and barrel."

"He's good," said Sam. "But not good enough." He looked at Cooley. "I want more on Brogan. I want you and your team to get the names of every friend, every acquaintance Brogan had. Talk to them all. It looks like our janitor got mixed up with the wrong guy. Maybe someone knows something, saw something."

"Won't the boys in Homicide be beating those bushes?"

"We'll beat 'em as well. They may miss something. And don't get into any turf battles, okay? We're not trying to steal their glory. We just want the bomber."

Cooley sighed and rose to his feet. "Guess it's back to the ol' widow Brogan."

"Gillis," said Sam, "I need you to talk to the best man and the matron of honor again. See if they have any links to Brogan. Or recognize his photo. I'll go back to the hospital and talk to Reverend Sullivan. And I'll talk to Dr. Bledsoe as well."

"What about the bride?" asked Gillis.

"I've pressed the questions a couple times already. She denies knowing anything about him."

"She seems to be the center of it all."

"I know. And she hasn't the foggiest idea why. But maybe her ex-bridegroom does."

The meeting broke up and everyone headed off to their respective tasks. It would take teamwork to find this bomber, and although he had good people working with him, Sam knew they were stretched thin. Since that rookie cop's death in the warehouse blast a week ago, Homicide had stepped into the investigation, and they were sucking up men and resources like crazy. As far as Homicide was concerned, the Bomb Task Force was little more than a squad of "techies"—the guys you called in when you didn't want your own head blown off.

The boys in Homicide were smart enough.

But the boys in Bombs were smarter.

That's why Sam himself drove out to Maine Medical Center to reinterview Reverend Sullivan. This latest information on Jimmy Brogan's death had opened up a whole new range of possibilities. Perhaps Brogan had been a completely innocent patsy. Perhaps he'd witnessed something—and had mentioned it to the minister.

At the hospital, Sam learned that Reverend Sullivan had been transferred out of Intensive Care that morning. A heart attack had been ruled out, and Sullivan was now on a regular ward.

When Sam walked in the man's room, he found the minister sitting up in bed, looking glum. There was a visitor there already—Dick Yeats of Homicide. Not one of Sam's favorite people.

"Hey, Navarro," said Yeats in that cocky tone of his. "No need to spin your wheels here. We're on the Brogan case."

"I'd like to talk to Reverend Sullivan myself."

"He doesn't know anything helpful."

"Nevertheless," said Sam, "I'd like to ask my own questions."

"Suit yourself," Yeats said as he headed out the door. "Seems to me, though, that you boys in Bombs could make better use of your time if you'd let Homicide do its job."

Sam turned to the elderly minister, who was looking very unhappy about talking to yet another cop.

"I'm sorry, Reverend," said Sam. "But I'm afraid I'm going to have to ask you some more questions."

Reverend Sullivan sighed, the weariness evident in his lined face. "I can't tell you more than I already have."

"You've been told about Brogan's death?"

"Yes. That policeman—that Homicide person—"

"Detective Yeats."

"He was far more graphic than necessary. I didn't need all the...details."

Sam sat down in a chair. The minister's color was better today, but he still looked frail. The events of the last twenty-four hours must be devastating for him. First the destruction of his church building, and then the violent death of his handyman. Sam hated to flog the old man with yet more questions, but he had no choice.

Unfortunately, he could elicit no new answers. Reverend Sullivan knew nothing about Jimmy Brogan's private life. Nor could he think of a single reason why Brogan, or anyone else for that matter, would attack the Good Shepherd Church. There had been minor incidents, of course. A few acts of vandalism and petty theft. That's why he had started locking the church doors at night, a move that grieved him deeply as he felt churches should be open to those in need, day or night. But the insurance company had insisted, and so Reverend Sullivan had instructed his staff to lock up every evening at 6:00 p.m., and reopen every morning at 7:00 a.m.

"And there've been no acts of vandalism since?" asked Sam.

"None whatsoever," affirmed the minister. "That is, until the bomb."

This was a dead end, thought Sam. Yeats was right. He was just spinning his wheels.

As he rose to leave, there was a knock on the door. A heavyset woman poked her head in the room.

"Reverend Sullivan?" she said. "Is this a good time to visit?"

The gloom on the minister's face instantly transformed to a look of relief. Thankfulness. "Helen! I'm so glad you're back! Did you hear what happened?"

"On the television, this morning. As soon as I saw it, I packed my things and started straight back for home." The woman, carrying a bundle of carnations, crossed to the bed and gave Reverend Sullivan a tearful hug. "I just saw the church. I drove right past it. Oh, what a mess."

"You don't know the worst of it," said Reverend Sullivan. He swallowed. "Jimmy's dead."

"Dear God." Helen pulled back in horror. "Was it...in the explosion?"

"No. They're saying he shot himself. I didn't even know he had a gun."

Helen took an unsteady step backward. At once Sam

grasped her ample arm and guided her into the chair from which he'd just risen. She sat quivering, her face white with shock.

"Excuse me, ma'am," said Sam gently. "I'm Detective Navarro, Portland Police. May I ask your full name?"

She swallowed. "Helen Whipple."

"You're the church secretary?"

She looked up at him with dazed eyes. "Yes. Yes."

"We've been trying to contact you, Miss Whipple."

"I was—I was at my sister's house. In Amherst." She sat twisting her hands together, shaking her head. "I can't believe this. I saw Jimmy only yesterday. I can't believe he's gone."

"You saw Brogan? What time?"

"It was in the morning. Just before I left town." She began digging in her purse, desperately fishing for tissues. "I stopped in to pay a few bills before I left."

"Did you two speak?"

"Naturally. Jimmy's such..." She gave a soft sob. "*Was* such...a friendly man. He was always coming up to the office to chat. Since I was leaving on vacation, and Reverend Sullivan wasn't in yet. I asked Jimmy to do a few things for me."

"What things?"

"Oh, there was so much confusion. The wedding, you know. The florist kept popping in to use the phone. The men's bathroom sink was leaking and we needed some plumbing done quick. I had to give Jimmy some last minute instructions. Everything from where to put the wedding gifts to which plumber to call. I was so relieved when Reverend Sullivan arrived, and I could leave."

"Excuse me, ma'am," Sam cut in. "You said something about wedding gifts."

"Yes. It's a nuisance, how some people have gifts delivered to the church instead of the bride's home."

"How many gifts arrived at the church?"

"There was only one. Jimmy—oh, poor Jimmy. It's so unfair. A wife and all…"

Sam fought to maintain his patience. "What about the gift?"

"Oh. That. Jimmy said a man brought it by. He showed it to me. Very nicely wrapped, with all these pretty silver bells and foil ribbons."

"Mrs. Whipple," Sam interrupted again. "What happened to that gift?"

"Oh, I don't know. I told Jimmy to give it to the bride's mother. I assume that's what he did."

"But the bride's mother hadn't arrived yet, right? So what would Jimmy do with it?"

Helplessly Helen Whipple shrugged her shoulders. "I suppose he'd leave it where she'd be sure to find it. In the front pew."

The front pew. The center of the blast.

Sam said, sharply, "Who was the gift addressed to?"

"The bride and groom, of course."

"Dr. Bledsoe and his fiancée?"

"Yes. That was on the card. Dr. and Mrs. Robert Bledsoe."

IT WAS STARTING to come together now, Sam thought as he got back in his car. The method of delivery. The time of planting. But the target wasn't quite clear yet. Was Nina Cormier or Robert Bledsoe supposed to die? Or was it both of them?

Nina, he knew, had no answers, no knowledge of any enemies. She couldn't help him.

So Sam drove to Ocean View Drive, to Robert Bledsoe's house. This time Bledsoe was damn well going to answer some questions, the first two being: Who was the other woman he'd been seeing, and was she jealous enough to sabotage her lover's wedding—and kill off a dozen people in the process?

Two blocks before he got there, he knew something was wrong. There were police lights flashing ahead and spectators gathered on the sidewalks.

Sam parked the car and quickly pushed his way through the crowd. At the edge of Bledsoe's driveway, a yellow police tape had been strung between wooden stakes. He flashed his badge to the patrolman standing guard and stepped across the line.

Homicide Detective Dick Yeats greeted him in the driveway with his usual I'm-in-charge tone of superiority.

"Hello again, Navarro. We have it all under control."

"You have *what* under control? What happened?"

Yeats nodded toward the BMW in the driveway.

Slowly Sam circled around the rear bumper. Only then did he see the blood. It was all over the steering wheel and the front seat. A small pool of it had congealed on the driveway pavement.

"Robert Bledsoe," said Yeats. "Shot once in the temple. The ambulance just left. He's still alive, but I don't expect he'll make it. He'd just pulled into his driveway and was getting out of his car. There's a sack of groceries in the trunk. Ice cream barely melted. The neighbor saw a green Jeep take off, just before she noticed Bledsoe's body. She thinks it was a man behind the wheel, but she didn't see his face."

"A man?" Sam's head snapped up. "Dark hair?"

"Yeah."

"Oh, God." Sam turned and started toward his car. *Nina,* he thought, and suddenly he was running. A dark-haired man had forced Nina off the road. Now Bledsoe was dead. Was Nina next?

Sam heard Yeats yell, "Navarro!" By then, he was already scrambling into his car. He made a screeching U-turn and headed away from Ocean View Drive.

He drove with his emergency lights flashing all the way to George Cormier's house.

It seemed he was ringing the bell forever before anyone answered the door. Finally it swung open and Daniella appeared, her flawless face arranged in a smile. "Why, hello, Detective."

"Where's Nina?" he demanded, pushing past her into the house.

"She's upstairs. Why?"

"I need to talk to her. *Now.*" He started for the stairway, then halted when he heard footsteps creak on the landing above. Glancing up, he saw Nina standing on the steps, her hair a tumble of black silk.

She's okay, he thought with relief. *She's still okay.*

She was dressed casually in jeans and a T-shirt, and she had a purse slung over her shoulder, as if she were just about to leave the house.

As she came down the stairs, she brought with her the elusive fragrance of soap and shampoo. Nina's scent, he thought with a pleasurable thrill of recognition. Since when had he committed her fragrance to memory?

By the time she reached the bottom step, she was frowning at him. "Has something happened?" she asked.

"Then no one's called you?"

"About what?"

"Robert."

She went very still, her dark eyes focused with sudden intensity on his face. He could see the questions in her eyes, and knew she was too afraid to ask them.

He reached for her hand. It was cold. "You'd better come with me."

"Where?"

"The hospital. That's where they took him." Gently he led her to the door.

"Wait!" called Daniella.

Sam glanced back. Daniella stood frozen, staring after them in panic. "What about Robert? What happened?"

"He's been shot. It happened a short while ago, just outside his house. I'm afraid it doesn't look good."

Daniella took a step backward, as though slapped. It was her reaction, that expression of horror in her eyes, that told Sam what he needed to know. *So she was the other woman,* he thought. *This blonde with her sculpted body and her perfect face.*

He could feel Nina's arm trembling in his grasp. He turned her toward the door. "We'd better go," he said. "There may not be much time."

Chapter Six

They spent the next four hours in a hospital waiting room.

Though Nina wasn't part of the medical team now battling to save Robert's life, she could picture only too vividly what was going on at that moment in the trauma suite. The massive infusions of blood and saline. The scramble to control the patient's bleeding, to keep his pressure up, his heart beating. She knew it all well because, at other times, on other patients, she had been part of the team. Now she was relegated to this useless task of waiting and worrying. Though her relationship with Robert was irrevocably broken, though she hadn't forgiven him for the way he'd betrayed her, she certainly didn't want him hurt.

Or dead.

It was only Sam's presence that kept her calm and sane during that long evening. Other cops came and went. As the hours stretched on, only Sam stayed next to her on the couch, his hand clasping hers in a silent gesture of support. She could see that he was tired, but he didn't leave her. He stayed right beside her as the night wore on toward ten o'clock.

And he was there when the neurosurgeon came out to inform them that Robert had died on the operating table.

Nina took the blow in numb silence. She was too

stunned to shed any tears, to say much more than "Thank you for trying." She scarcely realized Sam had his arm around her. Only when she sagged against him did she feel his support, steadying her.

"I'm going to take you home," he said softly. "There's nothing more you can do here."

Mutely she nodded. He helped her to her feet and guided her toward the exit. They were halfway across the room when a voice called, "Miss Cormier? I need to ask you some more questions."

Nina turned and looked at the rodent-faced man who'd just spoken to her. She couldn't remember his name, but she knew he was a cop; he'd been in and out of the waiting room all evening. Now he was studying her closely, and she didn't like the look in his eyes.

"Not now, Yeats," said Sam, nudging her to the exit. "It's a bad time."

"It's the best time to ask questions," said the other cop. "Right after the event."

"She's already told me she knew nothing about it."

"She hasn't told *me*." Yeats turned his gaze back to Nina. "Miss Cormier, I'm with Homicide. Your fiancé never regained consciousness, so we couldn't question him. That's why I need to talk to you. Where were you this afternoon?"

Bewildered, Nina shook her head. "I was at my father's house. I didn't know about it until…"

"Until I told her," filled in Sam.

"*You* did, Navarro?"

"I went straight from the crime scene to her father's house. Nina was there. You can ask Daniella Cormier to confirm it."

"I will." Yeats's gaze was still fixed on Nina. "I understand you and Dr. Bledsoe just called off the engagement. And you were in the process of moving out of his house."

Softly Nina said, "Yes."

"I imagine you must have been pretty hurt. Did you ever consider, oh…getting back at him?"

Horrified by his implication, she gave a violent shake of her head. "You don't really think that—that I had something to do with this?"

"Did you?"

Sam stepped between them. "That's enough, Yeats."

"What are you, Navarro? Her lawyer?"

"She doesn't have to answer these questions."

"Yes, she does. Maybe not tonight. But she does have to answer questions."

Sam took Nina's arm and propelled her toward the exit.

"Watch it, Navarro!" Yeats yelled as they left the room. "You're on thin ice!"

Though Sam didn't answer, Nina could sense his fury just by the way he gripped her arm all the way to the parking lot.

When they were back in his car, she said, quietly, "Thank you, Sam."

"For what?"

"For getting me away from that awful man."

"Eventually, you *will* have to talk to him. Yeats may be a pain in the butt, but he has a job to do."

And so do you, she thought with a twinge of sadness. She turned to look out the window. He was the cop again, always the cop, trying to solve the puzzle. She was merely one of the pieces.

"You're going to have to talk to him tomorrow," said Sam. "Just a warning—he can be a tough interrogator."

"There's nothing I have to tell him. I was at my father's house. You know that. And Daniella will confirm it."

"No one can knock your alibi. But murder doesn't have to be done in person. Killers can be hired."

She turned to him with a look of disbelief. "You don't think I'd—"

"I'm just saying that's the logic Yeats will use. When someone gets murdered, the number one suspect is always the spouse or lover. You and Bledsoe just broke up. And it happened in the most public and painful way possible. It doesn't take a giant leap of logic to come up with murderous intent on your part."

"I'm not a murderer. You know I'm not!"

He didn't answer. He just went on driving as though he had not registered a word.

"Navarro, did you hear me? I'm not a murderer!"

"I heard you."

"Then why aren't you saying anything?"

"Because I think something else just came up."

Only then did she notice that he was frowning at the rearview mirror. He picked up his car phone and dialed. "Gillis?" he said. "Do me a favor. Find out if Yeats has a tail on Nina Cormier. Yeah, right now. I'm in the car. Call me back." He hung up.

Nina turned and looked out the rear window, at a pair of headlights behind them. "Is someone following us?"

"I'm not sure. I do know that car pulled out behind ours when we left the hospital. And it's been there ever since."

"Your buddy in Homicide must really think I'm dangerous if he's having me followed."

"He's just keeping tabs on his suspect."

Me, she thought, and sank back against the seat, grateful that the darkness hid her face. *Am I your suspect as well?*

He drove calmly, making no sudden moves to alarm whoever was in the car behind them. In that tense stillness, the ringing of the phone was startling.

He picked up the receiver. "Navarro." There was a pause, then he said, "You're sure?" Again he glanced in the mirror. "I'm at Congress and Braeburn, heading west. There's a dark truck—looks like a Jeep Cherokee—right behind me. I'll swing around, make a pass by Houlton. If you can be ready and waiting, we'll sandwich this guy. Don't scare him off. For now, just move in close enough to get a good look. Okay, I'm making my turn now. I'll be there in five minutes." He hung up and shot Nina a tense glance. "You pick up what's happening?"

"What *is* happening?"

"That's not a cop behind us."

She looked back at the headlights. Not a cop. "Then who is it?"

"We're going to find out. Now listen good. In a minute I'll want you down near the floor. Not yet—I don't want to make him suspicious. But when Gillis pulls in behind him, things could get exciting. Are you ready for this?"

"I don't think I have much of a choice…"

He made his turn. Not too fast—a casual change of direction to make it seem as if he'd just decided on a different route.

The other car made the turn as well.

Sam turned again, back onto Congress Street. They were headed east now, going back the way they'd come. The pair of headlights was still behind them. At 10:30 on a Sunday, traffic was light and it was easy to spot their pursuer.

"There's Gillis," Sam stated. "Right on schedule." He

nodded at the blue Toyota idling near the curb. They drove past it.

A moment later, the Toyota pulled into traffic, right behind the Jeep.

"Perp sandwich," said Sam with a note of triumph. They were coming on a traffic light, just turning yellow. Purposely he slowed down, to keep the other two cars on his tail.

Without warning, the Cherokee suddenly screeched around them and sped straight through the intersection just as the light turned red.

Sam uttered an oath and hit the accelerator. They, too, lurched through the intersection just as a pickup truck barreled in from a side street. Sam swerved around it and took off after the sedan.

A block ahead, the Cherokee screeched around a corner.

"This guy's smart," muttered Sam. "He knew we were moving in on him."

"Watch out!" cried Nina as a car pulled out of a parking space, right in front of them.

Sam leaned on his horn and shot past.

This is crazy, she thought. *I'm riding with a maniac cop at the wheel.*

They spun around the corner into an alley. Nina, clutching the dashboard, caught a dizzying view of trash cans and Dumpsters as they raced through.

At the other end of the alley, Sam screeched to a halt.

There was no sign of the Cherokee. In either direction.

Gillis's Toyota squealed to a stop just behind them. "Which way?" they heard Gillis call.

"I don't know!" Sam yelled back. "I'll head east."

He turned right. Nina glanced back and saw Gillis turn

left, in the other direction. A two-pronged search. Surely one of them would spot the quarry.

Four blocks later, there was still no sign of the Cherokee. Sam reached for the car phone and dialed Gillis.

"No luck here," he said. "How about you?" At the answer, he gave a grunt of disappointment. "Okay. At least you got the license number. I'll check back with you later." He hung up.

"So he did catch the number?" Nina asked.

"Massachusetts plate. APB's going out now. With any luck, they'll pick him up." He glanced at Nina. "I'm not so sure you should go back to your father's house."

Their gazes locked. What she saw, in his eyes, confirmed her fears.

"You think he was following me," she said softly.

"What I want to know is, why? There's something weird going on here, something that involves both you and Robert. You must have *some* idea what it is."

She shook her head. "It's a mistake," she whispered. "It must be."

"Someone's gone to a lot of trouble to ensure your deaths. I don't think he—or she—would mistake the target."

"She? Do you really think…"

"As I said before, murder needn't be done in person. It can be bought and paid for. And that could be what we're dealing with. I'm more and more certain of it. A professional."

Nina was shaking now, unable to answer him. Unable to argue. The man next to her was talking so matter-of-factly. *His* life didn't hang in the balance.

"I know it's hard to accept any of this yet," he added. "But in your case, denial could be fatal. So let me lay it out for you. The brutal facts. Robert's already dead. And you could be next."

But I'm not worth killing! she thought. *I'm no threat to anyone.*

"We can't pin the blame on Jimmy Brogan," said Sam. "I think he's the innocent in all this. He saw something he shouldn't have, so he was disposed of. And then his death was set up to look like a suicide, to throw us off the track. Deflect our bomb investigation. Our killer's very clever. And very specific about his targets." He glanced at her, and she heard, in his voice, pure, passionless logic. "There's something else I learned today," he told her. "The morning of your wedding, a gift was delivered to the church. Jimmy Brogan may have seen the man who left it. We think Brogan put the parcel somewhere near the front pews. Right near the blast center. The gift was addressed specifically to you and Robert." He paused, as though daring her to argue that away.

She couldn't. The information was coming too fast, and she was having trouble dealing with the terrifying implications.

"Help me out, Nina," he urged. "Give me a name. A motive."

"I told you," she said, her voice breaking to a sob. "I don't know!"

"Robert admitted there was another woman. Do you know who that might be?"

She was hugging herself, huddling into a self-protective ball against the seat. "No."

"Did it ever seem to you that Daniella and Robert were particularly close?"

Nina went still. *Daniella?* Her father's wife? She thought back over the past six months. Remembered the evenings she and Robert had spent at her father's house. All the invitations, the dinners. She'd been pleased that her fiancé had been so quickly accepted by her father and Daniella, pleased that, for once, harmony had been achieved in the Cormier family. Daniella, who'd never been particularly warm toward her stepdaughter, had suddenly started including Nina and Robert in every social function.

Daniella and Robert.

"That's another reason," he said, "why I don't think you should go back to your father's house tonight."

She turned to him. "You think Daniella…"

"We'll be questioning her again."

"But why would she kill Robert? If she loved him?"

"Jealousy? If she couldn't have him, no one could?"

"But he'd already broken off our engagement! It was over between us!"

"Was it really?"

Though the question was asked softly, she sensed at once an underlying tension in his voice.

She said, "You were there, Sam. You heard our argument. He didn't love me. Sometimes I think he never did." Her head dropped. "For him it was definitely over."

"And for you?"

Tears pricked her eyes. All evening she'd managed not to cry, not to fall apart. During those endless hours in the hospital waiting room, she'd withdrawn so completely into numbness that when they'd told her Robert was dead, she'd registered that fact in some distant corner of her mind, but she hadn't *felt* it. Not the shock, nor the grief. She knew she *should* be grieving. No matter how much Robert had hurt her, how bitterly their affair had ended, he was still the man with whom she'd spent the last year of her life.

Now it all seemed like a different life. Not hers. Not Robert's. Just a dream, with no basis in reality.

She began to cry. Softly. Wearily. Not tears of grief, but tears of exhaustion.

Sam said nothing. He just kept driving while the woman beside him shed soundless tears. There was plenty he *wanted* to say. He wanted to point out that Robert Bledsoe had been a first-class rat, that he was scarcely worth grieving over. But women in love weren't creatures you could deal with on a logical level. And he was sure she did love Bledsoe; it was the obvious explanation for those tears.

He tightened his grip on the steering wheel as frustration surged through him. Frustration at his own inability to comfort her, to assuage her grief. The Roberts of the world didn't deserve any woman's tears. Yet they were the men whom women always seemed to cry over. The golden boys. He glanced at Nina, huddled against the door, and he felt a rush of sympathy. And something more, something that surprised him. Longing.

At once he quelled the feeling. It was yet another sign that he should not be in this situation. It was fine for a cop to sympathize, but when the feelings crossed that invisible line into more dangerous emotions, it was time to pull back.

But I can't pull back. Not tonight. Not until I make sure she's safe.

Without looking at her, he said, "You can't go to your father's. Or your mother's for that matter—her house isn't secure. No alarm system, no gate. And it's too easy for the killer to find you."

"I—I signed a lease on a new apartment today. It doesn't have any furniture yet, but—"

"I assume Daniella knows about it?"

She paused, then replied, "Yes. She does."

"Then that's out. What about friends?"

"They all have children. If they knew a killer was trying to find me…" She took a deep breath. "I'll go to a hotel."

He glanced at her and saw that her spine was suddenly stiff and straight. And he knew she was fighting to put on a brave front. That's all it was, a front. God, what was he supposed to do now? She was scared and she had a right to be. They were both exhausted. He couldn't just dump her at some hotel at this hour. Nor could he leave her alone. Whoever was stalking her had done an efficient job of dispatching both Jimmy Brogan and Robert Bledsoe. For such a killer, tracking down Nina would be no trouble at all.

The turnoff to Route 1 north was just ahead. He took it.

Twenty minutes later they were driving past thick stands of trees. Here the houses were few and far between, all the lots heavily forested. It was the trees that had first attracted Sam to this neighborhood. As a boy, first in Boston, then in Portland, he'd always lived in the heart of the city. He'd grown up around concrete and asphalt, but he'd always felt the lure of the woods. Every summer, he'd head north to fish at his lakeside camp.

The rest of the year, he had to be content with his home in this quiet neighborhood of birch and pine.

He turned onto his private dirt road, which wound a short way into the woods before widening into his gravel driveway. Only as he turned off the engine and looked at his house did the first doubts assail him. The place wasn't much to brag about. It was just a two-bedroom cottage of precut cedar hammered together three summers ago. And as for the interior, he wasn't exactly certain how presentable he'd left it.

Oh, well. There was no changing plans now.

He got out and circled around to open her door. She stepped out, her gaze fixed in bewilderment on the small house in the woods.

"Where are we?" she asked.

"A safe place. Safer than a hotel anyway." He gestured toward the front porch. "It's just for tonight. Until we can make other arrangements."

"Who lives here?"

"I do."

If that fact disturbed her, she didn't show it. Maybe she was too tired and frightened to care. In silence she waited while he unlocked the door. He stepped inside after her and turned on the lights.

At his first glimpse of the living room, he gave a silent prayer of thanks. No clothes on the couch, no dirty dishes on the coffee table. Not that the place was pristine. With newspapers scattered about and dust bunnies in the corners, the room had that unmistakable look of a sloppy bachelor. But at least it wasn't a major disaster area. A minor one, maybe.

He locked the door and turned the dead bolt.

She was just standing there, looking dazed. Maybe by the condition of his house? He touched her shoulder and she flinched.

"You okay?" he asked.

"I'm fine."

"You don't look so fine."

In fact she looked pretty pitiful, her eyes red from crying, her cheeks a bloodless white. He had the sudden urge to take her face in his hands and warm it with his touch. Not a good idea. He was turning into a sucker for women in distress, and this woman was most certainly in distress.

Instead he turned and went into the spare bedroom.

One glance at the mess and he nixed that idea. It was no place to put up a guest. Or an enemy, for that matter. There was only one solution. He'd sleep on the couch and let her have his room.

Sheets. Oh Lord, did he have any clean sheets?

Frantically he rummaged in the linen closet and found a fresh set. He was on top of things after all. Turning, he found himself face-to-face with Nina.

She held out her arms for the sheets. "I'll make up the couch."

"These are for the bed. I'm putting you in my room."

"No, Sam. I feel guilty enough as it is. Let me take the couch."

Something in the way she looked at him—that upward tilt of her chin—told him she'd had enough of playing the object of pity.

He gave her the sheets and added a blanket. "It's a lumpy couch. You don't mind?"

"I've taken a lot of lumps lately. I'll hardly notice a few more."

Almost a joke. That was good. She was pulling herself together—an act of will he found impressive.

While she made up the couch, he went to the kitchen and called Gillis at home.

"We got the info on that Massachusetts plate," Gillis told him. "It was stolen two weeks ago. APB hasn't netted the Cherokee yet. Man, this guy's quick."

"And dangerous."

"You think he's our bomber?"

"Our shooter, too. It's all tangled together, Gillis. It has to be."

"How does last week's warehouse bombing fit in? We figured that was a mob hit."

"Yeah. A nasty message to Billy Binford's rivals."

"Binford's in jail. His future's not looking so bright. Why would he order a church bombed?"

"The church wasn't the target, Gillis. I'm almost certain the target was Bledsoe or Nina Cormier. Or both."

"How does that tie in with Binford?"

"I don't know. Nina's never heard of Binford." Sam rubbed his face and felt the stubble of beard. God, he was tired. Too tired to figure anything out tonight. He said, "There's one other angle we haven't ruled out. The old crime of passion. You interviewed Daniella Cormier."

"Yeah. Right after the bombing. What a looker."

"You pick up anything odd about her?"

"What do you mean?"

"Anything that didn't sit right? Her reactions, her answers?"

"Not that I recall. She seemed appropriately stunned. What are you thinking?"

"I'm thinking Homicide should get their boys over there to question her tonight."

"I'll pass that message along to Yeats. What's your hunch?"

"She and Robert Bledsoe had a little thing going on the side."

"And she blew up the church out of jealousy?" Gillis laughed. "She didn't seem the type."

"Remember what they say about the female of the species."

"Yeah, but I can't imagine that gorgeous blonde—"

"Watch the hormones, Gillis."

His partner snorted. "If anyone better watch his hormones, it's you."

That's what I keep telling myself, thought Sam as he

hung up. He paused for a moment in the kitchen, giving himself the same old lecture he'd given himself a dozen times since meeting Nina. *I'm a cop, I'm here to serve and protect. Not seduce.*

Not fall in love.

He went into the living room. At his first sight of Nina, he felt his resolve crumble. She was standing at the window, peering out at the darkness. He'd hung no curtains; here in the woods, he'd never felt the need for them. But now he realized just how open and vulnerable she was. And that worried him—more than he cared to admit.

He said, "I'd feel better if you came away from those windows."

She turned, a startled look in her eyes. "You don't think someone could have followed us?"

"No. But I'd like you to stay away from the windows all the same."

Shuddering, she moved to the couch and sat down. She'd already made the couch into a bed, and only now did he realize how tattered the blanket was. Tattered furniture, tattered linens. Those were details that had never bothered him before. So many things about his life as a bachelor had not bothered him, simply because he'd never stopped to think how much better, sweeter, his life could be. Only now, as he saw Nina sitting on his couch, did it occur to him how stark the room was. It was only the presence of this woman that gave it any life. Any warmth.

Too soon, she'd be gone again.

The sooner the better, he told himself. Before she grew on him. Before she slipped too deeply into his life.

He paced over to the fireplace, paced back toward the kitchen door, his feet restless, his instincts telling him to say something.

"You must be hungry," he said.

She shook her head. "I can't think about food. I can't think about anything except..."

"Robert?"

She lowered her head and didn't answer. Was she crying again? She had a right to. But she just sat very still and silent, as though struggling to hold her emotions in check.

He sat down in the chair across from her. "Tell me about Robert," he prompted. "Tell me everything you know about him."

She took a shaky breath, then said softly, "I don't know what to say. We lived together a year. And now I feel as if I never knew him at all."

"You met at work?"

She nodded. "The Emergency Room. Evening shift. I'd been working there for three years. Then Robert joined the ER staff. He was a good doctor. One of the best I'd ever worked with. And he was so fun to talk to. He'd traveled everywhere, done everything. I remember how surprised I was to learn he wasn't married."

"Never?"

"Never. He told me he was holding out for the best. That he just hadn't found the woman he wanted to spend his life with."

"At forty-one, he must've been more than a little picky."

Her glance held a trace of amusement. "*You're* not married, Detective. Does that make you more than a little picky?"

"Guilty as charged. But then, I haven't really been looking."

"Not interested?"

"Not enough time for romance. It's the nature of the job."

She gave a sigh. "No, it's the nature of the beast. Men don't really want to be married."

"Did I say that?"

"It's something I've finally figured out after years of spinsterhood."

"We're all rats, that kind of thing? Let's get back to one specific rat. Robert. You were telling me you two met in the ER. Was it love at first sight?"

She leaned back, and he could clearly see the remembered pain on her face. "No. No, it wasn't. At least, not for me. I thought he was attractive, of course."

Of course, thought Sam with an undeniable twinge of cynicism.

"But when he asked me out, that first time, I didn't really think it would go anywhere. It wasn't until I introduced him to my mother that I began to realize what a catch he was. Mom was thrilled with Robert. All these years, I'd been dating guys she considered losers. And here I show up with a doctor. It was more than she'd ever expected of me, and she was already hearing wedding bells."

"What about your father?"

"I think he was just plain relieved I was dating someone who wouldn't marry me for *his* money. That's always been Dad's preoccupation. His money. And his wives. Or rather, whichever wife he happens to be married to at the time."

Sam shook his head. "After what you've seen of your parents' marriages, I'm surprised you wanted to take the plunge at all."

"But that's exactly why I *did* want to be married!" She looked at him. "To make it *work.* I never had that stability in my family. My parents were divorced when I was eight, and after that it was a steady parade of stepmothers and mother's boyfriends. I didn't want to live my own life that way." Sighing, she looked down at her ringless left hand. "Now I wonder if it's just another urban myth. A stable marriage."

"My parents had one. A good one."

"Had?"

"Before my dad died. He was a cop, in Boston. Didn't make it to his twentieth year on the force." Now Sam was the one who wasn't looking at *her*. He was gazing, instead, at some distant point in the room, avoiding her look of sympathy. He didn't feel he particularly needed her sympathy. One's parents died, and one went on with life. There was no other choice.

"After my dad died, Mom and I moved to Portland," he continued. "She wanted a safer town. A town where she wouldn't have to worry about her kid being shot on the street." He gave a rueful smile. "She wasn't too happy when I became a cop."

"Why did you become a cop?"

"I guess it was in the genes. Why did you become a nurse?"

"It was definitely *not* in the genes." She sat back, thinking it over for a moment. "I guess I wanted that one-on-one sense of helping someone. I like the contact. The touching. That was important to me, that it be hands-on. Not some vague idea of service to humanity." She gave a wry smile. "You said your mother didn't want you to be a cop. Well, my mother wasn't too happy about *my* career choice, either."

"What does she have against nursing?"

"Nothing. Just that it's not an appropriate profession for her daughter. She thinks of it as manual labor, something other women do. I was expected to marry well, entertain with flair, and help humanity by hosting benefits. That's why she was so happy about my engagement. She thought I was finally on the right track. She was actually...*proud* of me for the first time."

"That's not why you wanted to marry Robert, was it? To please your mother?"

"I don't know." She looked at him with genuine puzzlement. "I don't know anymore."

"What about love? You must have loved him."

"How can I be sure of anything? I've just found out he was seeing someone else. And now it seems as if I were caught up in some fantasy. In love with a man I made up." She leaned back and closed her eyes. "I don't want to talk about him anymore."

"It's important you tell me everything you know. That you consider all the possible reasons someone wanted him dead. A man doesn't just walk up to a stranger and shoot him in the head. The killer had a reason."

"Maybe he didn't. Maybe he was crazy. Or high on drugs. Robert could have been in the wrong place at the wrong time."

"You don't really believe that. Do you?"

She paused. Then, softly, she said, "No, I guess I don't."

He watched her for a moment, thinking how very vulnerable she looked. Had he been any other man, he would be taking her in his arms, offering her comfort and warmth.

Suddenly he felt disgusted with himself. This was the wrong time to be pressing for answers, the wrong time to be doing the cop act. Yet that act was the only thing that kept him comfortably at a distance. It protected him, insulated him. From her.

He rose from the chair. "I think we both need to get some sleep."

Her response was a silent nod.

"If you need anything, my room's at the end of the hall. Sure you wouldn't rather take my bed? Give me the couch?"

"I'll be fine here. Good night."

That was his cue to retreat. He did.

In his bedroom, he paced between the closet and the dresser, unbuttoning his shirt. He felt more restless than tired, his brain moving a mile a minute. In the last two days, a church had been bombed, a man shot to death, and a woman run off the road in an apparent murder attempt. He felt certain it was all linked, perhaps even linked to that warehouse bombing a week ago, but he couldn't see the connection. Maybe he was too dense. Maybe his brain was too drunk on hormones to think straight.

It was all her fault. He didn't need or want this complication. But he couldn't seem to think about this case without lingering on thoughts of her.

And now she was in his house.

He hadn't had a woman sleeping under his roof since… well, it was longer than he cared to admit. His last fling had amounted to little more than a few weeks of lust with a woman he'd met at some party. Then, by mutual agreement, it was over. No complications, no broken hearts.

Not much satisfaction, either.

These days, what satisfaction he got came from the challenge of his work. That was one thing he could count on: the world would never run out of perps.

He turned off the lights and stretched out on the bed, but still he wasn't ready to sleep. He thought of Nina, just down the hall. Thought of what a mismatch they'd be together. And how horrified her mother would be if a cop started squiring around her daughter. If a cop even had a chance.

What a mistake, bringing her here. Lately it seemed he was making a lot of mistakes. He wasn't going to compound this one by falling in love or lust or whatever it was he felt himself teetering toward.

Tomorrow, he thought, *she's out of here.*

And I'm back in control.

Chapter Seven

Nina knew she ought to be crying, but she couldn't. In darkness she lay on the couch and thought about those months she'd lived with Robert. The months she'd thought of as stepping stones to their marriage. When had it fallen apart? When had he stopped telling her the truth? She should have noticed the signs. The avoided looks, the silences.

She remembered that two weeks ago, he'd suggested the wedding be postponed. She'd assumed it was merely bridegroom jitters. By then, the arrangements were all made, the date set in stone.

How trapped he must have felt.

Oh Robert. If only you'd come out and told me.

She could have dealt with the truth. The pain, the rejection. She was strong enough and adult enough. What she couldn't deal with was the fact that, all these months, she'd been living with a man she scarcely knew.

Now she'd never know what he really felt about her. His death had cut off any chance she had to make peace with him.

At last she did fall asleep, but the couch was lumpy and the dreams kept waking her up.

Dreams not of Robert, but of Sam Navarro.

He was standing before her, silent and unsmiling. She saw no emotion in his eyes, just that flat, unreadable gaze of a stranger. He reached out to her, as though to take her hand. But when she looked down, there were handcuffs circling her wrists.

"You're guilty," he said. And he kept repeating the word. *Guilty. Guilty.*

She awakened with tears in her eyes. Never had she felt so alone. And she *was* alone, reduced to the pitiful state of seeking refuge in the home of a cop who cared nothing at all about her. Who considered her little more than an added responsibility. An added bother.

It was a flicker of shadow across the window that drew her attention. She would not have noticed it at all, save for the fact it had passed just to the right of her, a patch of darkness moving across her line of vision. Suddenly her heart was thudding. She stared at the curtainless squares of moonlight, watching for signs of movement.

There it was again. A shadow, flitting past.

In an instant she was off the couch and running blindly up the hallway to Sam's room. She didn't stop to knock, but pushed right inside.

"Sam?" she whispered. He didn't answer. Frantic to wake him, she reached down to give him a shake, and her hands met warm, bare flesh. "Sam?"

At her touch, he awoke with such a violent start she jerked away in fright. "What?" he said. "What is it?"

"I think there's someone outside!"

At once he seemed to snap fully awake. He rolled off the bed and grabbed his trousers from a chair. "Stay here," he whispered. "Don't leave the room."

"What are you going to do?"

She was answered by a metallic click. A gun. Of course he had a gun. He was a cop.

"Just stay here," he ordered, and slipped out of the room.

She wasn't crazy; she wasn't going to go wandering around a dark house when there was a cop with a loaded gun nearby. Chilled and shivering, she stood by the door and listened. She heard Sam's footsteps creak down the hall toward the living room. Then there was silence, a silence so deep it made every breath she took seem like a roar. Surely he hadn't left the house? He wouldn't go outside, would he?

The creak of returning footsteps made her back away from the door. She scurried to the far side of the bed. At the first glimpse of a figure entering the room, she ducked behind the mattress. Only when she heard Sam say, "Nina?" did she dare raise her head.

"Here," she whispered, suddenly feeling ridiculous as she emerged from her hiding place.

"There's no one out there."

"But I saw someone. Something."

"It could have been a deer. An owl flying past." He set his gun down on the nightstand. The solid clunk of metal on wood made her flinch. She hated guns. She wasn't sure she wanted to be anywhere near a man who owned one. Tonight, though, she didn't have a choice.

"Nina, I know you're scared. You have a right to be. But I've checked, and there's no one out there." He reached toward her. At the first touch of his hand on her arm, he gave a murmur of alarm. "You're freezing."

"I'm scared. Oh God, Sam. I'm so scared…"

He took her by the shoulders. By now she was shaking so hard she could barely form any words. Awkwardly, he drew her against him, and she settled, trembling, against his chest. If only he'd hold her. If only he'd put his arms around her. When at last he did, it was like being welcomed home. Enclosed in warmth and safety. This was not the man she'd dreamed about, not the cold, unsmiling cop. This was a man who held her and murmured comforting sounds. A man whose face nuzzled her hair, whose lips, even now, were lowering toward hers.

The kiss was gentle. Sweet. Not the sort of kiss she ever imagined Sam Navarro capable of. Certainly she never imagined being hugged by him, comforted by him. But here she was, in his arms, and she had never felt so protected.

He coaxed her, still shivering, to the bed. He pulled the covers over them both. Again, he kissed her. Again the kiss was gently undemanding. The heat of the bed, of their bodies, banished her chill. And she became aware of so many other things: the scent of his bare skin, the bristly plane of his chest. And most of all, the touch of his lips, lingering against hers.

They had their arms wrapped around each other now, and their legs were slowly twining together. The kiss had gone beyond sweetness, beyond comfort. This was transforming to lust, pure and simple, and she was responding with such a rush of eagerness it astonished her. Her lips parted, welcoming the thrust of his tongue. Through the tangle of sheets, the barrier of her clothes, she felt the undeniable evidence of his arousal burgeoning against her.

She had not meant for this to happen, had not expected this to happen. But as their kiss deepened, as his hand slid hungrily down the curve of her waist, the flare of her hips, she knew that this had been inevitable. That for all his cool, unreadable looks, Sam Navarro harbored more passion than any man she'd ever known.

He regained control first. Without warning, he broke off the kiss. She heard his breathing, harsh and rapid, in the darkness.

"Sam?" she whispered.

He pulled away from her and sat up on the side of the bed. She watched his silhouette in the darkness, running his hands through his hair. "God," he murmured. "What am I doing?"

She reached out toward the dark expanse of his back. As her fingers brushed his skin, she felt his shudder of pleasure. He wanted her—that much she was certain of. But he was right, this was a mistake, and they both knew it. She'd been afraid and in need of a protector. He was a man alone, in need of no one, but still a man with needs. It was natural they'd seek each other's arms for comfort, however temporary it might be.

Staring at him now, at the shadow huddled at the side of the bed, she knew she still wanted him. The longing was so intense it was a physical ache.

She said, "It's not so awful, is it? What just happened between us?"

"I'm not getting sucked into this again. I can't."

"It doesn't have to mean anything, Sam. Not if you don't want it to."

"Is that how you see it? Quick and meaningless?"

"No. No, that's not at all what I said."

"But that's how it'd end up." He gave a snort of self-disgust. "This is the classic trap, you know. I want to keep you safe. You want a white knight. It's good only as long as that lasts. And then it falls apart." He rose from the bed and moved to the door. "I'll sleep on the couch."

He left the room.

She lay alone in his bed, trying to sort out the confusing whirl of emotions. Nothing made sense to her. Nothing was under her control. She tried to remember a time when her life was in perfect order. It was before Robert. Before she'd let herself get caught up in those fantasies of the perfect marriage. That was where she'd gone wrong. Believing in fantasies.

Her reality was growing up in a broken home, living with a succession of faceless stepparents, having a mother and father who despised each other. Until she'd met Robert, she hadn't expected to marry at all. She'd been content enough with her life, her job. That's what had always sustained her: her work.

She could go back to that. She *would* go back to that.

That dream of a happy marriage, that fantasy, was dead.

SAM WAS UP at dawn. The couch had been even more uncomfortable than he'd expected. His sleep had been fitful, his shoulder ached, and at 7:00 a.m., he was unfit for human companionship. So when the phone rang, he was hard-pressed to answer with a civil "Hello."

"Navarro, you've got some explaining to do," said Abe Coopersmith.

Sam sighed. "Good morning, Chief."

"I just got an earful from Yeats in Homicide. I shouldn't have to tell you this, Sam. Back off the Cormier woman."

"You're right. You shouldn't have to tell me. But you did."

"Anything going on between you two?"

"I felt she was in danger. So I stepped in."

"Where is she right now?"

Sam paused. He couldn't avoid this question; he had to answer it. "She's here," he admitted. "My house."

"Damn."

"Someone was following us last night. I didn't think it was prudent to leave her alone. Or unprotected."

"So you brought her to *your* house? Where, exactly, did you happen to park your common sense?"

I don't know, thought Sam. *I lost track of it when I looked into Nina Cormier's big brown eyes.*

"Don't tell me you two are involved. Please don't tell me that," said Coopersmith.

"We're not involved."

"I hope to God you're not. Because Yeats wants her in here for questioning."

"For Robert Bledsoe's murder? Yeats is fishing. She doesn't know anything about it."

"He wants to question her. Bring her in. One hour."

"She has an airtight alibi—"

"*Bring her in,* Navarro." Coopersmith hung up.

There was no way around this. Much as he hated to do it, he'd have to hand Nina over to the boys in Homicide. Their questioning might be brutal, but they had their job to do. As a cop, he could hardly stand in their way.

He went up the hall to the bedroom door and knocked. When she didn't answer, he cautiously cracked open the door and peeked inside.

She was sound asleep, her hair spread across the pillow in a luxurious fan of black. Just the sight of her, lying so peacefully in his bed, in his house, sent a rush of yearning through him. It was so intense he had to grip the doorknob just to steady himself. Only when it had passed, when he had ruthlessly suppressed it, did he dare enter the room.

She awakened with one gentle shake of the shoulder. Dazed by sleep, she looked at him with an expression of utter vulnerability, and he cleared his throat just to keep his voice steady.

"You'll have to get up," he told her. "The detectives in Homicide want to see you downtown."

"When?"

"One hour. You have time to take a shower. I've already got coffee made."

She didn't say anything. She just looked at him with an expression of bewilderment. And no wonder. Last night they had held each other like lovers.

This morning, he was behaving like a stranger.

This was a mistake, coming into her room. Approaching the bed. At once he put distance between them and went to the door. "I'm sure it'll just be routine questions," he said. "But if you feel you need a lawyer—"

"Why should I need a lawyer?"

"It's not a bad idea."

"I don't need one. I didn't do anything." Her gaze was direct and defiant. He'd only been trying to protect her rights, but she had taken his suggestion the wrong way, had interpreted it as an accusation.

He didn't have the patience right now to set her straight. "They'll be waiting for us," was all he said, and he left the room.

While she showered, he tried to scrounge together a breakfast, but could come up with only frozen French bread and a months-old box of cornflakes. Both the pantry and the refrigerator looked pretty pathetic; bachelorhood was showing, and he wasn't at all proud of it.

In disgust, he went outside to fetch the newspaper, which had been delivered to its usual spot at the end of the driveway. He was walking back toward the house when he abruptly halted and stared at the ground.

There was a footprint.

Or, rather, a series of footprints. They tracked through

the soft dirt, past the living room window, and headed off among the trees. A man's shoes, thick soled. Size eleven at least.

He glanced toward the house and thought about what the man who'd made those prints could have seen last night, through the windows. Only darkness? Or had he seen Nina, a moving target as she walked around the living room?

He went to his car, parked near the front porch. Slowly, methodically, he examined it from bumper to bumper. He found no signs of tampering.

Maybe I'm paranoid. Maybe those footprints mean nothing.

He went back inside, into the kitchen, and found Nina finishing up her cup of coffee. Her face was flushed, her hair still damp from the shower. At her first look at him, she frowned. "Is something wrong?" she asked.

"No, everything's fine." He carried his cup to the sink. There he looked out the window and thought about how isolated this house was. How open those windows were to the sight of a gunman.

He turned to her and said, "I think it's time to leave."

I SHOULD HAVE taken Sam's advice. I should have hired a lawyer.

That was the thought that now crossed Nina's mind as she sat in an office at the police station and faced the three Homicide detectives seated across the table from her. They were polite enough, but she sensed their barely restrained eagerness. Detective Yeats in particular made her think of an attack dog—leashed, but only for the moment.

She glanced at Sam, hoping for moral support. He gave her none. Throughout the questioning, he hadn't even looked at her. He stood at the window, his shoulders rigid, his gaze focused outside. He'd brought her here, and now he was abandoning her. The cop, of course, had his duty to perform. And at this moment, he was playing the cop role to the hilt.

She said to Yeats, "I've told you everything I know. There's nothing else I can think of."

"You were his fiancée. If anyone would know, you would."

"I don't. I wasn't even there. If you'd just talk to Daniella—"

"We have. She confirms your alibi," Yeats admitted.

"Then why do you keep asking me these questions?"

"Because murder doesn't have to be done in person," one of the other cops said.

Now Yeats leaned forward, his gaze sympathetic, his voice quietly coaxing. "It must have been pretty humiliating for you," he persisted. "To be left at the altar. To have the whole world know he didn't want you."

She said nothing.

"Here's a man you trusted. A man you loved. And for weeks, maybe months, he was cheating on you. Probably laughing at you behind your back. A man like that doesn't deserve a woman like you. But you loved him anyway. And all you got for it was pain."

She lowered her head. She still didn't speak.

"Come on, Nina. Didn't you want to hurt him back? Just a little?"

"Not—not that way," she whispered.

"Even when you found out he was seeing someone else? Even when you learned it was your own stepmother?"

She looked up sharply at Yeats.

"It's true. We spoke to Daniella and she admitted it.

They'd been meeting on the sly for some time. While you were at work. You didn't know?"

Nina swallowed. In silence she shook her head.

"I think maybe you *did* know. Maybe you found out on your own. Maybe he told you."

"No."

"And how did it make you feel? Hurt? Angry?"

"I didn't know."

"Angry enough to strike back? To find someone who'd strike back *for* you?"

"I didn't know!"

"That's simply not believable, Nina. You expect us to accept your word that you knew nothing about it?"

"I didn't!"

"You *did*. You—"

"That's *enough*." It was Sam's voice that cut in. "What the hell do you think you're doing, Yeats?"

"My job," Yeats shot back.

"You're badgering her. Interrogating without benefit of counsel."

"Why should she need a lawyer? She claims she's innocent."

"She *is* innocent."

Yeats glanced smugly at the other Homicide detectives. "I think it's pretty obvious, Navarro, that you no longer belong on this investigation."

"You don't have the authority."

"Abe Coopersmith's given me the authority."

"Yeats, I don't give a flying—"

Sam's retort was cut off by the beeping of his pocket pager. Irritably he pressed the Silence button. "I'm not through here," he snapped. Then he turned and left the room.

Yeats turned back to Nina. "Now, Miss Cormier," he said. All trace of sympathy was gone from his expression. In its place was the razor-tooth smile of a pit bull. "Let's get back to the questions."

THE PAGE WAS from Ernie Takeda in the crime lab, and the code on the beeper readout told Sam it was an urgent message. He made the call from his own desk.

It took a few dialings to get through; the line was busy. When the usually low-key Takeda finally answered, there was an uncharacteristic tone of excitement in his voice.

"We've got something for you, Sam," said Takeda. "Something that'll make you happy."

"Okay. Make me happy."

"It's a fingerprint. A partial, from one of the device fragments from the warehouse bomb. It could be enough to ID our bomber. I've sent the print off to NCIC. It'll take a few days to run it through the system. So be patient. And let's hope our bomber is on file somewhere."

"You're right, Ernie. You've made me a happy man."

"Oh, one more thing. About that church bomb."

"Yes?"

"Based on the debris, I'd say the device had some sort of gift wrapping around it. Also, since it had no timing elements, my guess is, it was designed to be triggered on opening. But it went off prematurely. Probably a short circuit of some kind."

"You mentioned gift wrapping."

"Yeah. Silver-and-white paper."

Wedding wrap, thought Sam, remembering the gift that had been delivered that morning to the church. If the bomb was meant to explode on opening, then there was no longer any doubt who the intended victims were.

But why kill Nina? he wondered as he headed back to the conference room. Could this whole mess be attributed to another woman's jealousy? Daniella Cormier had a motive, but would she have gone so far as to hire a bomber?

What was he missing here?

He opened the office door and halted. The three homicide detectives were still sitting at the table. Nina wasn't. She was gone.

"Where is she?" Sam asked.

Yeats shrugged. "She left."

"What?"

"She got fed up with our questions, so she walked out."

"You *let* her leave?"

"We haven't charged her with anything. Are you saying we should have, Navarro?"

Sam's reply was unrepeatable. With a sudden sense of anxiety, he left Yeats and headed out the front entrance of police headquarters. He stood on the sidewalk, looking up and down the street.

Nina was nowhere in sight.

Someone's trying to kill her, he thought as he headed for his car. *I have to reach her first.*

From his car phone, he called Nina's father's house. She wasn't there. He called Robert Bledsoe's house. No answer. He called Lydia Warrenton's house. Nina wasn't there either.

On a hunch, he drove to Lydia's Cape Elizabeth home anyway. People in distress often flee home for comfort, he reasoned. Eventually, Nina might wind up at her mother's.

He found Lydia at home. But no Nina—not yet, at least.

"I haven't spoken to her since yesterday morning," said Lydia, ushering Sam into the seaview room. "I'm not sure she *would* come here."

"Do you know where she might go?" Sam asked. "Someone she might turn to?"

Lydia shook her head. "I'm afraid my daughter and I aren't very close. We never were. The truth is, she wasn't the easiest child."

"What do you mean, Mrs. Warrenton?"

Lydia seated herself on the white couch. Her silk pantsuit was a startling slash of purple against the pale cushions. "What I mean to say—I know it sounds awful—is that Nina was something of a disappointment to me. We offered her so many opportunities. To study abroad, for instance. At a boarding school in Switzerland. Her sister Wendy went and benefited wonderfully. But Nina refused to go. She insisted on staying home. Then there were the other things. The boys she brought home. The ridiculous outfits she'd wear. She could be doing so much with her life, but she never achieved much."

"She earned a nursing degree."

Lydia gave a shrug. "So do thousands of other girls."

"She's not any other girl, Mrs. Warrenton. She's your daughter."

"That's why I expected more. Her sister speaks three languages and plays the piano and cello. She's married to an attorney who's in line for a judicial seat. While Nina…" Lydia sighed. "I can't imagine how sisters could be so different."

"Maybe the real difference," said Sam, rising to his feet, "was in how you loved them." He turned and walked out of the room.

"Mr. Navarro!" he heard Lydia call as he reached the front door.

He looked back. She was standing in the hallway, a

woman of such perfectly groomed elegance that she didn't seem real or alive. Or touchable.

Not like Nina at all.

"I think you have entirely the wrong idea about me and my daughter," Lydia said.

"Does it really matter what I think?"

"I just want you to understand that I did the best I could, under the circumstances."

"Under the circumstances," replied Sam, "so did she." And he left the house.

Back in his car, he debated which way to head next. Another round of phone calls came up empty. Where the hell was she?

The only place he hadn't checked was her new apartment. She'd told him it was on Taylor Street. There was probably no phone in yet; he'd have to drive there to check it out.

On his way over, he kept thinking about what Lydia Warrenton had just told him. He thought about what it must have been like for Nina to grow up the black sheep, the unfavored child. Always doing the wrong thing, never meeting Mommy's approval. Sam had been fortunate to have a mother who'd instilled in him a sense of his own competence.

I understand now, he thought, *why you wanted to marry Robert.* Marrying Robert Bledsoe was the one sure way to gain her mother's approval. And even that had collapsed in failure.

By the time he pulled up at Nina's new apartment building, he was angry. At Lydia, at George Cormier and his parade of wives, at the entire Cormier family for its battering of a little girl's sense of self-worth.

He knocked harder at the apartment door than he had to.

There was no response. She wasn't here, either.

Where are you, Nina?

He was about to leave when he impulsively gave the knob a turn. It was unlocked.

He pushed the door open. "Nina?" he called.

Then his gaze focused on the wire. It was almost invisible, a tiny line of silver that traced along the doorframe and threaded toward the ceiling.

Oh, my God...

In one fluid movement he pivoted away and dived sideways, down the hallway.

The force of the explosion blasted straight through the open door and ripped through the wall in a flying cloud of wood and plaster.

Deafened, stunned by the blast, Sam lay facedown in the hallway as debris rained onto his back.

Chapter Eight

"Man, oh man," said Gillis. "You sure did bring down the house."

They were standing outside, behind the yellow police line, waiting for the rest of the search team to assemble. The apartment house—what was left of it—had been cleared of any second devices, and now it was Ernie Takeda's show. Takeda was, at that moment, diagramming the search grid, handing out evidence bags, and assigning his lab crew to their individual tasks.

Sam already knew what they'd find. Residue of Dupont label dynamite. Scraps of green two-inch-wide electrical tape. And Prima detonating cord. The same three components as the church bomb and the warehouse bomb.

And every other bomb put together by the late Vincent Spectre.

Who's your heir apparent, Spectre? Sam wondered. *To whom did you bequeath your tricks of the trade? And why is Nina Cormier the target?*

Just trying to reason it through made his head pound. He was still covered in dust, his cheek was bruised and swollen, and he could barely hear out of his left ear. But he had nothing to complain about. He was alive.

Nina would not have been so fortunate.

"I've got to find her," he said. "Before he does."

"We've checked with the family again," said Gillis. "Father, mother, sister. She hasn't turned up anywhere."

"Where the hell could she have gone?" Sam began to pace along the police line, his worry turning to agitation. "She walks out of headquarters, maybe she catches a cab or a bus. Then what? What would she do?"

"Whenever my wife gets mad, she goes shopping," Gillis offered helpfully.

"I'm going to call the family again." Sam turned to his car. "Maybe she's finally shown up somewhere."

He was about to reach inside the Taurus for the car phone when he froze, his gaze focused on the edge of the crowd. A small, dark-haired figure stood at the far end of the street. Even from that distance, Sam could read the fear, the shock, in her pale face.

"Nina," he murmured. At once he began to move toward her, began to push, then shove his way through the crowd. "Nina!"

She caught sight of him, struggling to reach her. Now she was moving as well, frantically plunging into the gathering of onlookers. They found each other, fell into each other's embrace. And at that moment, there was no one else in the world for Sam, no one but the woman he was holding. She felt so very precious in his arms, so easily taken from him.

With a sudden start, he became acutely aware of the crowd. All these people, pressing in on them. "I'm getting you out of here," he said. Hugging her close to his side, he guided her toward his car. The whole time, he was scanning faces, watching for any sudden movements.

Only when he'd bundled her safely into the Taurus did he allow himself a deep breath of relief.

"Gillis!" he called. "You're in charge here!"

"Where you going?"

"I'm taking her somewhere safe."

"But—"

Sam didn't finish the conversation. He steered the car out of the crowd and they drove away.

Drove north.

Nina was staring at him. At the bruise on his cheek, the plaster dust coating his hair. "My God, Sam," she murmured. "You've been hurt—"

"A little deaf in one ear, but otherwise I'm okay." He glanced at her and saw that she didn't quite believe him. "I ducked out just before it blew. It was a five-second delay detonator. Set off by opening the door." He paused, then added quietly, "It was meant for you."

She said nothing. She didn't have to; he could read the comprehension in her gaze. This bombing was no mistake, no random attack. She was the target and she could no longer deny it.

"We're chasing down every lead we have," he said. "Yeats is going to question Daniella again, but I think that's a dead end. We did get a partial fingerprint off the warehouse bomb, and we're waiting for an ID. Until then, we've just got to keep you alive. And that means you have to cooperate. Do exactly what I tell you to do." He gave an exasperated sigh and clutched the steering wheel tighter. "That was *not* smart, Nina. What you did today."

"I was angry. I needed to get away from all you cops."

"So you storm out of headquarters? Without telling me where you're going?"

"You threw me to the wolves, Sam. I expected Yeats to clap the handcuffs on me. And you delivered me to him."

"I had no choice. One way or the other, he was going to question you."

"Yeats thinks I'm guilty. And since *he* was so sure of it, I thought…I thought you must have your doubts as well."

"I have no doubts," he said, his voice absolutely steady. "Not about you. And after this latest bomb, I don't think Yeats'll have any doubts either. You're the target."

The turnoff to Route 95—the Interstate—was just ahead. Sam took it.

"Where are we going?" she asked.

"I'm getting you out of town. Portland isn't a safe place for you. So I have another spot in mind. A fishing camp on Coleman Pond. I've had it for a few years. You'll be roughing it there, but you can stay as long as you need to."

"You won't be staying with me?"

"I have a job to do, Nina. It's the only way we'll get the answers. If I do my job."

"Of course, you're right." And she looked straight ahead at the road. "I forget sometimes," she said softly, "that you're a cop."

Across the street from the police line, he stood in the thick of the crowd, watching the bomb investigators scurry about with their evidence bags and their notebooks. Judging by the shattered glass, the debris in the street, the blast had been quite impressive. But of course he'd planned it that way.

Too bad Nina Cormier was still alive.

He'd spotted her just moments before, being escorted through the crowd by Detective Sam Navarro. He'd recognized Navarro at once. For years he'd followed the man's career, had read every news article ever written about the Bomb Squad. He knew about Gordon Gillis and Ernie

Takeda as well. It was his business to know. They were the enemy, and a good soldier must know his enemy.

Navarro helped the woman into a car. He seemed unusually protective—not like Navarro at all, to be succumbing to romance on the job. Cops like him were supposed to be professionals. What had happened to the quality of civil servants these days?

Navarro and the woman drove away.

There was no point trying to follow them; another opportunity would arise.

Right now he had a job to do. And only two days in which to finish it.

He gave his gloves a little tug. And he walked away, unnoticed, through the crowd.

BILLY "THE SHOWMAN" Binford was happy today. He was even grinning at his attorney, seated on the other side of the Plexiglas barrier.

"It's gonna be all right, Darien," said Billy. "I got everything taken care of. You just get ready to negotiate that plea bargain. And get me out of here, quick."

Darien shook his head. "I told you, Liddell's not in a mood to cut any deals. He's out to score big with your conviction."

"Darien, Darien. You got no faith."

"What I got is a good grip on reality. Liddell's aiming for a higher office. For that, he's got to put you away."

"He won't be putting anyone away. Not after Saturday."

"What?"

"You didn't hear me say nothing, okay? I didn't say nothing. Just believe me, Liddell won't be a problem."

"I don't want to know. Don't tell me about it."

Billy regarded his attorney with a look of both pity

and amusement. "You know what? You're like that monkey with his paws over his ears. Hear no evil. That's you."

"Yeah," Darien agreed. And he nodded miserably. "That's me exactly."

A FIRE CRACKLED in the hearth, but Nina felt chilled to the bone. Outside, dusk had deepened, and the last light was fading behind the dense silhouettes of pine trees. The cry of a loon echoed, ghostlike, across the lake. She'd never been afraid of the woods, or the darkness, or of being alone. Tonight, though, she *was* afraid, and she didn't want Sam to leave.

She also knew he had to.

He came tramping back into the cottage, carrying an armload of firewood, and began to stack it by the hearth. "This should do you for a few days," he said. "I just spoke to Henry Pearl and his wife. Their camp's up the road. They said they'd check up on you a few times a day. I've known them for years, so I know you can count on them. If you need anything at all, just knock on their door."

He finished stacking the wood and clapped the dirt from his hands. With his shirtsleeves rolled up and sawdust clinging to his trousers, he looked more like a woodsman than a city cop. He threw another birch log on the fire and the flames shot up in a crackle of sparks. He turned to look at her, his expression hidden against the backlight of fire.

"You'll be safe here, Nina. I wouldn't leave you alone if I had even the slightest doubt."

She nodded. And smiled. "I'll be fine."

"There's a fishing pole and tackle box in the kitchen, if you feel like wrestling with a trout. And feel free to wear anything you find in the closet. None of it'll fit, but at least you'll be warm. Henry's wife'll drop by some, uh, women's wear tomorrow." He paused and laughed. "Those probably won't fit either. Since she's twice *my* size."

"I'll manage, Sam. Don't worry about me."

There was a long silence. They both knew there was nothing more to say, but he didn't move. He glanced around the room, as though reluctant to leave. Almost as reluctant as she was to see him go.

"It's a long drive back to the city," she said. "You should eat before you go. Can I interest you in dinner? Say, a gourmet repast of macaroni and cheese?"

He grinned. "Make it anything else and I'll say yes."

In the kitchen, they rummaged through the groceries they'd bought at a supermarket on the way. Mushroom omelets, a loaf of French bread, and a bottle of wine soon graced the tiny camp table. Electricity had not yet made it to this part of the lake, so they ate by the light of a hurricane lamp. Outside, dusk gave way to a darkness alive with the chirp of crickets.

She gazed across the table at him, watching the way his face gleamed in the lantern light. She kept focusing on that bruise on his cheek, thinking about how close he'd come to dying that afternoon. But that was exactly the sort of work he did, the sort of risk he took all the time. Bombs. Death. It was insane, and she didn't know why any man in his right mind would take those risks. *Crazy cop,* she thought. *And I must be just as insane, because I think I'm falling for this guy.*

She took a sip of wine, the whole time intensely, almost painfully aware of his presence. And of her attraction toward him, an attraction so strong she was having trouble remembering to eat.

She had to remind herself that he was just doing his job, that to him, she was nothing more than a piece of the puzzle he was trying to solve, but she couldn't help picturing other meals, other nights they might spend together. Here, on the lake. Candlelight, laughter. Children. She thought he'd be good with children. He'd be patient and kind, just as he was with her.

How would I know that? I'm dreaming. Fantasizing again.

She reached across to pour him more wine.

He put his hand over the glass. "I have to be driving back."

"Oh. Of course." Nervously she set the bottle down again. She folded and refolded her napkin. For a whole minute they didn't speak, didn't look at each other. At least, she didn't look at him.

But when she finally raised her eyes, she saw that he was watching her. Not the way a cop looks at a witness, at a piece of a puzzle.

He was watching her the way a man watches a woman he wants.

He said, quickly, "I should leave now—"

"I know."

"—before it gets too late."

"It's still early."

"They'll need me, back in the city."

She bit her lip and said nothing. Of course he was right. The city did need him. Everyone needed him. She was just one detail that required attending to. Now she was safely tucked away and he could go back to his real business, his real concerns.

But he didn't seem at all eager to leave. He hadn't moved from the chair, hadn't broken eye contact. She was the one who looked away, who nervously snatched up her wineglass.

She was startled when he reached over and gently caught her hand. Without a word he took the glass and set it down. He raised her hand, palm side up, and pressed a kiss, ever so light, to her wrist. The lingering of lips, the tickle of his breath, was the sweetest torture. If he could wreak such havoc kissing that one square inch of skin, what could he do with the rest of her?

She closed her eyes and gave a small, soft moan. "I don't want you to leave," she whispered.

"It's a bad idea. For me to stay."

"Why?"

"Because of this." He kissed her wrist again. "And this." His lips skimmed up her arm, his beard delightfully rough against her sensitive skin. "It's a mistake. You know it. I know it."

"I make mistakes all the time," she replied. "I don't always regret them."

His gaze lifted to hers. He saw both her fear and her fearlessness. She was hiding nothing now, letting him read all. Her hunger was too powerful to hide.

He rose from the table. So did she.

He pulled her toward him, cupped her face in his hands, and pressed his lips to hers. The kiss, sweet with the taste of wine and desire, left her legs unsteady. She swayed against him, her arms reaching up to clutch his shoulders. Before she could catch her breath, he was kissing her again, deeper. As their mouths joined, so did their bodies. His hands slid down her waist, to her hips. He didn't need to pull her against him; she could already feel him, hard and aroused. And that excited her even more.

"If we're going to stop," he breathed, "it had better be now...."

She responded with a kiss that drowned out any more

words between them. Their bodies did all the talking, all the communicating.

They were tugging at each other's clothes, feverish for the touch of bare skin. First her sweater came off, then his shirt. They kissed their way into the next room, where the fire had quieted to a warm glow. Still kissing her, he pulled the afghan off the couch and let it fall onto the floor by the hearth.

Facing each other, they knelt before the dying fire. His bare shoulders gleamed in the flickering light. She was eager, starved for his touch, but he moved slowly, savoring every moment, every new experience of her. He watched with longing as she unhooked her bra and shrugged the straps off her shoulders. When he reached out to cup her breast, to tug at her nipple, she let her head sag back with a moan. His touch was ever so gentle, yet it left her feeling weak. Conquered. He tipped her back and lowered her onto the afghan.

Her body was pure liquid now, melting under his touch. He unzipped her jeans, eased them off her hips. Her underwear slid off with the hiss of silk. She lay unshielded to his gaze now, her skin rosy in the firelight.

"I've had so many dreams about you," he whispered as his hand slid exploringly down her belly, toward the dark triangle of hair. "Last night, when you were in my house, I dreamed of holding you. Touching you just the way I am now. But when I woke up, I told myself it could never happen. That it was all fantasy. All longing. And here we are..." He bent forward, his kiss tender on her lips. "I shouldn't be doing this."

"I want you to. I want us to."

"I want it just as much. More. But I'm afraid we're going to regret it."

"Then we'll regret it later. Tonight, let's just be you and me. Let's pretend there's nothing else, no one else."

He kissed her again. And this time his hand slipped between her thighs, his finger dipping into her wetness, sliding deep into her warmth. She groaned, helpless with delight. He slid another finger in, and felt her trembling, tightening around him. She was ready, so ready for him, but he wanted to take his time, to make this last.

He withdrew his hand, just long enough to remove the rest of his clothes. As he knelt beside her, she couldn't help drawing in a sharp breath of admiration. What a beautiful man he was. Not just his body, but his soul. She could see it in his eyes: the caring, the warmth. Before it had been hidden from her, concealed behind that tough-cop mask of his. Now he was hiding nothing. Revealing everything.

As she was revealing everything to him.

She was too lost in pleasure to feel any modesty, any shame. She lay back, whimpering, as his fingers found her again, withdrew, teased, plunged back in. Already she was slick with sweat and desire, her hips arching against him.

"Please," she murmured. "Oh, Sam. I—"

He kissed her, cutting off any protest. And he continued his torment, his fingers dipping, sliding, until she was wound so tight she thought she'd shatter.

Only then, only as she reached the very edge, did he take away his hand, fit his hips to hers, and thrust deep inside her.

She gripped him, crying out as he swept her, and himself, toward climax. And when it came, when she felt herself tumbling into that wondrous free fall, they clung to each other and they tumbled together, to a soft and ever-so-gentle landing.

She fell asleep, warm and safe, in his arms.

It was later, much later, when she awakened in the deepest chill of night.

The fire had died out. Although she was cocooned in the afghan, she found herself shivering.

And alone.

Hugging the afghan to her shoulders, she went into the kitchen and peered out the window. By the light of the moon, she could see that Sam's car was gone. He had returned to the city.

Already I miss him, she thought. Already his absence was like a deep, dark gulf in her life.

She went into the bedroom, climbed under the blankets, and tried to stop shivering, but she could not. When Sam had left, he had taken with him all the warmth. All the joy.

It scared her, how much she felt his absence. She was not going to fall in love with him; she could not afford to. What they'd experienced tonight was pleasure. The enjoyment of each other's bodies. As a lover, he was superb.

But as a man to love, he was clearly wrong for her.

No wonder he'd stolen away like a thief in the night. He'd known it was a mistake, just as she did. At this moment, he was probably regretting what they'd done.

She burrowed deeper under the blankets and waited for sleep, for dawn—whichever came first. Anything to ease the ache of Sam's departure.

But the night, cold and lonely, stretched on.

It was mistake. A stupid, crazy mistake.

All the way back to Portland, on the drive down that long, dark highway, Sam kept asking himself how he could have let it happen.

No, he *knew* how it happened. The attraction between them was just too strong. It had been pulling them together from the first day they'd met. He'd fought it, had never stopped reminding himself that he was a cop, and she was an important element in his investigation. Good cops did not fall into this trap.

He used to think he was a good cop. Now he knew he was far too human, that Nina was a temptation he couldn't resist, and that the whole investigation would probably suffer because he'd lost his sense of objectivity.

All because she'd come to mean too much to him.

Not only would the investigation suffer, *he* would as well, and he had only himself to blame. Nina was scared and vulnerable; naturally she'd turn to her protector for comfort. He should have kept her at arm's length, should have kept his own urges in check. Instead he'd succumbed, and now she was all he could think about.

He gripped the steering wheel and forced himself to focus on the road. On the case.

By 1:00 a.m., he was back in the city. By 1:30, he was at his desk, catching up on the preliminary reports from Ernie Takeda. As he'd expected, the bomb in Nina's apartment was similar to the devices that blew up the church and the warehouse. The difference between the three was in the method of detonation. The warehouse device had had a simple timer. The church device was a package bomb, designed to explode on opening. Nina's apartment had been wired to blow after the door opened. This bomber was a versatile fellow. He could trigger a blast in any number of ways. He varied his device according to the situation, and that made him both clever and extremely dangerous.

He went home at 5:00 a.m., caught a few hours of sleep, and was back at headquarters for an eight o'clock meeting.

With three bombings in two weeks, the pressure was on,

and the tension showed in the faces around the conference table. Gillis looked beat, Chief Coopersmith was testy, and even the normally unemotional Ernie Takeda was showing flashes of irritation. Part of that irritation was due to the presence of two federal agents from Alcohol, Tobacco and Firearms. Both the men from ATF wore expressions of big-time experts visiting Hicksville.

But the most annoying source of irritation was the presence of their esteemed D.A. and perpetual pain in the neck, Norm Liddell.

Liddell was waving the morning edition of the *New York Times*. "Look at the headline," he said. "'Portland, Maine, the new bombing capital?' New York's saying that about us? *Us?*" He threw the newspaper down on the table. "What the hell is going on in this town? Who *is* this bomber?"

"We can give you a likely psychological profile," said one of the ATF agents. "He's a white male, intelligent—"

"I already know he's intelligent!" snapped Liddell. "A hell of a lot more intelligent than we are. I don't want some psychological profile. I want to know who he *is*. Does anyone have any idea about his identity?"

There was a silence at the table. Then Sam said, "We know who he's trying to kill."

"You mean the Cormier woman?" Liddell snorted. "So far, no one's come up with a single good reason why she's the target."

"But we know she is. She's our one link to the bomber."

"What about the warehouse bomb?" said Coopersmith. "How's that connect to Nina Cormier?"

Sam paused. "That I don't know," he admitted.

"I'd lay ten-to-one odds that Billy Binford's people ordered that warehouse bombing," said Liddell. "It was a logical move on his part. Scare off a prosecution witness. Does the Cormier woman have any connection to Binford?"

"All she knows about him is what she's read in the newspapers," said Sam. "There's no link."

"What about her family? Are they linked at all to Binford?"

"No link there, either," spoke up Gillis. "We've checked into the finances of the whole family. Nina Cormier's father, mother, stepfather, stepmother. No connection to Binford. Her ex-fiancé was just as clean."

Liddell sat back. "Something's coming. I can feel it. Binford's got something big planned."

"How do you know?" asked Coopersmith.

"I have sources." Liddell shook his head in disgust. "Here I finally get The Snowman behind bars, and he's still pulling strings, still making mincemeat of the court system. I'm convinced that warehouse bomb was an intimidation tactic. He's trying to scare all my witnesses. If I don't get a conviction, he'll be a free man in a few months. And he'll be scaring them in person."

"But chances are good you'll get that conviction," Coopersmith reassured him. "You've got credible witnesses, financial records. And you've drawn a law-and-order judge."

"Even so," countered Liddell, "Binford's not finished maneuvering. He's got something up his sleeve. I just wish I knew what it was." He looked at Sam. "Where are you hiding Nina Cormier?"

"A safe place," said Sam.

"You keeping it top secret or something?"

"Under the circumstances, I'd prefer to keep it known

only to myself and Gillis. If you have questions to ask her, I can ask them for you."

"I just want to know what her connection is to these bombings. Why The Snowman wants her dead."

"Maybe this has nothing to do with Binford," suggested Sam. "He's in jail, and there's another party involved here. The bomber."

"Right. So find him for me," snapped Liddell. "Before Portland gets known as the American Beirut." He rose from his chair, his signal that the meeting was over. "Binford goes to trial in a month. I don't want my witnesses scared off by any more bombs. So *get* this guy, before he destroys my case." With that, Liddell stalked out.

"Man, election year is hell," muttered Gillis.

As the others filed out of the room, Coopersmith said, "Navarro, a word with you."

Sam waited, knowing full well what was coming. Coopersmith shut the door and turned to look at him.

"You and Nina Cormier. What's going on?"

"She needs protection. So I'm looking out for her."

"Is that all you're doing?"

Sam let out a weary sigh. "I...may be more involved than I should be."

"That's what I figured." Coopersmith shook his head. "You're too smart for this, Sam. This is the sort of mistake rookies make. Not you."

"I know."

"It could put you both in a dangerous situation. I ought to yank you off the case."

"I need to stay on it."

"Because of the woman?"

"Because I want to nail this guy. I'm *going* to nail him."

"Fine. Just keep your distance from Nina Cormier. I

shouldn't have to tell you this. This kind of thing happens, someone always gets hurt. Right now she thinks you're John Wayne. But when this is all over, she's gonna see you're human like the rest of us. Don't set yourself up for this, Sam. She's got looks, she's got a daddy with lots of money. She doesn't want a cop."

I know he's right, thought Sam. *I know it from personal experience. Someone's going to get hurt. And it'll be me.*

The conference room door suddenly swung open and an excited Ernie Takeda stuck his head in the room. "You're not gonna believe this," he said, waving a sheet of fax paper.

"What is it?" asked Coopersmith.

"From NCIC. They just identified that fingerprint off the bomb fragment."

"And?"

"It's a match. With Vincent Spectre."

"That's impossible!" exclaimed Sam. He snatched the sheet from Ernie's grasp and stared at the faxed report. What he read there left no doubt that the ID was definite.

"There has to be a mistake," said Coopersmith. "They found his body. Spectre's been dead and buried for months."

Sam looked up. "Obviously not," he growled.

Chapter Nine

The rowboat was old and well used, but the hull was sound. At least, it didn't leak as Nina rowed it out into the lake. It was late afternoon and a pair of loons were paddling lazily through the water, neither one alarmed by the presence of a lone rower. The day was utter stillness, utter peace, as warm as a summer day should be.

Nina guided the boat to the center of the pond, where sunlight rippled on the water, and there she let the boat drift. As it turned lazy circles, she lay back and stared up at the sky. She saw birds winging overhead, saw a dragonfly hover, iridescent in the slanting light.

And then she heard a voice, calling her name.

She sat up so sharply the boat rocked. She saw him then, standing at the water's edge, waving to her.

As she rowed the boat back to shore, her heart was galloping, more from anticipation than exertion. Why had he returned so soon? Last night he'd left without a word of goodbye, the way a man leaves a woman he never intends to see again.

Now here he was, standing silent and still on the shore, his gaze as unreadable as ever. She couldn't figure him out. She'd never be able to figure him out. He was a man designed to drive her crazy, and as she glided across the last yards of water, she could already feel that lovely insanity take hold of her. It required all her willpower to suppress it.

She tossed him the painter rope. He hauled the rowboat up onto the shore and helped her step out. Just the pressure of his hand grasping her arm gave her a thrill of delight. But one look at his face quelled any hopes that he was here as a lover. This was the cop, impersonal, businesslike. Not at all the man who'd held her in his arms.

"There's been a new development," he said.

Just as coolly, she met his gaze. "What development?"

"We think we know who the bomber is. I want you to take a look at some photographs."

On the couch by the fireplace—the same fireplace that had warmed them when they'd made love the night before—Nina sat flipping through a book of mug shots. The hearth was now cold, and so was she, both in body and in spirit. Sam sat a good foot away, not touching her, not saying a word. But he was watching her expectantly, waiting for some sign that she recognized a face in that book.

She forced herself to concentrate on the photos. One by one she scanned the faces, carefully taking in the features of each man pictured there. She reached the last page. Shaking her head, she closed the cover.

"I don't recognize anyone," she declared.

"Are you certain?"

"I'm certain. Why? Who am I supposed to recognize?"

His disappointment was apparent. He opened the book to the fourth page and handed it back to her. "Look at this face. Third one down, first column. Have you ever seen this man?"

She spent a long time studying the photo. Then she said, "No. I don't know him."

With a sigh of frustration, Sam sank back against the couch. "This doesn't make any sense at all."

Nina was still focused on the photograph. The man in the picture appeared to be in his forties, with sandy hair, blue eyes, and hollow, almost gaunt, cheeks. It was the eyes that held her attention. They stared straight at her, a look of intimidation that burned, lifelike, from a mere two-dimensional image. Nina gave an involuntary shiver.

"Who is he?" she asked.

"His name is—or was—Vincent Spectre. He's five foot eleven, 180 pounds, forty-six years old. At least, that's what he would be now. If he's still alive."

"You mean you don't know if he is?"

"We thought he was dead."

"You're not sure?"

"Not any longer." Sam rose from the couch. It was getting chilly in the cabin; he crouched at the hearth and began to arrange kindling in the fireplace.

"For twelve years," he said, "Vincent Spectre was an army demolitions expert. Then he got booted out of the service. Dishonorable discharge, petty theft. It didn't take him long to launch a second career. He became what we call a specialist. Big bangs, big bucks. Hired himself out to anyone who'd pay for his expertise. He worked for terrorist governments. For the mob. For crime bosses all over the country.

"For years he raked in the money. Then his luck ran out. He was recognized on a bank security camera. Arrested, convicted, served only a year. Then he escaped."

Sam struck a match and lit the kindling. It caught fire in a crackle of sparks and flames. He lay a log on top and turned to look at her.

"Six months ago," he continued, "Spectre's remains

were found in the rubble after one of his bombs blew up a warehouse. That is, authorities *thought* it was his body. Now we think it might have been someone else's. And Spectre's still alive."

"How do you know that?"

"Because his fingerprint just turned up. On a fragment of the warehouse bomb."

She stared at him. "You think he also blew up the church?"

"Almost certainly. Vincent Spectre's trying to kill you."

"But I don't know any Vincent Spectre! I've never even heard his name before!"

"And you don't recognize his photo."

"No."

Sam stood up. Behind him, the flames were now crackling, consuming the log. "We've shown Spectre's photo to the rest of your family. They don't recognize him, either."

"It must be a mistake. Even if the man's alive, he has no reason to kill me."

"Someone else could have hired him."

"You've already explored that. And all you came up with was Daniella."

"That's still a possibility. She denies it, of course. And she passed the polygraph test."

"She let you hook her up to a *polygraph?*"

"She consented. So we did it."

Nina shook her head in amazement. "She must have been royally ticked off."

"As a matter of fact, I think she rather enjoyed giving the performance. She turned every male head in the department."

"Yes, she's good at that. She certainly turned my father's head. And Robert's, too," Nina added softly.

Sam was moving around the room now, pacing a slow circle around the couch. "So we're back to the question of Vincent Spectre," he said. "And what his connection is to you. Or Robert."

"I told you, I've never heard his name before. I don't remember Robert ever mentioning the name, either."

Sam paced around the couch, returned to stand by the fireplace. Against the background of flames, his face was unreadable. "Spectre *is* alive. And he built a bomb intended for you and Robert. Why?"

She looked down again at the photo of Vincent Spectre. Try as she might, she could conjure up no memory of that face. The eyes, perhaps, seemed vaguely familiar. That stare was one she might have seen before. But not the face.

"Tell me more about him," she suggested.

Sam went to the couch and sat down beside her. Not quite close enough to touch her, but close enough to make her very aware of his presence.

"Vincent Spectre was born and raised in California. Joined the army at age nineteen. Quickly showed an aptitude for explosives work, and was trained in demolitions. Saw action in Grenada and Panama. That's where he lost his finger—trying to disarm a terrorist explosive. At that point, he could have retired on disability but—"

"Wait. Did you just say he was missing a finger?"

"That's right."

"Which hand?"

"The left. Why?"

Nina went very still. Thinking, remembering. A missing finger. Why did that image seem so vividly familiar?

Softly she said, "Was it the left middle finger?"

Frowning, Sam reached for his briefcase and took out

a file folder. He flipped through the papers contained inside. "Yes," he said. "It was the middle finger."

"No stump at all? Just...missing entirely."

"That's right. They had to amputate all the way back to the knuckle." He was watching her, his eyes alert, his voice quiet with tension. "So you *do* know him."

"I—I'm not sure. There was a man with an amputated finger—the left middle finger—"

"What? Where?"

"The Emergency Room. It was a few weeks ago. I remember he was wearing gloves, and he didn't want to take them off. But I had to check his pulse. So I pulled off the left glove. And I was so startled to see he was missing a finger. He'd stuffed the glove finger with cotton. I think I...I must have stared. I remember I asked him how he lost it. He told me he'd caught it in some machinery."

"Why was he in the ER?"

"It was—I think an accident. Oh, I remember. He was knocked down by a bicycle. He'd cut his arm and needed stitches put in. The strange part about it all was the way he vanished afterward. Right after the cut was sutured, I left the room to get something. When I came back, he was gone. No thank you, nothing. Just—disappeared. I thought he was trying to get away without paying his bill. But I found out later that he did pay the clerk. In cash."

"Do you remember his name?"

"No." She gave a shrug. "I'm terrible with names."

"Describe him for me. Everything you remember."

She was silent for a moment, struggling to conjure up the face of a man she'd seen weeks ago, and only once. "I remember he was fairly tall. When he lay down on the treatment table, his feet hung over the edge." She looked at Sam. "He'd be about your height."

"I'm six feet. Vincent Spectre's five-eleven. What about his face? Hair, eyes?"

"He had dark hair. Almost black. And his eyes..." She sat back, frowning in concentration. Remembered how startled she'd been by the missing finger. That she'd looked up and met the patient's gaze. "I think they were blue."

"The blue eyes would match Spectre's. The black hair doesn't. He could've dyed it."

"But the face was different. It didn't look like this photo."

"Spectre has resources. He could've paid for plastic surgery, completely changed his appearance. For six months we assumed he was dead. During that time he could've remade himself into an entirely different man."

"All right, what if it *was* Spectre I saw in the ER that day? Why does that make me a target? Why would he want to kill me?"

"You saw his face. You could identify him."

"A lot of people must have seen his face!"

"You're the only one who could connect that face with a man who was missing a finger. You said he was wearing gloves, that he didn't want to remove them."

"Yes, but it was part of his uniform. Maybe the only reason for the gloves was—"

"What uniform?"

"Some sort of long-sleeved jacket with brass buttons. White gloves. Pants with this side stripe. You know, like an elevator operator. Or a bellhop."

"Was there a logo embroidered on the jacket? A building or hotel name?"

"No."

Sam was on his feet now, pacing back and forth with new excitement. "Okay. Okay, he has a minor accident.

Cuts his arm, has to go to the ER for stitches. You see that he's missing a finger. You see his face. And you see he's wearing some sort of uniform...."

"It's not enough to make me a threat."

"Maybe it is. Right now, he's operating under a completely new identity. The authorities have no idea what he looks like. But that missing finger is a giveaway. You saw it. And his face. You could identify him for us."

"I didn't know anything about Vincent Spectre. I wouldn't have thought to go to the police."

"We were already raising questions about his so-called death. Wondering if he was still alive and operating. Another bombing, and we might have figured out the truth. All we had to do was tell the public we were looking for a man missing his left middle finger. You would have come forward. Wouldn't you?"

She nodded. "Of course."

"That may be what he was afraid of. That you'd tell us the one thing we didn't know. What he looks like."

For a long moment she was silent. She was staring down at the book of mug shots, thinking about that day in the ER. Trying to remember the patients, the crises. Sore throats and sprained ankles. She'd been a nurse for eight years, had treated so many patients, that the days all seemed to blend together. But she did remember one more detail about that visit from the man with the gloves. A detail that left her suddenly chilled.

"The doctor," she said softly. "The doctor who sutured the cut—"

"Yes? Who was it?"

"Robert. It was Robert."

Sam stared at her. In that instant, he understood. They both did. Robert had been in the same room as well. He'd seen the patient's face, had seen the mutilated left hand. He, like Nina, could have identified Vincent Spectre.

Now Robert was dead.

Sam reached down to take Nina's hand. "Come on." He pulled her to her feet.

They were standing face-to-face now, and she felt her body respond immediately to his nearness, felt her stomach dance that little dance of excitement. Arousal.

"I'm driving you back to Portland," he said.

"Tonight?"

"I want you to meet with our police artist. See if you two can come up with a sketch of Spectre's face."

"I'm not sure I can. If I saw him, I'd recognize him. But just to describe his face—"

"The artist will walk you through it. The important thing is that we have something to work with. Also, I need you to help me go through the ER records. Maybe there's some information you've forgotten."

"We keep a copy of all the encounter forms. I can find his record for you." *I'll do anything you want me to do,* she thought, *if only you'll stop this tough-cop act.*

As they stood gazing at each other, she thought she saw a ripple of longing in his eyes. Too quickly, he turned away to get a jacket from the closet. He draped it over her shoulders. Just the brushing of his fingers against her skin made her quiver.

She shifted around to face him. To confront him.

"Has something happened between us?" she asked softly.

"What do you mean?"

"Last night. I didn't imagine it, Sam. We made love, right here in this room. Now I'm wondering what I did wrong. Why you seem so...indifferent."

He sighed, a sound of weariness. And perhaps regret. "Last night," he began, "shouldn't have happened. It was a mistake."

"I didn't think so."

"Nina, it's always a mistake to fall in love with the investigating cop. You're scared, you're looking for a hero. I happen to fall into the role."

"But you're not playing a role! Neither am I. Sam, I care about you. I think I'm falling in love with you."

He just looked at her without speaking, his silence as cutting as any words.

She turned away, so that she wouldn't have to see that flat, emotionless gaze of his. With a forced laugh she said, "God, I feel like such an idiot. Of course, this must happen to you all the time. Women throwing themselves at you."

"It's not like that."

"Isn't it? The hero cop. Who could resist?" She turned back to him. "So, how do I compare with all the others?"

"There aren't any others! Nina, I'm not trying to shove you away. I just want you to understand that it's the situation that's pulled us together. The danger. The intensity. You look at me and you completely miss all the flaws. All the reasons I'm not the right guy for you. You were engaged to Robert Bledsoe. Ivy League. Medical degree. House on the water. What the hell am I but a civil servant?"

She shook her head, tears suddenly filling her eyes. "Do you really think that's how I see you? As just a civil servant? Just a cop?"

"It's what I am."

"You're so much more." She reached up to touch his face. He flinched, but didn't pull away as her fingers caressed the roughness of his jaw. "Oh, Sam. You're kind.

And gentle. And brave. I haven't met any other man like you. Okay, so you're a cop. It's just part of who you are. You've kept me alive. You've watched over me…."

"It was my job."

"Is that all it was?"

He didn't answer right away. He just looked at her, as though reluctant to tell the truth.

"Is it, Sam? Just a part of your job?"

He sighed. "No," he admitted. "It was more than that. You're more than that."

Pure joy made her smile. Last night she'd felt it—his warmth, his caring. For all his denials, there was a living, breathing man under that mask of indifference. She wanted so badly to fall into his arms, to coax the real Sam Navarro out from his hiding place.

He reached up for her hand and gently but firmly lowered it from his face. "Please, Nina," he said. "Don't make this hard for both of us. I have a job to do, and I can't be distracted. It's dangerous. For you and for me."

"But you do care. That's all I need to know. That you care."

He nodded. It was the most she could hope for.

"It's getting late. We should leave," he mumbled. And he turned toward the door. "I'll be waiting for you in the car."

NINA FROWNED AT the computer-generated sketch of the suspect's face. "It's not quite right," she said.

"What's not right about it?" asked Sam.

"I don't know. It's not easy to conjure up a man's face. I saw him only that one time. I didn't consciously register the shape of his nose or jaw."

"Does he look anything like this picture?"

She studied the image on the computer screen. For an hour, they'd played with different hairlines, noses, shapes of jaws and chins. What they'd come up with seemed generic, lifeless. Like every other police sketch she'd ever seen.

"To be honest," she admitted with a sigh, "I can't be sure this is what he looks like. If you put the real man in a lineup, I think I'd be able to identify him. But I'm not very good at re-creating what I saw."

Sam, obviously disappointed, turned to the computer technician. "Print it up anyway. Send copies to the news stations and wire services."

"Sure thing, Navarro," the tech replied and he flipped on the printer switch.

As Sam led Nina away, she said miserably, "I'm sorry. I guess I wasn't much help."

"You did fine. And you're right, it's not easy to re-create a face. Especially one you saw only once. You really think you'd know him if you saw him?"

"Yes. I'm pretty sure of it."

He gave her arm a squeeze. "That may be all we'll need from you. Assuming we ever get our hands on him. Which leads to the next item on our agenda."

"What's that?"

"Gillis is already at the hospital, pulling those treatment records. He'll need you to interpret a few things on the encounter form."

She nodded. "*That* I know I can do."

They found Gillis sitting in a back room of the ER, papers piled up on the table in front of him. His face was pasty with fatigue under the fluorescent lights. It was nearly midnight, and he'd been on the job since 7:00 a.m. So had Sam.

For both of them, the night was just beginning.

"I pulled what I think is the right encounter form," said Gillis. "May 29, 5:00 p.m. Sound about right, Miss Cormier?"

"It could be."

Gillis handed her the sheet. It was the one-page record of an ER visit. On top was the name Lawrence Foley, his address, and billing information. On the line Chief Complaint, she recognized her own handwriting: Laceration, left forearm. Below that, she had written: forty-six-year-old white male hit by bicycle in crosswalk. Fell, cut arm on fender. No loss of consciousness."

She nodded. "This is the one. Here's Robert's signature, on the bottom. Treating physician. He sutured the cut—four stitches, according to his notes."

"Have we checked out this name, Lawrence Foley?" Sam asked Gillis.

"No one by that name living at that address," Gillis informed him. "And that's a nonexistent phone number."

"Bingo," said Sam. "False address, false identity. This is our man."

"But we're no closer to catching him," stressed Gillis. "He left no trail, no clues. Where are we supposed to look?"

"We have a sketch of his face circulating. We know he was wearing some sort of uniform, possibly a bellhop's. So we check all the hotels. Try to match the sketch with any of their employees." Sam paused, frowning. "A hotel. Why would he be working at a hotel?"

"He needed a job?" Gillis offered.

"As a bellhop?" Sam shook his head. "If this is really Vincent Spectre, he had a reason to be there. A contract. A target..." He sat back and rubbed his eyes. The late hour, the stress, was showing in his face. All those shadows, all those lines of weariness. Nina longed to reach out to him, to stroke away the worry she saw there, but she didn't dare. Not in front of Gillis. Maybe not ever. He'd made it perfectly clear she was a distraction to him, to his work, and that distractions were dangerous. That much she accepted.

Yet how she ached to touch him.

Sam rose to his feet and began to move about, as though forcing himself to stay awake. "We need to check all the hotels. Set up a lineup of bellhops. And we need to check police reports. Maybe someone called in that bicycle accident."

"Okay, I'll get Cooley on it."

"What we really need to know is—who is he after? Who's the target?"

"We're not going to figure that out tonight," said Gillis. "We need more to go on." He yawned, and added, "And we need some sleep. Both of us."

"He's right," said Nina. "You can't function without rest, Sam. You need to sleep on this."

"In the meantime, Spectre's at work on God knows what catastrophe. So far we've been lucky. Only one bombing casualty. But the next time…" Sam stopped pacing. Stopped because he'd simply run out of steam. He was standing in one spot, his shoulders slumped, his whole body drooping.

Gillis looked at Nina. "Get him home, will ya? Before he keels over and I have to drag him."

Nina rose from her chair. "Come on, Sam," she said softly. "I'll drive you home."

Heading out to the car, he kept insisting he could drive, that he was in perfectly good shape to take the wheel.

She, just as insistently, pointed out that he was a menace on the road.

He let her drive.

Scarcely after she'd pulled out of the hospital parking lot, he was sound asleep.

At his house, she roused him just long enough to climb out of the car and walk in the front door. In his bedroom, he shrugged off his gun holster, pulled off his shoes, and collapsed on the bed. His last words were some sort of apology. Then he was fast asleep.

Smiling, she pulled the covers over him and went out to check the windows and doors. Everything was locked tight; the house was secure—as secure as it could be.

Back in Sam's room, she undressed in the dark and climbed into bed beside him. He didn't stir. Gently she stroked her fingers through his hair and thought, *My poor, exhausted Sam. Tonight, I'll watch over you.*

Sighing, he turned toward her, his arm reaching out to hug her against him. Even in his sleep, he was trying to protect her.

Like no other man I've ever known.

Nothing could hurt her. Not tonight, not in his arms. She'd stake her life on it.

THEY WERE SHOWING his picture on the morning news.

Vincent Spectre took one look at the police sketch on the TV screen and he laughed softly. What a joke. The picture looked nothing like him. The ears were too big, the jaw was too wide, and the eyes looked beady. He did not have beady eyes. How had they gotten it so wrong? What had happened to the quality of law enforcement?

"Can't catch me, I'm the gingerbread man," he murmured.

Sam Navarro was slipping, if that drawing was the best he could come up with. A pity. Navarro had seemed such a clever man, a truly worthy opponent. Now it appeared he was as dumb a cop as all the others. Though he *had* managed to draw one correct conclusion.

Vincent Spectre was alive and back in the game.

"Just wait till you see how alive I am," he said.

That Cormier woman must have described his face to the police artist. Although the sketch wasn't anything for him to worry about, Nina Cormier did concern him. Chances were, she'd recognize him in a room of anonymous strangers. She was the only one who could link his face to his identity, the only one who could ruin his plan. She would have to be disposed of.

Eventually.

He turned off the TV and went into the apartment bedroom, where the woman was still asleep. He'd met Marilyn Dukoff three weeks ago at the Stop Light Club, where he'd gone to watch the topless dance revue. Marilyn had been the blonde in the purple-sequined G-string. Her face was coarse, her IQ a joke, but her figure was a marvel of nature and silicone. Like so many other women on the exotic dance circuit, she was in desperate need of money and affection.

He'd offered her both, in abundance.

She'd accepted his gifts with true gratitude. She was like a puppy who'd been neglected too long, loyal and hungry for approval. Best of all, she asked no questions. She knew enough not to.

He sat down beside her on the bed and nudged her awake. "Marilyn?"

She opened one sleepy eye and smiled at him. "Good morning."

He returned her smile. And followed it with a kiss. As usual, she responded eagerly. Gratefully. He removed his clothes and climbed under the sheets, next to that architecturally astonishing body. It took no coaxing at all to get her into the mood.

When they had finished, and she lay smiling and satisfied beside him, he knew it was the right time to ask.

And he said, "I need another favor from you."

TWO HOURS LATER, a blond woman in a gray suit presented her ID to the prison official. "I'm an attorney with Frick and Darien," she said. "Here to see our client, Billy Binford."

Moments later she was escorted to the visiting room. Billy "The Snowman" took a seat on the other side of the Plexiglas. He regarded her for a moment, then said, "I been watching the news on TV. What the hell's all this other stuff going on?"

"He says it's all necessary," said the blonde.

"Look, I just wanted the job done like he promised."

"It's being taken care of. Everything's on schedule. All you have to do is sit back and wait."

Billy glanced at the prison guard, who was standing off to the side and obviously bored. "I got everything riding on this," he muttered.

"It will happen. But he wants to make sure you keep up your end of the bargain. Payment, by the end of the week."

"Not yet. Not till I'm sure it's done. I got a court date coming up fast—too fast. I'm counting on this."

The blonde merely smiled. "It'll happen," she said. "He guarantees it."

Chapter Ten

Sam woke up to the smell of coffee and the aroma of something cooking, something delicious. It was Saturday. He was alone in the bed, but there was no question that someone else was in the house. He could hear the bustle in the kitchen, the soft clink of dishes. For the first time in months, he found himself smiling as he rose from bed and headed to the shower. There was a woman in the kitchen, a woman who was actually cooking breakfast. Amazing how different that made the whole house feel. Warm. Welcoming.

He came out of the shower and stood in front of the mirror to shave. That's when his smile faded. He suddenly wondered how long he'd been asleep. He'd slept so heavily he hadn't heard Nina get out of bed this morning, hadn't even heard her take a shower. But she'd been in here; the shower curtain had already been damp when he stepped in.

Last night someone could have broken into the house, and he would have slept right through it.

I'm useless to her, he thought. He couldn't track down Spectre and keep Nina safe at the same time. He didn't have the stamina or the objectivity. He was worse than useless; he was endangering her life.

This was exactly what he'd been afraid would happen.

He finished shaving, got dressed, and went into the kitchen.

Just the sight of her standing at the stove was enough to shake his determination. She turned and smiled at him.

"Good morning," she murmured, and wrapped her arms around him in a sweetly scented hug. Lord, this was every man's fantasy. Or, at least, it was *his* fantasy: a gorgeous woman in his kitchen. The good morning smile. Pancakes cooking in the skillet.

A woman in the house.

Not just any woman. Nina. Already he felt his resistance weakening, felt the masculine urges taking over again. This was what always happened when he got too close to her.

He took her by the shoulders and stepped away. "Nina, we have to talk."

"You mean…about the case?"

"No. I mean about you. And me."

All at once that radiant smile was gone from her face. She'd sensed that a blow was about to fall, a blow that would be delivered by *him*. Mutely she turned, lifted the pancake from the skillet, and slid it onto a plate. Then she just stood there, looking at it lying on the countertop.

He hated himself at that moment. At the same time he knew there was no other way to handle this—not if he really cared about her.

"Last night shouldn't have happened," he said.

"But nothing *did* happen between us. I just brought you home and put you to bed."

"That's exactly what I'm talking about. Nina, I was so exhausted last night, someone could've driven a damn train through my bedroom and I wouldn't have moved a muscle. How am I supposed to keep you safe when I can't even keep my eyes open?"

"Oh, Sam." She stepped toward him, her hands rising to caress his face. "I don't expect you to be my guardian. Last night, I wanted to take care of *you*. I was so happy to do it."

"I'm the cop, Nina. I'm responsible for your safety."

"For once, can't you stop being a cop? Can't you let me take care of *you?* I'm not so helpless. And you're not so tough that you don't need someone. When I was scared, you were there for me. And I want to be here for *you*."

"I'm not the one who could get killed." He took both her hands and firmly lowered them from his face. "This isn't a good idea, getting involved, and we both know it. I can't watch out for you the way I should. Any other cop could do a better job."

"I don't trust any other cop. I trust you."

"And that could be a fatal mistake." He pulled away, gaining himself some breathing space. Anything to put distance between them. He couldn't think clearly when she was so near; her scent, her touch, were too distracting. He turned and matter-of-factly poured himself a cup of coffee, noting as he did it that his hand wasn't quite steady. Her effect, again. Not looking at her, he said, "It's time to focus on the case, Nina. On finding Spectre. That's the best way to ensure your safety. By doing my job and doing it right."

She said nothing.

He turned and saw that she was gazing listlessly at the table. It had already been set with silverware and napkins, glasses of juice, and a small crock of maple syrup. Again he felt that stab of regret. *I've finally found a woman I care about, a woman I could love, and I'm doing my best to push her away.*

"So," she said softly. "What do you propose, Sam?"

"I think another man should be assigned to protect you. Someone who has no personal involvement with you."

"Is that what we have? A personal involvement?"

"What else would you call it?"

She shook her head. "I'm beginning to think we have no involvement at all."

"For God's sake, Nina. We slept with each other! How can two people get more involved than that?"

"For some people, sex is purely a physical act. And that's all it is." Her chin tilted up in silent inquiry. *For some people.*

Meaning me?

Damn it, he refused to get caught up in this hopeless conversation. She was baiting him, trying to get him to admit there was more to that act of lovemaking than just sex. He was not about to admit the truth, not about to let her know how terrified he was of losing her.

He knew what had to be done.

He crossed the kitchen to the telephone. He'd call Coopersmith, ask him to assign a man to pull guard duty. He was about to pick up the receiver when the phone suddenly rang.

He answered it with a curt "Navarro."

"Sam, it's me."

"Morning, Gillis."

"Morning? It's nearly noon. I've already put in a full day here."

"Yeah, I'm hanging my head in shame."

"You should. We've got that lineup scheduled for one o'clock. Bellhops from five different hotels. You think you can bring Nina Cormier down here to take a look? That is, if she's there with you."

"She's here," admitted Sam.

"That's what I figured. Be here at one o'clock, got it?"

"We'll be there." He hung up and ran his hand through his damp hair. God. Nearly noon? He was getting lazy. Careless. All this agonizing over him and Nina, over a relationship that really had nowhere to go, was cutting into his effectiveness as a cop. If he didn't do his job right, *she* was the one who'd suffer.

"What did Gillis say?" he heard her ask.

He turned to her. "They've scheduled a lineup at one o'clock. Want you to look at a few hotel bellhops. You up to it?"

"Of course. I want this over with as much as you do."

"Good."

"And you're right about turning me over to another cop. It's all for the best." She met his gaze with a look of clear-eyed determination. "You have more important things to do than baby-sit me."

He didn't try to argue with her. In fact, he didn't say a thing. But as she walked out of the kitchen, leaving him standing alone by that cozily set breakfast table, he thought, *You're wrong. There's no more important job in the world to me than watching over you.*

EIGHT MEN STOOD on the other side of the one-way mirror. All of them were facing forward. All of them looked a little sheepish about being there.

Nina carefully regarded each man's uniform in turn, searching for any hint of familiarity. Any detail at all that might trip a memory.

She shook her head. "I don't see the right uniform."

"You're absolutely certain?" asked Gillis.

"I'm certain. It wasn't any of those."

She heard an undisguised snort of disappointment. It

came from Norm Liddell, the D.A. who was standing next to Gillis. Sam, poker-faced, said nothing.

"Well, this was a big waste of my time," muttered Liddell. "Is this all you've come up with, Navarro? A bellhop roundup?"

"We know Spectre was wearing some sort of uniform similar to a bellhop's," said Sam. "We just wanted her to look over a few."

"We did track down a police report of that bike accident," said Gillis. "The bicyclist himself called it in. I think he was worried about a lawsuit, so he made a point of stating that he hit the man outside a crosswalk. Apparently, Spectre was jaywalking when he was hit on Congress Street."

"Congress?" Liddell frowned.

"Right near the Pioneer Hotel," said Sam. "Which, we've found out, is where the Governor plans to stay day after tomorrow. He's the guest speaker at some small business seminar."

"You think Spectre's target is the Governor?"

"It's a possibility. We're having the Pioneer checked and double-checked. Especially the Governor's room."

"What about the Pioneer's bellhops?"

"We eliminated all of them, just based on height and age. No one's missing any fingers. That one there—number three—is the closest to Spectre's description. But he has all his fingers, too. We just wanted Nina to take a look at the uniform, see if it jogged a memory."

"But no one in that lineup is Spectre."

"No. We've looked at everyone's hands. No missing fingers."

Nina's gaze turned to number three in the lineup. He

was dressed in a bellhop's red jacket and black pants. "Is that what all the Pioneer's bellhops wear?" she asked.

"Yeah," said Gillis. "Why?"

"I don't think that's the uniform I saw."

"What's different about it?"

"The man I saw in the ER—I'm just remembering it— his jacket was green. Sort of a forest green. It was definitely not red."

Gillis shook his head. "We got us a problem then. The Holiday Inn's uniform is red, too. Marriott's green, but it's not located anywhere near the bicycle accident."

"Check out their staff anyway," Liddell ordered. "If you have to interview every bellhop in town, I want this guy caught. And I sure as hell want him caught before he blows up some high-muck-a-muck. When's the Governor arriving tomorrow?"

"Sometime in the afternoon," said Gillis.

Liddell glanced at his watch. "We have a full twenty-four hours. If anything comes up, I get called. Got it?"

"Yes, sir, your highness," muttered Gillis.

Liddell glanced sharply at him, but obviously decided to drop it. "My wife and I'll be at the Brant Theater tonight. I'll have my beeper with me, just in case."

"You'll be first on our list to call," said Sam.

"We're in the spotlight on this. So let's not screw up." It was Liddell's parting shot, and the two cops took it in silence.

Only after Liddell had left the room did Gillis growl, "I'm gonna get that guy. I swear, I'm gonna get him."

"Cool it, Gillis. He may be governor someday."

"In which case, I'll help Spectre plant the damn bomb myself."

Sam took Nina's arm and walked her out of the room.

"Come on. I have my hands full today. I'll introduce you to your new watchdog."

Passing me off already, she thought. Was she such a nuisance to him?

"For now, we're keeping you in a hotel," he said. "Officer Pressler's been assigned to watch over you. He's a sharp cop. I trust him."

"Meaning I should, too?"

"Absolutely. I'll call you if we turn up any suspects. We'll need you to identify them."

"So I may not be seeing you for a while."

He stopped in the hallway and looked at her. "No. It may be a while."

They faced each other for a moment. The hallway was hardly private; certainly this wasn't the time or the place to confess how she felt about him. *She* wasn't even sure how she felt about him. All she knew was that it hurt to say goodbye. What hurt even worse was to look in his eyes and see no regret, no distress. Just that flat, unemotional gaze.

So it was back to Mr. Civil Servant. She could deal with that. After the trauma of this last week, she could deal with anything, including the realization that she had, once again, gotten involved with the wrong man.

She met his gaze with one just as cool and said, "You find Spectre. I'll identify him. Just do it soon, okay? So I can get on with my life."

"We're working on it round the clock. We'll keep you informed."

"Can I count on that?"

He answered with a curt dip of the head. "It's part of my job."

Officer Leon Pressler was not a conversationalist. In fact, whether he could converse at all was in question. For the past three hours, the muscular young cop had done a terrific sphinx imitation, saying nary a word as he roamed the hotel room, alternately checking the door and glancing out the third floor window. The most he would say was "Yes, ma'am," or "No, ma'am," and that was only in response to a direct question. Was the strong, silent bit some kind of cop thing? Nina wondered. Or was he under orders not to get too chatty with the witness?

She tried to read a novel she'd picked up in the hotel gift shop, but after a few chapters she gave up. His silence made her too nervous. It was simply not natural to spend a day in a hotel room with another person and not, at the very least, talk to each other. Lord knew, she tried to draw him out.

"Have you been a cop a long time, Leon?" she asked.

"Yes, ma'am."

"Do you enjoy it?"

"Yes, ma'am."

"Does it ever scare you?"

"No, ma'am."

"Never?"

"Sometimes."

Now they were getting somewhere, she thought.

But then Officer Pressler crossed the room and peered out the window, ignoring her.

She put her book aside and launched another attempt at conversation.

"Does this sort of assignment bore you?" she asked.

"No, ma'am."

"It would bore me. Spending all day in a hotel room doing nothing."

"Things could happen."

"And I'm sure you'll be ready for it." Sighing, she

reached for the remote and clicked on the TV. Five minutes of channel surfing turned up nothing of interest. She clicked it off again. "Can I make a phone call?" she asked.

"Sorry."

"I just want to call my nursing supervisor at Maine Medical. To tell her I won't be coming in next week."

"Detective Navarro said no phone calls. It's necessary for your safety. He was very specific on that."

"What else did the good detective tell you?"

"I'm to keep a close eye. Not let my guard down for a minute. Because if anything happened to you..." He paused and gave a nervous cough.

"What?"

"He'd, uh, have my hide."

"That's quite an incentive."

"He wanted to make sure I took special care. Not that I'd let anything happen. I owe him that much."

She frowned at him. He was at the window again, peering down at the street. "What do you mean, you owe him?"

Officer Pressler didn't move from the window. He stood looking out, as though unwilling to meet her gaze. "It was a few years back. I was on this domestic call. Husband didn't much like me sticking my nose into his business. So he shot me."

"My god."

"I radioed for help. Navarro was first to respond." Pressler turned and looked at her. "So you see, I do owe him." Calmly he turned back to the window.

"How well do you know him?" she asked softly.

Pressler shrugged. "He's a good cop. But real private. I'm not sure anyone knows him very well."

Including me, she thought. Sighing, she clicked on the boob tube again and channel surfed past a jumble of daytime soaps, a TV court show and a golf tournament. She could almost feel another few brain cells collapse into mush.

What was Sam doing right now? she wondered.

And ruthlessly suppressed the thought. Sam Navarro was his own man. That much was perfectly clear.

She would have to be her own woman.

I WONDER WHAT Nina's doing right now. At once Sam tried to suppress the thought, tried to concentrate instead on what was being said at the meeting, but his mind kept drifting back to the subject of Nina. Specifically, her safety. He had every reason to trust Leon Pressler. The young cop was sharp and reliable, and he owed his life to Sam. If anyone could be trusted to keep Nina out of harm's way, it would be Pressler.

Still, he couldn't shake that lingering sense of uneasiness. And fear. It was one more indication that he'd lost his objectivity, that his feelings were way out of control. To the point of affecting his work...

"...the best we can do? Sam?"

Sam suddenly focused on Abe Coopersmith. "Excuse me?"

Coopersmith sighed. "Where the hell are you, Navarro?"

"I'm sorry. I let my attention drift for a moment."

Gillis said, "Chief asked if we're following any other leads."

"We're following every lead we have," Sam informed him. "The sketch of Spectre is circulating. We've checked all the hotels in Portland. So far, no employees with a missing finger. Problem is, we're operating blind. We don't know Spectre's target, when he plans to strike, or where he plans to strike. All we have is a witness who's seen his face."

"And this bit about the bellhop's uniform."

"That's right."

"Have you shown all those uniforms to Miss Cormier? To help us identify which hotel we're talking about?"

"We're getting together a few more samples for her to look at," said Gillis. "Also, we've interviewed that bicyclist. He doesn't remember much about the man he hit. It happened so fast, he didn't really pay attention to the face. But he does back up Miss Cormier's recollection that the uniform jacket was green. Some shade of it, anyway. And he confirms that it happened on Congress Street, near Franklin Avenue."

"We've combed that whole area," said Sam. "Showed the sketch to every shopkeeper and clerk within a five-block radius. No one recognized the face."

Coopersmith gave a grunt of frustration. "We've got the Governor arriving tomorrow afternoon. And a bomber somewhere in the city."

"We don't know if there's a connection. Spectre could be targeting someone else entirely. It all depends on who hired him."

"He may not even plan a hit at all," suggested Gillis. "Maybe he's finished his job. Maybe he's left town."

"We have to assume he's still here," cautioned Coopersmith. "And up to no good."

Sam nodded in agreement. "We have twenty-four hours before the Governor's meeting. By then, something's bound to turn up."

"God, I hope so," said Coopersmith, and he rose to leave. "If there's one thing we don't need, it's another bomb going off. And a dead Governor."

"LET'S TAKE IT from the top. Measure 36." The conductor raised his baton, brought it down again. Four beats later, the trumpets blared out the opening notes of "Wrong Side of the Track Blues," to be joined seconds later by wood-winds and bass. Then the sax slid in, its plaintive whine picking up the melody.

"Never did understand jazz," complained the Brant Theater manager, watching the rehearsal from the middle aisle. "Lotta sour notes if you ask me. All the instruments fighting with each other."

"I like jazz," said the head usher.

"Yeah, well, you like rap, too. So I don't think much of your taste." The manager glanced around the theater, surveying the empty seats. He noted that everything was clean, that there was no litter in the aisles. The audience tonight would be a discriminating crowd. Bunch of lawyer types. They wouldn't appreciate sticky floors or wadded up programs in the chairs.

Just a year ago, this building had been a porn palace, showing X-rated films to an audience of nameless, face-less men. The new owner had changed all that. Now, with a little private money from a local benefactor, the Brant Theater had been rehabilitated into a live performance center, featuring stage plays and musical artists. Unfor-tunately, the live performances brought in fewer crowds than the porn had. The manager wasn't surprised.

Tonight, at least, a big audience was assured—five hun-dred paid and reserved seats, with additional walk-ins ex-pected, to benefit the local Legal Aid office. Imagine that. All those lawyers actually paying to hear jazz. He didn't get it. But he was glad these seats would be filled.

"Looks like we may be short a man tonight," said the head usher.

"Who?"

"That new guy you hired. You know, the one from the Agency. Showed up for work two days ago. Haven't heard from him since. I tried calling him, but no luck."

The manager cursed. "Can't rely on these agency hires."

"That's for sure."

"You just gotta work the crowd with four men tonight."

"Gonna be a bear. Five hundred reserved seats and all."

"Let some of 'em find their own seats. They're lawyers. They're supposed to have brains." The manager glanced at his watch. It was six-thirty. He'd have just enough time to wolf down that corned beef sandwich in his office. "Doors open in an hour," he said. "Better get your supper now."

"Sure thing," replied the head usher. He swept up the green uniform jacket from the seat where he'd left it. And, whistling, he headed up the aisle for his dinner.

AT SEVEN-THIRTY, OFFICER Pressler escorted Nina back to police headquarters. The building was quieter than it had been that afternoon, most of the desks deserted, and only an occasional clerk circulating in the halls. Pressler brought Nina upstairs and ushered her into an office.

Sam was there.

He gave her only the most noncommittal of greetings: a nod, a quiet hello. She responded in kind. Pressler was in the room too, as were Gillis and another man in plainclothes, no doubt a cop as well. With an audience watching, she was not about to let her feelings show. Obviously Sam wasn't, either.

"We wanted you to take a look at these uniforms," Sam said, gesturing to the long conference table. Laid out on the table were a half dozen uniform jackets of various colors. "We've got bellhops, an elevator operator, and an usher's uniform from the downtown Cineplex. Do any of them strike you as familiar?"

Nina approached the table. Thoughtfully she eyed each one, examining the fabrics, the buttons. Some of them had embroidered hotel logos. Some were trimmed with gold braid or nametags.

She shook her head. "It wasn't one of these."

"What about that green one, on the end?"

"It has gold braid. The jacket I remember had black braid, sort of coiled up here, on the shoulder."

"Geez," murmured Gillis. "Women remember the weirdest things."

"Okay," Sam said with a sigh. "That's it for this session. Thanks, everyone. Pressler, why don't you take a break and get some supper. I'll bring Miss Cormier back to her hotel. You can meet us there in an hour or so."

The room emptied out. All except Sam and Nina.

For a moment, they didn't speak to each other. They didn't even look at each other. Nina almost wished that the earnest Officer Pressler was back with her again; at least *he* didn't make her feel like turning tail and running.

"I hope your hotel room's all right," he finally said.

"It's fine. But I'll be going stir crazy in another day. I have to get out of there."

"It's not safe yet."

"When will it be safe?"

"When we have Spectre."

"That could be never." She shook her head. "I can't live this way. I have a job. I have a life. I can't stay in a hotel room with some cop who drives me up a wall."

Sam frowned. "What's Pressler done?"

"He won't sit still! He never stops checking the windows. He won't let me touch the phone. And he can't carry on a decent conversation."

"Oh." Sam's frown evaporated. "That's just Leon doing his job. He's good."

"Maybe he is. But he still drives me crazy." Sighing, she took a step toward him. "Sam, I can't stay cooped up. I have to get on with my life."

"You will. But we have to get you through this part alive."

"What if I left town? Went somewhere else for a while—"

"We might need you here, Nina."

"You don't. You have his prints. You know he's missing a finger. You could identify him without any question—"

"But we need to spot him first. And for that, we might need you to pick him out of a crowd. So you have to stay in town. Available. We'll keep you safe, I promise."

"I suppose you'll have to. If you want to catch your man."

He took her by the shoulders. "That's not the only reason, and you know it."

"Do I?"

He leaned closer. For one astonishing moment she thought he was going to kiss her. Then a rap on the door made them both jerk apart.

Gillis, looking distinctly ill at ease, stood in the doorway. "Uh…I'm heading over to get a burger. You want I should get you something, Sam?"

"No. We'll pick something up at her hotel."

"Okay." Gillis gave an apologetic wave. "I'll be back here in an hour." He departed, leaving Sam and Nina alone once again.

But the moment was gone forever. If he'd intended to kiss her, she saw no hint of it in his face.

He said, simply, "I'll drive you back now."

In Sam's car, she felt as if they'd reverted right back to the very first day they'd met, to the time when he'd been the stone-faced detective and she'd been the bewildered citizen. It was as if all the events of the past week—their nights together, their lovemaking—had never happened. He seemed determined to avoid any talk of feelings tonight, and she was just as determined not to broach the subject.

The only safe topic was the case. And even on that topic, he was not very forthcoming.

"I notice you've circulated the police sketch," she said.

"It's been everywhere. TV, the papers."

"Any response?"

"We've been inundated by calls. We've spent all day chasing them down. So far, nothing's panned out."

"I'm afraid my description wasn't very helpful."

"You did the best you could."

She looked out the window, at the streets of downtown Portland. It was already eight o'clock, the summer dusk just slipping into night. "If I saw him again, I'd know him. I'm sure I would."

"That's all we need from you, Nina."

All you want from me, too, she thought sadly. She asked, "What happens tomorrow?"

"More of the same. Chase down leads. Hope someone recognizes that sketch."

"Do you know if Spectre's even in the city?"

"No. He may be long gone. In which case we're just spinning our wheels. But my instincts are telling me he's still here somewhere. And he's got something planned, something big." He glanced at her. "*You* could be the wrench in the works. The one person who can recognize him. That's why we have to keep you under wraps."

"I can't stand much more of this. I'm not even allowed to make a phone call."

"We don't want people to know your whereabouts."

"I won't tell anyone. I promise. It's just that I feel so cut off from everyone."

"Okay." He sighed. "Who do you want to call?"

"I could start with my sister, Wendy."

"I thought you two didn't get along."

"We don't. But she's still my sister. And she can tell the rest of the family I'm okay."

He thought it over for a moment, then said, "All right, go ahead and call her. You can use the car phone. But don't—"

"I know, I know. Don't tell her where I am." She picked up the receiver and dialed Wendy's number. She heard three rings, and then a woman's voice answered—a voice she didn't recognize.

"Hayward residence."

"Hello, this is Nina. I'm Wendy's sister. Is she there?"

"I'm sorry, but Mr. and Mrs. Hayward are out for the evening. I'm the baby-sitter."

That's how worried she is about me, thought Nina with an irrational sense of abandonment.

"Would you like her to call you back?" asked the baby-sitter.

"No, I, uh, won't be available. But maybe I can call her later. Do you know what time she'll be home?"

"They're at the Brant Theater for that Legal Aid benefit. I think it runs till ten-thirty. And then they usually go out for coffee and dessert, so I'd expect them home around midnight."

"Oh. That's too late. I'll call tomorrow, thanks." She hung up and gave a sigh of disappointment.

"Not home?"

"No. I should have guessed they'd be out. In Jake's law firm, the business day doesn't end at five. The evenings are taken up by business affairs, too."

"Your brother-in-law's an attorney?"

"With ambitions of being a judge. And he's only thirty years old."

"Sounds like a fast-tracker."

"He is. Which means he needs a fast-track wife. Wendy's perfect that way. I'll bet you that right at this moment, she's at the theater charming the socks off some judge. And she can do it without even trying. She's the politician in the family." She glanced at Sam and saw that he was frowning. "Is something wrong?" she asked.

"What theater? Where did they go tonight?"

"The Brant Theater. That's where the benefit is."

"Benefit?"

"The baby-sitter said it was for Legal Aid. Why?"

Sam stared ahead at the road. "The Brant Theater. Didn't it just reopen?"

"A month ago. It was a disgrace before. All those porn flicks."

"Damn. Why didn't I think of it?"

Without warning, he made a screeching U-turn and headed the car the way they'd come, back toward the downtown district.

"What are you doing?" she demanded.

"The Brant Theater. A Legal Aid benefit. Who do you suppose'll be there?"

"A bunch of lawyers?"

"Right. As well as our esteemed D.A., Norm Liddell. Now, I'm not particularly fond of lawyers, but I'm not crazy about picking up their dead bodies, either."

She stared at him. "You think that's the target? The Brant Theater?"

"They'll need ushers tonight. Think about it. What does an usher wear?"

"Sometimes it's just black pants and a white shirt."

"But in a grand old theater like the Brant? They just might be dressed in green jackets with black braid...."

"That's where we're going?"

He nodded. "I want you to take a look. Tell me if we're warm. Tell me if that uniform you saw could've been a theater usher's."

By the time they pulled up across the street from the Brant Theater, it was 8:20. Sam didn't waste his time looking for a parking space; he left the car angled against the red-painted curb. As he and Nina climbed out, they heard a doorman yell, "Hey, you can't park there!"

"Police!" Sam answered, waving his badge. "We need to get in the theater."

The doorman stepped aside and waved them in.

The lobby was deserted. Through the closed aisle doors, they could hear the bluesy wail of clarinets, the syncopated beats of a snare drum. No ushers were in sight.

Sam yanked open an aisle door and slipped into the theater. Seconds later, he reemerged with a short and loudly protesting usher in tow. "Look at the uniform," he said to Nina. "Look familiar?"

Nina took one glance at the short green jacket, the black braid and brass buttons, and she nodded. "That's it. That's the one I saw."

"*What's* the one?" demanded the usher, yanking himself free.

"How many ushers working here tonight?" snapped Sam.

"Who are you, anyway?"

Again Sam whipped out his badge. "Police. There's a chance you have a bomb somewhere in there. So tell me quick. How many ushers?"

"A bomb?" The man's gaze darted nervously toward the lobby exit. "Uh, we got four working tonight."

"That's it?"

"Yeah. One didn't show up."

"Did he have a missing finger?"

"Hell, I don't know. We all wear gloves." The usher looked again toward the exit. "You really think there could be a bomb in there?"

"We can't afford to make a wrong guess. I'm evacuating the building." He glanced at Nina. "Get out of here. Wait in the car."

"But you'll need help—"

He was already pushing through the door, into the darkened theater. From the open doorway, she watched him walk swiftly down the aisle. He climbed up to the stage and crossed to the conductor, who regarded him with a look of startled outrage.

The musicians, just as startled, stopped playing.

Sam grabbed the conductor's microphone. "Ladies and gentlemen," he said curtly. "This is the Portland Police. We have had a bomb threat. Calmly, but without delay, will everyone please evacuate the building. I repeat, stay calm, but please evacuate the building."

Almost immediately the exodus began. Nina had to scramble backward out of the doorway to avoid the first rush of people heading up the aisle. In the confusion, she lost sight of Sam, but she could still hear his voice over the speaker system.

"Please remain calm. There is no immediate danger. Exit the building in an orderly fashion."

He's going to be the last one out, she thought. *The one most likely hurt if a bomb does go off.*

The exodus was in full force now, a rush of frightened men and women in evening clothes. The first hint of disaster happened so quickly Nina didn't even see it. Perhaps someone had tripped over a long hem; perhaps there were simply too many feet storming the doorway. Suddenly people were stumbling, falling over each other. A woman screamed. Those still backed up in the aisle instantly panicked.

And rushed for the door.

Chapter Eleven

Nina watched in horror as a woman in a long evening gown fell beneath the stampede. Struggling to reach her, Nina shoved through the crowd, only to be swept along with them and forced out the lobby doors and into the street. To get back inside the building was impossible; she'd be moving against the crowd, against the full force of panic.

Already the street was filling up with evacuees, everyone milling about looking dazed. To her relief, she caught sight of Wendy and Jake among the crowd; at least her sister was safe and out of the building. The flood of people out the doors gradually began to ebb.

But where was Sam? Had he made it out yet?

Then, through the crowd, she spotted him emerging from the lobby door. He had his arm around an elderly man, whom he hauled to the sidewalk and set down against the lamppost.

As Nina started toward him, Sam spotted her and yelled, "This one needs attention. Take care of him!"

"Where are you going?"

"Back inside. There are a few more in there."

"I can help you—"

"Help me by staying *out* of the building. And see to that man."

He has his job to do, she thought, watching Sam head back into the theater. *So do I.*

She turned her attention to the elderly man propped up against the lamppost. Kneeling beside him she asked, "Sir, are you all right?"

"My chest. It hurts…"

Oh, no. A coronary. And no ambulance in sight. At once she lowered his head onto the sidewalk, checked his pulse, and unbuttoned his shirt. She was so busy attending to her patient she scarcely noticed when the first patrol car pulled up in front of the theater. By then the crowd was a mass of confusion, everyone demanding to know what was going on.

She looked up to see Sam push out the lobby door again, this time carrying the woman in the evening dress. He lay the woman down beside Nina.

"One more inside," he said, turning back to the building. "Check the lady out."

"Navarro!" yelled a voice.

Sam glanced back as a man in a tuxedo approached.

"What the hell is going on?"

"Can't talk, Liddell. I've got work to do."

"Was there a bomb call or not?"

"Not a call."

"Then why'd you order an evacuation?"

"The usher's uniform." Again Sam turned toward the building.

"Navarro!" Liddell yelled. "I want an explanation! People have been hurt because of this! Unless you can justify it—"

Sam had vanished through the lobby doors.

Liddell paced the sidewalk, waiting to resume his

harangue. At last, in frustration, he shouted, "I'm going to have your ass for this, Navarro!"

Those were the last words out of Liddell's mouth before the bomb exploded.

The force of the blast threw Nina backward, onto the street. She landed hard, her elbows scraping across the pavement, but she felt no pain. The shock of the impact left her too stunned to feel anything at all except a strange sense of unreality. She saw broken glass pelt the cars in the street. Saw smoke curl through the air and scores of people lying on the road, all of them just as stunned as she was. And she saw that the lobby door of the Brant Theater was tilted at a crazy angle and hanging by one hinge.

Through the pall of silence, she heard the first moan. Then another. Then came sobs, cries from the injured. Slowly she struggled to sit up. Only then did she feel the pain. Her elbows were torn and bleeding. Her head ached so badly she had to clutch it just to keep from throwing up. But as the awareness of pain crept into her consciousness, so too did the memory of what had happened just before the blast.

Sam. Sam had gone into the building.

Where was he? She scanned the road, the sidewalk, but her vision was blurry. She saw Liddell, sitting up now and groaning by the lamppost. Next to him was the elderly man whom Sam had dragged out of the theater. He, too, was conscious and moving. But there was no Sam.

She stumbled to her feet. A wave of dizziness almost sent her back down to her knees. Fighting it, she forced herself to move toward that open door and stepped inside.

It was dark, too dark to see anything. The only light was the faint glow from the street, shining through the doorway. She stumbled across debris and landed on her knees. Quickly she rose back to her feet, but she knew it was hopeless. It was impossible to navigate, much less find anyone in this darkness.

"Sam?" she cried, moving deeper into the shadows. *"Sam?"*

Her own voice, thick with despair, echoed back at her.

She remembered that he'd stepped into the lobby a moment before the blast. He could be anywhere in the building, or he could be somewhere nearby. Somewhere she could reach him.

Again she cried out, "Sam!"

This time, faintly, she heard a reply. "Nina?" It didn't come from inside the building. It came from the outside. From the street.

She turned and felt her way back toward the exit, guided by the glow of the doorway. Even before she reached it, she saw him standing there, silhouetted in the light from the street.

"Nina?"

"I'm here. I'm here…." She stumbled through the last stretch of darkness dividing them and was instantly swept into an embrace that was too fierce to be gentle, too terrified to be comforting.

"What the hell were you doing in *there?*" he demanded.

"Looking for you."

"You were supposed to stay outside. Away from the building. When I couldn't find you…" His arms tightened around her, drawing her so close she felt as though it were his heart hammering in her chest. "Next time, you *listen* to me."

"I thought you were inside—"

"I came out the other door."

"I didn't see you!"

"I was dragging the last man out. I'd just got out when the bomb went off. It blew us both out onto the sidewalk." He pulled back and looked at her. Only then did she see the blood trickling down his temple.

"Sam, you need to see a doctor—"

"We have a lot of people here who need a doctor." He glanced around at the street. "I can wait."

Nina, too, focused on the chaos surrounding them. "We've got to get people triaged for the ambulances. I'll get to work."

"You feeling up to it?"

She gave him a nod. And a quick smile. "This is my forte, Detective. Disasters." She waded off into the crowd.

Now that she knew Sam was alive and safe, she could concentrate on what needed to be done. And one glance at the scene told her this was the start of a busy night. Not just here, in the street, but in the ER as well. All the area hospitals would need to call in every ER nurse they had to attend to these people.

Her head was starting to ache worse than ever, her scraped elbows stung every time she bent her arms. But at this moment, as far as she knew, she was the only nurse on the scene.

She focused on the nearest victim, a woman whose leg was cut and bleeding. Nina knelt down, ripped a strip of fabric from the victim's hem, and quickly wrapped a makeshift pressure bandage around the bleeding limb. When she'd finished tying it off, she noted to her satisfaction that the flow of blood had stopped.

That was only the first, she thought, and she looked around for the next patient. There were dozens more to go....

Across the street, his face hidden in the shadows, Vincent Spectre watched the chaos and muttered a curse. Both Judge Stanley Dalton and Norm Liddell were still alive. Spectre could see the young D.A. sitting against the lamp-post, clutching his head. The blond woman sitting beside him must be Liddell's wife. They were right in the thick of things, surrounded by dozens of other injured theater patrons. Spectre couldn't just walk right over and dispatch Liddell, not without being seen by a score of witnesses. Sam Navarro was just a few yards from Liddell, and Navarro would certainly be armed.

Another humiliation. This would destroy his reputation, not to mention his back account. The Showman had prom-ised four hundred thousand dollars for the deaths of Dalton and Liddell. Spectre had thought this an elegant solution: to kill both of them at once. With so many other victims, the identity of the targets might never be pinpointed.

But the targets were still alive, and there'd be no pay-ment forthcoming.

The job had become too risky to complete, especially with Navarro on the scent. Thanks to Navarro, Spectre would have to bow out. And kiss his four hundred thou-sand goodbye.

He shifted his gaze, refocusing on another figure in the crowd. It was that nurse, Nina Cormier, bandaging one of the injured. This fiasco was her fault, too; he was sure of it. She must've given the police just enough info to tip them off to the bomb. The usher's uniform, no doubt, had been the vital clue.

She was another detail he hadn't bothered to clean up, and look at the result. No hit, no money. Plus, she could identify him. Though that police sketch was hopelessly generic, Spectre had a feeling that, if Nina Cormier ever saw his face, she would remember him. That made her a threat he could no longer ignore.

But now was not the opportunity. Not in this crowd, in this street. The ambulances were arriving, siren after siren whooping to a stop. And the police had cordoned off the street from stray vehicles.

Time to leave.

Spectre turned and walked away, his frustration mounting with every step he took. He'd always prided himself on paying attention to the little things. Anyone who worked with explosives had to have a fetish for details, or they didn't last long. Spectre intended to hang around in this business, which meant he would continue to fuss over the details.

And the next detail to attend to was Nina Cormier.

SHE WAS MAGNIFICENT. Sam paused wearily amid the broken glass and shouting voices and he gazed in Nina's direction. It was ten-thirty, an hour and a half since the explosion, and the street was still a scene of confusion. Police cars and ambulances were parked haphazardly up and down the block, their lights flashing like a dozen strobes. Emergency personnel were everywhere, picking through the wreckage, sorting through the victims. The most seriously injured had already been evacuated, but there were dozens more still to be transported to hospitals.

In the midst of all that wreckage, Nina seemed an island of calm efficiency. As Sam watched, she knelt down beside a groaning man and dressed his bleeding arm with a makeshift bandage. Then, with a reassuring pat and a soft word, she moved on to the next patient. As though sensing she was being watched, she suddenly glanced in Sam's direction. Just for a moment their gazes locked across the chaos, and she read the question in his eyes: *Are you holding up okay?*

She gave him a wave, a nod of reassurance. Then she turned back to her patient.

They both had their work cut out for them tonight. He focused his attention, once again, on the bomb scene investigation.

Gillis had arrived forty-five minutes ago with the personal body armor and mask. The rest of the team had straggled in one by one—three techs, Ernie Takeda, Detective Cooley. Even Abe Coopersmith had appeared, his presence more symbolic than practical. This was Sam's show, and everyone knew it. The bomb disposal truck was in place and parked nearby. Everyone was waiting.

It was time to go in the building. Time to search for any second device.

Sam and Gillis, both of them wearing headlamps, entered the theater.

The darkness made the search slow and difficult. Stepping gingerly over debris, Sam headed down the left aisle, Gillis the right. The back rows of seats had sustained damage only to the upholstery—shredded fabric and stuffing. The further they advanced the more severe the damage.

"Dynamite," Gillis noted, sniffing the air.

"Looks like the blast center's near the front."

Sam moved slowly toward the orchestra pit, the beam of his headlamp slicing the darkness left and right as he scanned the area around the stage—or what had once been the stage. A few splintered boards was all that remained.

"Crater's right here," observed Gillis.

Sam joined him. The two men knelt down for a closer inspection. Like the church bomb a week before, this one was shallow—a low-velocity blast. Dynamite.

"Looks like the third row, center stage," said Sam. "Wonder who was sitting here."

"Assigned seating, you figure?"

"If so, then we'll have ourselves a convenient list of potential targets."

"Looks all clear to me," Gillis declared.

"We can call in the searchers." Sam rose to his feet and at once felt a little dizzy. The aftereffects of the blast. He'd been in so many bombs lately, his brain must be getting scrambled. Maybe some fresh air would clear his head.

"You okay?" asked Gillis.

"Yeah. I just need to get out of here for a moment." He stumbled back up the aisle and through the lobby doors. Outside he leaned against a lamppost, breathing gulps of night air. His dizziness faded and he became aware, once again, of the activity in the street. He noticed that the crowds had thinned, and that the injured had all been evacuated. Only one ambulance was still parked in the road.

Where was Nina?

That one thought instantly cleared his head. He glanced up and down the street, but caught no glimpse of her. Had she left the scene? Or was she taken from it?

A young cop manning the police line glanced up as Sam approached. "Yes, sir?"

"There was a woman—a nurse in street clothes—working out here. Where'd she go?"

"You mean the dark-haired lady? The pretty one?"

"That's her."

"She left in one of the ambulances, about twenty minutes ago. I think she was helping with a patient."

"Thanks." Sam went to his car and reached inside for his cellular phone. He was not taking any chances; he had to be sure she was safe. He dialed Maine Med ER.

The line was busy.

In frustration he climbed in the car. "I'm heading to the hospital!" he yelled to Gillis. "Be right back."

Ignoring his partner's look of puzzlement, Sam lurched away from the curb and steered through the obstacle course of police vehicles. Fifteen minutes later, he pulled into a parking stall near the hospital's emergency entrance.

Even before he walked in the doors, he could hear the sounds of frantic activity inside. The waiting area was mobbed. He pushed his way through the crowd until he'd reached the triage desk, manned by a clearly embattled nurse.

"I'm Detective Navarro, Portland Police," he said. "Is Nina Cormier working here?"

"Nina? Not tonight, as far as I know."

"She came in with one of the ambulances."

"I might have missed her. Let me check." She punched the intercom button and said, "There's a policeman out here. Wants to speak to Nina. If she's back there, can you ask her to come out?"

For a good ten minutes, he waited with growing impatience. Nina didn't appear. The crowd in the ER seemed to grow even larger, packing into every available square inch of the waiting area. Even worse, the reporters had shown up, TV cameras and all. The triage nurse had her hands full; she'd forgotten entirely about Sam.

Unable to wait any longer, he pushed past the front desk. The nurse was calming down a hysterical family member; she didn't even notice Sam had crossed into the inner sanctum and was heading up the ER corridor.

Treatment rooms lined both sides of the halls. He glanced in each one as he passed. All were occupied and overflowing with victims from the bombing. He saw stunned faces, bloodied clothes. But no Nina.

He turned, retraced his steps down the hall, and paused outside a closed door. It was the trauma room. From beyond the door came the sound of voices, the clang of cabinets. He knew that a crisis was in full swing, and he was reluctant to intrude, but he had no alternative. He had to confirm that Nina was here, that she'd made it safely to the ER.

He pushed open the door.

A patient—a man—was lying on the table, his body white and flaccid under the lights. Half a dozen medical personnel were laboring over him, one performing CPR, the others scurrying about with IV's and drugs. Sam paused, momentarily stunned by the horror of the scene.

"Sam?"

Only then did he notice Nina moving toward him from the other side of the room. Like all the other nurses, she was dressed in scrub clothes. He hadn't even noticed her in that first glimpse of blue-clad personnel.

She took his arm and quickly tugged him out of the room. "What are you doing here?" she whispered.

"You left the blast site. I wasn't sure what happened to you."

"I rode here in one of the ambulances. I figured they needed me." She glanced back at the door to the trauma room. "I was right."

"Nina, you can't just take off without telling me! I had no idea if you were all right."

She regarded him with an expression of quiet wonder, but didn't say a thing.

"Are you listening to me?" he said.

"Yes," she replied softly. "But I don't believe what I'm hearing. You actually sound scared."

"I wasn't scared. I was just— I mean—" He shook his head in frustration. "Okay, I was worried. I didn't want something to happen to you."

"Because I'm your witness?"

He looked into her eyes, those beautiful, thoughtful eyes. Never in his life had he felt so vulnerable. This was a new feeling for him and he didn't like it. He was not a man who was easily frightened, and the fact that he had experienced such fear at the thought of losing her told him he was far more deeply involved than he'd ever intended to be.

"Sam?" She reached up and touched his face.

He grasped her hand and gently lowered it. "Next time," he instructed, "I want you to tell me where you're going. It's *your* life at stake. If you want to risk it, that's your business. But until Spectre's under arrest, your safety's my concern. Do you understand?"

She withdrew her hand from his. The retreat was more than physical; he could feel her pulling away emotionally as well, and it hurt him. It was a pain of his own choosing, and that made it even worse.

She said, tightly, "I understand perfectly well."

"Good. Now, I think you should go back to the hotel where we can keep an eye on you tonight."

"I can't leave. They need me here."

"I need you, too. Alive."

"Look at this place!" She waved toward the waiting area, crowded with the injured. "These people all have to be examined and treated. I can't walk out now."

"Nina, I have a job to do. And your safety is part of that job."

"I have a job to do, too!" she asserted.

They faced each other for a moment, neither one willing to back down.

Then Nina snapped, "I don't have time for this," and she turned back toward the trauma room.

"Nina!"

"I'll do my job, Sam. You do yours."

"Then I'm sending a man over to keep an eye on you."

"Do whatever you want."

"When will you be finished here?"

She stopped and glanced at the waiting patients. "My guess? Not till morning."

"Then I'll be back to get you at 6:00 a.m."

"Whatever you say, Detective," she retorted and pushed into the trauma room. He caught a fleeting glimpse of her as she rejoined the surgical team, and then the door closed behind her.

I'll do my job. You do yours, she'd told him.

She's right, he thought. *That's exactly what I should be focusing on. My job.*

From his car phone, he put in a call to Officer Pressler and told him to send his relief officer down to Maine Med ER, where he'd be the official baby-sitting service for the night. Then, satisfied that Nina was in good hands, he headed back to the bomb scene.

It was eleven-thirty. The night was just beginning.

NINA MADE IT through the next seven hours on sheer nerve. Her conversation with Sam had left her hurt and angry, and she had to force herself to concentrate on the work at hand—tending to the dozens of patients who now filled the waiting area. Their injuries, their discomfort, had to take priority. But every so often, when she'd pause to collect her thoughts or catch her breath, she'd find herself thinking about Sam, about what he'd said.

I have a job to do. And your safety is part of that job.

Is that all I am to you? she wondered as she signed her name to yet another patient instruction sheet. A job, a burden? And what had she expected, anyway? From the beginning, he'd been the unflappable public official, Mr. Cool himself. There'd been flashes of warmth, of course, even the occasional glimpse of the man inside, a man of genuine kindness. But every time she thought she'd touched the real Sam Navarro, he'd pull away from her as though scalded by the contact.

What am I to do with you, Sam? she wondered sadly. And what was she to do with all the feelings she had for him?

Work was all that kept her going that night. She never even noticed when the sun came up.

By the time 6:00 a.m. rolled around, she was so tired she could scarcely walk without weaving, but at last the waiting room was empty and the patients all sent home. Most of the ER staff had gathered, shell-shocked, in the employee lounge for a well-deserved coffee break. Nina was about to join them when she heard her name called.

She turned. Sam was standing in the waiting room.

He looked every bit as exhausted as she felt, his eyes bleary, his jaw dark with a day's growth of beard. At her first sight of his face, all the anger she'd felt the night before instantly evaporated.

My poor, poor Sam, she thought. *You give so much of yourself. And what comfort do you have at the end of the day?*

She went to him. He didn't speak; he just looked at her with that expression of weariness. She put her arms around him. For a moment they held each other, their bodies trembling with fatigue. Then she heard him say, softly, "Let's go home."

"I'd like that," she said. And smiled.

She didn't know how he managed to pilot the car to his house. All she knew was that a moment after she dozed off, they were in his driveway, and he was gently prodding her awake. Together they dragged themselves into the house, into his bedroom. No thoughts of lust crossed her mind, even as they undressed and crawled into bed together, even as she felt his lips brush her face, felt his breath warm her hair.

She fell asleep in his arms.

SHE FELT SO warm, so perfect, lying beside him. As if she belonged here, in his bed.

Sam gazed through drowsy eyes at Nina, who was still sound asleep. It was already afternoon. He should have been up and dressed hours ago, but sheer exhaustion had taken its toll.

He was getting too old for this job. For the past eighteen years, he'd been a cop through and through. Though there were times when he hated the work, when the ugly side of it seemed to overwhelm his love for the job, he'd never once doubted that a cop was exactly what he was meant to be. And so it dismayed him now that, at this moment, being a cop was the furthest thing from his mind.

What he wanted, really wanted, was to spend eternity in this bed, gazing at this woman. Studying her face, enjoying the view. Only when Nina was asleep did he feel it was safe to really look at her. When she was awake, he felt too vulnerable, as though she could read his thoughts, could see past his barriers, straight to his heart. He was afraid to admit, even to himself, the feelings he harbored there.

As he studied her now, he realized there was no point denying it to himself: he couldn't bear the thought of her walking out of his life. Did that mean he loved her? He didn't know.

He did know this was not the turn of events he'd wanted or expected.

But last night he'd watched her at work in the wreckage of the bomb site, and he'd admired a new dimension of Nina, one he saw for the first time. A woman with both compassion and strength.

It would be so easy to fall in love with her. It would be such a mistake.

In a month, a year, she'd come to see him for what he was: no hero with a badge, but an everyday guy doing his job the best way he knew how. And there she'd be in that hospital, working side by side with men like Robert Bledsoe. Men with medical degrees and houses on the water. How long would it take for her to grow weary of the cop who just happened to love her?

He sat up on the side of the bed and ran his hands through his hair, trying to shake off the last vestiges of sleep. His brain wasn't feeling alert yet. He needed coffee, food, anything to snap him back into gear. There were so many details to follow up on, so many leads still to check out.

Then he felt a touch, soft as silk, caress his bare back. All at once, work was the last thing on his mind.

He turned and met her gaze. She was looking drowsily at him, her smile relaxed and contented. "What time is it?" she murmured.

"Almost three."

"We slept that long?"

"We needed it. Both of us. It was okay to let our guard down. Pressler was watching the house."

"You mean he was outside all day?"

"I made the arrangements last night. Before he went off duty. I knew I wanted to bring you home with me."

She opened her arms to him. That gesture of invitation was too tempting to resist. With a groan of surrender, he lay down beside her and met her lips with a kiss. At once his body was responding, and so was she. Their arms were entwined now, their warmth mingling. He couldn't stop, couldn't turn back; he wanted her too badly. He wanted to feel their bodies join, just one last time. If he couldn't have her for the rest of his life, at least he would have her for this moment. And he'd remember, always, her face, her smile, her sweet moans of desire as he thrust, hard and deep, inside her.

They both took. They both gave.

But even as he reached his climax, even as he felt the first glorious release, he thought, *This is not enough. This could never be enough.* He wanted to know more than just her body; he wanted to know her soul.

His passion was temporarily sated, yet he felt both un-satisfied and depressed as he lay beside her afterward. Not at all what the carefree bachelor should expect to feel after a conquest. If anything, he was angry at himself for sliding into this situation. For allowing this woman to be-come so important to him.

And here she was, smiling, working her way even deeper into his life.

His response was to pull away, to rise from the bed and head into the shower. When he reemerged, clean and still damp, she was sitting up on the side of the bed, watching him with a look of bewilderment.

"I have to get back to work," he said, pulling on a clean shirt. "I'll invite Pressler inside to sit with you."

"The bombing's over and done with. Spectre's probably a thousand miles away by now."

"I can't take that chance."

"There are others who know his face. The theater ushers. They could identify him."

"One of them hit his head on the sidewalk. He's still in and out of consciousness. The other one can't even decide on the color of Spectre's eyes. That's how helpful the ushers are."

"Nevertheless, you've got other witnesses and Spectre knows it." She paused. "I'd say that lets both of us off the hook."

"What do you mean?"

"I can stop worrying about being a target. And you can stop worrying about keeping me alive. And go back to your real job."

"This is part of my job."

"So you've told me." She tilted her chin up, and he saw the brief gleam of tears in her eyes. "I wish I was more than that. God, I wish…"

"Nina, please. This doesn't help either one of us."

Her head drooped. The sight of her, hurt, silent, was almost more than he could stand. He knelt down before her and took her hands in his. "You know I'm attracted to you."

She gave a softly ironic laugh. "That much, I guess, is obvious to us both."

"And you also know that I think you're a terrific woman. If I ever get hauled to the ER in an ambulance, I hope you're the nurse who takes care of me."

"But?"

"But…" He sighed. "I just don't see us together. Not for the long haul."

She looked down again, and he could sense her struggle for composure. He'd hurt her, and he hated himself for it, hated his own cowardice. That's what it was, of course. He didn't believe hard enough in their chances. He didn't believe in *her.*

All he was certain of was that he'd never, ever get over her.

He rose to his feet. She didn't react, but just sat on the bed, staring down. "It's not you, Nina," he said. "It's *me.* It's something that happened to me years ago. It convinced me that this situation we're in—it doesn't last. It's artificial. A scared woman. And a cop. It's a setup for all kinds of unrealistic expectations."

"Don't give me the old psychology lecture, Sam. I don't need to hear about transference and misplaced affections."

"You have to hear it. And understand it. Because the effect goes both ways. How you feel about me, and how I feel about you. My wanting to take care of you, protect you. It's something I can't help, either." He sighed, a sound of both frustration and despair. *It's too late,* he thought. *We both feel things we shouldn't be feeling. And it's impossible to turn back the clock.*

"You were saying something happened to you. Years ago," she said. "Was it…another woman?"

He nodded.

"The same situation? Scared woman, protective cop?"

Again he nodded.

"Oh." She shook her head and murmured in a tone of self-disgust, "I guess I fell right into it."

"We both did."

"So who left whom, Sam? The last time this happened?"

"It was the only time it happened. Except for you." He turned away, began to move around the room. "I was just a rookie patrolman. Twenty-two years old. Assigned to protect a woman being stalked. She was twenty-eight going on forty when it came to sophistication. It's not surprising I got a little infatuated. The surprising part was that she seemed to return the sentiment. At least, until the crisis was over. Then she decided I wasn't so impressive after all. And she was right." He stopped and looked at her. "It's that damn thing called reality. It has a way of stripping us all down to what we really are. And in my case, I'm just a hardworking cop. Honest for the most part. Brighter than some, dumber than others. In short, I'm not anyone's hero. And when she finally saw that, she turned right around and walked out, leaving behind one sadder but wiser rookie."

"And you think that's what I'm going to do."

"It's what you should do. Because you deserve so much, Nina. More than I can ever give you."

She shook her head. "What I really want, Sam, has nothing to do with what a man can *give* me."

"Think about Robert. What you could have had with him."

"Robert was the perfect example! He had it all. Everything except what I wanted from him."

"What did you want, Nina?"

"Love. Loyalty." She met his gaze. "Honesty."

What he saw in her eyes left him shaken. Those were the things he wanted to give her. The very things he was afraid to give her.

"Right now you think it's enough," he remarked. "But maybe you'll find out it's not."

"It's more than I ever got from Robert." *More than I'll ever get from you, too,* was what her eyes said.

He didn't try to convince her otherwise. Instead, he turned toward the door.

"I'm going to call Pressler inside," he told her. "Have him stay with you all day today."

"There's no need."

"You shouldn't be alone, Nina."

"I won't be." She looked up at him. "I can go back to my father's house. He has that fancy security system. Not to mention a few dogs. Now that we know Daniella isn't the one running around planting bombs, I should be perfectly safe there." She glanced around the room. "I shouldn't be staying here, anyway. Not in your house."

"You can. As long as you need to."

"No." She met his gaze. "I don't really see the point, Sam. Since it's so apparent to us both that this is a hopeless relationship."

He didn't argue with her. And that, more than anything else, was what hurt her. He could see it in her face.

He simply said, "I'll drive you there." Then he turned and left the room. He had to.

He couldn't bear to see the look in her eyes.

Chapter Twelve

"We think we know who the target was," reported Sam. "It was our wonderful D.A., Liddell."

Chief Coopersmith stared across the conference table at Sam and Gillis. "Are you certain?"

"Everything points that way. We pinpointed the bomb placement to somewhere in Row Three, Seats G through J. The seating last night was reserved weeks in advance. We've gone over the list of people sitting in that row and section. And Liddell and his wife were right smack in the center. They would've been killed instantly."

"Who else was in that row?"

"Judge Dalton was about six seats away," said Gillis. "Chances are, he would've been killed, too. Or at least seriously maimed."

"And the other people in that row?"

"We've checked them all out. A visiting law professor from California. A few relatives of Judge Dalton's. A pair of law clerks. We doubt any of them would've attracted the interest of a hired killer. Oh, and you may be interested to hear Ernie Takeda's latest report. He called it in from the lab this afternoon. It was dynamite, Dupont label. Prima detonating cord. Green electrical tape."

"Spectre," said Coopersmith. He leaned back and exhaled a loud sigh of weariness. They were all tired. Every one of them had worked straight through the night, caught a few hours of sleep, and then returned to the job. Now it was 5:00 p.m., and another night was just beginning. "God, the man is back with a vengeance."

"Yeah, but he's not having much luck," commented Gillis. "His targets keep surviving. Liddell. Judge Dalton. Nina Cormier. I'd say that the legendary Vincent Spectre must be feeling pretty frustrated about now."

"Embarrassed, too," added Sam. "His reputation's on the line, if it isn't already shot. After this fiasco, he's washed up as a contract man. Anyone with the money to hire will go elsewhere."

"Do we know who *did* hire him?"

Sam and Gillis glanced at each other. "We can make a wild guess," said Gillis.

"Billy Binford?"

Sam nodded. "The Snowman's trial is coming up in a month. And Liddell was dead set against any plea bargains. Rumor has it, he was going to use a conviction as a jumping-off place for some political campaign. I think The Snowman knows he's in for a long stay in jail. I think he wants Liddell off the prosecution team. Permanently."

"If Sam hadn't cleared that theater," added Gillis, "we could have lost half our prosecutors. The courts would've been backed up for months. In that situation, Binford's lawyers could've written the plea bargain for him."

"Any way we can pin this down with proof?"

"Not yet. Binford's attorney, Albert Darien, denies any knowledge of this. We're not going to be able to shake a word out of him. ATF's going over the videotapes from the prison surveillance cameras, looking over all the visitors that Binford had. We may be able to identify a go-between."

"You think it's someone other than his attorney?"

"Possibly. If we can identify that go-between, we may have a link to Spectre."

"Go for it," said Coopersmith. "I want this guy, and I want him bad."

At five-thirty, the meeting broke up and Sam headed for the coffee machine in search of a caffeine boost that would keep him going for the next eight hours. He was just taking his first sip when Norm Liddell walked into the station. Sam couldn't help feeling a prick of satisfaction at the sight of the bruises and scrapes on Liddell's face. The injuries were minor, but last night, after the bomb, Liddell had been among those screaming the loudest for medical assistance. His own wife, who'd sustained a broken arm, had finally told her husband to shut up and act like a man.

Now here he was, sporting a few nasty scrapes on his face as well as a look of—could it be? Contrition?

"Afternoon, Navarro," said Liddell, his voice subdued.

"Afternoon."

"I, uh…" Liddell cleared his throat and glanced around the hall, as though to check if anyone was listening. No one was.

"How's the wife doing?" asked Sam.

"Fine. She'll be in a cast for a while. Luckily, it was just a closed fracture."

"She handled herself pretty well last night, considering her injury," Sam commented. *Unlike you.*

"Yes, well, my wife's got a spine of steel. In fact, that's sort of why I want to talk to you."

"Oh?"

"Look, Navarro. Last night…I guess I jumped on you

prematurely. I mean, I didn't realize you had information about any bomb."

Sam didn't say a word. He didn't want to interrupt this enjoyable performance.

"So when I got on your case last night—about evacuating the building—I should've realized you had your reasons. But damn it, Navarro, all I could see was all those people hurt in the stampede. I thought you'd gotten them panicked for nothing, and I—" He paused, obviously struggling to bite back his words. "Anyway, I apologize."

"Apology accepted."

Liddell gave a curt nod of relief.

"Now you can tell your wife you're off the hook."

The look on Liddell's face was all Sam needed to know that he'd guessed right. This apology had been Mrs. Liddell's idea, bless her steely spine. He couldn't help grinning as he watched the other man turn and walk stiffly toward Chief Coopersmith's office. The good D.A., it appeared, was not the one wearing the pants in the family.

"Hey, Sam!" Gillis was heading toward him, pulling on his jacket. "Let's go."

"Where?"

"Prison's got a surveillance videotape they want us to look at. It's The Snowman and some unknown visitor from a few days ago."

Sam felt a sudden adrenaline rush. "Was it Spectre?"

"No. It was a woman."

"THERE. THE BLONDE." said Detective Cooley.

Sam and Gillis leaned toward the TV screen, their gazes fixed on the black-and-white image of the woman. The view of her face was intermittently blocked by other visitors moving in the foreground, but from what they could see, the woman was indeed a blonde, twenties to thirties, and built like a showgirl.

"Okay, freeze it there," Cooley said to the video tech. "That's a good view of her."

The woman was caught in a still frame, her face turned to the surveillance camera, her figure momentarily visible between two passersby. She was dressed in a skirt suit, and she appeared to be carrying a briefcase. Judging by her attire, she might be an attorney or some other professional. But two details didn't fit.

One was her shoes. The camera's angle, facing downward, captured a view of her right foot, perched atop a sexy spike-heeled sandal with a delicate ankle strap.

"Not the kind of shoes you wear to court," noted Sam.

"Not unless you're out to give the judge a thrill," Gillis said. "And look at that makeup."

It was the second detail that didn't fit. This woman was made up like no lawyer Sam had ever seen. Obviously false eyelashes. Eyeshadow like some tropical fish. Lipstick painted on in bold, broad smears.

"Man, she sure ain't the girl next door," Gillis observed.

"What's the name on the visitor log?" asked Sam.

Cooley glanced at a sheet of paper. "She signed in as Marilyn Dukoff. Identified her purpose for visiting The Snowman as attorney-client consultation."

Gillis laughed. "If she's an attorney, then I'm applying to law school."

"Which law firm did she say she was with?" asked Sam.

"Frick and Darien."

"Not true?"

Cooley shook his head. "She's not on the firm's list of partners, associates or clerks. But…" He leaned forward, a grin on his face. "We think we know where she *did* work."

"Where?"

"The Stop Light."

Gillis shot Sam a look of *Didn't I tell ya?* No one had to explain a thing. They knew all about the Stop Light and its stage shows, pasties optional.

"Let me guess," said Sam. "Exotic dancer."

"You got it," affirmed Cooley.

"Are we sure we're talking about the right Marilyn Dukoff?"

"I think we are," Cooley answered. "See, all visitors to the prison have to present ID, and that's the name she gave, backed up by a Maine driver's license. We've pulled the license file. And here's the photo." Cooley passed a copy of the photo to Sam and Gillis.

"It's her," said Gillis.

"Which means we're talking about the right Marilyn Dukoff," said Cooley. "I think she just waltzed in under her own name and didn't bother with fake IDs. All she faked was her profession."

"Which is obviously not in the legal field," Gillis drawled.

Sam gave a nod to Cooley. "Good work."

"Unfortunately," added the younger detective, "I can't seem to locate the woman herself. We know where she *was* employed, but she left the job two weeks ago. I sent a man to the address listed on her license. She doesn't answer the door. And her phone's just been disconnected." He paused. "I think it's time for a search warrant."

"Let's get it." Sam rose to his feet and glanced at Gillis. "Meet you in the car, ten minutes."

"The blonde's?"

"Unless you've got somewhere better to go."

Gillis looked back at the video screen. At that still

shot of a slim ankle, a sexy shoe. "Better than *that?*" He laughed. "I don't think so."

THE POLICE WERE getting too close for comfort.

Spectre slouched in the doorway of an apartment building half a block away and watched the cops come out of Marilyn's old building. Only moments before, Spectre had been inside that apartment, checking to make sure Marilyn hadn't left behind any clues to her current whereabouts. Luckily for him, he'd slipped out just ahead of Navarro's arrival.

They'd been inside almost an hour. They were good, all right—but Spectre was cleverer. Hours after the theater bombing, he'd hustled Marilyn into a different apartment across town. He'd known that his target might become apparent once they'd pinpointed the bomb placement in the theater. And that Marilyn would inevitably come under their scrutiny. Luckily, she'd been cooperative.

Unfortunately, her usefulness was just about over, and the time had come to end their association. But first, he needed her for one more task.

His face tightened as he spotted a familiar figure emerge from the building. Navarro again. The detective had come to represent all the failures that Spectre had suffered over the past week. Navarro was the brains behind the investigation, the one man responsible for Liddell still being alive.

No hit. No fee. Navarro had cost him money—a lot of it.

Spectre watched the cops confer on the sidewalk. There were five of them, three in plain clothes, two in uniform, but it was Navarro on whom he focused his rage. This had turned into a battle of wits between them, a test of determination. In all his years as a "fuse" man, Spectre had never matched skills with such a wily opponent.

The safe thing to do was merely to slip away from this town and seek out contracts elsewhere. Miami or New Orleans. But his reputation had suffered a serious blow here; he wasn't sure he could land a job in Miami. And he had the feeling Navarro wouldn't give up the pursuit, that, wherever Spectre went, the detective would be dogging his trail.

And then, there was the matter of getting even. Spectre wasn't going to walk away without exacting some kind of payback.

The three plainclothes cops climbed into an unmarked car and drove away. A moment later, the uniformed cops were gone as well. They had found nothing in Marilyn's apartment; Spectre had seen to it.

Catch me if you can, Navarro, he thought. *Or will I catch you first?*

He straightened and stamped his feet, feeling the blood return to his legs. Then he left the doorway and walked around the corner, to his car.

Navarro. Once and for all, he had to take care of Navarro. And he had the perfect plan. It would require Marilyn's help. One little phone call—that's all he'd ask. And then he'd ask no more of her.

Ever again.

THE DINNER WAS excellent. The company was wretched.

Daniella, dressed in an iridescent green leotard and a slinky wraparound skirt, sullenly picked at her salad, ignoring the platter of roast duckling and wild rice. She was not speaking to her husband, and he was not speaking to her, and Nina was too uncomfortable to speak to either one of them.

After all those questions by the police, the matter of Daniella's affair with Robert had come to light. While Nina would never forgive Daniella for that betrayal, at least she could manage to pull off a civil evening with the woman.

Nina's father could not. He was still in a state of shock from the revelation. His showpiece wife, the stunning blonde thirty years his junior, had not been satisfied with marrying mere wealth. She'd wanted a younger man. After four marriages, George Cormier still didn't know how to choose the right wife.

Now it looks like this will be his fourth divorce, Nina thought. She glanced at her father, then at Daniella. Though she loved her father, she couldn't help feeling that he and Daniella deserved each other. In the worst possible way.

Daniella set down her fork. "If you'll excuse me," she said, "I don't really have much of an appetite. I think I'll skip out for a movie."

"What about me?" snapped George. "I know I'm just your husband, but a few evenings a week with your boring old spouse isn't too much to ask, is it? Considering all the benefits you get in exchange."

"Benefits? *Benefits?*" Daniella drew herself to her feet in anger. "All the money in the world can't make up for being married to an old goat like you."

"Goat?"

"An old goat. Do you hear me? *Old.*" She leaned across the table. "In every sense of the word."

He, too, rose to his feet. "Why, you bitch..."

"Go ahead. Call me names. I can think of just as many

to call you back." With a whisk of her blond hair, she turned and walked out of the dining room.

George stared after her for a moment. Slowly, he sank back in his chair. "God," he whispered. "What was I thinking when I married her?"

You weren't thinking at all, Nina felt like saying. She touched her father's arm. "Seems like neither one of us is any good at picking spouses. Are we, Dad?"

He regarded his daughter with a look of shared misery. "I sincerely hope you haven't inherited my bad luck with love, sweetheart."

They sat for a moment without speaking. Their supper lay, almost untouched, on the table. In another room, music had started up, the fast and thumping rhythm of an aerobics tape. Daniella was at it again, working off her anger by sculpting a new and better body. Smart girl; she was going to come out of a divorce looking like a million bucks.

Nina sighed and leaned back. "Whether it's bad luck or character flaws, Dad, maybe some people are just meant to be single."

"Not you, Nina. You *need* to love someone. You always have. And that's what makes you so easy to love."

She gave a sad laugh but said nothing. *Easy to love, easy to leave,* she thought.

Once again, she found herself wondering what Sam was doing. What he was thinking. Not about her, surely; he was too much the cop to be bothered by minor distractions.

Yet when the phone rang, she couldn't suppress the sudden hope that he was calling. She sat at the table, heart thumping hard as she listened to Daniella's voice in the next room talking on the phone.

A moment later, Daniella appeared in the doorway and

said, "It's for you, Nina. The hospital. They said they've been trying to reach you."

Disappointed, Nina rose to take the call. "Hello?"

"Hi, this is Gladys Power, the night nursing supervisor. Sorry to bother you—we got your phone number from your mother. We have a number of staff out sick tonight, and we were wondering if you could come in to cover for the ER."

"Night shift?"

"Yes. We could really use you."

Nina glanced toward Daniella's exercise room, where the music was playing louder than ever. She had to get out of this house. Away from this emotional battleground.

She said, "Okay, I'll take the shift."

"See you at eleven o'clock."

"Eleven?" Nina frowned. The night shift usually started at midnight. "You want me there an hour early?"

"If you could manage it. We're shorthanded on the evening shift as well."

"Right. I'll be there, eleven o'clock." She hung up and breathed a soft sigh of relief. Work was exactly what she needed. Maybe eight hours of crises, major and minor, would get her mind back on track.

And off the subject of Sam Navarro.

MARILYN HUNG UP the phone. "She said she'd be there."

Spectre gave a nod of approval. "You handled it well."

"Of course." Marilyn favored him with that satisfied smile of hers. A smile that said, *I'm worth every penny you pay me.*

"Did she seem at all suspicious?" he asked.

"Not a bit. I'm telling you, she'll be there. Eleven o'clock, just like you wanted." Marilyn tilted back her head and gave her lips a predatory lick. "Now, do I get what I want?"

He smiled. "What *do* you want?"

"You know." She sidled toward him and unbuckled his belt. His breath caught in an involuntary gasp as that hot little hand slid inside his trousers. Her touch was delicious, expert, her technique designed to reduce a man to begging. Oh yes, he knew exactly what she was asking for.

And it wasn't sex.

Why not enjoy the moment? he thought. She was willing, and he still had the time to spare. Three hours until Nina Cormier showed up for her shift at the hospital. Some quick amusement with Marilyn, and then on to more serious business.

She dropped to her knees before him. "You said you'd pay me what I was worth," she whispered.

He groaned. "I promised…"

"I'm worth a lot. Don't you think?"

"Absolutely."

"I can be worth even more to you."

He gave a jerk of pleasure and grasped her face. Breathing heavily, he stroked down her cheek, her jaw, to her neck. Such a long, slender neck. How easy it should be to finish it. First, though, he'd let *her* finish…

"Oh, yes," she murmured. "You're ready for me."

He pulled her, hard, against him. And he thought, *A pity you won't be ready for me.*

IT WAS TEN-THIRTY by the time a weary Sam stepped through his front door. The first thing he noticed was the silence. The emptiness. It was a house that had somehow lost its soul.

He turned on the lights, but even the glow of all those

lamps couldn't seem to dispel the shadows. For the past three years, this was the house he'd called home, the house he'd returned to every evening after work. Now the place felt cold to him, like the house of a stranger. Not a home at all.

He poured himself a glass of milk and drank it in a few thirsty gulps. So much for supper; he didn't have the energy to cook. He poured a second glass and carried it over to the telephone. All evening, he'd been itching to make this call, but something had always interrupted him. Now that he had a few blessed moments of peace, he was going to call Nina. He was going to tell her what he'd been afraid to tell her, what he could no longer deny to her, or to himself.

It had come to him this afternoon, a realization that had struck him, oddly enough, in the midst of searching Marilyn Dukoff's apartment. He'd stood in the woman's bedroom and gazed at the empty bureau drawers, the stripped mattress. And without warning, he'd been struck by a sense of loneliness so intense it made his chest ache. Because that abandoned room had suddenly come to represent his life. It had a purpose, a function, but it was nevertheless empty.

I've been a cop too long, he'd thought. *I've let it take over my life.* Only at that moment, standing in that empty bedroom, did it occur to him how little of his own life he really had. No wife, no kids, no family.

Nina had opened his eyes to the possibilities. Yes, he was scared. Yes, he knew just how much, how deeply, he would be hurt if she ever left him. But the alternative was just as bleak; that he would never even give it a chance.

He'd been a coward. But no longer.

He picked up the phone and dialed Nina's father's house.

A few rings later, the call was answered by a bland "Hello?" Not Nina but Daniella, the fitness freak.

"This is Sam Navarro," he said. "Sorry to call so late. May I speak to Nina?"

"She's not here."

His immediate pang of disappointment was quickly followed by a cop's sense of dismay. How could she not be there? She was supposed to stay in a safe place tonight, not run around unprotected.

"Mind telling me where she went?" he asked.

"The hospital. They called her in to work the night shift."

"The Emergency Room?"

"I guess so."

"Thanks." He hung up, his disappointment so heavy it felt like a physical weight on his shoulders. What the hell. He was not going to hold off any longer. He was going to tell her now. Tonight.

He dialed Maine Medical ER.

"Emergency Room."

"This is Detective Sam Navarro, Portland Police. May I speak with Nina Cormier?"

"Nina's not here tonight."

"Well, when she gets there, could you ask her to call me at home?"

"She's not scheduled to come in."

"Excuse me?"

"I have the time sheet right in front of me. Her name's not down here for tonight."

"I was told someone called her in to work the night shift."

"I don't know anything about that."

"Well, can you find out? This is urgent."

"Let me check with the supervisor. Can you hold?"

In the silence that followed, Sam could hear his own blood rushing through his ears. Something was wrong. That old instinct of his was tingling.

The woman came back on the line. "Detective? I've checked with the supervisor. She says she doesn't know anything about it, either. According to her schedule, Nina isn't listed for any shifts until next week."

"Thank you," said Sam softly.

For a moment he sat thinking about that phone call from the hospital. Someone had known enough to locate Nina at her father's house. Someone had talked her into leaving those protective gates at an hour of night when there'd be few witnesses to see what was about to happen.

Not just someone. Spectre.

It was 10:45.

In a heartbeat, he was out the door and running to his car. Even as he roared out of his driveway, he knew he might already be too late. Racing for the freeway, he steered with one hand and dialed his car phone with the other.

"Gillis here," answered a weary voice.

"I'm on my way to Maine Med," Sam said. "Spectre's there."

"What?"

"Nina got a bogus call asking her to come in to work. I'm sure it was him. She's already left the house—"

Gillis replied, "I'll meet you there," and hung up.

Sam turned his full attention to the road. The speedometer hit seventy. Eighty.

Don't let me be too late, he prayed.

He floored the accelerator.

THE HOSPITAL PARKING garage was deserted, a fact that scarcely concerned Nina as she drove through the automatic gate. She had often been in this garage late at night, either coming to, or leaving from, her shifts in the ER, and she'd never encountered any problems. Portland, after all, was one of the safest towns in America.

Provided you're not on someone's hit list, she reminded herself.

She pulled into a parking stall and sat there for a moment, trying to calm her nerves. She wanted to start her shift with her mind focused clearly on the job. Not on death threats. Not on Sam Navarro. Once she walked in those doors, she was first and foremost a professional. People's lives depended on it.

She opened the door and stepped out of the car.

It was still an hour before the usual shift change. Come midnight, this garage would be busy with hospital staff coming or going. But at this moment, no one else was around. She quickened her pace. The hospital elevator was just ahead; the way was clear. Only a dozen yards to go.

She never saw the man step out from behind the parked car.

But she felt a hand grasp her arm, felt the bite of a gun barrel pressed against her temple. Her scream was cut off by the first words he uttered.

"Not a sound or you're dead." The gun at her head was all the emphasis needed to keep her silent.

He yanked her away from the elevator, shoved her toward a row of parked cars. She caught a fleeting glimpse of his face as she was spun around. *Spectre.* They were moving now, Nina sobbing as she stumbled forward, the man gripping her arm with terrifying strength.

He's going to kill me now, here, where no one will see it....

The pounding of her own pulse was so loud at first, she didn't hear the faint squeal of tires across pavement.

But her captor did. Spectre froze, his grip still around her arm.

Now Nina heard it, too: car tires, screeching up the garage ramp.

With savage force, Spectre wrenched her sideways, toward the cover of a parked car. *This is my only chance to escape,* she thought.

In an instant she was fighting back, struggling against his grip. He was going to shoot her anyway. Whether it happened in some dark corner or out here, in the open, she would not go down without a fight. She kicked, flailed, clawed at his face.

He swung at her, a swift, ugly blow that slammed against her chin. The pain was blinding. She staggered, felt herself falling. He grasped her arm and began dragging her across the pavement. She was too stunned to fight now, to save herself.

Light suddenly glared in her eyes, a light so bright it seemed to stab straight through her aching head. She heard tires screech and realized she was staring at a pair of headlights.

A voice yelled, *"Freeze!"*

Sam. It was Sam.

"Let her go, Spectre!" Sam shouted.

The gun barrel was back at Nina's head, pressing harder than ever. "What superb timing, Navarro," Spectre drawled without a trace of panic in his voice.

"I said, *let her go.*"

"Is that a command, Detective? I certainly hope not. Because, considering the young woman's situation—" Spectre grabbed her by the chin and turned her face toward Sam "—offending me could prove hazardous to her health."

"I know your face. So do the ushers at the Brant Theater. You have no reason to kill her now!"

"No reason? Think again." Spectre, still holding the gun to Nina's head, nudged her forward. Toward Sam. "Move out of the way, Navarro."

"She's worthless to you—"

"But not to you."

Nina caught a glimpse of Sam's face, saw his look of helpless panic. He was gripping his gun in both hands, the barrel aimed, but he didn't dare shoot. Not with her in the line of fire.

She tried to go limp, tried to slump to the ground. No good; Spectre was too strong and he had too firm a grip around her neck. He simply dragged her beside him, his arm like a vise around her throat.

"Back off!" Spectre yelled.

"You don't want her!"

"Back off or it ends here, with her brains all over the ground!"

Sam took a step back, then another. Though his gun was still raised, it was useless to him. In that instant, Nina's gaze locked with his, and she saw more than fear, more than panic in his eyes. She saw despair.

"Nina," he said. "Nina—"

It was her last glimpse of Sam before Spectre pulled her into Sam's car. He slammed the door shut and threw the car in Reverse. Suddenly they were screeching backward down the ramp. She caught a fast-moving view of parked cars and concrete pillars, and then they crashed through the arm of the security gate.

Spectre spun the car around to face forward and hit the accelerator. They roared out of the driveway and onto the road.

Before she could recover her wits, the gun was back at her head. She looked at him, and saw a face that was frighteningly calm. The face of a man who knows he's in complete control.

"I have nothing to lose by killing you," he said.

"Then why don't you?" she whispered.

"I have plans. Plans that happen to include you."

"What plans?"

He gave a low, amused laugh. "Let's just say they involve Detective Navarro, his Bomb Squad, and a rather large amount of dynamite. I like spectacular endings, don't you?" He smiled at her.

That's when she realized whom she was looking at. What she was looking at.

A monster.

Chapter Thirteen

Sam raced down the parking garage ramp, his legs pumping with desperate speed. He emerged from the building just in time to see his car, Spectre at the wheel, careening out of the driveway and taking off down the road.

I've lost her, he thought as the taillights winked into the night. *My God. Nina...*

He sprinted to the sidewalk and ran halfway down the block before he finally came to a stop. The taillights had vanished.

The car was gone.

He gave a shout of rage, of despair, and heard his voice echo in the darkness. Too late. He was too late.

A flash of light made him spin around. A pair of headlights had just rounded the corner. Another car was approaching—one he recognized.

"Gillis!" he shouted.

The car braked to a stop near the curb. Sam dashed to the passenger door and scrambled inside.

"Go. *Go!*" he barked.

A perplexed Gillis stared at him. "What?"

"Spectre's got Nina! Move it!"

Gillis threw the car into gear. They screeched away from the curb. "Which way?"

"Left. Here!"

Gillis swerved around the corner.

Sam caught a glimpse of his own car, two blocks ahead, as it moved into an intersection and turned right.

"There!"

"I see it," Gillis said, and made the same turn.

Spectre must have spotted them, too. A moment later he accelerated and shot through a red light. Cars skidded to a stop in the intersection.

As Gillis steered through the maze of vehicles and pressed his pursuit, Sam picked up the car phone and called for assistance from all available patrol cars. With a little help, they could have Spectre boxed in.

For now, they just had to keep him in sight.

"This guy's a maniac," Gillis muttered.

"Don't lose her."

"He's gonna get us all killed. Look!"

Up ahead, Spectre swerved into the left lane, passed a car, and swerved back to the right just as a truck barreled down on him.

"Stay with them!" Sam ordered.

"I'm trying, I'm trying," Gillis, too, swerved left to pass. Too much traffic was heading toward them; he swerved back.

Seconds were lost. Seconds that Spectre pushed to his advantage.

Gillis tried again, this time managing to scoot back into his lane before colliding head-on with an oncoming van.

Spectre was nowhere in sight.

"What the hell?" muttered Gillis.

They stared at the road, saw stray taillights here and there, but otherwise it was an empty street. They drove on, through intersection after intersection, scanning the side roads. With every block they passed, Sam's panic swelled.

A half mile later, he was forced to accept the obvious. They had lost Spectre.

He had lost Nina.

Gillis was driving in grim silence now. Sam's despair had rubbed off on him as well. Neither one said it, but both of them knew. Nina was as good as dead.

"I'm sorry, Sam," murmured Gillis. "God, I'm sorry."

Sam could only stare ahead, wordless, his view blurring in a haze of tears. Moments passed. An eternity.

Patrol cars reported in. No trace of the car. Or Spectre.

Finally, at midnight, Gillis pulled over and parked at the curb. Both men sat in silence.

Gillis said, "There's still a chance."

Sam dropped his head in his hands. *A chance.* Spectre could be fifty miles away by now. Or he could be right around the corner. *What I would give for one, small chance....*

His gaze fell and he focused on Gillis's car phone. *One small chance.*

He picked up the phone and dialed.

"Who're you calling?" asked Gillis.

"Spectre."

"What?"

"I'm calling my car phone." He listened as it rang. Five, six times.

Spectre answered, his voice raised in a bizarre falsetto. "Hello, you have reached the Portland Bomb Squad. No one's available to answer your call, as we seem to have misplaced our damn telephone."

"This is Navarro," growled Sam.

"Why hello, Detective Navarro. How *are* you?"

"Is she all right?"

"Who?"

"Is she all right?"

"Ah, you must be referring to the young lady. Perhaps I'll let her speak for herself."

There was a pause. He heard muffled voices, some sort of scraping sound. A soft, distant whine. Then Nina's voice came on, quiet, frightened. "Sam?"

"Are you hurt?"

"No. No, I'm fine."

"Where are you? Where's he taken you?"

"Oops," cut in Spectre. "Forbidden topic, Detective. Afraid I must abort this phone call."

"Wait. *Wait!*" cried Sam.

"Any parting words?"

"If you hurt her, Spectre—if anything happens to her—I swear I'll kill you."

"Is this a *law* enforcement officer I'm speaking to?"

"I mean it. I'll *kill* you."

"I'm shocked. *Shocked,* I tell you."

"Spectre!"

He was answered by laughter, soft and mocking. And then, abruptly, the line went dead.

Frantically Sam redialed and got a busy signal. He hung up, counted to ten, and dialed once more.

Another busy signal. Spectre had taken the phone off the hook.

Sam slammed the receiver down. "She's still alive."

"Where are they?"

"She never got the chance to tell me."

"It's been an hour. They could be anywhere within a fifty-mile radius."

"I know, I know." Sam sat back, trying to think through

his swirl of panic. During his years as a cop, he'd always managed to keep his head cool, his thoughts focused. But tonight, for the first time in his career, he felt paralyzed by fear. By the knowledge that, with every moment that passed, every moment he did nothing, Nina's chances for survival faded.

"Why hasn't he killed her?" murmured Gillis. "Why is she still alive?"

Sam looked at his partner. At least Gillis still had a functioning brain. And he was thinking. Puzzling over a question that should've been obvious to them both.

"He's keeping her alive for a reason," said Gillis.

"A trump card. Insurance in case he's trapped."

"No, he's already home free. Right now, she's more of a liability than a help. Hostages slow you down. Complicate things. But he's allowed her to live."

So far, thought Sam with a wave of helpless rage. *I'm losing it, losing my ability to think straight. Her life depends on me. I can't afford to blow it.*

He looked at the phone again, and a memory echoed in his head. Something he'd heard over the phone during that brief pause between hearing Spectre's voice and Nina's. That distant wail, rising and falling.

A siren.

He reached for the phone again and dialed 911.

"Emergency operator," answered a voice.

"This is Detective Sam Navarro, Portland Police. I need a list of all emergency dispatches made in the last twenty minutes. Anywhere in the Portland-South Portland area."

"Which vehicles, sir?"

"Everything. Ambulance, fire, police. All of them."

There was a brief silence, then another voice came on the line. Sam had his notepad ready.

"This is the supervisor, Detective Navarro," a woman said. "I've checked with the South Portland dispatcher. Combined, we've had three dispatches in the last twenty minutes. At 11:55, an ambulance was sent to 2203 Green Street in Portland. At 12:10, the police were dispatched to a burglar alarm at 751 Bickford Street in South Portland. And at 12:13, a squad car was called to the vicinity of Munjoy Hill for a report of some disturbance of the peace. There were no fire trucks dispatched during that period."

"Okay, thanks." Sam hung up and rifled through the glove compartment for a map. Quickly he circled the three dispatch locations.

"What now?" asked Gillis.

"I heard a siren over the phone, when I was talking to Spectre. Which means he had to be within hearing distance of some emergency vehicle. And these are the only three locations vehicles were dispatched to."

Gillis glanced at the map and shook his head. "We've got dozens of city blocks covered there! From point of dispatch to destination."

"But these are starting points."

"Like a haystack's a starting point."

"It's all we have to go on. Let's start at Munjoy Hill."

"This is crazy. The APB's out on your car. We've got people looking for it already. We'd be running ourselves ragged trying to chase sirens."

"Munjoy Hill, Gillis. Go."

"You're beat. I'm beat. We should go back to HQ and wait for things to develop."

"You want me to drive? Then move the hell over."

"Sam, are you *hearing* me?"

"Yes, damn you!" Sam shouted back in a sudden outburst of rage. Then, with a groan, he dropped his head in

his hands. Quietly he said, "It's my fault. My fault she's going to die. They were right there in front of me. And I couldn't think of any way to save her. Any way to keep her alive."

Gillis gave a sigh of comprehension. "She means that much to you?"

"And Spectre knows it. Somehow he knows it. That's why he's keeping her alive. To torment me. Manipulate me. He has the winning hand and he's using it." He looked at Gillis. "We have to find her."

"Right now, he has the advantage. He has someone who means a lot to you. And *you're* the cop he seems to be focused on. The cop he wants to get back at." He glanced down at his car phone. It was ringing.

He answered it. "Gillis here." A moment later he hung up and started the car. "Jackman Avenue," he said, pulling into the road. "It could be our break."

"What's on Jackman Avenue?"

"An apartment, unit 338-D. They just found a body there."

Sam went very still. A sense of dread had clamped down on his chest, making it difficult to breathe. He asked, softly, "Whose body?"

"Marilyn Dukoff's."

HE WAS SINGING "Dixie!" as he worked, stringing out wire in multicolored lengths along the floor. Nina, hands and feet bound to a heavy chair, could only sit and watch helplessly. Next to Spectre was a toolbox, a soldering iron, and two dozen dynamite sticks.

"In Dixieland where I was born, early on a frosty mornin'…"

Spectre finished laying out the wire and turned his

attention to the dynamite. With green electrical tape, he neatly bundled the sticks together in groups of three and set the bundles in a cardboard box.

"In Dixieland we'll make our stand, to live and die in Dixie. Away, away, away down south, in DIXIE!" he boomed out, and his voice echoed in the far reaches of the vast and empty warehouse. Then, turning to Nina, he dipped his head in a bow.

"You're crazy," whispered Nina.

"But what is madness? Who's to say?" Spectre wound green tape around the last three dynamite sticks. Then he gazed at the bundles, admiring his work. "What's that saying? 'Don't get mad, get even'? Well, I'm not mad, in any sense of the word. But I *am* going to get even."

He picked up the box of dynamite and was carrying it toward Nina when he seemed to stumble. Nina's heart almost stopped as the box of explosives tilted toward the floor. Toward her.

Spectre gave a loud gasp of horror just before he caught the box. To Nina's astonishment, he suddenly burst out laughing. "Just an old joke," he admitted. "But it never fails to get a reaction."

He really was crazy, she thought, her heart thudding.

Carrying the box of dynamite, he moved about the warehouse, laying bundles of explosives at measured intervals around the perimeter. "It's a shame, really," he said, "to waste so much quality dynamite on one building. But I do want to leave a good impression. A lasting impression. And I've had quite enough of Sam Navarro and his nine lives. This should take care of any extra lives he still has."

"You're laying a trap."

"You're so clever."

"Why? Why do you want to kill him?"

"Because."

"He's just a policeman doing his job."

"*Just* a policeman?" Spectre turned to her, but his expression remained hidden in the shadows of the warehouse. "Navarro is more than that. He's a challenge. My nemesis. To think, after all these years of success in cities like Boston and Miami, I should find my match in a small town like this. Not even Portland, Oregon, but Portland, *Maine*." He gave a laugh of self-disgust. "It ends here, in this warehouse. Between Navarro and me."

Spectre crossed toward her, carrying the final bundle of dynamite. He knelt beside the rocking chair where Nina sat with hands and ankles bound. "I saved the last blast for you, Miss Cormier," he said. And he taped the bundle under Nina's chair. "You won't feel a thing," he assured her. "It will happen so fast, why, the next thing you know, you'll be sprouting angel's wings. So will Navarro. If he gets his wings at all."

"He's not stupid. He'll know you've set a trap."

Spectre began stringing out more color-coded wire now, yards and yards of it. "Yes, it should be quite obvious this isn't any run-of-the-mill bomb. All this wire, tangled up to confuse him. Circuitry that makes no sense..." He snipped a white wire, then a red one. With his soldering iron, he connected the ends. "And the time ticking away. Minutes, then seconds. Which is the detonator wire? Which wire should he cut? The wrong one, and it all goes up in smoke. The warehouse. You. And him—if he has nerve enough to see it to the end. It's a hopeless dilemma, you see. He stays to disarm it and you could both die. He chickens out and runs, and *you* die, leaving him with guilt he'll never forget. Either way, Sam Navarro suffers. And I win."

"You can't win."

"Spare me the moralistic warnings. I have work to do. And not much time to do it." He strung the wires out to the other dynamite bundles, crisscrossing colors, splicing ends to blasting caps.

Not much time to do it, he had said. How much time was he talking about?

She glanced down at the other items laid out on the floor. A digital timer. A radio transmitter. It was to be a timed device, she realized, the countdown triggered by that transmitter. Spectre would be safely out of the building when he armed the bomb. Out of harm's way when it exploded.

Stay away, Sam, she thought. *Please stay away. And live.*

Spectre rose to his feet and glanced at his watch. "Another hour and I should be ready to make the call." He looked at her and smiled. "Three in the morning, Miss Cormier. That seems as good an hour as any to die, don't you think?"

THE WOMAN WAS nude from the waist down, her body crumpled on the wood floor. She had been shot once, in the head.

"The report came in at 10:45," said Yeats from Homicide. "Tenant below us noticed bloodstains seeping across the ceiling and called the landlady. She opened the door, saw the body and called us. We found the victim's ID in her purse. That's why we called you."

"Any witnesses? Anyone see anything, hear anything?" asked Gillis.

"No. He must've used a silencer. Then slipped out without being seen."

Sam gazed around at the sparsely furnished room.

The walls were bare, the closets half empty, and there were boxes of clothes on the floor—all signs that Marilyn Dukoff had not yet settled into this apartment.

Yeats confirmed it. "She moved in a day ago, under the name Marilyn Brown. Paid the deposit and first month's rent in cash. That's all the landlady could tell me."

"She have any visitors?" asked Gillis.

"Next-door tenant heard a man's voice in here yesterday. But never saw him."

"Spectre," said Sam. He focused once again on the body. The criminalists were already combing the room, dusting for prints, searching for evidence. They would find none, Sam already knew; Spectre would've seen to it.

There was no point hanging around here; they'd be better off trying to chase sirens. He turned to the door, then paused as he heard one of the detectives say, "Not much in the purse. Wallet, keys, a few bills—"

"What bills?" asked Sam.

"Electric, phone. Water. Look like they're to the old apartment. The name Dukoff's on them. Delivered to a PO box."

"Let me see the phone bill."

At his first glance at the bill, Sam almost uttered a groan of frustration. It was two sheets long and covered with long distance calls, most of them to Bangor numbers, a few to Massachusetts and Florida. It would take hours to track all those numbers down, and the chances were it would simply lead them to Marilyn Dukoff's bewildered friends or family.

Then he focused on one number, at the bottom of the bill. It was a collect call charge, from a South Portland prefix, dated a week and a half ago at 10:17 p.m. Someone had called collect and Marilyn Dukoff had accepted the charges.

"This could be something," Sam noted. "I need the location of this number."

"We can call the operator from my car," said Gillis. "but I don't know what it's going to get you."

"A hunch. That's what I'm going on," Sam admitted.

Back in Gillis's car, Sam called the Directory Assistance supervisor.

After checking her computer, she confirmed it was a pay phone. "It's near the corner of Calderwood and Hardwick, in South Portland."

"Isn't there a gas station on that corner?" asked Sam. "I seem to remember one there."

"There may be, Detective. I can't tell you for certain."

Sam hung up and reached for the South Portland map. Under the dome light, he pinpointed the location of the pay phone. "Here it is," he said to Gillis.

"There's just some industrial buildings out there."

"Yeah, which makes a collect call at 10:17 p.m. all the more interesting."

"Could've been anyone calling her. Friends, family. For all we know—"

"It was Spectre," Sam said. His head jerked up in sudden excitement. "South Portland. Let's *go*."

"What?"

Sam thrust the map toward Gillis. "Here's Bickford Street. A squad car was dispatched there at 12:10. And here's Calderwood and Hardwick. The squad car would've gone right through this area."

"You think Spectre's holed up around there?"

Sam scrawled a circle on the map, a three-block radius

around Calderwood and Hardwick. "He's here. He's got to be around here."

Gillis started the car. "I think our haystack just got a hell of a lot smaller."

Twenty minutes later, they were at the corner of Hardwick and Calderwood. There was, indeed, a gas station there, but it had been closed down and a For Sale—Commercial Property sign was posted in the scraggly strip of a garden near the road. Sam and Gillis sat in their idling car for a moment, scanning the street. There was no other traffic in sight.

Gillis began to drive up Hardwick. The neighborhood was mostly industrial. Vacant lots, a boating supply outlet. A lumber wholesaler. A furniture maker. Everything was closed for the night, the parking lots empty, the buildings dark. They turned onto Calderwood.

A few hundred yards later, Sam spotted the light. It was faint, no more than a yellowish glow from a small window—the only window in the building. As they pulled closer, Gillis cut his headlights. They stopped half a block away.

"It's the old Stimson warehouse," said Sam.

"No cars in the lot," Gillis noted. "But it looks like someone's home."

"Didn't the Stimson cannery close down last year?"

Sam didn't answer; he was already stepping out of the car.

"Hey!" whispered Gillis. "Shouldn't we call for backup?"

"You call. I'm checking it out."

"Sam!" Gillis hissed. "Sam!"

Adrenaline pumping, Sam ignored his partner's warnings and started toward the warehouse. The darkness was in his favor; whoever was inside wouldn't be able to spot his approach. Through the cracks in the truck bay doors, he saw more light, vertical slivers of yellow.

He circled the building, but spotted no ground floor windows, no way to look inside. There was a back door and a front door, but both were locked.

At the front of the building, he met up with Gillis.

"Backup's on the way," Gillis informed him.

"I have to get in there."

"We don't know what we'll find in there—" Gillis suddenly paused and glanced at his car.

The phone was ringing.

Both men scurried back to answer it.

Sam grabbed the receiver. "Navarro here."

"Detective Navarro," said the police operator. "We have an outside phone call for you. The man says it's urgent. I'll put it through."

There was a pause, a few clicks, and then a man's voice said, "I'm so glad to reach you, Detective. This car phone of yours is coming in handy."

"Spectre?"

"I'd like to issue a personal invitation, Detective. To you and you alone. A reunion, with a certain someone who's right here beside me."

"Is she all right?"

"She's perfectly fine." Spectre paused and added with a soft tone of threat. "For the moment."

"What do you want from me?"

"Nothing at all. I'd just like you to come and take Miss Cormier off my hands. She's becoming an inconvenience. And I have other places to go to."

"Where is she?"

"I'll give you a clue. Herring."

"What?"

"Maybe the name *Stimson* rings a bell? You can look up the address. Sorry I won't be here to greet you, but I really *must* be going."

SPECTRE HUNG UP the phone and smiled at Nina. "Time for me to go. Lover boy should be here any minute." He picked up his toolbox and set it in the car, which he'd driven through the loading bay to keep it out of sight.

He's leaving, she thought. *Leaving me as bait for the trap.*

It was cool in the warehouse, but she felt a drop of sweat slide down her temple as she watched Spectre reach down for the radio transmitter. All he had to do was flick one switch on that radio device, and the bomb would be armed, the countdown started.

Ten minutes later, it would explode.

Her heart gave a painful thud as she saw him reach for the radio switch. Then he smiled at her.

"Not yet," he said. "I wouldn't want things to happen prematurely."

Turning, he walked toward the truck bay door. He gave Nina a farewell salute. "Say goodbye to Navarro for me. Tell him I'm so sorry to miss the big kaboom." He unlatched the bay door and gave the handle a yank. It slid up with the sound of grating metal. It was almost open when Spectre suddenly froze.

Right in front of him, a pair of headlights came on.

"Freeze, Spectre!" came a command from somewhere in the darkness. "Hands over your head!"

Sam, thought Nina. *You found me....*

"Hands up!" yelled Sam. "Do it!"

Silhouetted against the headlights, Spectre seemed to

hesitate for a few seconds. Then, slowly, he raised his hands over his head.

He was still holding the transmitter.

"Sam!" cried Nina. "There's a bomb! He's got a transmitter!"

"Put it down," Sam ordered. "Put it down or I shoot!"

"Certainly," agreed Spectre. Slowly he dropped to a crouch and lowered the transmitter toward the floor. But as he lay it down, there was a distinct *click* that echoed through the warehouse.

My God, he's armed the bomb, thought Nina.

"Better run," said Spectre. And he dived sideways, toward a stack of crates.

He wasn't fast enough. In the next instant, Sam squeezed off two shots. Both bullets found their target.

Spectre seemed to stumble. He dropped to his knees and began to crawl forward, but his limbs were moving drunkenly, like a swimmer trying to paddle across land. He was making gurgling sounds now, gasping out curses with his last few breaths.

"Dead," wheezed Spectre, and it was almost a laugh. "You're all dead...."

Sam stepped over Spectre's motionless body and started straight toward Nina.

"No!" she cried. "Stay away!"

He stopped dead, staring at her with a look of bewilderment. "What is it?"

"He's wired a bomb to my chair," sobbed Nina. "If you try to cut me loose it'll go off!"

At once Sam's gaze shot to the coils of wire ringing her chair, then followed the trail of wire to the warehouse wall, to the first bundle of dynamite, lying in plain view.

"He has eighteen sticks planted all around the building," she said. "Three are under my chair. It's set to go off in ten minutes. Less, now."

Their gazes met. And in that one glance she saw his look of panic. It was quickly suppressed. He stepped across the wire and crouched by her chair.

"I'm getting you out of here," he vowed.

"There's not enough time!"

"Ten minutes?" He gave a terse laugh. "That's loads of time." He knelt down and peered under the seat. He didn't say a thing, but when he rose again, his expression was grim. He turned and called, "Gillis?"

"Right here," Gillis answered, stepping gingerly over the wires. "I got the toolbox. What do we have?"

"Three sticks under the chair, and a digital timer." Sam gently slid out the timing device, bristling with wires, and set it carefully on the floor. "It looks like a simple series-parallel circuit. I'll need time to analyze it."

"How long do we have?"

"Eight minutes and forty-five seconds and counting."

Gillis cursed. "No time to get the bomb truck."

A wail of a siren suddenly cut through the night. Two police cruisers pulled up outside the bay door.

"Backup's here," Gillis said. He hurried over to the doors, waving at the other cops. "Stay back!" he yelled. "We got a bomb in here! I want a perimeter evac *now!* And get an ambulance here on standby."

I won't need an ambulance, thought Nina. *If this bomb goes off, there'll be nothing left of me to pick up.*

She tried to calm her racing heart, tried to stop her slide toward hysteria, but sheer terror was making it hard for her to breathe. There was nothing she could do to save herself. Her wrists were tightly bound; so were her ankles.

If she so much as shifted too far in her chair, the bomb could be triggered.

It was all up to Sam.

Chapter Fourteen

Sam's jaw was taut as he studied the tangle of wires and circuitry. There were so many wires! It would take an hour just to sort them all out. But all they had were minutes. Though he didn't say a word, she could read the urgency in his face, could see the first droplets of sweat forming on his forehead.

Gillis returned to his partner's side. "I checked the perimeter. Spectre's got the building wired with fifteen or more sticks. No other action fuses as far as I can see. The brain to this whole device is right there in your hands."

"It's too easy," muttered Sam, scanning the circuitry. "He *wants* me to cut this wire."

"Could it be a double feint? He knew we'd be suspicious. So he made it simple on purpose—just to throw us?"

Sam swallowed. "This looks like the arming switch right here. But over here, he's got the cover soldered shut. He could have a completely different switch inside. Magnetic reed or a Castle-Robins device. If I pry off that cap, it could fire."

Gillis glanced at the digital timer. "Five minutes left."

"I know, I know." Sam's voice was hoarse with tension, but his hands were absolutely steady as he traced the circuitry. One tug on the wrong wire, and all three of them could be instantly vaporized.

Outside, more sirens whined to a stop. Nina could hear voices, the sounds of confusion.

But inside, there was silence.

Sam took a breath and glanced up at her. "You okay?"

She gave a tense nod. And she saw, in his face, the first glimpse of panic. *He won't figure this out in time, and he knows it.*

This was just what Spectre had planned. The hopeless dilemma. The fatal choice. Which wire to cut? One? None? Does he gamble with his own life? Or does he make the rational choice to abandon the building—and her?

She knew the choice he would make. She could see it in his eyes.

They were both going to die.

"Two and a half minutes," said Gillis.

"Go on, get out of here," Sam ordered.

"You need an extra pair of hands."

"And your kids need a father. Get the hell out."

Gillis didn't budge.

Sam picked up the wire cutters and isolated a white wire.

"You're guessing, Sam. You don't know."

"Instinct, buddy. I've always had good instincts. Better leave. We're down to two minutes. And you're not doing me any good."

Gillis rose to his feet, but lingered there, torn between leaving and staying. "Sam—"

"Move."

Gillis said, softly, "I'll have a bottle of Scotch waiting for you, buddy."

"You do that. Now get out of here."

Without another word, Gillis left the building.

Only Sam and Nina remained. *He doesn't have to stay,* she thought. *He doesn't have to die.*

"Sam," she whispered.

He didn't seem to hear her; he was concentrating too hard on the circuit board, his wire cutters hovering between a life-and-death choice.

"Leave, Sam," she begged.

"This is my job, Nina."

"It's not your job to die!"

"We're not going to die."

"You're right. *We* aren't. *You* aren't. If you leave now—"

"I'm not leaving. You understand? I'm *not*." His gaze rose to meet hers. And she saw, in those steady eyes, that he had made up his mind. He'd made the choice to live— or die—with her. This was not the cop looking at her, but the man who loved her. The man *she* loved.

She felt tears trickle down her face. Only then did she realize she was crying.

"We're down to a minute. I'm going to make a guess here," he said. "If I'm right, cutting this wire should do the trick. If I'm wrong…" He let out a breath. "We'll know pretty quick one way or the other." He slipped the teeth of the cutter around the white wire. "Okay, I'm going with this one."

"Wait."

"What is it?"

"When Spectre was putting it together, he soldered a white wire to a red one, then he covered it all up with green tape. Does that make a difference?"

Sam stared down at the wire he'd been about to cut. "It does," he said softly. "It makes a hell of a lot of difference."

"Sam!" came Gillis's shout through a megaphone. "You've got ten seconds left!"

Ten seconds to run.

Sam didn't run. He moved the wire cutter to a black wire and positioned the jaws to cut. Then he stopped and looked up at Nina.

They stared at each other one last time.

"I love you," he said.

She nodded, the tears streaming down her face. "I love you too," she whispered.

Their gazes remained locked, unwavering, as he slowly closed the cutter over the wire. Even as the jaws came together, even as the teeth bit into the plastic coating, Sam was looking at her, and she at him.

The wire snapped in two.

For a moment neither one of them moved. They were still frozen in place, still paralyzed by the certainty of death.

Then, outside, Gillis yelled, "Sam? You're past countdown! *Sam!*"

All at once, Sam was cutting the bonds from her hands, her ankles. She was too numb to stand, but she didn't need to. He gathered her up into his arms and carried her out of the warehouse, into the night.

Outside, the street was ablaze with the flashing lights of emergency vehicles: squad cars, ambulances, fire trucks. Sam carried her safely past the yellow police tape and set her down on her feet.

Instantly they were surrounded by a mob of officials, Chief Coopersmith and Liddell among them, all clamoring to know the bomb's status. Sam ignored them all. He just stood there with his arms around Nina, shielding her from the chaos.

"Everyone back!" shouted Gillis, waving the crowd away. "Give 'em some breathing space!" He turned to Sam. "What about the device?"

"It's disarmed," said Sam. "But be careful. Spectre may have left us one last surprise."

"I'll take care of it." Gillis started toward the warehouse, then turned back. "Hey, Sam?"

"Yeah?"

"I'd say you just earned your retirement." Gillis grinned. And then he walked away.

Nina looked up at Sam. Though the danger was over, she could still feel his heart pounding, could feel her own heart beating just as wildly.

"You didn't leave me," she whispered, new tears sliding down her face. "You could have—"

"No, I couldn't."

"I told you to go! I *wanted* you to go."

"And I wanted to stay." He took her face in his hands. Firmly, insistently. "There was no other place I'd be but right there beside you, Nina. There's no other place I ever want to be."

She knew a dozen pairs of eyes were watching them. Already the news media had arrived with their camera flashbulbs and their shouted questions. The night was alive with voices and multicolored lights. But at that moment, as he held her, as they kissed, there was no one else but Sam.

When dawn broke, he would still be holding her.

Epilogue

The wedding was on. No doubt about it.

Accompanied by a lilting Irish melody played by flute and harp, Nina and her father walked arm in arm into the forest glade. There, beneath the fiery brilliance of autumn foliage, stood Sam. Just as she knew he would be.

He was grinning, as nervous as a rookie cop on his first beat. Beside him stood his best man, Gillis, and Reverend Sullivan, both wearing smiles. A small circle of friends and family stood gathered under the trees: Wendy and her husband. Chief Coopersmith. Nina's colleagues from the hospital. Also among the guests was Lydia, looking quietly resigned to the fact her daughter was marrying a mere cop.

Some things in life, thought Nina, cannot be changed. She had accepted that. Perhaps Lydia, some day, would learn to be as accepting.

The music faded, and the leaves of autumn drifted down in a soft rain of red and orange. Sam reached out to her. His smile told her all she needed to know. This was right; this was meant to be.

She took his hand.

* * * * *

Whistleblower

To Fiens and Frans

Prologue

Branches whipped his face, and his heart was pounding so hard he thought his chest would explode, but he couldn't stop running. Already, he could hear the man gaining on him, could almost imagine the bullet slicing through the night and slamming into his back. Maybe it already had. Maybe he was trailing a river of blood; he was too numb with terror to feel anything now, except the desperate hunger to live. The rain was pouring down his face, icy, blinding sheets of it, rattling on the dead leaves of winter. He stumbled through a pool of darkness and found himself sprawled flat on his belly in the mud. The sound of his fall was deafening. His pursuer, alerted by the sharp crack of branches, altered course and was now headed straight for him. The thud of a silencer, the zing of a bullet past his cheek, told him he'd been spotted. He forced himself to his feet and made a sharp right, zigzagging back toward the highway. Here in the woods, he was a dead man. But if he could flag down a car, if he could draw someone's attention, he might have a chance.

A crash of branches, a coarse oath, told him his pursuer had stumbled. He'd gained a few precious seconds. He kept running, moving only by an instinctive sense of direction. There was no light to guide his way, nothing except the dim glow of the clouds in the night sky. The road had to be just ahead. Any second now, his feet would hit pavement.

And then what? What if there's no car to flag down, no one to help me?

Then, through the trees ahead, he saw a faint flickering, two watery beams of light.

With a desperate burst of speed, he sprinted toward the car. His lungs were on fire, his eyes blinded by the lash of branches and rain. Another bullet whipped past him and thudded into a tree trunk, but the gunman behind him had suddenly lost all importance. All that mattered was those lights, beckoning him through the darkness, taunting him with the promise of salvation.

When his feet suddenly hit the pavement, he was shocked. The lights were still ahead, bobbing somewhere beyond the trees. Had he missed the car? Was it already moving away, around a curve? No, there it was, brighter now. It was coming this way. He ran to meet it, following the bend of the road and knowing all the time that here in the open, he was an easy target. The sound of his shoes slapping the wet road filled his ears. The lights twisted toward him. At that instant, he heard the gun fire a third time. The force of the impact made him stumble to his knees, and he was vaguely aware of the bullet tearing through his shoulder, of the warmth of his own blood dribbling down his arm, but he was oblivious to pain. He could focus only on staying alive. He struggled back to his feet, took a stumbling step forward...

And was blinded by the onrush of headlights. There was no time to throw himself out of the way, no time even to register panic. Tires screamed across the pavement, throwing up a spray of water.

He didn't feel the impact. All he knew was that he was

suddenly lying on the ground and the rain was pouring into his mouth and he was very, very cold.

And that he had something to do, something important.

Feebly, he reached into the pocket of his windbreaker, and his fingers curled around the small plastic cylinder. He couldn't quite remember why it mattered so much, but it was still there and he was relieved. He clutched it tightly in his palm.

Someone was calling to him. A woman. He couldn't see her face through the rain, but he could hear her voice, hoarse with panic, floating through the buzz in his head. He tried to speak, tried to warn her that they had to get away, that death was waiting in the woods. But all that came out was a groan.

Chapter One

Three miles out of Redwood Valley, a tree had fallen across the road, and with the heavy rains and backed-up cars, it took Catherine Weaver nearly three hours to get past the town of Willits. By then it was already ten o'clock and she knew she wouldn't reach Garberville till midnight. She hoped Sarah wouldn't sit up all night waiting for her. But knowing Sarah, there'd be a supper still warm in the oven and a fire blazing in the hearth. She wondered how pregnancy suited her friend. Wonderfully, of course. Sarah had talked about this baby for years, had chosen its name—Sam or Emma—long before it was conceived. The fact she no longer had a husband was a minor point. "You can only wait around so long for the right father," Sarah had said. "Then you have to take matters into your own hands."

And she had. With her biological clock furiously ticking its last years away, Sarah had driven down to visit Cathy in San Francisco and had calmly selected a fertility clinic from the yellow pages. A liberal-minded one, of course. One that would understand the desperate longings of a thirty-nine-year-old single woman. The insemination itself had been a coolly clinical affair, she'd said later. Hop on the table, slip your feet into the stirrups, and five minutes later, you were pregnant. Well, almost. But it was a simple procedure, the donors were certifiably healthy, and best of all, a woman could fulfill her maternal instincts without all that foolishness about marriage.

Yes, the old marriage game. They'd both suffered through it. And after their divorces, they'd both carried on, albeit with battle scars.

Brave Sarah, thought Cathy. *At least she has the courage to go through with this on her own.*

The old anger washed through her, still potent enough to make her mouth tighten. She could forgive her ex-husband Jack for a lot of things. For his selfishness. His demands. His infidelity. But she could never forgive him for denying her the chance to have a child. Oh, she could have gone against his wishes and had a baby anyway, but she'd wanted him to want one as well. So she'd waited for the time to be right. But during their ten years of marriage, he'd never been "ready," never felt it was the "right time."

What he should have told her was the truth: that he was too self-centered to be bothered with a baby.

I'm thirty-seven years old, she thought. *I no longer have a husband. I don't even have a steady boyfriend. But I could be content, if only I could hold my own child in my arms.*

At least Sarah would soon be blessed.

Four months to go and then the baby was due. Sarah's baby. Cathy had to smile at that thought, despite the rain now pouring over her windshield. It was coming down harder now; even with the wipers thrashing at full speed, she could barely make out the road. She glanced at her watch and saw it was already eleven-thirty; there were no other cars in sight. If she had engine trouble out here, she'd probably have to spend the night huddled in the backseat, waiting for help to arrive.

Peering ahead, she tried to make out the road's dividing line and saw nothing but a solid wall of rain. This was ridiculous. She really should have stopped at that motel in

Willits, but she hated the thought of being only fifty miles from her goal, especially when she'd already driven so far.

She spotted a sign ahead: Garberville, 10 Miles. So she was closer than she'd thought. Twenty-five miles more, then there'd be a turnoff and a five-mile drive through dense woods to Sarah's cedar house. The thought of being so close fueled her impatience. She fed the old Datsun some gas and sped up to forty-five miles an hour. It was a reckless thing to do, especially in these conditions, but the thought of a warm house and hot chocolate was just too tempting.

The road curved unexpectedly; startled, she jerked the wheel to the right and the car slid sideways, tobogganing wildly across the rain-slicked pavement. She knew enough not to slam on the brakes. Instead, she clutched the wheel, fighting to regain control. The tires skidded a few feet, a heart-stopping ride that took her to the very edge of the road. Just as she thought she'd clip the trees, the tires gripped the pavement. The car was still moving twenty miles an hour, but at least it was headed in a straight line. With clammy hands, she managed to negotiate the rest of the curve.

What happened next caught her completely by surprise. One instant she was congratulating herself for averting disaster, the next, she was staring ahead in disbelief.

The man had appeared out of nowhere. He was crouched in the road, captured like a wild animal in the glare of her headlights. Reflexes took over. She slammed on the brakes, but it was already too late. The screech of her tires was punctuated by the thud of the man's body against the hood of her car.

For what seemed like eternity, she sat frozen and unable to do anything but clutch the steering wheel and stare at the windshield wipers skating back and forth. Then, as the reality of what she'd just done sank in, she shoved the door open and dashed out into the rain.

At first she could see nothing through the downpour, only a glistening strip of blacktop lit by the dim glow of her taillights. *Where is he?* she thought frantically. With water streaming past her eyes, she traced the road backward, struggling to see in the darkness. Then, through the pounding rain, she heard a low moan. It came from somewhere off to the side, near the trees.

Shifting direction, she plunged into the shadows and sank ankle-deep in mud and pine needles. Again she heard the moan, closer now, almost within reach.

"Where are you?" she screamed. "Help me find you!"

"Here…" The answer was so weak she barely heard it, but it was all she needed. Turning, she took a few steps and practically stumbled over his crumpled body in the darkness. At first, he seemed to be only a confusing jumble of soaked clothes, then she managed to locate his hand and feel for his pulse. It was fast but steady, probably steadier than her own pulse, which was skipping wildly. His fingers suddenly closed over hers in a desperate grip. He rolled against her and struggled to sit up.

"Please! Don't move!" she said.

"Can't—can't stay here—"

"Where are you hurt?"

"No time. Help me. Hurry—"

"Not till you tell me where you're hurt!"

He reached out and grabbed her shoulder in a clumsy attempt to rise to his feet. To her amazement, he managed to pull himself halfway up. For an instant they wobbled against each other, then his strength seemed to collapse and they both slid to their knees in the mud. His breathing had turned harsh and irregular and she wondered about his injuries. If he was bleeding internally he could die within minutes. She had to get him to a hospital now, even if it meant dragging him back to the car.

"Okay. Let's try again," she said, grabbing his left arm and draping it around her neck. She was startled by his gasp of agony. Immediately she released him. His arm left a sticky trail of warmth around her neck. *Blood.*

"My other side's okay," he grunted. "Try again."

She shifted to his right side and pulled his arm over her neck. If she weren't so frantic, it would have struck her as a comical scene, the two of them struggling like drunkards to stand up. When at last he was on his feet and they stood swaying together in the mud, she wondered if he even had the strength to put one foot in front of the other. She certainly couldn't move them both. Though he was slender, he was also a great deal taller than she'd expected, and much more than her five-foot-five frame could support.

But something seemed to compel him forward, a kindling of some hidden reserves. Even through their soaked clothes, she could feel the heat of his body and could sense the urgency driving him onward. A dozen questions formed in her head, but she was breathing too hard to voice them. Her every effort had to be concentrated on getting him to the car, and then to a hospital.

Gripping him around the waist, she latched her fingers through his belt. Painfully they made their way to the road, struggling step by step. His arm felt taut as wire over her neck. It seemed everything about him was wound up tight. There was something desperate about the way his muscles strained to move forward. His urgency penetrated right through to her skin. It was a panic as palpable as the warmth of his body, and she was suddenly infected with his need to flee, a need made more desperate by the fact they could move no faster than they already were. Every few feet she had to stop and shove back her dripping hair just to see where she was going. And all around them, the rain and darkness closed off all view of whatever danger pursued.

The taillights of her car glowed ahead like ruby eyes winking in the night. With every step the man grew heavier and her legs felt so rubbery she thought they'd both topple in the road. If they did, she wouldn't have the strength to haul him back up again. Already, his head was sagging against her cheek and water trickled from his rain-matted hair down her neck. The simple act of putting one foot in front of the other was so automatic that she never even considered dropping him on the road and backing the car to him instead. And the taillights were already so close, just beyond the next veil of rain.

By the time she'd guided him to the passenger side, her arm felt ready to fall off. With the man on the verge of sliding from her grasp, she barely managed to wrench the door open. She had no strength left to be gentle; she simply shoved him inside.

He flopped onto the front seat with his legs still hanging out. She bent down, grabbed his ankles, and heaved them one by one into the car, noting with a sense of detachment that no man with feet this big could possibly be graceful.

As she slid into the driver's seat, he made a feeble attempt to raise his head, then let it sink back again. "Hurry," he whispered.

At the first turn of the key in the ignition, the engine sputtered and died. Dear God, she pleaded. Start. *Start!* She switched the key off, counted slowly to three, and tried again. This time the engine caught. Almost shouting with relief, she jammed it into gear and made a tire-screeching takeoff toward Garberville. Even a town that small must have a hospital or, at the very least, an emergency clinic. The question was: could she find it in this downpour? And what if she was wrong? What if the nearest medical help was in Willits, the other direction? She might be wasting precious minutes on the road while the man bled to death.

Suddenly panicked by that thought, she glanced at her passenger. By the glow of the dashboard, she saw that his head was still flopped back against the seat. He wasn't moving.

"Hey! Are you all right?" she cried.

The answer came back in a whisper. "I'm still here."

"Dear God. For a minute I thought…" She looked back at the road, her heart pounding. "There's got to be a clinic somewhere—"

"Near Garberville—there's a hospital—"

"Do you know how to find it?"

"I drove past it—fifteen miles…"

If he drove here, where's his car? she thought. "What happened?" she asked. "Did you have an accident?"

He started to speak but his answer was cut off by a sudden flicker of light. Struggling to sit up, he turned and stared at the headlights of another car far behind them. His whispered oath made her look sideways in alarm.

"What is it?"

"That car."

She glanced in the rearview mirror. "What about it?"

"How long's it been following us?"

"I don't know. A few miles. Why?"

The effort of keeping his head up suddenly seemed too much for him, and he let it sink back down with a groan. "Can't think," he whispered. "Christ, I can't think…"

He's lost too much blood, she thought. In a panic, she shoved hard on the gas pedal. The car seemed to leap through the rain, the steering wheel vibrating wildly as sheets of spray flew up from the tires. Darkness flew at dizzying speed against their windshield. *Slow down, slow down! Or I'll get us both killed.*

Easing back on the gas, she let the speedometer fall to a more manageable forty-five miles per hour. The man was struggling to sit up again.

"Please, keep your head down!" she pleaded.

"That car—"

"It's not there anymore."

"Are you sure?"

She looked at the rearview mirror. Through the rain, she saw only a faint twinkling of light, but nothing as definite as headlights. "I'm sure," she lied and was relieved to see him slowly settle back again. *How much farther?* she thought. *Five miles? Ten?* And then the next thought forced its way into her mind: *He might die before we get there.*

His silence terrified her. She needed to hear his voice, needed to be reassured that he hadn't slipped into oblivion. "Talk to me," she urged. "Please."

"I'm tired...."

"Don't stop. Keep talking. What—what's your name?"

The answer was a mere whisper: "Victor."

"Victor. That's a great name. I like that name. What do you do, Victor?"

His silence told her he was too weak to carry on any conversation. She couldn't let him lose consciousness! For some reason it suddenly seemed crucial to keep him awake, to keep him in touch with a living voice. If that fragile connection was broken, she feared he might slip away entirely.

"All right," she said, forcing her voice to remain low and steady. "Then *I'll* talk. You don't have to say a thing. Just listen. Keep listening. My name is Catherine. Cathy Weaver. I live in San Francisco, the Richmond district. Do you know the city?" There was no answer, but she sensed some movement in his head, a silent acknowledgement of her words. "Okay," she went on, mindlessly filling the silence. "Maybe you don't know the city. It really doesn't matter. I work with an independent film company. Actually, it's Jack's company. My ex-husband. We make horror films. Grade B, really, but they turn a profit. Our last one was *Reptilian*. I did the special-effects makeup. Really gruesome stuff. Lots of green scales and slime..." She laughed—it was a strange, panicked sound. It had an unmistakable note of hysteria.

She had to fight to regain control.

A wink of light made her glance up sharply at the rearview mirror. A pair of headlights was barely discernible through the rain. For a few seconds she watched them, debating whether to say anything to Victor. Then, like phantoms, the lights flickered off and vanished.

"Victor?" she called softly. He responded with an unintelligible grunt, but it was all she needed to be reassured that he was still alive. That he was listening. *I've got to keep him awake,* she thought, her mind scrambling for some new topic of conversation. She'd never been good at the glib sort of chitchat so highly valued at filmmakers' cocktail parties. What she needed was a joke, however stupid, as long as it was vaguely funny. *Laughter heals.* Hadn't she read it somewhere? That a steady barrage of comedy could shrink tumors? *Oh sure,* she chided herself. *Just make him laugh and the bleeding will miraculously stop....*

But she couldn't think of a joke, anyway, not a single damn one. So she returned to the topic that had first come to mind: her work.

"Our next project's slated for January. *Ghouls.* We'll be filming in Mexico, which I hate, because the damn heat always melts the makeup...."

She looked at Victor but saw no response, not even a flicker of movement. Terrified that she was losing him, she reached out to feel for his pulse and discovered that his hand was buried deep in the pocket of his windbreaker. She tried to tug it free, and to her amazement he reacted to her invasion with immediate and savage resistance. Lurching awake, he blindly lashed at her, trying to force her away.

"Victor, it's all right!" she cried, fighting to steer the car and protect herself at the same time. "It's all right! It's me, Cathy. I'm only trying to help!"

At the sound of her voice, his struggles weakened. As the tension eased from his body, she felt his head settle slowly against her shoulder. "Cathy," he whispered. It was a sound of wonder, of relief. "Cathy..."

"That's right. It's only me." Gently, she reached up and brushed back the tendrils of his wet hair. She wondered what color it was, a concern that struck her as totally irrelevant but nonetheless compelling. He reached for her hand. His fingers closed around hers in a grip that was surprisingly strong and steadying. *I'm still here,* it said. *I'm warm and alive and breathing.* He pressed her palm to his lips. So tender was the gesture, she was startled by the roughness of his unshaven jaw against her skin. It was a caress between strangers, and it left her shaken and trembling.

She returned her grip to the steering wheel and shifted her full attention back to the road. He had fallen silent again, but she couldn't ignore the weight of his head on her shoulder or the heat of his breath in her hair.

The torrent eased to a slow but steady rain, and she coaxed the car to fifty. The Sunnyside Up cafe whipped past, a drab little box beneath a single streetlight, and she caught a glimpse of Victor's face in the brief glow of light. She saw him only in profile: a high forehead, sharp nose, a jutting chin, and then the light was gone and he was only a shadow breathing softly against her. But she'd seen enough to know she'd never forget that face. Even as she peered through the darkness, his profile floated before her like an image burned into her memory.

"We have to be getting close," she said, as much to reassure herself as him. "Where a cafe appears, a town is sure to follow." There was no response. "Victor?" Still no response. Swallowing her panic, she sped up to fifty-five.

Though they'd passed the Sunnyside Up over a mile ago, she could still make out the streetlight winking on and off in her mirror. It took her a few seconds to realize it wasn't just one light she was watching but two, and that they were moving—a pair of headlights, winding along the highway. Was it the same car she'd spotted earlier?

Mesmerized, she watched the lights dance like twin wraiths among the trees, then, suddenly, they vanished and she saw only darkness. A ghost? she wondered irrationally. Any instant she expected the lights to rematerialize, to resume their phantom twinkling in the woods. She was watching the mirror so intently that she almost missed the road sign:

Garberville, Pop, 5,750
Gas—Food—Lodging

A half mile later streetlights appeared, glowing a hazy yellow in the drizzle; a flatbed truck splashed by, headed in the other direction. Though the speed limit had dropped to thirty-five, she kept her foot firmly on the gas pedal and for once in her life prayed for a police car to give chase.

The *Hospital* road sign seemed to leap out at her from nowhere. She braked and swerved onto the turnoff. A quarter mile away, a red *Emergency* sign directed her up a driveway to a side entrance. Leaving Victor in the front seat, she ran inside, through a deserted waiting room, and cried to a nurse sitting at her desk: "Please, help me! I've got a man in my car...."

The nurse responded instantly. She followed Cathy outside, took one look at the man slumped in the front seat, and yelled for assistance.

Even with the help of a burly ER physician, they had difficulty pulling Victor out of the car. He had slid sideways, and his arm was wedged under the emergency hand brake.

"Hey, Miss!" the doctor barked at Cathy. "Climb in the other side and free up his arm!"

Cathy scrambled to the driver's seat. There she hesitated. She would have to manipulate his injured arm. She took his elbow and tried to unhook it from around the brake, but discovered his wristwatch was snagged in the pocket of his windbreaker. After unsnapping the watchband, she took hold of his arm and lifted it over the brake. He responded with a groan of pure agony. The arm slid limply toward the floor.

"Okay!" said the doctor. "Arm's free! Now, just ease him toward me and we'll take it from there."

Gingerly, she guided Victor's head and shoulders safely past the emergency brake. Then she scrambled back outside to help load him onto the wheeled stretcher. Three straps were buckled into place. Everything became a blur of noise and motion as the stretcher was wheeled through the open double doors into the building.

"What happened?" the doctor barked over his shoulder at Cathy.

"I hit him—on the road—"

"When?"

"Fifteen—twenty minutes ago."

"How fast were you driving?"

"About thirty-five."

"Was he conscious when you found him?"

"For about ten minutes—then he sort of faded—"

A nurse said: "Shirt's soaked with blood. He's got broken glass in his shoulder."

In that mad dash beneath harsh fluorescent lights, Cathy had her first clear look at Victor, and she saw a lean, mud-streaked face, a jaw tightly squared in pain, a broad forehead matted damply with light brown hair. He reached out to her, grasping for her hand.

"Cathy—"

"I'm here, Victor."

He held on tightly, refusing to break contact. The pressure of his fingers in her flesh was almost painful. Squinting through the pain, he focused on her face. "I have to—have to tell you—"

"Later!" snapped the doctor.

"No, wait!" Victor was fighting to keep her in view, to hold her beside him. He struggled to speak, agony etching lines on his face.

Cathy bent close, drawn by the desperation of his gaze. "Yes, Victor," she whispered, stroking his hair, longing to ease his pain. This link between their hands, their gazes, felt forged in timeless steel. "Tell me."

"We can't delay!" barked the doctor. "Get him in the room."

All at once, Victor's hand was wrenched away from her as they whisked him into the trauma suite, a nightmarish room of stainless steel and blindingly bright lights. He was lifted onto the surgical table.

"Pulse 110," said a nurse. "Blood pressure eight-five over fifty!"

The doctor ordered, "Let's get two IVs in. Type and cross six units of blood. And get hold of a surgeon. We're going to need help...."

The machine-gun fire of voices, the metallic clang of cabinets and IV poles and instruments was deafening. No one seemed to notice Cathy standing in the doorway, watching in horrified fascination as a nurse pulled out a knife and began to tear off Victor's bloody clothing. With each rip, more and more flesh was exposed, until the shirt and windbreaker were shredded off, revealing a broad chest thickly matted with tawny hair. To the doctors and nurses, this was just another body to labor over, another patient to be saved. To Cathy, this was a living, breathing man, a man she cared about, if only because they had shared those last harrowing moments. The nurse shifted her attention to his belt, which she quickly unbuckled. With a few firm tugs, she peeled off his trousers and shorts and threw them into a pile with the other soiled clothing. Cathy scarcely noticed the man's nakedness, or the nurses and technicians shoving past her into the room. Her shocked gaze had focused on Victor's left shoulder, which was oozing fresh blood onto the table. She remembered how his whole body had resonated with pain when she'd grabbed that shoulder; only now did she understand how much he must have suffered.

A sour taste flooded her throat. She was going to be sick.

Struggling against the nausea, she somehow managed to stumble away and sink into a nearby chair. There she sat for a few minutes, oblivious to the chaos whirling around her. Looking down, she noted with instinctive horror the blood on her hands.

"There you are," someone said. A nurse had just emerged from the trauma room, carrying a bundle of the patient's belongings. She motioned Cathy over to a desk. "We'll need your name and address in case the doctors have any more questions. And the police will have to be notified. Have you called them?"

Cathy shook her head numbly. "I—I guess I should…"

"You can use this phone."

"Thank you."

It rang eight times before anyone answered. The voice that greeted her was raspy with sleep. Obviously, Garberville provided little late-night stimulation, even for the local police. The desk officer took down Cathy's report and told her he'd be in touch with her later, after they'd checked the accident scene.

The nurse had opened Victor's wallet and was flipping through the various ID cards for information. Cathy watched her fill in the blanks on a patient admission form: *Name: Victor Holland. Age: 41. Occupation: Biochemist. Next of kin: Unknown.*

So that was his full name. Victor Holland. Cathy stared down at the stack of ID cards and focused on what appeared to be a security pass for some company called Viratek. A color photograph showed Victor's quietly sober face, its green eyes gazing straight into the camera. Even if she had never seen his face, this was exactly how she would have pictured him, his expression unyielding, his gaze unflinchingly direct. She touched her palm, where he had kissed her. She could still recall how his beard had stung her flesh.

Softly, she asked, "Is he going to be all right?"

The nurse continued writing. "He's lost a lot of blood. But he looks like a pretty tough guy...."

Cathy nodded, remembering how, even in his agony, Victor had somehow dredged up the strength to keep moving through the rain. Yes, she knew just how tough a man he was.

The nurse handed her a pen and the information sheet. "If you could write your name and address at the bottom. In case the doctor has any more questions."

Cathy fished out Sarah's address and phone number from her purse and copied them onto the form. "My name's Cathy Weaver. You can get hold of me at this number."

"You're staying in Garberville?"

"For three weeks. I'm just visiting."

"Oh. Terrific way to start a vacation, huh?"

Cathy sighed as she rose to leave. "Yeah. Terrific."

She paused outside the trauma room, wondering what was happening inside, knowing that Victor was fighting for his life. She wondered if he was still conscious, if he would remember her. It seemed important that he *did* remember her.

Cathy turned to the nurse. "You will call me, won't you? I mean, you'll let me know if he…"

The nurse nodded. "We'll keep you informed."

Outside, the rain had finally stopped and a belt of stars twinkled through a parting in the clouds. To Cathy's weary eyes, it was an exhilarating sight, that first glimpse of the storm's end. As she drove out of the hospital parking lot, she was shaking from fatigue. She never noticed the car parked across the street or the brief glow of the cigarette before it was snuffed out.

Chapter Two

Barely a minute after Cathy left the hospital, a man walked into the emergency room, sweeping the smells of a stormy night in with him through the double doors. The nurse on duty was busy with the new patient's admission papers. At the sudden rush of cold air, she looked up to see a man approach her desk. He was about thirty-five, gaunt-faced, silent, his dark hair lightly feathered by gray. Droplets of water sparkled on his tan Burberry raincoat.

"Can I help you, sir?" she asked, focusing on his eyes, which were as black and polished as pebbles in a pond.

Nodding, he said quietly, "Was there a man brought in a short time ago? Victor Holland?"

The nurse glanced down at the papers on her desk. That was the name. Victor Holland. "Yes," she said. "Are you a relative?"

"I'm his brother. How is he?"

"He just arrived, sir. They're working on him now. If you'll wait, I can check on how he's doing—" She stopped to answer the ringing telephone. It was a technician calling with the new patient's laboratory results. As she jotted down the numbers, she noticed out of the corner of her eye that the man had turned and was gazing at the closed door to the trauma room. It suddenly swung open as an orderly emerged carrying a bulging plastic bag streaked with blood. The clamor of voices spilled from the room:

"Pressure up to 110 over 70!"

"OR says they're ready to go."

"Where's that surgeon?"

"On his way. He had car trouble."

"Ready for X rays! Everyone back!"

Slowly the door closed, muffling the voices. The nurse hung up just as the orderly deposited the plastic bag on her desk. "What's this?" she asked.

"Patient's clothes. They're a mess. Should I just toss 'em?"

"I'll take them home," the man in the raincoat cut in. "Is everything here?"

The orderly flashed the nurse an uncomfortable glance. "I'm not sure he'd want to…I mean, they're kind of…uh, dirty…."

The nurse said quickly, "Mr. Holland, why don't you let us dispose of the clothes for you? There's nothing worth keeping in there. I've already collected his valuables." She unlocked a drawer and pulled out a sealed manila envelope labeled: Holland, Victor. Contents: Wallet, Wristwatch. "You can take these home. Just sign this receipt."

The man nodded and signed his name: David Holland. "Tell me," he said, sliding the envelope in his pocket. "Is Victor awake? Has he said anything?"

"I'm afraid not. He was semiconscious when he arrived."

The man took this information in silence, a silence that the nurse found suddenly and profoundly disturbing. "Excuse me, Mr. Holland?" she asked. "How did you hear your brother was hurt? I didn't get a chance to contact any relatives…."

"The police called me. Victor was driving my car. They found it smashed up at the side of the road."

"Oh. What an awful way to be notified."

"Yes. The stuff of nightmares."

"At least someone was able to get in touch with you." She sifted through the sheaf of papers on her desk. "Can we get your address and phone number? In case we need to reach you?"

"Of course." The man took the ER papers, which he quickly scanned before scrawling his name and phone number on the blank marked Next of Kin. "Who's this Catherine Weaver?" he asked, pointing to the name and address at the bottom of the page.

"She's the woman who brought him in."

"I'll have to thank her." He handed back the papers.

"Nurse?"

She looked around and saw that the doctor was calling to her from the trauma room doorway. "Yes?"

"I want you to call the police. Tell them to get in here as soon as possible."

"They've been called, Doctor. They know about the accident—"

"Call them again. This is no accident."

"What?"

"We just got the X rays. The man's got a bullet in his shoulder."

"A *bullet?*" A chill went through the nurse's body, like a cold wind sweeping in from the night. Slowly, she turned toward the man in the raincoat, the man who'd claimed to be Victor Holland's brother. To her amazement, no one was there. She felt only a cold puff of night air, and then she saw the double doors quietly slide shut.

"Where the hell did he go?" the orderly whispered.

For a few seconds she could only stare at the closed doors. Then her gaze dropped and she focused on the empty spot on her desk. The bag containing Victor Holland's clothes had vanished.

"WHY DID THE police call again?"

Cathy slowly replaced the telephone receiver. Even though she was bundled in a warm terry-cloth robe, she was shivering. She turned and stared across the kitchen at Sarah. "That man on the road—they found a bullet in his shoulder."

In the midst of pouring tea, Sarah glanced up in surprise. "You mean—someone *shot* him?"

Cathy sank down at the kitchen table and gazed numbly at the cup of cinnamon tea that Sarah had just slid in front of her. A hot bath and a soothing hour of sitting by the fireplace had made the night's events seem like nothing more than a bad dream. Here in Sarah's kitchen, with its chintz curtains and its cinnamon and spice smells, the violence of the real world seemed a million miles away.

Sarah leaned toward her. "Do they know what happened? Has he said anything?"

"He just got out of surgery." She turned and glanced at the telephone. "I should call the hospital again—"

"No. You shouldn't. You've done everything you possibly can." Sarah gently touched her arm. "And your tea's getting cold."

With a shaking hand, Cathy brushed back a strand of damp hair and settled uneasily in her chair. A bullet in his shoulder, she thought. Why? Had it been a random attack, a highway gunslinger blasting out the car window at a total stranger? She'd read about it in the newspapers, the stories of freeway arguments settled by the pulling of a trigger.

Or had it been a deliberate attack? Had Victor Holland been targeted for death?

Outside, something rattled and clanged against the house. Cathy sat up sharply. "What was that?"

"Believe me, it's not the bogeyman," said Sarah, laughing. She went to the kitchen door and reached for the bolt.

"Sarah!" Cathy called in panic as the bold slid open. "Wait!"

"Take a look for yourself." Sarah opened the door. The kitchen light swung across a cluster of trash cans sitting in the carport. A shadow slid to the ground and scurried away, trailing food wrappers across the driveway. "Raccoons," said Sarah. "If I don't tie the lids down, those pests'll scatter trash all over the yard." Another shadow popped its head out of a can and stared at her, its eyes glowing in the darkness. Sarah clapped her hands and yelled, "Go on, get lost!" The raccoon didn't budge. "Don't you have a home to go to?" At last, the raccoon dropped to the ground and ambled off into the trees. "They get bolder every year," Sarah sighed, closing the door. She turned and winked at Cathy. "So take it easy. This isn't the big city."

"Keep reminding me." Cathy took a slice of banana bread and began to spread it with sweet butter. "You know, Sarah, I think it'll be a lot nicer spending Christmas with you than it ever was with old Jack."

"Uh-oh. Since we're now speaking of ex-husbands—" Sarah shuffled over to a cabinet "—we might as well get in the right frame of mind. And tea just won't cut it." She grinned and waved a bottle of brandy.

"Sarah, you're not drinking alcohol, are you?"

"It's not for *me*." Sarah set the bottle and a single wine glass in front of Cathy. "But I think *you* could use a nip. After all, it's been a cold, traumatic night. And here we are, talking about turkeys of the male variety."

"Well, since you put it that way…" Cathy poured out a

generous shot of brandy. "To the turkeys of the world," she declared and took a sip. It felt just right going down.

"So how *is* old Jack?" asked Sarah.

"Same as always."

"Blondes?"

"He's moved on to brunettes."

"It took him only a year to go through the world's supply of blondes?"

Cathy shrugged. "He might have missed a few."

They both laughed then, light and easy laughter that told them their wounds were well on the way to healing, that men were now creatures to be discussed without pain, without sorrow.

Cathy regarded her glass of brandy. "Do you suppose there *are* any good men left in the world? I mean, shouldn't there be *one* floating around somewhere? Maybe a mutation or something? One measly decent guy?"

"Sure. Somewhere in Siberia. But he's a hundred-and-twenty years old."

"I've always liked older men."

They laughed again, but this time the sound wasn't as lighthearted. So many years had passed since their college days together, the days when they had *known,* had never doubted, that Prince Charmings abounded in the world.

Cathy drained her glass of brandy and set it down. "What a lousy friend I am. Keeping a pregnant lady up all night! What time is it, anyway?"

"Only two-thirty in the morning."

"Oh, Sarah! Go to bed!" Cathy went to the sink and began wetting a handful of paper towels.

"And what are you going to do?" Sarah asked.

"I just want to clean up the car. I didn't get all the blood off the seat."

"I already did it."

"What? When?"

"While you were taking a bath."

"Sarah, you idiot."

"Hey, I didn't have a miscarriage or anything. Oh, I almost forgot." Sarah pointed to a tiny film canister on the counter. "I found that on the floor of your car."

Cathy shook her head and sighed. "It's Hickey's."

"Hickey! Now *there's* a waste of a man."

'He's also a good friend of mine."

"That's all Hickey will ever be to a woman. A *friend.* So what's on the roll of film? Naked women, as usual?"

"I don't even want to know. When I dropped him off at the airport, he handed me a half-dozen rolls and told me he'd pick them up when he got back. Guess he didn't want to lug 'em all the way to Nairobi."

"Is that where he went? Nairobi?"

"He's shooting 'gorgeous ladies of Africa' or something." Cathy slipped the film canister into her bathrobe pocket. "This must've dropped out of the glove compartment. Gee. I hope it's not pornographic."

"Knowing Hickey, it probably is."

They both laughed at the irony of it all. Hickman Von Trapp, whose only job it was to photograph naked females in erotic poses, had absolutely no interest in the opposite sex, with the possible exception of his mother.

"A guy like Hickey only goes to prove my point," Sarah said over her shoulder as she headed up the hall to bed.

"What point is that?"

"There really *are* no good men left in the world!"

IT WAS THE light that dragged Victor up from the depths of unconsciousness, a light brighter than a dozen suns, beating against his closed eyelids. He didn't want to wake up; he knew, in some dim, scarcely functioning part of his brain, that if he continued to struggle against this blessed oblivion he would feel pain and nausea and something else, something much, much worse: terror. Of what, he couldn't remember. Of death? No, no, this was death, or as close as one could come to it, and it was warm and black and comfortable. But he had something important to do, something that he couldn't allow himself to forget. He tried to think, but all he could remember was a hand, gentle but somehow strong, brushing his forehead, and a voice, reaching to him softly in the darkness.

My name is Catherine....

As her touch, her voice, flooded his memory, so too did the fear. Not for himself (he was dead, wasn't he?) but for her. Strong, gentle Catherine. He'd seen her face only briefly, could scarcely remember it, but somehow he knew she was beautiful, the way a blind man knows, without benefit of vision, that a rainbow or the sky or his own dear child's face is beautiful. And now he was afraid for her.

Where are you? he wanted to cry out.

"He's coming around," said a female voice (not Catherine's, it was too hard, too crisp) followed by a confusing rush of other voices.

"Watch that IV!"

"Mr. Holland, hold still. Everything's going to be all right—"

"I said, watch the IV!"

"Hand me that second unit of blood—"

"Don't move, Mr. Holland—"

Where are you, Catherine? The shout exploded in his head. Fighting the temptation to sink back into unconsciousness, he struggled to lift his eyelids. At first, there was only a blur of light and color, so harsh he felt it stab through his sockets straight to his brain. Gradually the blur took the shape of faces, strangers in blue, frowning down at him. He tried to focus but the effort made his stomach rebel.

"Mr. Holland, take it easy," said a quietly gruff voice. "You're in the hospital—the recovery room. They've just operated on your shoulder. You just rest and go back to sleep...."

No. No, I can't, he tried to say.

"Five milligrams of morphine going in," someone said, and Victor felt a warm flush creep up his arm and spread across his chest.

"That should help," he heard. "Now, sleep. Everything went just fine...."

You don't understand, he wanted to scream. *I have to warn her*—It was the last conscious thought he had before the lights once again were swallowed by the gentle darkness.

ALONE IN HER husbandless bed, Sarah lay smiling. No, laughing! Her whole body seemed filled with laughter tonight. She wanted to sing, to dance. To stand at the open window and shout out her joy! It was all hormonal, she'd been told, this chemical pandemonium of pregnancy, dragging her body on a roller coaster of emotions. She knew she should rest, she should work toward serenity, but tonight she wasn't tired at all. Poor exhausted Cathy had dragged herself up the attic steps to bed. But here was Sarah, still wide awake.

She closed her eyes and focused her thoughts on the child resting in her belly. *How are you, my love? Are you asleep? Or are you listening, hearing my thoughts even now?*

The baby wiggled in her belly, then fell silent. It was a reply, secret words shared only between them. Sarah was almost glad there was no husband to distract her from this silent conversation, to lie here in jealousy, an outsider. There was only mother and child, the ancient bond, the mystical link.

Poor Cathy, she thought, riding those roller coaster emotions from joy to sadness for her friend. She knew Cathy yearned just as deeply for a child, but eventually time would snatch the chance away from her. Cathy was too much of a romantic to realize that the man, the circumstances, might never be right. Hadn't it taken Cathy ten long years to finally acknowledge that her marriage was a miserable failure? Not that Cathy hadn't tried to make it work. She had tried to the point of developing a monumental blind spot to Jack's faults, primarily his selfishness. It was surprising how a woman so bright, so intuitive, could have let things drag on as long as she did. But that was Cathy. Even at thirty-seven she was open and trusting and loyal to the point of idiocy.

The clatter of gravel outside on the driveway pricked Sarah's awareness. Lying perfectly still, she listened and for a moment heard only the familiar creak of the trees, the rustle of branches against the shake roof. Then—there it was again. Stones skittering across the road, and then the faint squeal of metal. Those raccoons again. If she didn't shoo them off now, they'd litter garbage all over the driveway.

Sighing, she sat up and hunted in the darkness for her slippers. Shuffling quietly out of her bedroom, she navigated instinctively down the hallway and into the kitchen. Her eyes found the night too comfortable; she didn't want to assault them with light. Instead of flipping on the carport switch, she grabbed the flashlight from its usual spot on the kitchen shelf and unlocked the door.

Outside, moonlight glowed dimly through the clouds. She pointed the flashlight at the trash cans, but her beam caught no raccoon eyes, no telltale scattering of garbage, only the dull reflection of stainless steel. Puzzled, she crossed the carport and paused next to the Datsun that Cathy had parked in the driveway.

That was when she noticed the light glowing faintly inside the car. Glancing through the window, she saw that the glove compartment was open. Her first thought was that it had somehow fallen open by itself or that she or Cathy had forgotten to close it. Then she spotted the road maps strewn haphazardly across the front seat.

With fear suddenly hissing in her ear, she backed away, but terror made her legs slow and stiff. Only then did she sense that someone was nearby, waiting in the darkness; she could feel his presence, like a chill wind in the night.

She wheeled around for the house. As she turned, the beam of her flashlight swung around in a wild arc, only to freeze on the face of a man. The eyes that stared down at her were as slick and as black as pebbles. She scarcely focused on the rest of his face: the hawk nose, the thin, bloodless lips. It was only the eyes she saw. They were the eyes of a man without a soul.

"Hello, Catherine," he whispered, and she heard, in his voice, the greeting of death.

Please, she wanted to cry out as she felt him wrench her hair backward, exposing her neck. *Let me live!*

But no sound escaped. The words, like his blade, were buried in her throat.

CATHY WOKE UP to the quarreling of blue jays outside her window, a sound that brought a smile to her lips for it struck her as somehow whimsical, this flap and flutter of wings across the panes, this maniacal crackling of feathered enemies. So unlike the morning roar of buses and cars she was accustomed to. The blue jays' quarrel moved to the rooftop, and she heard their claws scratching across the shakes in a dance of combat. She trailed their progress across the ceiling, up one side of the roof and down the other. Then, tired of the battle, she focused on the window.

Morning sunlight cascaded in, bathing the attic room in a soft haze. Such a perfect room for a nursery! She could see all the changes Sarah had already made here—the Jack-and-Jill curtains, the watercolor animal portraits. The very prospect of a baby sleeping in this room filled her with such joy that she sat up, grinning, and hugged the covers to her knees. Then she glanced at her watch on the nightstand and saw it was already nine-thirty—half the morning gone!

Reluctantly, she left the warmth of her bed and poked around in her suitcase for a sweater and jeans. She dressed to the thrashing of blue jays in the branches, the battle having moved from the roof to the treetops. From the window, she watched them dart from twig to twig until one finally hoisted up the feathered version of a white flag and took off, defeated. The victor, his authority no longer in question, gave one last screech and settled back to preen his feathers.

Only then did Cathy notice the silence of the house, a stillness that magnified her every heartbeat, her every breath.

Leaving the room, she descended the attic steps and confronted the empty living room. Ashes from last night's fire mounded the grate. A silver garland drooped from the Christmas tree. A cardboard angel with glittery wings winked on the mantelpiece. She followed the hallway to Sarah's room and frowned at the rumpled bed, the coverlet flung aside. "Sarah?"

Her voice was swallowed up in the stillness. How could a cottage seem so immense? She wandered back through the living room and into the kitchen. Last night's teacups still sat in the sink. On the windowsill, an asparagus fern trembled, stirred by a breeze through the open door.

Cathy stepped out into the carport where Sarah's old Dodge was parked. "Sarah?" she called.

Something skittered across the roof. Startled, Cathy looked up and suddenly laughed as she heard the blue jay chattering in the tree above—a victory speech, no doubt. Even the animal kingdom had its conceits.

She started to head back into the house when her gaze swept past a stain on the gravel near the car's rear tire. For a few seconds she stared at the blot of rust-brown, unable to comprehend its meaning. Slowly, she moved alongside the car, her gaze tracing the stain backward along its meandering course.

As she rounded the rear of the car, the driveway came into full view. The dried rivulet of brown became a crimson lake in which a single swimmer lay open-eyed and still.

The blue jay's chatter abruptly ceased as another sound rose up and filled the trees. It was Cathy, screaming.

"HEY, MISTER. HEY, mister."

Victor tried to brush off the sound but it kept buzzing in his ear, like a fly that can't be shooed away.

"Hey, mister. You awake?"

Victor opened his eyes and focused painfully on a wry little face stubbled with gray whiskers. The apparition grinned, and darkness gaped where teeth should have been. Victor stared into that foul black hole of a mouth and thought: *I've died and gone to hell.*

"Hey, mister, you got a cigarette?"

Victor shook his head and barely managed to whisper: "I don't think so."

"Well, you got a dollar I could borrow?"

"Go away," groaned Victor, shutting his eyes against the daylight. He tried to think, tried to remember where he was, but his head ached and the little man's voice kept distracting him.

"Can't get no cigarettes in this place. Like a jail in here. Don't know why I don't just get up and walk out. But y'know, streets are cold this time of year. Been rainin' all night long. Least in here it's warm...."

Raining all night long... Suddenly Victor remembered. The rain. Running and running through the rain.

Victor's eyes shot open. "Where am I?"

"Three East. Land o' the bitches."

He struggled to sit up and almost gasped from the pain. Dizzily, he focused on the metal pole with its bag of fluid dripping slowly into the plastic intravenous tube, then stared at the bandages on his left shoulder. Through the window, he saw that the day was already drenched in sunshine. "What time is it?"

"Dunno. Nine o'clock, I guess. You missed breakfast."

"I've got to get out of here." Victor swung his legs out of bed and discovered that, except for a flimsy hospital gown, he was stark naked. "Where's my clothes? My wallet?"

The old man shrugged. "Nurse'd know. Ask her."

Victor found the call button buried among the bed sheets. He stabbed it a few times, then turned his attention to peeling off the tape affixing the IV tube to his arm.

The door hissed open and a woman's voice barked, *"Mr. Holland! What do you think you're doing?"*

"I'm getting out of here, that's what I'm doing," said Victor as he stripped off the last piece of tape. Before he could pull the IV out, the nurse rushed across the room as fast as her stout legs could carry her and slapped a piece of gauze over the catheter.

"Don't blame me, Miss Redfern!" screeched the little man.

"Lenny, go back to your own bed this instant! And as for you, Mr. Holland," she said, turning her steel-blue eyes on Victor, "you've lost too much blood." Trapping his arm against her massive biceps, she began to retape the catheter firmly in place.

"Just get me my clothes."

"Don't argue, Mr. Holland. You have to stay."

"Why?"

"Because you've got an IV, that's why!" she snapped, as if the plastic tube itself was some sort of irreversible condition.

"I want my clothes."

"I'd have to check with the ER. Nothing of yours came up to the floor."

"Then call the ER, damn you!" At Miss Redfern's disapproving scowl, he added with strained politeness, _"If_ you don't mind."

It was another half hour before a woman showed up from the business office to explain what had happened to Victor's belongings.

"I'm afraid we—well, we seem to have…lost your clothes, Mr. Holland," she said, fidgeting under his astonished gaze.

"What do you mean, _lost?"_

"They were—" she cleared her throat "—er, stolen. From the emergency room. Believe me, this has never happened before. We're really very sorry about this, Mr. Holland, and I'm sure we'll be able to arrange a purchase of replacement clothing…."

She was too busy trying to make excuses to notice that Victor's face had frozen in alarm. That his mind was racing as he tried to remember, through the blur of last night's events, just what had happened to the film canister. He knew he'd had it in his pocket during the endless drive to the hospital. He remembered clutching it there, remembered flailing senselessly at the woman when she'd tried to pull his hand from his pocket. After that, nothing was clear, nothing was certain. *Have I lost it?* he thought. *Have I lost my only evidence?*

"...While the money's missing, your credit cards seem to be all there, so I guess that's something to be thankful for."

He looked at her blankly. "What?"

"Your valuables, Mr. Holland." She pointed to the wallet and watch she'd just placed on the bedside table. "The security guard found them in the trash bin outside the hospital. Looks like the thief only wanted your cash."

"And my clothes. Right."

The instant the woman left, Victor pressed the button for Miss Redfern. She walked in carrying a breakfast tray. "Eat, Mr. Holland" she said. "Maybe your behavior's all due to hypoglycemia."

"A woman brought me to the ER," he said. "Her first name was Catherine. I have to get hold of her."

"Oh, look! Eggs and Rice Krispies! Here's your fork—"

"Miss Redfern, will you forget the damned Rice Krispies!"

Miss Redfern slapped down the cereal box. "There is no need for profanity!"

"I have to find that woman!"

Without a word, Miss Redfern spun around and marched out of the room. A few minutes later she returned and brusquely handed him a slip of paper. On it was written the name Catherine Weaver followed by a local address.

"You'd better eat fast," she said. "There's a policeman coming over to talk to you."

"Fine," he grunted, stuffing a forkful of cold, rubbery egg in his mouth.

"And some man from the FBI called. He's on his way, too."

Victor's head jerked up in alarm. "The FBI? What was his name?"

"Oh, for heaven's sake, how should I know? Something Polish, I think."

Staring at her, Victor slowly put down his fork. "Polowski," he said softly.

"That sounds like it. Polowski." She turned and headed out of the room. "The FBI indeed," she muttered. "Wonder what he did to get *their* attention...."

Before the door had even swung shut behind her, Victor was out of bed and tearing at his IV. He scarcely felt the sting of the tape wrenching the hair off his arm; he had to concentrate on getting the hell out of this hospital before Polowski showed up. He was certain the FBI agent had set him up for that ambush last night, and he wasn't about to wait around for another attack.

He turned and snapped at his roommate, "Lenny, where are your clothes?"

Lenny's gaze traveled reluctantly to a cabinet near the sink. "Don't got no other clothes. Besides, they wouldn't fit you, mister..."

Victor yanked open the cabinet door and pulled out a frayed cotton shirt and a pair of baggy polyester pants. The pants were too short and about six inches of Victor's hairy legs stuck out below the cuffs, but he had no trouble fastening the belt. The real trouble was going to be finding a pair of size twelve shoes. To his relief, he discovered that the cabinet also contained a pair of Lenny's thongs. His heels hung at least an inch over the back edge, but at least he wouldn't be barefoot.

"Those are mine!" protested Lenny.

"Here. You can have this." Victor tossed his wristwatch to the old man. "You should be able to hock that for a whole new outfit."

Suspicious, Lenny put the watch up against his ear. "Piece of junk. It's not ticking."

"It's quartz."

"Oh. Yeah. I knew that."

Victor pocketed his wallet and went to the door. Opening it just a crack, he peered down the hall toward the nurses' station. The coast was clear. He glanced back at Lenny. "So long, buddy. Give my regards to Miss Redfern."

Slipping out of the room, Victor headed quietly down the hall, away from the nurses' station. The emergency stairwell door was at the far end, marked by the warning painted in red: Alarm Will Sound If Opened. He walked steadily towards it, willing himself not to run, not to attract attention. But just as he neared the door, a familiar voice echoed in the hall.

"Mr. Holland! You come back here this instant!"

Victor lunged for the door, slammed against the closing bar, and dashed into the stairwell.

His footsteps echoed against the concrete as he pounded down the stairs. By the time he heard Miss Redfern scramble after him into the stairwell, he'd already reached the first floor and was pushing through the last door to freedom.

"Mr. Holland!" yelled Miss Redfern.

Even as he dashed across the parking lot, he could still hear Miss Redfern's outraged voice echoing in his ears.

Eight blocks away he turned into a K Mart, and within ten minutes had bought a shirt, blue jeans, underwear, socks and a pair of size-twelve tennis shoes, all of which he paid for with his credit card. He tossed Lenny's old clothes into a trash can.

Before emerging back outside, he peered through the store window at the street. It seemed like a perfectly normal mid-December morning in a small town, shoppers strolling beneath a tacky garland of Christmas decorations, a half-dozen cars waiting patiently at a red light. He was just about to step out the door when he spotted the police car creeping down the road. Immediately he ducked behind an undressed mannequin and watched through the nude plastic limbs as the police car made its way slowly past the K Mart and continued in the direction of the hospital. They were obviously searching for someone. Was he the one they wanted?

He couldn't afford to risk a stroll down Main Street. There was no way of knowing who else besides Polowski was involved in the double cross.

It took him at least an hour on foot to reach the outskirts of town, and by then he was so weak and wobbly he could barely stand. The surge of adrenaline that had sent him dashing from the hospital was at last petering out. Too tired to take another step, he sank onto a boulder at the side of the highway and halfheartedly held out his thumb. To his immense relief, the next vehicle to come along—a pickup truck loaded with firewood—pulled over. Victor climbed in and collapsed gratefully on the seat.

The driver spat out the window, then squinted at Victor from beneath an Agway Seeds cap. "Goin' far?"

"Just a few miles. Oak Hill Road."

"Yep. I go right past it." The driver pulled back onto the road. The truck spewed black exhaust as they roared down the highway, country music blaring from the radio.

Through the plucked strains of guitar music, Victor heard a sound that made him sit up sharply. A siren. Whipping his head around, he saw a patrol car zooming up fast behind them. *That's it,* thought Victor. *They've found me. They're going to stop this truck and arrest me....*

But for what? For walking away from the hospital? For insulting Miss Redfern? Or had Polowski fabricated some charge against him?

With a sense of impending doom, he waited for the patrol car to overtake them and start flashing its signal to pull over. In fact, he was so certain they *would* be pulled over that when the police car sped right past them and roared off down the highway, he could only stare ahead in amazement.

"Must be some kinda trouble," his companion said blandly, nodding at the rapidly vanishing police car.

Victor managed to clear his throat. "Trouble?"

"Yep. Don't get much of a chance to use that siren of theirs but when they do, boy oh boy, do they go to town with it."

With his heart hammering against his ribs, Victor sat back and forced himself to calm down. He had nothing to worry about. The police weren't after him, they were busy with some other concern. He wondered what sort of small-town catastrophe could warrant blaring sirens. Probably nothing more exciting than a few kids out on a joyride.

By the time they reached the turnoff to Oak Hill Road, Victor's pulse had settled back to normal. He thanked the driver, climbed out, and began the trek to Catherine Weaver's house. It was a long walk, and the road wound through a forest of pines. Every so often he'd pass a mailbox along the road and, peering through the trees, would spot a house. Catherine's address was coming up fast.

What on earth should he say to her? Up till now he'd concentrated only on reaching her house. Now that he was almost there, he had to come up with some reasonable explanation for why he'd dragged himself out of a hospital bed and trudged all this way to see her. A simple *thanks for saving my life* just wouldn't do it. He had to find out if she had the film canister. But she, of course, would want to know why the damn thing was so important.

You could tell her the truth.

No, forget that. He could imagine her reaction if he were to launch into his wild tale about viruses and dead scientists and double-crossing FBI agents. *The FBI is out to get you? I see. And who else is after you, Mr. Holland?* It was so absurdly paranoid he almost felt like laughing. No, he couldn't tell her any of it or he'd end up right back in a hospital, and this time in a ward that would make Miss Redfern's Three East look like paradise.

She didn't need to know any of it. In fact, she was better off ignorant. The woman had saved his life, and the last thing he wanted to do was put her in any danger. The film was all he wanted from her. After today, she'd never see him again.

He was so busy debating what to tell her that he didn't notice the police cars until well after he'd rounded the road's bend. Suddenly he froze, confronted by three squad cars— probably the entire police fleet of Garberville—parked in front of a rustic cedar house. A half-dozen neighbors lingered in the gravel driveway, shaking their heads in disbelief. Good God, had something happened to Catherine?

Swallowing the urge to turn and flee, Victor propelled himself forward, past the squad cars and through the loose gathering of onlookers, only to be stopped by a uniformed officer.

"I'm sorry, sir. No one's allowed past this point."

Dazed, Victor stared down and saw that the police had strung out a perimeter of red tape. Slowly, his gaze moved beyond the tape, to the old Datsun parked near the carport. Was that Catherine's car? He tried desperately to remember if she'd driven a Datsun, but last night it had been so dark and he'd been in so much pain that he hadn't bothered to pay attention. All he could remember was that it was a compact model, with scarcely enough room for his legs. Then he noticed the faded parking sticker on the rear bumper: Parking Permit, Studio Lot A.

I work for an independent film company, she'd told him last night.

It was Catherine's car.

Unwillingly, he focused on the stained gravel just beside the Datsun, and even though the rational part of him knew that that peculiar brick red could only be dried blood, he wanted to deny it. He wanted to believe there was some other explanation for that stain, for this ominous gathering of police.

He tried to speak, but his voice sounded like something dragged up through gravel.

"What did you say, sir?" the police officer asked.

"What—what happened?"

The officer shook his head sadly. "Woman was killed here last night. Our first murder in ten years."

"Murder?" Victor's gaze was still fixed in horror on the bloodstained gravel. "But—*why?*"

The officer shrugged. "Don't know yet. Maybe robbery, though I don't think he got much." He nodded at the Datsun. "Car was the only thing broken into."

If Victor said anything at that point, he never remembered what it was. He was vaguely aware of his legs carrying him back through the onlookers, past the three police cars, toward the road. The sunshine was so brilliant it hurt his eyes and he could barely see where he was going.

I killed her, he thought. *She saved my life and I killed her....*

Guilt slashed its way to his throat and he could scarcely breathe, could barely take another step for the pain. For a long time he stood there at the side of the road, his head bent in the sunshine, his ears filled with the sound of blue jays, and mourned a woman he'd never known.

When at last he was able to raise his head again, rage fueled the rest of his walk back to the highway, rage against Catherine's murderer. Rage at himself for having put her in such danger. It was the film the killer had been searching for, and he'd probably found it in the Datsun. If he hadn't, the house would have been ransacked, as well.

Now what? thought Victor. He dismissed the possibility that his briefcase—with most of the evidence—might still be in his wrecked car. That was the first place the killer would have searched. Without the film, Victor was left with no evidence at all. It would all come down to his word against Viratek's. The newspapers would dismiss him as nothing more than a disgruntled ex-employee. And after Polowski's double cross, he couldn't trust the FBI.

At that last thought, he quickened his pace. The sooner he got out of Garberville, the better. When he got back to the highway, he'd hitch another ride. Once safely out of town, he could take the time to plan his next move.

He decided to head south, to San Francisco.

Chapter Three

From the window of his office at Viratek, Archibald Black watched the limousine glide up the tree-lined driveway and pull to a stop at the front entrance. Black snorted derisively. The cowboy was back in town, damn him. And after all the man's fussing about the importance of secrecy, about keeping his little visit discreet, the idiot had the gall to show up in a limousine—with a uniformed driver, no less.

Black turned from the window and paced over to his desk. Despite his contempt for the visitor, he had to acknowledge the man made him uneasy, the way all so-called men of action made him uneasy. Not enough brains behind all that muscle. Too much power in the hands of imbeciles, he thought. Is this an example of who we have running the country?

The intercom buzzed. "Mr. Black?" said his secretary. "A Mr. Tyrone is here to see you."

"Send him in, please," said Black, smoothing the scorn from his expression. He was wearing a look of polite deference when the door opened and Matthew Tyrone walked into the office.

They shook hands. Tyrone's grip was unreasonably firm, as though he was trying to remind Black of their relative positions of power. His bearing had all the spit and polish of an ex-marine, which Tyrone was. Only the thickening waist betrayed the fact that Tyrone's marine days had been left far behind.

"How was the flight from Washington?" inquired Black as they sat down.

"Terrible service. I tell you, commercial flights aren't what they used to be. To think the average American pays good money for the privilege."

"I imagine it can't compare with Air Force One."

Tyrone smiled. "Let's get down to business. Tell me where things stand with this little crisis of yours."

Black noted Tyrone's use of the word *yours. So now it's my problem,* he thought. Naturally. That's what they meant by deniability: When things go wrong, the other guy gets the blame. If any of this leaked out, Black's head would be the one to fall. But then, that's why this contract was so lucrative—because he—meaning Viratek—was willing to take that risk.

"We've recovered the documents," said Black. "And the film canisters. The negatives are being developed now."

"And your two employees?"

Black cleared his throat. "There's no need to take this any further."

"They're a risk to national security."

"You can't just kill them off!"

"Can't we?" Tyrone's eyes were a cold, gun-metal gray. An appropriate color for someone who called himself "the Cowboy." You didn't argue with anyone who had eyes like that. Not if you had an instinct for self-preservation.

Black dipped his head deferentially. "I'm not accustomed to this sort of…business. And I don't like dealing with your man Savitch."

"Mr. Savitch has performed well for us before."

"He killed one of my senior scientists!"

"I assume it was necessary."

Black looked down unhappily at his desk. Just the thought of that monster Savitch made him shudder.

"Why, exactly, did Martinique go bad?"

Because he had a conscience, thought Black. He looked at Tyrone. "There was no way to predict it. He'd worked in commercial R and D for ten years. He'd never presented a security problem before. We only found out last week that he'd taken classified documents. And then Victor Holland got involved...."

"How much does Holland know?"

"Holland wasn't involved with the project. But he's clever. If he looked over those papers, he might have pieced it together."

Now Tyrone was agitated, his fingers drumming the desktop. "Tell me about Holland. What do you know about him?"

"I've gone over his personnel file. He's forty-one years old, born and raised in San Diego. Entered the seminary but dropped out after a year. Went on to Stanford, then MIT. Doctorate in biochemistry. He was with Viratek for four years. One of our most promising researchers."

"What about his personal life?"

"His wife died three years ago of leukemia. Keeps pretty much to himself these days. Quiet kind of guy, likes classical jazz. Plays the saxophone in some amateur group."

Tyrone laughed. "Your typical nerd scientist." It was just the sort of moronic comment an ex-marine like Tyrone would make. It was an insult that grated on Black. Years ago, before he created Viratek Industries, Black too had been a research biochemist.

"He should be a simple matter to dispose of," said Tyrone. "Inexperienced. And probably scared." He reached for his briefcase. "Mr. Savitch is an expert on these matters. I suggest you let him take care of the problem."

"Of course." In truth, Black didn't think he had any choice. Nicholas Savitch was like some evil, frightening force that, once unleashed, could not be controlled.

The intercom buzzed. "Mr. Gregorian's here from the photo lab," said the secretary.

"Send him in." Black glanced at Tyrone. "The film's been developed. Let's see just what Martinique managed to photograph."

Gregorian walked in carrying a bulky envelope. "Here are those contact prints you requested," he said, handing the bundle across the desk to Black. Then he cupped his hand over his mouth, muffling a sound suspiciously like laughter.

"Yes, Mr. Gregorian?" inquired Black.

"Nothing, sir."

Tyrone cut in, "Well, let's see them!"

Black removed the five contact sheets and lay them out on the desk for everyone to see. The men stared.

For a long time, no one spoke. Then Tyrone said, "Is this some sort of joke?"

Gregorian burst out laughing.

Black said, "What the hell is this?"

"Those are the negatives you gave me, sir," Gregorian insisted. "I processed them myself."

"These are the photos you got back from Victor Holland?" Tyrone's voice started soft and rose slowly to a roar. "Five rolls of *naked women?*"

"There's been a mistake," said Black. "It's the wrong film—"

Gregorian laughed harder.

"Shut up!" yelled Black. He looked at Tyrone. "I don't know how this happened."

"Then the roll we want is still out there?"

Black nodded wearily.

Tyrone reached for the phone. "We need to clean things up. Fast."

"Who are you calling?" asked Black.

"The man who can do the job," said Tyrone as he punched in the numbers. "Savitch."

IN HIS MOTEL room on Lombard Street, Victor paced the avocado-green carpet, wracking his brain for a plan. Any plan. His well-organized scientist's mind had already distilled the situation into the elements of a research project. Identify the problem: someone is out to kill me. State your hypothesis: Jerry Martinique uncovered something dangerous and he was killed for it. Now they think I have the information—and the evidence. Which I don't. Goal: Stay alive. Method: *Any damn way I can!*

For the last two days, his only strategy had consisted of holing up in various cheap motel rooms and pacing the carpets. He couldn't hide out forever. If the feds were involved, and he had reason to believe they were, they'd soon have his credit card charges traced, would know exactly where to find him.

I need a plan of attack.

Going to the FBI was definitely out. Sam Polowski was the agent Victor had contacted, the one who'd arranged to meet him in Garberville. No one else should have known about that meeting. Sam Polowski had never shown up.

But someone else had. Victor's aching shoulder was a constant reminder of that near-disastrous rendezvous.

I could go to the newspapers. But how would he convince some skeptical reporter? Who would believe his stories of a project so dangerous it could kill millions? They would think his tale was some fabrication of a paranoid mind.

And I am not paranoid.

He paced over to the TV and switched it on to the five o'clock news. A perfectly coiffed anchorwoman smiled from the screen as she read a piece of fluff about the last day of school, happy children, Christmas vacation. Then her expression sobered. Transition. Victor found himself staring at the TV as the next story came on.

"And in Garberville, California, there have been no new leads in the murder investigation of a woman found slain Wednesday morning. A houseguest found Sarah Boylan, 39, lying in the driveway, dead of stab wounds to the neck. The victim was five months pregnant. Police say they are puzzled by the lack of motive in this terrible tragedy, and at the present time there are no suspects. Moving on to national news..."

No, no, no! Victor thought. She wasn't pregnant. Her name wasn't Sarah. It's a mistake....

Or was it?

My name is Catherine, she had told him.

Catherine Weaver. Yes, he was sure of the name. He'd remember it till the day he died.

He sat on the bed, the facts spinning around in his brain. Sarah. Cathy. A murder in Garberville.

When at last he rose to his feet, it was with a swelling sense of urgency, even panic. He grabbed the hotel room phone book and flipped to the *W*s. He understood now. The killer had made a mistake. If Cathy Weaver was still alive, she might have that roll of film—or know where to find it. Victor had to reach her.

Before someone else did.

NOTHING COULD HAVE prepared Cathy for the indescribable sense of gloom she felt upon returning to her flat in San Francisco. She had thought she'd cried out all her tears that night in the Garberville motel, the night after Sarah's death. But here she was, still bursting into tears, then sinking into deep, dark meditations. The drive to the city had been temporarily numbing. But as soon as she'd climbed the steps to her door and confronted the deathly silence of her second-story flat, she felt overwhelmed once again by grief. And bewilderment. Of all the people in the world to die, why Sarah?

She made a feeble attempt at unpacking. Then, forcing herself to stay busy, she surveyed the refrigerator and saw that her shelves were practically empty. It was all the excuse she needed to flee her apartment. She pulled a sweater over her jeans and, with a sense of escape, walked the four blocks to the neighborhood grocery store. She bought only the essentials, bread and eggs and fruit. Enough to tide her over for a few days, until she was back on her feet and could think clearly about any sort of menu.

Carrying a sack of groceries in each arm, she walked through the gathering darkness back to her apartment building. The night was chilly, and she regretted not wearing a coat. Through an open window, a woman called, "Time for dinner!" and two children playing kickball in the street turned and scampered for home.

By the time Cathy reached her building, she was shivering and her arms were aching from the weight of the groceries. She trudged up the steps and, balancing one sack on her hip, managed to pull out her keys and unlock the security door. Just as she swung through, she heard footsteps, then glimpsed a blur of movement rushing toward her from the side. She was swept through the doorway, into the building. A grocery bag tumbled from her arms, spilling apples across the floor. She stumbled forward, catching herself on the wood banister. The door slammed shut behind her.

She spun around, ready to fight off her attacker.

It was Victor Holland.

"You!" she whispered in amazement.

He didn't seem so sure of *her* identity. He was frantically searching her face, as though trying to confirm he had the right woman. "Cathy Weaver?"

"What do you think you're—"

"Where's your apartment?" he cut in.

"What?"

"We can't stand around out here."

"It's—it's upstairs—"

"Let's go." He reached for her arm but she pulled away.

"My groceries," she said, glancing down at the scattered apples.

He quickly scooped up the fruit, tossed it in one of the bags, and nudged her toward the stairs. "We don't have a lot of time."

Cathy allowed herself to be herded up the stairs and halfway down the hall before she stopped dead in her tracks. "Wait a minute. You tell me what this is all about, Mr. Holland, and you tell me right now or I don't move another step!"

"Give me your keys."

"You can't just—"

"Give me your keys!"

She stared at him, shocked by the command. Suddenly she realized that what she saw in his eyes was panic. They were the eyes of a hunted man.

Automatically she handed him her keys.

"Wait here," he said. "Let me check the apartment first."

She watched in bewilderment as he unlocked her door and cautiously eased his way inside. For a few moments she heard nothing. She pictured him moving through the flat, tried to estimate how many seconds each room would require for inspection. It was a small flat, so why was he taking so long?

Slowly she moved toward the doorway. Just as she reached it, his head popped out. She let out a little squeak of surprise. He barely caught the bag of groceries as it slipped from her grasp.

"It's okay," he said. "Come on inside."

The instant she stepped over the threshold, he had the door locked and bolted behind her. Then he quickly circled the living room, closing the drapes, locking windows.

"Are you going to tell me what's going on?" she asked, following him around the room.

"We're in trouble."

"You mean *you're* in trouble."

"No. I mean *we*. Both of us." He turned to her, his gaze clear and steady. "Do you have the film?"

"What are you talking about?" she asked, utterly confused by the sudden shift of conversation.

"A roll of film. Thirty-five millimeter. In a black plastic container. Do you have it?"

She didn't answer. But an image from that last night with Sarah had already taken shape in her mind: a roll of film on the kitchen counter. Film she'd thought belonged to her friend Hickey. Film she'd slipped into her bathrobe pocket and later into her purse. But she wasn't about to reveal any of this, not until she found out why he wanted it. The gaze she returned to him was purposefully blank and unrevealing.

Frustrated, he forced himself to take a deep breath, and started over. "That night you found me—on the highway—I had it in my pocket. It wasn't with me when I woke up in the hospital. I might have dropped it in your car."

"Why do you want this roll of film?"

"I need it. As evidence—"

"For what?"

"It would take too long to explain."

She shrugged. "I've got nothing better to do at the moment—"

"Damn it!" He stalked over to her. Taking her by the shoulders, he forced her to look at him. "Don't you understand? That's why your friend was killed! The night they broke into your car, they were looking for that film!"

She stared at him, a look of sudden comprehension and horror. "Sarah…"

"Was in the wrong place at the wrong time. The killer must have thought she was *you*."

Cathy felt trapped by his unrelenting gaze. And by the inescapable threat of his revelation. Her knees wobbled, gave way. She sank into the nearest chair and sat there in numb silence.

"You have to get out of here," he said. "Before they find you. Before they figure out you're the Cathy Weaver they're looking for."

She didn't move. She couldn't move.

"Come on, Cathy. There isn't much time!"

"What was on that roll of film?" she asked softly.

"I told you. Evidence. Against a company called Viratek."

She frowned. "Isn't—isn't that the company you work for?"

"Used to work for."

"What did they do?"

"They're involved in some sort of illegal research project. I can't tell you the particulars."

"Why not?"

"Because I don't know them. I'm not the one who gathered the evidence. A colleague—a friend—passed it to me, just before he was killed."

"What do you mean by killed?"

"The police called it an accident. I think otherwise."

"You're saying he was murdered over a research project?" She shook her head. "Must have been dangerous stuff he was working on."

"I know this much. It involves biological weapons. Which makes the research illegal. And incredibly dangerous."

"Weapons? For what government?"

"Ours."

"I don't understand. If this is a federal project, that makes it all legal, right?"

"Not by a long shot. People in high places have been known to break the rules."

"How high are we talking about?"

"I don't know. I can't be sure of anyone. Not the police, not the Justice Department. Not the FBI."

Her eyes narrowed. The words she was hearing sounded like paranoid ravings. But the voice—and the eyes—were perfectly sane. They were sea-green, those eyes. They held an honesty, a steadiness that should have been all the assurance she needed.

It wasn't. Not by a long shot.

Quietly she said, "So you're telling me the FBI is after you. Is that correct?"

Sudden anger flared in his eyes, then just as quickly, it was gone. Groaning, he sank onto the couch and ran his hands through his hair. "I don't blame you for thinking I'm nuts. Sometimes I wonder if I'm all there. I thought if I could trust anyone, it'd be you...."

"Why me?"

He looked at her. "Because you're the one who saved my life. You're the one they'll try to kill next."

She froze. No, no, this was insane. Now he was pulling her into his delusion, making her believe in his nightmare world of murder and conspiracy. She wouldn't let him! She stood up and started to walk away, but his voice made her stop again.

"Cathy, think about it. Why was your friend Sarah killed? Because they thought she was *you*. By now they've figured out they killed the wrong woman. They'll have to come back and do the job right. Just in case you know something. In case you have evidence—"

"This is crazy!" she cried, clapping her hands over her ears. "No one's going to—"

"They already have!" He whipped out a scrap of newspaper from his shirt pocket. "On my way over here, I happened to pass a newsstand. This was on the front page." He handed her the piece of paper.

She stared in bewilderment at the photograph of a middle-aged woman, a total stranger. "San Francisco woman shot to death on front doorstep," read the accompanying headline.

"This has nothing to do with me," she said.

"Look at her name."

Cathy's gaze slid to the third paragraph, which identified the victim.

Her name was Catherine Weaver.

The scrap of newsprint slipped from her grasp and fluttered to the floor.

"There are three Catherine Weavers in the San Francisco phone book," he said. "That one was shot to death at nine o'clock this morning. I don't know what's happened to the second. She might already be dead. Which makes you next on the list. They've had enough time to locate you."

"I've been out of town—I only got back an hour ago—"

"Which explains why you're still alive. Maybe they came here earlier. Maybe they decided to check out the other two women first."

She shot to her feet, suddenly frantic with the need to flee. "I have to pack my things—"

"No. Let's just get the hell out of here."

Yes, do what he says! an inner voice screamed at her.

She nodded. Turning, she headed blindly for the door. Halfway there, she halted. "My purse—"

"Where is it?"

She headed back, past a curtained window. "I think I left it by the—"

Her next words were cut off by an explosion of shattering glass. Only the closed curtains kept the shards from piercing her flesh. Pure reflex sent Cathy diving to the floor just as the second gun blast went off. An instant later she found Victor Holland sprawled on top of her, covering her body with his as the third bullet slammed into the far wall, splintering wood and plaster.

The curtains shuddered, then hung still.

For a few seconds Cathy was paralyzed by terror, by the weight of Victor's body on hers. Then panic took hold. She squirmed free, intent on fleeing the apartment.

"Stay down!" Victor snapped.

"They're trying to kill us!"

"Don't make it easy for them!" He dragged her back to the floor. "We're getting out. But not through the front door."

"How—"

"Where's your fire escape?"

"My bedroom window."

"Does it go to the roof?"

"I'm not sure—I think so—"

"Then let's move it."

On hands and knees they crawled down the hall, into Cathy's unlit bedroom. Beneath the window they paused, listening. Outside, in the darkness, there was no sound.

Then, from downstairs in the lobby, came the tinkle of breaking glass.

"He's already in the building!" hissed Victor. He yanked open the window. "Out, out!"

Cathy didn't need to be prodded. Hands shaking, she scrambled out and lowered herself onto the fire escape. Victor was right behind her.

"Up," he whispered. "To the roof."

And then what? she wondered, climbing the ladder to the third floor, past Mrs. Chang's flat. Mrs. Chang was out of town this week, visiting her son in New Jersey. The apartment was dark, the windows locked tight. No way in there.

"Keep going," said Victor, nudging her forward.

Only a few more rungs to go.

At last, she pulled herself up and over the edge and onto the asphalt roof. A second later, Victor dropped down beside her. Potted plants shuddered in the darkness. It was Mrs. Chang's rooftop garden, a fragrant mélange of Chinese herbs and vegetables.

Together, Victor and Cathy weaved their way through the plants and crossed to the opposite edge of the roof, where the next building abutted theirs.

"All the way?" said Cathy.

"All the way."

They hopped onto the adjoining roof and ran across to the other side, where three feet of emptiness separated them from the next building. She didn't pause to think of the perils of that leap, she simply flung herself across the gap and kept running, aware that every step took her farther and farther from danger.

On the roof of the fourth building, Cathy finally halted and stared over the edge at the street below. End of the line. It suddenly occurred to her that it was a very long drop to the ground below. The fire escape looked as sturdy as a Tinkertoy.

She swallowed. "This probably isn't a good time to tell you this, but—"

"Tell me what?"

"I'm afraid of heights."

He clambered over the edge. "Then don't look down."

Right, she thought, slithering onto the fire escape. *Don't look down.* Her palms were so slick with sweat she could barely grip the rungs. Suddenly seized by an attack of vertigo, she froze there, clinging desperately to that flimsy steel skeleton.

"Don't stop now!" Victor whispered up to her. "Just keep moving!"

Still she didn't move. She pressed her face against the rung, so hard she felt the rough edge bite into her flesh.

"You're okay, Cathy!" he said. "Come on."

The pain became all-encompassing, blocking out the dizziness, even the fear. When she opened her eyes again, the world had steadied. On rubbery legs, she descended the ladder, pausing on the third floor landing to wipe her sweaty palms on her jeans. She continued downward, to the second-floor landing. It was still a good fifteen-foot drop to the ground. She unlatched the extension ladder and started to slide it down, but it let out such a screech that Victor immediately stopped her.

"Too noisy. We have to jump!"

"But—"

To her astonishment, he scrambled over the railing and dropped to the ground. "Come on!" he hissed from below. "It's not that far. I'll catch you."

Murmuring a prayer, she lowered herself over the side and let go.

To her surprise he did catch her—but held on only for

a second. The bullet wound had left his injured shoulder too weak to hold on. They both tumbled to the ground. She landed smack on top of him, her legs astride his hips, their faces inches apart. They stared at each other, so stunned they could scarcely breathe.

Upstairs, a window slid open and someone yelled, "Hey, you bums! If you don't clear out this instant, I'm calling the cops!"

Instantly Cathy rolled off Victor, only to stagger into a trash can. The lid fell off and slammed like a cymbal against the sidewalk.

"That's it for rest stops," Victor grunted and scrambled to his feet. *"Move it."*

They took off at a wild dash down the street, turned up an alley, and kept running. It was a good five blocks before they finally stopped to catch their breath. They glanced back.

The street was deserted.

They were safe!

NICHOLAS SAVITCH STOOD beside the neatly made bed and surveyed the room. It was every inch a woman's room, from the closet hung with a half-dozen simple but elegant dresses, to the sweetly scented powders and lotions lined up on the vanity table. It took only a single circuit around the room to tell him about the woman whose bedroom this was. She was slim, a size seven dress, size six-and-a-half shoe. The hairs on the brush were brown and shoulder-length. She owned only a few pieces of jewelry, and she favored natural scents, rosewater and lavender. Her favorite color was green.

Back in the living room, he continued to gather information. The woman subscribed to the Hollywood trade journals. Her taste in music, like her taste in books, was eclectic. He noticed a scrap of newspaper lying on the floor. He picked it up and glanced at the article. Now this was interesting. The death of Catherine Weaver I had not gone unnoticed by Catherine Weaver III.

He pocketed the article. Then he saw the purse, lying on the floor near the shattered window.

Bingo.

He emptied the contents on the coffee table. Out tumbled a wallet, checkbook, pens, loose change, and...an address book. He opened it to the *B*s. There he found the name he was looking for: Sarah Boylan.

He now knew this was the Catherine Weaver he'd been seeking. What a shame he'd wasted his time hunting down the other two.

He flipped through the address book and spotted a half dozen or so San Francisco listings. The woman may have been clever enough to slip away from him this time. But staying out of sight was a more difficult matter. And this little book, with its names of friends and relatives and colleagues, could lead him straight to her.

Somewhere in the distance, a police siren was wailing.

It was time to leave.

Savitch took the address book and the woman's wallet and headed out the door. Outside, his breath misted in the cold air as he walked at a leisurely pace down the street,

He could afford to take his time.

But for Catherine Weaver and Victor Holland, time was running out.

Chapter Four

There was no time to rest. They jogged for the next six blocks, miles and miles, it seemed to Cathy. Victor moved tirelessly, leading her down side streets, avoiding busy intersections. She let him do the thinking and navigating. Her terror slowly gave way to numbness and a disorienting sense of unreality. The city itself seemed little more than a dreamscape, asphalt and streetlights and endless twists and turns of concrete. The only reality was the man striding close beside her, his gaze alert, his movements swift and sure. She knew he too must be afraid, but she couldn't see his fear.

He took her hand; the warmth of that grasp, the strength of those fingers, seemed to flow into her cold, exhausted limbs.

She quickened her pace. "I think there's a police substation down that street," she said. "If we go a block or two further—"

"We're not going to the police."

"What?" She stopped dead, staring at him.

"Not yet. Not until I've had a chance to think this through."

"Victor," she said slowly. "Someone is trying to kill us. Trying to kill *me*. What do you mean, you need time to *think this through?*"

"Look, we can't stand around talking about it. We have to get off the streets." He grabbed her hand again. "Come on."

"Where?"

"I have a room. It's only a few blocks away."

She let him drag her only a few yards before she mustered the will to pull free. "Wait a minute. Just *wait*."

He turned, his face a mask of frustration, and confronted her. "Wait for what? For that maniac to catch up? For the bullets to start flying again?"

"For an explanation!"

"I'll explain it all. When we're safe."

She backed away. "Why are you afraid of the police?"

"I can't be sure of them."

"Do you have a reason to be afraid? What have you done?"

With two steps he closed the gap between them and grabbed her hard by the shoulders. "I just pulled you out of a death trap, remember? The bullets were going through your window, not mine!"

"Maybe they were aimed at you!"

"Okay!" He let her go, let her back away from him. "You want to try it on your own? Do it. Maybe the police'll be a help. Maybe not. But I can't risk it. Not until I know all the players behind this."

"You—you're letting me go?"

"You were never my prisoner."

"No." She took a breath—it misted in the cold air. She glanced down the street, toward the police substation. "It's…the reasonable thing to do," she muttered, almost to reassure herself. "That's what they're there for."

"Right."

She frowned, anticipating what lay ahead. "They'll ask a lot of questions."

"What are you going to tell them?"

She looked at him, her gaze unflinchingly meeting his. "The truth."

"Which'll be at best, incomplete. And at worst, unbelievable."

"I have broken glass all over my apartment to prove it."

"A drive-by shooting. Purely random."

"It's their job to protect me."

"What if they don't think you need protection?"

"I'll tell them about you! About Sarah."

"They may or may not take you seriously."

"They have to take me seriously! Someone's trying to kill me!" Her voice, shrill with desperation, seemed to echo endlessly through the maze of streets.

Quietly he said, "I know."

She glanced back toward the substation. "I'm going."

He said nothing.

"Where will you be?" she asked.

"On my own. For now."

She took two steps away, then stopped. "Victor?"

"I'm still here."

"You did save my life. Thank you."

He didn't respond. She heard his footsteps slowly walk away. She stood there thinking, wondering if she was doing the right thing. Of course she was. A man afraid of the police—with a story as paranoid as his was—had to be dangerous.

But he saved my life.

And once, on a rainy night in Garberville, she had saved his.

She replayed all the events of the last week. Sarah's murder, never explained. The other Catherine Weaver, shot to death on her front doorstep. The film canister that Sarah had retrieved from the car, the one Cathy had slipped into her bathrobe pocket...

Victor's footsteps had faded.

In that instant she realized she'd lost the only man who could help her find the answers to all those questions, the one man who'd stood by her in her darkest moment of terror. The one man she knew, by some strange intuition, she could trust. Facing that deserted street, she felt abandoned and utterly friendless. In sudden panic, she whirled around and called out: "Victor!"

At the far end of the block, a silhouette stopped and turned. He seemed an island of refuge in that crazy, dangerous world. She started toward him, her legs moving her faster and faster, until she was running, yearning for the safety of his arms, the arms of a man she scarcely knew. Yet it didn't feel like a stranger's arms gathering her to his chest, welcoming her into his protective embrace. She felt the pounding of his heart, the grip of his fingers against her back, and something told her that this was a man she could depend upon, a man who wouldn't fold when she needed him most.

"I'm right here," he murmured. "Right here." He stroked through her windblown hair, his fingers burying deep in the tangled strands. She felt the heat of his breath against her face, felt her own quick and shuddering response. And then, all at once, his mouth hungrily sought hers and he was kissing her. She responded with a kiss just as desperate, just as needy. Stranger though he was, he had been there for her and he was still here, his arms sheltering her from the terrors of the night.

She burrowed her face against his chest, longing to press ever deeper, ever closer. "I don't know what to do! I'm so afraid, Victor, and I don't know what to do...."

"We'll work this out together. Okay?" He cupped her face in his hands and tilted it up to his. "You and I, we'll beat this thing."

She nodded. Searching his eyes, connecting with that rock-solid gaze, she found all the assurance she needed.

A wind gusted down the street. She shivered in its wake. "What do we do first?" she whispered.

"First," he said, pulling off his windbreaker and draping it over her shoulders, "We get you warmed up. And inside." He took her hand. "Come on. A hot bath, a good supper, and you'll be operating on all cylinders again."

It was another five blocks to the Kon-Tiki Motel. Though not exactly a five-star establishment, the Kon-Tiki was comfortingly drab and anonymous, one of a dozen on motel row. They climbed the steps to Room 214, overlooking the half-empty parking lot. He unlocked the door and motioned her inside.

The rush of warmth against her cheeks was delicious. She stood in the center of that utterly charmless space and marveled at how good it felt to be safely surrounded by four walls. The furnishings were spare: a double bed, a dresser, two nightstands with lamps, and a single chair. On the wall was a framed print of some nameless South Pacific island. The only luggage she saw was a cheap nylon bag on the floor. The bedcovers were rumpled, recently napped in, the pillows punched up against the headboard.

"Not much," he said. "But it's warm. And it's paid for." He turned on the TV. "We'd better keep an eye on the news. Maybe they'll have something on the Weaver woman."

The Weaver woman, she thought. *It could have been me.* She was shivering again, but now it wasn't from the cold. Settling onto the bed she stared numbly at the TV, not really seeing what was on the screen. She was more aware of *him.* He was circling the room, checking the windows, fiddling with the lock on the door. He moved quietly, efficiently, his silence a testimony to the dangers of their situation. Most men she knew began to babble nonsense when they were scared; Victor Holland simply turned quiet. His mere presence was overwhelming. He seemed to fill the room.

He moved to her side. She flinched as he took her hands and gently inspected them, palm side up. Looking down, she saw the bloodied scratches, the flakes of rust from the fire escape embedded in her skin.

"I guess I'm a mess," she murmured.

He smiled and stroked her face. "You could use some washing up. Go ahead. I'll get us something to eat."

She retreated into the bathroom. Through the door she could hear the drone of the TV, the sound of Victor's voice ordering a pizza over the phone. She ran hot water over her cold, numb hands. In the mirror over the sink she caught an unflattering glimpse of herself, her hair a tangled mess, her chin smudged with dirt. She washed her face, rubbing new life, new circulation into those frigid cheeks. Glancing down, she noticed Victor's razor on the counter. The sight of that blade cast her situation into a new focus—a frightening one. She picked up the razor, thinking how lethal that blade looked, how vulnerable she would be tonight. Victor was a large man, at least six foot two, with powerful arms. She was scarcely five foot five, a comparative weakling. There was only one bed in the next room. She had come here voluntarily. What would he assume about her? That she was a willing victim? She thought of all the ways a man could hurt her, kill her. It wouldn't take a razor to finish the job. Victor could use his bare hands. *What am I doing here?* she wondered. *Spending the night with a man I scarcely know?*

This was not the time to have doubts. She'd made the decision. She had to go by her instincts, and her instincts told her Victor Holland would never hurt her.

Deliberately she set down the razor. She would have to trust him. She was afraid not to.

In the other room, a door slammed shut. Had he left?

Opening the door a crack, she peered out. The TV was still on. There was no sign of Victor. Slowly she emerged, to find she was alone. She began to circle the room, searching for clues, anything that would tell her more about the man. The bureau drawers were empty, and so was the closet. Obviously he had not moved into this room for a long stay. He'd planned only one night, maybe two. She went to the nylon bag and glanced inside. She saw a clean pair of socks, an unopened package of underwear, and a day-old edition of the *San Francisco Chronicle*. All it told her was that the man kept himself informed and he traveled light.

Like a man on the run.

She dug deeper and came up with a receipt from an automatic teller machine. Yesterday he'd tried to withdraw cash. The machine had printed out the message: *Transaction cannot be completed. Please contact your bank.* Why had it refused him the cash? she wondered. Was he overdrawn? Had the machine been out of order?

The sound of a key grating in the lock caught her by surprise. She glanced up as the door swung open.

The look he gave her made her cheeks flush with guilt. Slowly she rose to her feet, unable to answer that look of accusation in his eyes.

The door swung shut behind him.

"I suppose it's a reasonable thing for you to do," he said. "Search my things."

"I'm sorry. I was just…" She swallowed. "I had to know more about you."

"And what terrible things have you dug up?"

"Nothing!"

"No deep dark secrets? Don't be afraid. Tell me, Cathy."

"Only…only that you had trouble getting cash out of your account."

He nodded. "A frustrating state of affairs. Since by my

estimate I have a balance of six thousand dollars. And now I can't seem to touch it." He sat down in the chair, his gaze still on her face. "What else did you learn?"

"You—you read the newspaper."

"So do a lot of people. What else?"

She shrugged. "You wear boxer shorts."

Amusement flickered in his eyes. "Now we're getting personal."

"You…" She took a deep breath. "You're on the run."

He looked at her a long time without saying a word.

"That's why you won't go to the police," she said. "Isn't it?"

He turned away, gazing not at her but at the far wall. "There are reasons."

"Give me one, Victor. One good reason is all I need and then I'll shut up."

He sighed. "I doubt it."

"Try me. I have every reason to believe you."

"You have every reason to think I'm paranoid." Leaning forward, he ran his hands over his face. "Lord, sometimes *I* think I must be."

Quietly she went to him and knelt down beside his chair. "Victor, these people who are trying to kill me—who are they?"

"I don't know."

"You said it might involve people in high places."

"It's just a guess. It's a case of federal money going to illegal research. Deadly research."

"And federal money has to be doled out by someone in authority."

He nodded. "This is someone who's bent the rules. Someone who could be hurt by a political scandal. He just might try to protect himself by manipulating the Bureau.

Or even your local police. That's why I won't go to them. That's why I left the room to make my call."

"When?"

"While you were in the bathroom. I went to a pay phone and called the police. I didn't want it traced."

"You just said you don't want them involved."

"This call I had to make. There's a third Catherine Weaver in that phone book. Remember?"

A third victim on the list. Suddenly weak, she sat down on the bed. "What did you say?" she asked softly.

"That I had reason to think she might be in danger. That she wasn't answering her phone."

"You tried it?"

"Twice."

"Did they listen to you?"

"Not only did they listen, they demanded to know my name. That's when I picked up the cue that something must already have happened to her. At that point I hung up and hightailed it out of the booth. A call can be traced in seconds. They could've had me surrounded."

"That makes three," she whispered. "Those two other women. And me."

"They have no way of finding you. Not as long as you stay away from your apartment. Stay out of—"

They both froze in panic.

Someone was knocking on the door.

They stared at each other, fear mirrored in their eyes. Then, after a moment's hesitation, Victor said: "Who is it?"

"Domino's," called a thin voice.

Cautiously, Victor eased open the door. A teenage boy stood outside, wielding a bag and a flat cardboard box.

"Hi!" chirped the boy. "A large combo with the works, two Cokes and extra napkins. Right?"

"Right." Victor handed the boy a few bills. "Keep the

change," he said and closed the door. Turning, he gave Cathy a sheepish look. "Well," he admitted. "Just goes to show you. Sometimes a knock at the door really is just the pizza man."

They both laughed, a sound not of humor but of frayed nerves. The release of tension seemed to transform his face, melted his wariness to warmth. Erase those haggard lines, she thought, and he could almost be called a handsome man.

"I tell you what," he said. "Let's not think about this mess right now. Why don't we just get right down to the really important issue of the day. Food."

Nodding, she reached out for the box. "Better hand it over. Before I eat the damn bedspread."

While the ten o'clock news droned from the television set, they tore into the pizza like two ravenous animals. It was a greasy and utterly satisfying banquet on a motel bed. They scarcely bothered with conversation—their mouths were too busy devouring cheese and pepperoni. On the TV, a dapper anchorman announced a shakeup in the mayor's office, the resignation of the city manager, news that, given their current situation, seemed ridiculously trivial. Scarcely thirty seconds were devoted to that morning's killing of Catherine Weaver I; as yet, no suspects were in custody. No mention was made of any second victim by the same name.

Victor frowned. "Looks like the other woman didn't make it to the news."

"Or nothing's happened to her." She glanced at him questioningly. "What if the second Cathy Weaver is all right? When you called the police, they might've been asking you routine questions. When you're on edge, it's easy to—"

"Imagine things?" The look he gave her almost made her bite her tongue.

"No," she said quietly. "Misinterpret. The police can't

respond to every anonymous call. It's natural they'd ask for your name."

"It was more than a request, Cathy. They were champing at the bit to interrogate me."

"I'm not doubting your word. I'm just playing devil's advocate. Trying to keep things level and sane in a crazy situation."

He looked at her long and hard. At last he nodded. "The voice of a rational woman," he sighed. "Exactly what I need right now. To keep me from jumping at my own shadow."

"And remind you to eat." She held out another slice of pizza. "You ordered this giant thing. You'd better help me finish it."

The tension between them instantly evaporated. He settled onto the bed and accepted the proferred slice. "That maternal look becomes you," he noted wryly. "So does the pizza sauce."

"What?" She swiped at her chin.

"You look like a two-year-old who's decided to finger-paint her face."

"Good grief, can you hand me the napkins?"

"Let me do it." Leaning forward, he gently dabbed away the sauce. As he did, she studied his face, saw the laugh lines creasing the corners of his eyes, the strands of silver intertwined with the brown hair. She remembered the photo of that very face, pasted on a Viratek badge. How somber he'd looked, the unsmiling portrait of a scientist. Now he appeared young and alive and almost happy.

Suddenly aware that she was watching him, he looked up and met her gaze. Slowly his smile faded. They both went very still, as though seeing, in each other's eyes, something they had not noticed before. The voices on the television seemed to fade into a far-off dimension. She felt his fingers trace lightly down her cheek. It was only a touch, but it left her shivering.

She asked, softly, "What happens now, Victor? Where do we go from here?"

"We have several choices."

"Such as?"

"I have friends in Palo Alto. We could turn to them."

"Or?"

"Or we could stay right where we are. For a while."

Right where we are. In this room, on this bed. She wouldn't mind that. Not at all.

She felt herself leaning toward him, drawn by a force against which she could offer no resistance. Both his hands came up to cradle her face, such large hands, but so infinitely gentle. She closed her eyes, knowing that this kiss, too, would be a gentle one.

And it was. This wasn't a kiss driven by fear or desperation. This was a quiet melting together of warmth, of souls. She swayed against him, felt his arms circle behind her to pull her inescapably close. It was a dangerous moment. She could feel herself tottering on the edge of total surrender to this man she scarcely knew. Already, her arms had found their way around his neck and her hands were roaming through the silver-streaked thickness of his hair.

His kisses dropped to her neck, exploring all the tender rises and hollows of her throat. All the needs that had lain dormant these past few years, all the hungers and desires, seemed to stir inside her, awakening at his touch.

And then, in an instant, the magic slipped away. At first she didn't understand why he suddenly pulled back. He sat bolt upright. The expression on his face was one of frozen astonishment. Bewildered, she followed his gaze and saw that he was focused on the television set behind her. She turned to see what had captured his attention.

A disturbingly familiar face stared back from the screen. She recognized the Viratek logo at the top, the straight-ahead gaze of the man in the photo. Why on earth would they be broadcasting Victor Holland's ID badge?

"...Sought on charges of industrial espionage. Evidence now links Dr. Holland to the death of a fellow Viratek researcher, Dr. Gerald Martinique. Investigators fear the suspect has already sold extensive research data to a European competitor...."

Neither one of them seemed able to move from the bed. They could only stare in disbelief at the newscaster with the Ken doll haircut. The station switched to a commercial break, raisins dancing crazily on a field, proclaiming the wonders of California sunshine. The lilting music was unbearable.

Victor rose to his feet and flicked off the television.

Slowly he turned to look at her. The silence between them grew agonizing.

"It's not true," he said quietly. "None of it."

She tried to read those unfathomable green eyes, wanting desperately to believe him. The taste of his kisses were still warm on her lips. The kisses of a con artist? *Is this just another lie? Has everything you've told me been nothing but lies? Who and what are you, Victor Holland?*

She glanced sideways, at the telephone on the bedside stand. It was so close. One call to the police, that's all it would take to end this nightmare.

"It's a frame-up," he said. "Viratek's releasing false information."

"Why?"

"To corner me. What easier way to find me than to have the police help them?"

She edged toward the phone.

"Don't, Cathy."

She froze, startled by the threat in his voice.

He saw the instant fear in her eyes. Gently he said, "Please. Don't call. I won't hurt you. I promise you can walk right out that door if you want. But first listen to me. Let me tell you what happened. Give me a chance."

His gaze was steady and absolutely believable. And he was right beside her, ready to stop her from making a move. Or to break her arm, if need be. She had no other choice. Nodding, she settled back down on the bed.

He began to pace, his feet tracing a path in the dull green carpet.

"It's all some—some incredible lie," he said. "It's crazy to think I'd kill him. Jerry Martinique and I were the best of friends. We both worked at Viratek. I was in vaccine development, he was a microbiologist. His specialty was viral studies. Genome research."

"You mean—like chromosomes?"

"The viral equivalent. Anyway, Jerry and I, we helped each other through some bad times. He'd gone through a painful divorce and I…" He paused, his voice dropping. "I lost my wife three years ago. To leukemia."

So he'd been married. Somehow it surprised her. He seemed like the sort of man who was far too independent to have ever said,"I do."

"About two months ago," he continued, "Jerry was transferred to a new research department. Viratek had been awarded a grant for some defense project. It was top security—Jerry couldn't talk about it. But I could see he was bothered by something that was going on in that lab. All he'd say to me was, 'They don't understand the danger. They don't know what they're getting into.' Jerry's field was the alteration of viral genes. So I assume the project had something to do with viruses as weapons. Jerry was fully aware that those weapons are outlawed by international agreement."

"If he knew it was illegal, why did he take part in it?"

"Maybe he didn't realize at first what the project was aiming for. Maybe they sold it to him as purely defensive research. In any event, he got upset enough to resign from the project. He went right to the top—the founder of Viratek. Walked into Archibald Black's office and threatened to go public if the project wasn't terminated. Four days later he had an accident." Anger flashed in Victor's eyes. It wasn't directed at her, but the fury in that gaze was frightening all the same.

"What happened to him?" she asked.

"His wrecked car was found at the side of the road. Jerry was still inside. Dead, of course." Suddenly, the anger was gone, replaced by overwhelming weariness. He sank onto the bed. "I thought the accident investigation would blow everything into the open. It was a farce. The local cops did their best, but then some federal transportation "expert" showed up on the scene and took over. He said Jerry must've fallen asleep at the wheel. Case closed. That's when I realized just how deep this went. I didn't know who to go to, so I called the FBI in San Francisco. Told them I had evidence."

"You mean the film?" asked Cathy.

Victor nodded. "Just before he was killed, Jerry told me about some duplicate papers he'd stashed away in his garden shed. After the…accident, I went over to his house. Found the place ransacked. But they never bothered to search the shed. That's how I got hold of the evidence, a single file and a roll of film. I arranged a meeting with one of the San Francisco agents, a guy named Sam Polowski. I'd already talked to him a few times on the phone. He offered to meet me in Garberville. We wanted to keep it private, so we agreed to a spot just outside of town. I drove down, fully expecting him to show. Well, someone showed up, all right. Someone who ran me off the road." He paused and looked straight at her. "That's the night you found me."

The night my whole life changed, she thought.

"You have to believe me," he said.

She studied him, her instincts battling against logic. The story was just barely plausible, halfway between truth and fantasy. But the man looked solid as stone.

Wearily she nodded. "I do believe you, Victor. Maybe I'm crazy. Or just gullible. But I do."

The bed shifted as he sat down beside her. They didn't touch, yet she could almost feel the warmth radiating between them.

"That's all that matters to me right now," he said. "That you know, in your heart, I'm telling the truth."

"In my heart?" She shook her head and laughed. "My heart's always been a lousy judge of character. No, I'm guessing. I'm going by the fact you kept me alive. By the fact there's another Cathy Weaver who's now dead..."

Remembering the face of that other woman, the face in the newspaper, she suddenly began to shake. It all added up to the terrible truth. The gun blasts into her apartment, the other dead Cathy. And Sarah, poor Sarah.

She was gulping in shaky breaths, hovering on the verge of tears.

She let him take her in his arms, let him pull her down on the bed beside him. He murmured into her hair, gentle words of comfort and reassurance. He turned off the lamp. In darkness they held each other, two frightened souls joined against a terrifying world. She felt safe there, tucked away against his chest. This was a place where no one could hurt her. It was a stranger's arms, but from the smell of his shirt to the beat of his heart, it all seemed somehow familiar. She never wanted to leave that spot, ever.

She trembled as his lips brushed her forehead. He was stroking her face now, her neck, warming her with his touch. When his hand slipped beneath her blouse, she didn't protest. Somehow it seemed so natural, that that hand would come to lie at her breast. It wasn't the touch of a marauder, it was simply a gentle reminder that she was in safekeeping.

And yet, she found herself responding....

Her nipple tingled and grew taut beneath his cupping hand. The tingling spread, a warmth that crept to her face and flushed her cheeks. She reached for his shirt and began to unbutton it. In the darkness she was slow and clumsy. By the time she finally slid her hand under the fabric, they were both breathing hard and fast with anticipation.

She brushed through the coarse mat of hair, stroking her way across that broad chest. He took in a sharp breath as her fingers skimmed a delicate circle around his nipple.

If playing with fire had been her intention, then she had just struck the match.

His mouth was suddenly on hers, seeking, devouring. The force of his kiss pressed her onto her back, trapping her head against the pillows. For a dizzy eternity she was swimming in sensations, the scent of male heat, the unyielding grip of his hands imprisoning her face. Only when he at last drew away did they both come up for air.

He stared down at her, as though hovering on the edge of temptation.

"This is crazy," he whispered.

"Yes. Yes, it is—"

"I never meant to do this—"

"Neither did I."

"It's just that you're scared. We're both scared. And we don't know what the hell we're doing."

"No." She closed her eyes, felt the unexpected bite of

tears. "We don't. But I *am* scared. And I just want to be held. Please, Victor. Hold me, that's all. Just hold me."

He pulled her close, murmuring her name. This time the embrace was gentle, without the fever of desire. His shirt was still unbuttoned, his chest bared. And that's where she lay her head, against that curling nest of hair. Yes, he was right, so wise. They were crazy to be making love when they both knew it was fear, nothing else, that had driven their desire. And now the fever had broken.

A sense of peace fell over her. She curled up against him. Exhaustion robbed them both of speech. Her muscles gradually fell limp as sleep tugged her into its shadow. Even if she tried to, she could not move her arms or legs. Instead she was drifting free, like a wraith in the darkness, floating somewhere in a warm and inky sea.

Vaguely she was aware of light sliding past her eyelids.

The warmth encircling her body seemed to melt away. No, she wanted it back, wanted *him* back! An instant later she felt him shaking her.

"Cathy. Come on, wake up!"

Through drowsy eyes she peered at him. "Victor?"

"Something's going on outside."

She tumbled out of bed and followed him to the window. Through a slit in the curtains she spotted what had alarmed him: a patrol car, its radio crackling faintly, parked by the motel registration door. At once she snapped wide awake, her mind going over the exits from their room. There was only one.

"Out, now!" he ordered. "Before we're trapped."

He eased open the door. They scrambled out onto the walkway. The frigid night air was like a slap in the face. She was already shivering, more from fear than from the cold. Running at a crouch, they moved along the walkway, away from the stairs, and ducked past the ice machine.

Below, they heard the lobby door open and the voice of the motel manager: "Yeah, that'll be right upstairs. Gee, he sure seemed like a nice-enough guy...."

Tires screeched as another patrol car pulled up, lights flashing.

Victor gave her a push. *"Go!"*

They slipped into a breezeway and scurried through, to the other side of the building. No stairways there! They climbed over the walkway railing and dropped into the parking lot.

Faintly they heard a banging, then the command: "Open up! This is the police."

At once they were sprinting instinctively for the shadows. No one spotted them, no one gave chase. Still they kept running, until they'd left the Kon-Tiki Motel blocks and blocks behind them, until they were so tired they were stumbling.

At last Cathy slowed to a halt and leaned back against a doorway, her breath coming out in clouds of cold mist. "How did they find you?" she said between gasps.

"It couldn't have been the call...." Suddenly he groaned. "My credit card! I had to use it to pay the bill."

"Where now? Should we try another motel?"

He shook his head. "I'm down to my last forty bucks. I can't risk a credit card again."

"And I left my purse at the apartment. I—I'm not sure I want to—"

"We're not going back for it. They'll be watching the place."

They. Meaning the killers.

"So we're broke," she said weakly.

He didn't answer. He stood with his hands in his pockets, his whole body a study in frustration. "You have friends you can go to?"

"I think so. Uh, no. She's out of town till Friday. And what would I tell her? How would I explain you?"

"You can't. And we can't handle any questions right now."

That leaves out most of my friends, she thought. Nowhere to go, no one to turn to. Unless…

No, she'd promised herself never to sink that low, never to beg for *that* particular source of help.

Victor glanced up the street. "There's a bus stop over there." He reached in his pocket and took out a handful of money. "Here," he said. "Take it and get out of the city. Go visit some friends on your own."

"What about you?"

"I'll be okay."

"Broke? With everyone after you?" She shook her head.

"I'll only make things more dangerous for you." He pressed the money into her hand.

She stared down at the wad of bills, thinking: *This is all he has. And he's giving it to me.* "I can't," she said.

"You have to."

"But—"

"Don't argue with me." The look in his eyes left no alternative.

Reluctantly she closed her fingers around the money.

"I'll wait till you get on the bus. It should take you right past the station."

"Victor?"

He silenced her with a single look. Placing both hands on her shoulders, he stood her before him. "You'll be fine," he said. Then he pressed a kiss to her forehead. For a moment his lips lingered, and the warmth of his breath in her hair left her trembling. "I wouldn't leave you if I thought otherwise."

The roar of a bus down the block made them both turn.

"There's your limousine," he whispered. "Go." He gave her a nudge. "Take care of yourself, Cathy."

She started toward the bus stop. Three steps, four. She slowed and came to a halt. Turning, she saw that he had already edged away into the shadows.

"Get on it!" he called.

She looked at the bus. *I won't do it,* she thought.

She turned back to Victor. "I know a place! A place we can both stay!"

"What?"

"I didn't want to use it but—"

Her words were drowned out as the bus wheezed to the stop, then roared away.

"It's a bit of a walk," she said. "But we'd have beds and a meal. And I can guarantee no one would call the police."

He came out of the shadows. "Why didn't you think of this earlier?"

"I did think of it. But up till now, things weren't, well... desperate enough."

"Not desperate enough," he repeated slowly. He moved toward her, his face taut with incredulity. "Not *desperate* enough? Hell, lady. I'd like to know exactly what kind of crisis would qualify!"

"You have to understand, this is a last resort. It's not an easy place for me to turn to."

His eyes narrowed in suspicion. "This place is beginning to sound worse and worse. What are we talking about? A flophouse?"

"No, it's in Pacific Heights. You could even call the place a mansion."

"Who lives there? A friend?"

"Quite the opposite."

His eyebrow shot up. "An enemy?"

"Close." She let out a sigh of resignation. "My ex-husband."

Chapter Five

"Jack, open up! Jack!" Cathy banged again and again on the door of the formidable Pacific Heights home. There was no answer. Through the windows they saw only darkness.

"Damn you, Jack!" She gave the door a slap of frustration. "Why aren't you *ever* home when I need you?"

Victor glanced around at the neighborhood of elegant homes and neatly trimmed shrubbery. "We can't stand around out here all night."

"We're not going to," she muttered. Crouching on her knees, she began to dig around in a red-brick planter.

"What are you doing?"

"Something I swore I'd never do." Her fingers raked the loamy soil, searching for the key Jack kept buried under the geraniums. Sure enough, there it was, right where it had always been. She rose to her feet, clapping the dirt off her hands. "But there are limits to my pride. Threat of death being one of them." She inserted the key and felt a momentary dart of panic when it didn't turn. But with a little jiggling, the lock at last gave way. The door swung open to the faint gleam of a polished wood floor, a massive bannister.

She motioned Victor inside. The solid thunk of the door closing behind them seemed to shut out all the dangers of the night. Cloaked in the darkness, they both let out a sigh of relief.

"Just what kind of terms are you on with your ex-husband?" Victor asked, following her blindly through the unlit foyer.

"Speaking. Barely."

"He doesn't mind you wandering around his house?"

"Why not?" She snorted. "Jack lets half the human race wander through his bedroom. The only prerequisite being XX chromosomes."

She felt her way into the pitch-dark living room and flipped on the light switch. There she froze in astonishment and stared at the two naked bodies intertwined on the polar bear rug.

"Jack!" she blurted out.

The larger of the two bodies extricated himself and sat up. "Hello, Cathy!" He raked his hand through his dark hair and grinned. "Seems like old times."

The woman lying next to him spat out a shocking obscenity, scrambled to her feet, and stormed off in a blur of wild red hair and bare bottom toward the bedroom.

"That's Lulu," yawned Jack, by way of introduction.

Cathy sighed. "I see your taste in women hasn't improved."

"No, sweetheart, my taste in women hit a high point when I married you." Unmindful of his state of nudity, Jack rose to his feet and regarded Victor. The contrast between the two men was instantly apparent. Though both were tall and lean, it was Jack who possessed the striking good looks, and he knew it. He'd always known it. Vanity wasn't a label one could ever pin on Victor Holland.

"I see you brought a fourth," said Jack, giving Victor the once-over. "So, what'll it be, folks? Bridge or poker?"

"Neither," said Cathy.

"That opens up all *sorts* of possibilities."

"Jack, I need your help."

He turned and looked at her with mock incredulity. *"No!"*

"You know damn well I wouldn't be here if I could avoid it!"

He winked at Victor. "Don't believe her. She's still madly in love with me."

"Can we get serious?"

"Darling, you never did have a sense of humor."

"Damn you, Jack!" Everyone had a breaking point and Cathy had reached hers. She couldn't help it; without warning she burst into tears. "For once in your life will you *listen* to me?"

That's when Victor's patience finally snapped. He didn't need a degree in psychology to know this Jack character was a first-class jerk. Couldn't he see that Cathy was exhausted and terrified? Up till this moment, Victor had admired her for her strength. Now he ached at the sight of her vulnerability.

It was only natural to pull her into his arms, to ease her tear-streaked face against his chest. Over her shoulder, he growled out an oath that impugned not only Jack's name but that of Jack's mother as well.

The other man didn't seem to take offense, probably because he'd been called far worse names, and on a regular basis. He simply crossed his arms and regarded Victor with a raised eyebrow. "Being protective, are we?"

"She needs protection."

"From what, pray tell?"

"Maybe you haven't heard. Three days ago, someone murdered her friend Sarah."

"Sarah...Boylan?"

Victor nodded. "Tonight, someone tried to kill Cathy."

Jack stared at him. He looked at his ex-wife. "Is this true? What he's saying?"

Cathy, wiping away tears, nodded.

"Why didn't you tell me this to begin with?"

"Because you were acting like an ass to begin with!" she shot back.

Down the hall came the *click-click* of high-heeled shoes. "She's absolutely right!" yelled a female voice from the foyer. "You *are* an ass, Jack Zuckerman!" The front door opened and slammed shut again. The thud seemed to echo endlessly through the mansion.

There was a long silence.

Suddenly, through her tears, Cathy laughed. "You know what, Jack? I *like* that woman."

Jack crossed his arms and gave his ex-wife the critical once-over. "Either I'm going senile or you forgot to tell me something. Why haven't you gone to the police? Why bother old Jack about this?"

Cathy and Victor glanced at each other.

"We can't go to the police," Cathy said.

"I assume this has to do with *him?*" He cocked a thumb at Victor.

Cathy let out a breath. "It's a complicated story...."

"It must be. If you're afraid to go to the police."

"I can explain it," said Victor.

"Mm-hm. Well." Jack reached for the bathrobe lying in a heap by the polar bear rug. "Well," he said again, calmly tying the sash. "I've always enjoyed watching creativity at work. So let's have it." He sat down on the leather couch and smiled at Victor. "I'm waiting. It's showtime."

SPECIAL AGENT SAM Polowski lay shivering in his bed, watching the eleven o'clock news. Every muscle in his body ached, his head pounded, and the thermometer at his bed-

side read an irrefutable 101 degrees. So much for changing flat tires in the pouring rain. He wished he could get
his hands on the joker who'd punched that nail in his tire
while he was grabbing a quick bite at that roadside cafe.
Not only had the culprit managed to keep Sam from his
appointment in Garberville, thereby shredding the Viratek
case into confetti, Sam had also lost track of his only contact in the affair: Victor Holland. And now, the flu.

Sam reached over for the bottle of aspirin. To hell with
the ulcer. His head hurt. And when it came to headaches,
there was nothing like Mom's time-tested remedy.

He was in the midst of gulping down three tablets when
the news about Victor Holland flashed on the screen.

"...New evidence links the suspect to the murder of fellow Viratek researcher, Dr. Gerald Martinique...."

Sam sat up straight in bed. "What the hell?" he growled
at the TV.

Then he grabbed the telephone.

It took six rings for his supervisor to answer. "Dafoe?"
Sam said. "This is Polowski."

"Do you know what time it is?"

"Have you seen the late-night news?"

"I happen to be in bed."

"There's a story on Viratek."

A pause. "Yeah, I know. I cleared it."

"What's with this crap about industrial espionage?
They're making Holland out to be a—"

"Polowski, drop it."

"Since when did he become a murder suspect?"

"Look, just consider it a cover story. I want him brought
in. For his own good."

"So you sic him with a bunch of trigger-happy cops?"

"I said drop it."

"But—"

"You're off the case." Dafoe hung up.

Sam stared in disbelief at the receiver, then at the television, then back at the receiver.

Pull me off the case? He slammed the receiver down so hard the bottle of aspirin tumbled off the nightstand.

That's what you think.

"I THINK I'VE heard about enough," said Jack, rising to his feet. "I want this man out of my house. And I want him out now."

"Jack, please!" said Cathy. "Give him a chance—"

"You're buying this ridiculous tale?"

"I believe him."

"Why?"

She looked at Victor and saw the clear fire of honesty burning in his eyes. "Because he saved my life."

"You're a fool, babycakes." Jack reached for the phone. "You yourself saw the TV. He's wanted for murder. If you don't call the police, I will."

But as Jack picked up the receiver, Victor grabbed his arm. "No," he said. Though his voice was quiet, it held the unmistakable note of authority.

The two men stared at each other, neither willing to back down.

"This is more than just a case of murder," said Victor. "This is deadly research. The manufacture of illegal weapons. This could reach all the way to Washington."

"Who in Washington?"

"Someone in control. Someone with the federal funds to authorize that research."

"I see. Some lofty public servant is out knocking off scientists. With the help of the FBI."

"Jerry wasn't just any scientist. He had a conscience. He was a whistleblower who would've taken this to the press to stop that research. The political fallout would've been disastrous, for the whole administration."

"Wait. Are we talking Pennsylvania Avenue?"

"Maybe."

Jack snorted. "Holland, I *make* Grade B horror films. I don't live them."

"This isn't a film. This is real. Real bullets, real bodies."

"Then that's all the more reason I want nothing to do with it." Jack turned to Cathy. "Sorry, sweetcakes. It's nothing personal, but I detest the company you keep."

"Jack," she said. "You have to help us!"

"You, I'll help. Him—no way. I draw the line at lunatics and felons."

"You heard what he said! It's a frame-up!"

"You are so gullible."

"Only about you."

"Cathy, it's all right," said Victor. He was standing very still, very calm. "I'll leave."

"No, you won't." Cathy shot to her feet and stalked over to her ex-husband. She stared him straight in the eye, a gaze so direct, so accusing, he seemed to wilt right down into a chair. "You owe it to me, Jack. You owe me for all the years we were married. All the years I put into *your* career, *your* company, *your* idiotic flicks. I haven't asked for anything. You have the house. The Jaguar. The bank account. I never asked because I didn't want to take a damn thing from this marriage except my own soul. But now I'm asking. This man saved my life tonight. If you ever cared about me, if you ever loved me, even a little, then you'll do me this favor."

"Harbor a criminal?"

"Only until we figure out what to do next."

"And how long might that take? Weeks? Months?"

"I don't know."

"Just the kind of definite answer I like."

Victor said, "I need time to find out what Jerry was trying to prove. What it is Viratek's working on—"

"You had one of his files," said Jack. "Why didn't you read the blasted thing?"

"I'm not a virologist. I couldn't interpret the data. It was some sort of RNA sequence, probably a viral genome. A lot of the data was coded. All I can be sure of is the name: Project Cerberus."

"Where is all this vital evidence now?"

"I lost the file. It was in my car the night I was shot. I'm sure they have it back."

"And the film?"

Victor sank into a chair, his face suddenly lined by weariness. "I don't have it. I was hoping that Cathy…" Sighing, he ran his hands through his hair. "I've lost that, too."

"Well," said Jack. "Give or take a few miracles, I'd say this puts your chances at just about zero. And I'm known as an optimist."

"I know where the film is," said Cathy.

There was a long silence. Victor raised his head and stared at her. "What?"

"I wasn't sure about you—not at first. I didn't want to tell you until I could be certain—"

Victor shot to his feet. *"Where is it?"*

She flinched at the sharpness of his voice. He must have noticed how startled she was—his next words were quiet but urgent. "I need that film, Cathy. Before they find it. Where is it?"

"Sarah found it in my car. I didn't know it was yours! I thought it was Hickey's."

"Who's Hickey?"

"A photographer—a friend of mine—"

Jack snorted. "Hickey. Now *there's* a ladies' man."

"He was in a rush to get to the airport," she continued. "At the last minute he left me with some rolls of film. Asked me to take care of them till he got back from Nairobi. But all his film was stolen from my car."

"And my roll?" asked Victor.

"It was in my bathrobe pocket the night Sarah—the night she—" She paused, swallowing at the mention of her friend. "When I got back here, to the city, I mailed it to Hickey's studio."

"Where's the studio?"

"Over on Union Street. I mailed it this afternoon—"

"So it should be there sometime tomorrow." He began to pace the room. "All we have to do is wait for the mail to arrive."

"I don't have a key."

"We'll find a way in."

"Terrific," sighed Jack. "Now he's turning my ex-wife into a burglar."

"We're only after the film!" said Cathy.

"It's still breaking and entering, sweetie."

"You don't have to get involved."

"But you're asking me to harbor the breakers and enterers."

"Just one night, Jack. That's all I'm asking."

"That sounds like one of *my* lines."

"And your lines always work, don't they?"

"Not this time."

"Then here's another line to chew on: 1988. Your federal tax return. Or lack of one."

Jack froze. He glowered at Victor, then at Cathy. "That's below the belt."

"Your most vulnerable spot."

"I'll get around to filing—"

"More words to chew on. Audit. IRS. Jail."

"Okay, okay!" Jack threw his arms up in surrender. "God, I *hate* that word."

"What, *jail?*"

"Don't laugh, babycakes. The word could soon apply to all of us." He turned and headed for the stairs.

"Where are you going?" Cathy demanded.

"To make up the spare beds. Seems I have houseguests for the night...."

"Can we trust him?" Victor asked after Jack had vanished upstairs.

Cathy sank back on the couch, all the energy suddenly drained from her body, and closed her eyes. "We have to. I can't think of anywhere else to go...."

She was suddenly aware of his approach, and then he was sitting beside her, so close she could feel the overwhelming strength of his presence. He didn't say a word, yet she knew he was watching her.

She opened her eyes and met his gaze. So steady, so intense, it seemed to infuse her with new strength.

"I know it wasn't easy for you," he said. "Asking Jack for favors."

She smiled. "I've always wanted to talk tough with Jack." Ruefully she added, "Until tonight, I've never quite been able to pull it off."

"My guess is, talking tough isn't in your repertoire."

"No, it isn't. When it comes to confrontation, I'm a gutless wonder."

"For a gutless wonder, you did pretty well. In fact, you were magnificent."

"That's because I wasn't fighting for me. I was fighting for you."

"You don't consider yourself worth fighting for?"

She shrugged. "It's the way I was raised. I was always

told that sticking up for yourself was unladylike. Whereas sticking up for other people was okay."

He nodded gravely. "Self-sacrifice. A fine feminine tradition."

That made her laugh. "Spoken like a man who knows women well."

"Only two women. My mother and my wife."

At the mention of his dead wife, she fell silent. She wondered what the woman's name was, what she'd looked like, how much he'd loved her. He must have loved her a great deal—she'd heard the pain in his voice earlier that evening when he'd mentioned her death. She felt an unexpected stab of envy that this unnamed wife had been so loved. What Cathy would give to be as dearly loved by a man! Just as quickly she suppressed the thought, appalled that she could be jealous of a dead woman.

She turned away, her face tinged with guilt. "I think Jack will go along," she said. "Tonight, at least."

"That was blackmail, wasn't it? That stuff about the tax return?"

"He's a careless man. I just reminded him of his oversight."

Victor shook his head. "You are amazing. Jumping along rooftops one minute, blackmailing ex-husbands the next."

"You're so right," said Jack, who'd reappeared at the bottom of the stairs. "She is an amazing woman. I can't wait to see what she'll do next."

Cathy rose wearily to her feet. "At this point I'll do anything." She slipped past Jack and headed up the stairs. "Anything I have to to stay alive."

The two men listened to her footsteps recede along the hall. Then they regarded each other in silence.

"Well," said Jack with forced cheerfulness. "What's next on the agenda? Scrabble?"

"Try solitaire," said Victor, hauling himself off the couch. He was in no mood to share pleasantries with Jack Zuckerman. The man was slick and self-centered and he obviously went through women the way most men went through socks. Victor had a hard time imagining what Cathy had ever seen in the man. That is, aside from Jack's good looks and obvious wealth. There was no denying the fact he was a classic hunk, with the added attraction of money thrown in. Maybe it was that combination that had dazzled her.

A combination I'll certainly never possess, he thought.

He crossed the room, then stopped and turned. "Zuckerman?" he asked. "Do you still love your wife?"

Jack looked faintly startled by the question. "Do I still love her? Well, let me see. No, not exactly. But I suppose I have a sentimental attachment, based on ten years of marriage. And I respect her."

"Respect her? You?"

"Yes. Her talents. Her technical skill. After all, she's my number-one makeup artist."

That's what she meant to him. An asset he could use. *Thinking of himself, the jerk.* If there was anyone else Victor could turn to, he would. But the one man he would've trusted—Jerry—was dead. His other friends might already be under observation. Plus, they weren't in the sort of tax brackets that allowed private little hideaways in the woods. Jack, on the other hand, had the resources to spirit Cathy away to a safe place. Victor could only hope the man's sentimental attachment was strong enough to make him watch out for her.

"I have a proposition," said Victor.

Jack instantly looked suspicious. "What might that be?"

"I'm the one they're really after. Not Cathy. I don't want to make things any more dangerous for her than I already have."

"Big of you."

"It's better if I go off on my own. If I leave her with you, will you keep her safe?"

Jack shifted, looked down at his feet. "Well, sure. I guess so."

"Don't guess. Can you?"

"Look, we start shooting a film in Mexico next month. Jungle scenes, black lagoons, that sort of stuff. Should be a safe-enough place."

"That's next month. What about now?"

"I'll think of something. But first you get yourself out of the picture. Since you're the reason she's in danger in the first place."

Victor couldn't disagree with that last point. *Since the night I met her I've caused her nothing but trouble.*

He nodded. "I'm out of here tomorrow."

"Good."

"Take care of Cathy. Get her out of the city. Out of the country. Don't wait."

"Yeah. Sure."

Something about the way Jack said it, his hasty, what-ever-you-say tone, made Victor wonder if the man gave a damn about anyone but himself. But at this point Victor had no choice. He had to trust Jack Zuckerman.

As he climbed the stairs to the guest rooms, it occurred to him that, come morning, it would be goodbye. A quiet little bond had formed between them. He owed his life to her and she to him. That was the sort of link one could never break.

Even if we never see each other again.

In the upstairs hall, he paused outside her closed door. He could hear her moving around the room, opening and closing drawers, squeaking bedsprings.

He knocked on the door. "Cathy?"

There was a pause. Then, "Come in."

One dim lamp lit the room. She was sitting on the bed, dressed in a ridiculously huge man's shirt. Her hair hung in damp waves to her shoulders. The scent of soap and shampoo permeated the shadows. It reminded him of his wife, of the shower smells and feminine sweetness. He stood there, pierced by a sense of longing he hadn't felt in over a year, longing for the warmth, the love, of a woman. Not just any woman. He wasn't like Jack, to whom a soft body with the right equipment would be sufficient. What Victor wanted was the heart and soul; the package they came wrapped in was only of minor importance.

His own wife Lily hadn't been beautiful; neither had she been unattractive. Even at the end, when the ravages of illness had left her shrunken and bruised, there had been a light in her eyes, a gentle spirit's glow.

The same glow he'd seen in Catherine Weaver's eyes the night she'd saved his life. The same glow he saw now.

She sat with her back propped up on pillows. Her gaze was silently expectant, maybe a little fearful. She was clutching a handful of tissues. *Why were you crying?* he wondered.

He didn't approach; he stood just inside the doorway. Their gazes locked together in the gloom. "I've just talked with Jack," he said.

She nodded but said nothing.

"We both agree. It's better that I leave as soon as possible. So I'll be taking off in the morning."

"What about the film?"

"I'll get it. All I need is Hickey's address."

"Yes. Of course." She looked down at the tissues in her fist.

He could tell she wanted to say something. He went to the bed and sat down. Those sweet woman smells grew intoxicating. The neckline of her oversized shirt sagged low enough to reveal a tempting glimpse of shadow. He forced himself to focus on her face.

"Cathy, you'll be fine. Jack said he'd watch out for you. Get you out of the city."

"Jack?" What sounded like a laugh escaped her throat.

"You'll be safer with him. I don't even know where I'll be going. I don't want to drag you into this—"

"But you already have. You've dragged me in over my head, Victor. What am I supposed to do now? I can't just— just sit around and wait for you to fix things. I owe it to Sarah—"

"And I owe it to you not to let you get hurt."

"You think you can hand me over to Jack and make everything be fine again? Well, it won't be fine. Sarah's dead. Her baby's dead. And somehow it's not just your fault. It's mine as well."

"No, it's not. Cathy—"

"It is my fault! Did you know she was lying there in the driveway all night? In the rain. In the cold. There she was, dying, and I slept through the whole damn thing…." She dropped her face in her hands. The guilt that had been tormenting her since Sarah's death at last burst through. She began to cry, silently, ashamedly, unable to hold back the tears any longer.

Victor's response was automatic and instinctively male. He pulled her against him and gave her a warm, safe place to cry. As soon as he felt her settle into his arms, he knew it was a mistake. It was too perfect a fit. She felt as if she belonged there, against his heart, felt that if she ever pulled away there would be left a hole so gaping it could never be filled. He pressed his lips to her damp hair and inhaled her heady scent of soap and warm skin. That gentle fragrance was enough to drown a man with need. So was the softness of her face, the silken luster of that shoulder peeking out from beneath the shirt. And all the time he was stroking her hair, murmuring inane words of comfort, he was thinking: *I have to leave her. For her sake I have to abandon this woman. Or I'll get us both killed.*

"Cathy," he said. It took all the willpower he could muster to pull away. He placed his hands on her shoulders, made her look at him. Her gaze was confused and brimming with tears. "We have to talk about tomorrow."

She nodded and swiped at the tears on her cheeks.

"I want you out of the city, first thing in the morning. Go to Mexico with Jack. Anywhere. Just keep out of sight."

"What will you do?"

"I'm going to take a look at that roll of film, see what kind of evidence it has."

"And then?"

"I don't know yet. Maybe I'll take it to the newspapers. The FBI is definitely out."

"How will I know you're all right? How do I reach you?"

He thought hard, fighting the distraction of her scent, her hair. He found himself stroking the bare skin of her shoulder, marveling at how smooth it felt beneath his fingers.

He focused on her face, on the look of worry in her eyes. "Every other Sunday I'll put an ad in the Personals. *Los Angeles Times.* It'll be addressed to, let's say, Cora. Anything I need to tell you will be there."

"Cora." She nodded. "I'll remember."

They looked at each other, a silent acknowledgment that this parting had to be. He cupped her face and pressed a kiss to her mouth. She barely responded; already, it seemed, she had said her goodbyes.

He rose from the bed and started for the door. There he couldn't resist asking, one more time: "You'll be all right?"

She nodded, but it was too automatic. The sort of nod

one gave to dismiss an unimportant question. "I'll be fine. After all, I'll have Jack to watch over me."

He didn't miss the faint note of irony in her reply. Jack, it seemed, didn't inspire confidence in either of them. *What's my alternative? Drag her along with me as a moving target?*

He gripped the doorknob. No, it was better this way. He'd already ripped her life apart; he wasn't going to scatter the pieces as well.

As he was leaving, he took one last backward glance. She was still huddled on the bed, her knees drawn up to her chest. The oversized shirt had slid off one bare shoulder. For a moment he thought she was crying. Then she raised her head and met his gaze. What he saw in her eyes wasn't tears. It was something far more moving, something pure and bright and beautiful.

Courage.

IN THE PALE light of dawn, Savitch stood outside Jack Zuckerman's house. Through the fingers of morning mist, Savitch studied the curtained windows, trying to picture the inhabitants within. He wondered who they were, in which room they slept, and whether Catherine Weaver was among them.

He'd find out soon.

He pocketed the black address book he'd taken from the woman's apartment. The name C. Zuckerman and this Pacific Heights address had been written on the inside front cover. Then the Zuckerman had been crossed out and replaced with Weaver. She was a divorcée, he concluded. Under *Z,* he'd found a prominent listing for a man named Jack, with various phone numbers and addresses, both foreign and domestic. Her ex-husband, he'd confirmed, after a brief chat with another name listed in the book. Pumping strangers for information was a simple matter. All it took was an air of authority and a cop's ID. The same ID he was planning to use now.

He gave the house one final perusal, taking in the manicured lawns and shrubbery, the trellis with its vines of winter-dormant wisteria. A successful man, this Jack Zuckerman. Savitch had always admired men of wealth. He gave his jacket a final tug to assure himself that the shoulder holster was concealed. Then he crossed the street to the front porch and rang the doorbell.

Chapter Six

At first light, Cathy awakened. It wasn't a gentle return but a startling jerk back to consciousness. She was instantly aware that she was not in her own bed and that something was terribly wrong. It took her a few seconds to remember exactly what it was. And when she did remember, the sense of urgency was so compelling she rose at once from bed and began to dress in the semidarkness. *Have to be ready to run...*

The creak of floorboards in the next room told her that Victor was awake as well, probably planning his moves for the day. She rummaged through the closet, searching for things he might need in his flight. All she came up with was a zippered nylon bag and a raincoat. She searched the dresser next and found a few men's socks. She also found a collection of women's underwear. *Damn Jack and all his women,* she thought with sudden irritation and slammed the drawer shut. The thud was still resonating in the room when another sound echoed through the house.

The doorbell was ringing.

It was only seven o'clock, too early for visitors or deliverymen. Suddenly her door swung open. She turned to see Victor, his face etched with tension.

"What should we do?" she asked.

"Get ready to leave. Fast."

"There's a back door—"

"Let's go."

They hurried along the hall and had almost reached the top of the stairs when they heard Jack's sleepy voice below, grumbling: "I'm coming, dammit! Stop that racket, I'm coming!"

The doorbell rang again.

"Don't answer it!" hissed Cathy. "Not yet—"

Jack had already opened the door. Instantly Victor snatched Cathy back up the hall, out of sight. They froze with their backs against the wall, listening to the voices below.

"Yeah," they heard Jack say. "I'm Jack Zuckerman. And who are you?"

The visitor's voice was soft. They could tell only that it was a man.

"Is that so?" said Jack, his voice suddenly edged with panic. "You're with the *FBI,* you say? And what on earth would the *FBI* want with my *ex-wife?*"

Cathy's gaze flew to Victor. She read the frantic message in his eyes: *Which way out?*

She pointed toward the bedroom at the end of the hall. He nodded. Together they tiptoed along the carpet, all the time aware that one misstep, one loud creak, might be enough to alert the agent downstairs.

"Where's your warrant?" they heard Jack demand of the visitor. "Hey, wait a minute! You can't just barge in here without a court order or something!"

No time left! thought Cathy in panic as she slipped into the last room. They closed the door behind them.

"The window!" she whispered.

"You mean jump?"

"No." She hurried across the room and gingerly eased the window open. "There's a trellis!"

He glanced down dubiously at the tangled vines of wisteria. "Are you sure it'll hold us?"

"I know it will," she said, swinging her leg over the sill. "I caught one of Jack's blondes hanging off it one night. And believe me, she was a *big* girl." She glanced down at the ground far below and felt a sudden wave of nausea as the old fear of heights washed through her. "God," she muttered. "Why do we always seem to be hanging out of windows?"

From somewhere in the house came Jack's outraged shout: "You can't go up there! You haven't shown me your warrant!"

"Move!" snapped Victor.

Cathy lowered herself onto the trellis. Branches clawed her face as she scrambled down the vine. An instant after she landed on the dew-soaked grass, Victor dropped beside her.

At once they were on their feet and sprinting for the cover of shrubbery. Just as they rolled behind the azalea bushes, they heard a second-floor window slide open, and then Jack's voice complaining loudly: "I know my rights! This is an illegal search! I'm going to call my lawyer!"

Don't let him see us! prayed Cathy, burrowing frantically into the bush. She felt Victor's body curl around her back, his arms pulling her tightly to him, his breath hot and ragged against her neck. For an eternity they lay shivering in the grass as mist swirled around them.

"You see?" they heard Jack say. "There's no one here but me. Or would you like to check the garage?"

The window slid shut.

Victor gave Cathy a little push. "Go," he whispered. "The end of the hedge. We'll run from there."

On hands and knees she crawled along the row of azalea bushes. Her soaked jeans were icy and her palms scratched and bleeding, but she was too numbed by terror to feel any pain. All her attention was focused on moving forward. Victor was crawling close behind her. When she felt him bump up against her hip, it occurred to her what a ridiculous view he had, her rump swaying practically under his nose.

She reached the last bush and stopped to shove a handful of tangled hair off her face. "That house next?" she asked.

"Go for it!"

They both took off like scared rabbits, dashing across the twenty yards of lawn between houses. Once they reached the cover of the next house, they didn't stop. They kept running, past parked cars and early-morning pedestrians. Five blocks later, they ducked into a coffee shop. Through the front window, they glanced out at the street, watching for signs of pursuit. All they saw was the typical Monday morning bustle: the stop-and-go traffic, the passersby bundled up in scarves and overcoats.

From the grill behind them came the hiss and sizzle of bacon. The smell of freshly brewed coffee wafted from the counter burner. The aromas were almost painful; they reminded Cathy that she and Victor probably had a total of forty dollars between them. Damn it, why hadn't she begged, borrowed or stolen some cash from Jack?

"What now?" she asked, half hoping he'd suggest blowing the rest of their cash on breakfast.

He scanned the street. "Let's go on."

"Where?"

"Hickey's studio."

"Oh." She sighed. Another long walk, and all on an empty stomach.

Outside, a car passed by bearing the bumper sticker: Today is the First Day of the Rest of Your Life.

Lord, I hope it gets better than this, she thought. Then she followed Victor out the door and into the morning chill.

FIELD SUPERVISOR LARRY Dafoe was sitting at his desk, pumping away at his executive power chair. Upper body strength, he always said, was the key to success as a man. Bulk out those muscles *pull!*, fill out that size forty-four jacket *pull!*, and what you got was a pair of shoulders that'd impress any woman, intimidate any rival. And with this snazzy 700-buck model, you didn't even have to get out of your chair.

Sam Polowski watched his superior strain at the system of wires and pulleys and thought the device looked more like an exotic instrument of torture.

"What you gotta understand," gasped Dafoe, "is that there are other *pull!* issues at work here. Things you know nothing about."

"Like what?" asked Polowski.

Dafoe released the handles and looked up, his face sheened with a healthy sweat. "If I was at liberty to tell you, don't you think I already would've?"

Polowski looked at the gleaming black exercise handles, wondering whether he'd benefit from an executive power chair. Maybe a souped-up set of biceps was what he needed to get a little respect around this office.

"I still don't see what the point is," he said. "Putting Victor Holland in the hot seat."

"The point," said Dafoe, "is that you don't call the shots."

"I gave Holland my word he'd be left out of this mess."

"He's *part* of the mess! First he claims he has evidence, then he pulls a vanishing act."

"That's partly my fault. I never made it to the rendezvous."

"Why hasn't he tried to contact you?"

"I don't know." Polowski sighed and shook his head. "Maybe he's dead."

"Maybe we just need to find him." Dafoe reached for

the exercise handles. "Maybe you need to get to work on the Lanzano file. Or maybe you should just go home. You look terrible."

"Yeah. Sure." Polowski turned. As he left the office, he could hear Dafoe once again huffing and puffing. He went to his desk, sat down and contemplated his collection of cold capsules, aspirin and cough syrup. He took a double dose of each. Then he reached in his briefcase and pulled out the Viratek file.

It was his own private collection of scrambled notes and phone numbers and news clippings. He sifted through them, stopping to ponder once again the link between Holland and the woman Catherine Weaver. He'd first seen her name on the hospital admission sheet, and had later been startled to hear of her connection to the murdered Garberville woman. Too many coincidences, too many twists and turns. Was there something obvious here he was missing? Might the woman have an answer or two?

He reached for the telephone and dialed the Garberville police department. They would know how to reach their witness. And maybe she would know how to find Victor Holland. It was a long shot but Sam Polowski was an inveterate horseplayer. He had a penchant for long shots.

THE MAN RINGING his doorbell looked like a tree stump dressed in a brown polyester suit. Jack opened the door and said, "Sorry, I'm not buying today."

"I'm not selling anything, Mr. Zuckerman," said the man. "I'm with the FBI."

Jack sighed. "Not again."

"I'm Special Agent Sam Polowski. I'm trying to locate a woman named Catherine Weaver, formerly Zuckerman. I believe she—"

"Don't you guys ever know when to quit?"

"Quit what?"

"One of your agents was here this morning. Talk to him!"

The man frowned. "One of *our* agents?"

"Yeah. And I just might register a complaint against him. Barged right in here without a warrant and started tramping all over my house."

"What did he look like?"

"Oh, I don't know! Dark hair, terrific build. But he could've used a course in charm school."

"Was he about my height?"

"Taller. Skinnier. Lots more hair."

"Did he give you his name? It wasn't Mac Braden, was it?"

"Naw, he didn't give me any name."

Polowski pulled out his badge. Jack squinted at the words: Federal Bureau of Investigation. "Did he show you one of these?" asked Polowski.

"No. He just asked about Cathy and some guy named Victor Holland. Whether I knew how to find them."

"Did you tell him?"

"That jerk?" Jack laughed. "I wouldn't bother to give him the time of day. I sure as hell wasn't going to tell him about—" Jack paused and cleared his throat. "I wasn't going to tell him anything. Even if I knew. Which I don't."

Polowski slipped his badge into his pocket, all the time gazing steadily at Jack. "I think we should talk, Mr. Zuckerman."

"What about?"

"About your ex-wife. About the fact she's in big trouble."

"That," sighed Jack, "I already know."

"She's going to get hurt. I can't fill you in on all the details because I'm still in the dark myself. But I do know one woman's already been hit. Your wife—"

"My ex-wife."

"Your ex-wife could be next."

Jack, unconvinced, merely looked at him.

"It's your duty as a citizen to tell me what you know," Polowski reminded him.

"My duty. Right."

"Look, cooperate, and you and me, we'll get along just fine. Give me grief, and I'll give *you* grief." Polowski smiled. Jack didn't. "Now, Mr. Zuckerman. Hey, can I call you Jack? Jack, why don't you tell me where she is? Before it's too late. For both of you."

Jack scowled at him. He drummed his fingers against the door frame. He debated. At last he stepped aside. "As a law-abiding citizen, I suppose it is my duty." Grudgingly, he waved the man in. "Oh, just come in, Polowski. I'll tell you what I know."

The window shattered, raining slivers into the gloomy space beyond.

Cathy winced at the sound. "Sorry, Hickey," she said under her breath.

"We'll make it up to him," said Victor, knocking off the remaining shards. "We'll send him a nice fat check. You see anyone?"

She glanced up and down the alley. Except for a crumpled newspaper tumbling past the trash cans, nothing moved. A few blocks away, car horns blared, the sounds of another Union Street traffic jam.

"All clear," she whispered.

"Okay." Victor draped his windbreaker over the sill. "Up you go."

He gave her a lift to the window. She clambered through and landed among the glass shards. Seconds later, Victor dropped down beside her.

They were standing in the studio dressing room. Against

one wall hung a rack of women's lingerie; against the other
were makeup tables and a long mirror.

Victor frowned at a cloud of peach silk flung over one
of the chairs. "What kind of photos does your friend take,
anyway?"

"Hickey specializes in what's politely known as 'bou-
doir portraits.'"

Victor's startled gaze turned to a black lace negligee
hanging from a wall hook. "Does that mean what I think
it means?"

"What do you think it means?"

"You know."

She headed into the next room. "Hickey insists it's not
pornography. It's tasteful erotic art...." She stopped in her
tracks as she came face-to-face with a photo blowup on the
wall. Naked limbs—eight, maybe more—were entwined
in a sort of human octopus. Nothing was left to the imagination. Nothing at all.

"Tasteful," Victor said dryly.

"That must be one of his, uh, commercial assignments."

"I wonder what product they were selling."

She turned and found herself staring at another photograph. This time it was two women, drop-dead gorgeous
and wearing not a stitch.

"Another commercial assignment?" Victor inquired politely over her shoulder.

She shook her head. "Don't ask."

In the front room they found a week's worth of mail piled
up beneath the door slot, darkroom catalogues and adver-
tising flyers. The roll of film Cathy had mailed the day before was not yet in the mound.

"I guess we just sit around and wait for the postman,"
she said.

He nodded. "Seems like a safe-enough place. Any
chance your friend keeps food around?"

"I seem to remember a refrigerator in the other room."

She led Victor into what Hickey had dubbed his "shoot-ing gallery." Cathy flipped the wall switch and the vast room was instantly illuminated by a dazzling array of spot-lights.

"So this is where he does it," said Victor, blinking in the sudden glare. He stepped over a jumble of electrical cords and slowly circled the room, regarding with humorous dis-belief the various props. It was a strange collection of ob-jects: a genuine English phone booth, a street bench, an exercise bicycle. In a place of honor sat a four-poster bed. The ruffled coverlet was Victorian; the handcuffs dangling from the bedposts were not.

Victor picked up one of the cuffs and let it fall again. "Just how good a friend *is* this Hickey guy, anyway?"

"None of this stuff was here when he shot me a month ago."

"He photographed *you?*" Victor turned and stared at her.

She flushed, imagining the images that must be flash-ing through his mind. She could feel his gaze undressing her, posing her in a sprawl across that ridiculous four-poster bed. With the handcuffs, no less.

"It wasn't like—like these other photos," she protested. "I mean, I just did it as a favor...."

"A favor?"

"It was a purely *commercial* shot!"

"Oh."

"I was fully dressed. In overalls, as a matter of fact. I was supposed to be a plumber."

"A lady plumber?"

"I was an emergency stand-in. One of his models didn't show up that day, and he needed someone with an ordi-nary face. I guess that's me. Ordinary. And it really was just my face."

"And your overalls."

"Right."

They looked at each other and burst out laughing.

"I can guess what you were thinking," she said.

"I don't even want to *tell* you what I was thinking." He turned and glanced around the room. "Didn't you say there was some food around here?"

She crossed the room to the refrigerator. Inside she found a shelf of film plus a jar of sweet pickles, some rubbery carrots and half a salami. In the freezer they discovered real treasures: ground Sumatran coffee and a loaf of sourdough bread.

Grinning, she turned to him. "A feast!"

They sat together on the four-poster bed and gnawed on salami and half-frozen sourdough, all washed down with cups of coffee. It was a bizarre little picnic, paper plates with pickles and carrots resting in their laps, the spotlights glaring down like a dozen hot suns from the ceiling.

"Why did you say that about yourself?" he asked, watching her munch a carrot.

"Say what?"

"That you're ordinary. So ordinary that you get cast as the lady plumber?"

"Because I am ordinary."

"I don't think so. And I happen to be a pretty good judge of character."

She looked up at a wall poster featuring one of Hickey's super models. The woman stared back with a look of glossy confidence. "Well, I certainly don't measure up to *that*."

"*That*," he said, "is pure fantasy. *That* isn't a real woman, but an amalgam of makeup, hairspray and fake eyelashes."

"Oh, I know that. That's my job, turning actors into some moviegoer's fantasy. Or nightmare, as the case may be." She reached into the jar and fished out the last pickle. "No, I really meant *underneath* it all. Deep inside, I *feel* ordinary."

"I think you're quite extraordinary. And after last night, I should know."

She gazed down, at the limp carrot stretched out like a little corpse across the paper plate. "There was a time—I suppose there's always that time, for everyone, when we're still young, when we feel special. When we feel the world's meant just for us. The last time I felt that way was when I married Jack." She sighed. "It didn't last long."

"Why did you marry him?"

"I don't know. Dazzle? I was only twenty-three, a mere apprentice on the set. He was the director." She paused. "He was *God*."

"He impressed you, did he?"

"Jack can be very impressive. He can turn on the power, the charisma, and just overwhelm a gal. Then there was the champagne, the suppers, the flowers. I think what attracted him to me was that I didn't immediately fall for him. That I wasn't swooning at his every look. He thought of me as a challenge, the one he finally conquered." She gave him a rueful look. "That accomplished, he moved onto bigger and better things. That's when I realized that I wasn't particularly special. That I'm really just a perfectly ordinary woman. It's not a bad feeling. It's not as if I go through life longing to be someone different, someone special."

"Then who do you consider special?"

"Well, my grandmother. But she's dead."

"Venerable grandmothers always make the list."

"Okay, then. Mother Teresa."

"She's on everyone's list."

"Kate Hepburn. Gloria Steinem. My friend Sarah…" Her voice faded. Looking down, she added softly: "But she's dead, too."

Gently he took her hand. With a strange sense of wonder she watched his long fingers close over hers and thought about how the strength she felt in that grasp reflected the strength of the man himself. Jack, for all his dazzle and polish, had never inspired a fraction of the confidence she now felt in Victor. No man ever had.

He was watching her with quiet sympathy. "Tell me about Sarah," he said.

Cathy swallowed, trying to stem the tears. "She was absolutely lovely. I don't mean in *that* way." She nodded at the photo of Hickey's picture-perfect model. "I mean, in an inner sort of way. It was this look in her eyes. A perfect calmness. As though she'd found exactly what she wanted while all the rest of us were still grubbing around for lost treasure. I don't think she was born like that. She came to it, all by herself. In college, we were both pretty unsure of ourselves. Marriage certainly didn't help either of us. My divorce—it was nothing short of devastating. But Sarah's divorce only seemed to make her stronger. Better able to take care of herself. When she finally got pregnant, it was exactly as she planned it. There wasn't a father, you see, just a test tube. An anonymous donor. Sarah used to say that the primeval family unit wasn't man, woman and child. It was just woman and child. I thought she was brave, to take that step. She was a lot braver than I could ever be...." She cleared her throat. "Anyway, Sarah *was* special. Some people simply are."

"Yes," he said. "Some people are."

She looked up at him. He was staring off at the far wall, his gaze infinitely sad. What had etched those lines of pain in his face? She wondered if lines so deep could ever be erased. There were some losses one never got over, never accepted.

Softly she asked, "What was your wife like?"

He didn't answer at first. She thought: *Why did I ask that? Why did I have to bring up such terrible memories?*

He said, "She was a kind woman. That's what I'll always remember about her. Her kindness." He looked at Cathy and she sensed it wasn't sadness she saw in those eyes, but acceptance.

"What was her name?"

"Lily. Lillian Dorinda Cassidy. A mouthful for such a tiny woman." He smiled. "She was about five foot one, maybe ninety pounds sopping wet. It used to scare me, how small she always seemed. Almost breakable. Especially toward the end, when she'd lost all that weight. It seemed as if she'd shrunk down to nothing but a pair of big brown eyes."

"She must have been young when she died."

"Only thirty-eight. It seemed so unfair. All her life, she'd done everything right. Never smoked, hardly ever touched a glass of wine. She even refused to eat meat. After she was diagnosed, we kept trying to figure out how it could've happened. Then it occurred to us what might have caused it. She grew up in a small town in Massachusetts. Directly downwind from a nuclear power plant."

"You think that was it?"

"One can never be sure. But we asked around. And we learned that, just in her neighborhood, at least twenty families had someone with leukemia. It took four years and a class-action suit to force an investigation. What they found was a history of safety violations going back all the way to the plant's opening."

Cathy shook her head in disbelief. "And all those years they allowed it to operate?"

"No one knew about it. The violations were hushed up so well even the federal regulators were kept in the dark."

"They shut it down, didn't they?"

He nodded. "I can't say I got much satisfaction, seeing the plant finally close. By that time Lily was gone. And all the families, well, we were exhausted by the fight. Even though it sometimes felt as though we were banging our heads against a wall, we knew it was something we had to

do. *Somebody* had to do it, for all the Lilys of the world."
He looked up, at the spotlights shining above. "And here I
am again, still banging my head against walls. Only this
time, it feels like the Great Wall of China. And the lives at
stake are yours and mine."

Their gazes met. She sat absolutely still as he lightly
stroked down the curve of her cheek. She took his hand,
pressed it to her lips. His fingers closed over hers, refusing
to release her hand. Gently he tugged her close. Their lips
met, a tentative kiss that left her longing for more.

"I'm sorry you were pulled into this," he murmured.
"You and Sarah and those other Cathy Weavers. None of
you asked to be part of it. And somehow I've managed to
hurt you all."

"Not you, Victor. You're not the one to blame. It's this
windmill you're tilting at. This giant, dangerous windmill.
Anyone else would have dropped his lance and fled. You're
still going at it."

"I didn't have much of a choice."

"But you did. You could have walked away from your
friend's death. Turned a blind eye to whatever's going on
at Viratek. That's what Jack would have done."

"But I'm not Jack. There are things I can't walk away
from. I'd always be thinking of the Lilys. All the thousands
of people who might get hurt."

At the mention once again of his dead wife, Cathy
felt some unbreachable barrier form between them—the
shadow of Lily, the wife she'd never met. Cathy drew back,
at once aching from the loss of his touch.

"You think that many people could die?" she asked.

"Jerry must have thought so. There's no way to predict
the outcome. The world's never seen the effects of all-out
biological warfare. I like to think it's because we're too
smart to play with our own self-destruction. Then I think

of all the crazy things people have done over the years and it scares me...."

"Are viral weapons that dangerous?"

"If you alter a few genes, make it just a little more contagious, raise the kill ratio, you'd end up with a devastating strain. The research alone is hazardous. A single slip-up in lab security and you could have millions of people accidentally infected. And no means of treatment. It's the kind of worldwide disaster a scientist doesn't want to think about."

"Armageddon."

He nodded, his gaze frighteningly sane. "If you believe in such a thing. That's exactly what it'd be."

She shook her head. "I don't understand why these things are allowed."

"They aren't. By international agreement, they're outlawed. But there's always some madman lurking in the shadows who wants that extra bit of leverage, that weapon no one else has."

A madman. That's what one would have to be, to even think of unleashing such a weapon on the world. She thought of a novel she'd read, about just such a plague, how the cities had lain dead and decaying, how the very air had turned poisonous. But those were only the nightmares of science fiction. This was real.

From somewhere in the building came the sound of whistling.

Cathy and Victor both sat up straight. The melody traveled along the hall, closer and closer, until it stopped right outside Hickey's door. They heard a rustling, then the slap of magazines hitting the floor.

"It's here!" said Cathy, leaping to her feet.

Victor was right behind her as she hurried into the front room. She spotted it immediately, sitting atop the pile: a padded envelope, addressed in her handwriting. She scooped it up and ripped the envelope open. Out slid the roll of film. The note she'd scribbled to Hickey fluttered to the floor. Grinning in triumph, she held up the canister. "Here's your evidence!"

"We hope. Let's see what we've got on the roll. Where's the darkroom?"

"Next to the dressing room." She handed him the film. "Do you know how to process it?"

"I've done some amateur photography. As long as I've got the chemicals I can—" He stopped and glanced over at the desk.

The phone was ringing.

Victor shook his head. "Ignore it," he said and turned for the darkroom.

As they left the reception room, they heard the answering machine click on. Hickey's voice, smooth as silk, spoke on the recording. "This is the studio of Hickman Von Trapp, specializing in tasteful and artistic images of the female form...."

Victor laughed. "Tasteful?"

"It depends on your taste," said Cathy as she followed him up the hall.

They had just reached the darkroom when the recording ended and was followed by the message beep. An agitated voice rattled from the speaker. "Hello? Hello, Cathy? If you're there, answer me, will you? There's an FBI agent looking for you—some guy named Polowski—"

Cathy stopped dead. "It's Jack!" she said, turning to retrace her steps toward the front room.

The voice on the speaker had taken on a note of panic. "I couldn't help it—he made me tell him about Hickey. Get out of there now!"

The message clicked off just as Cathy grabbed the receiver. "Hello? *Jack?*"

She heard only the dial tone. He'd already hung up. Hands shaking, she began to punch in Jack's phone number.

"There's no time!" said Victor.

"I have to talk to him——"

He grabbed the receiver and slammed it down. "Later! We have to get out of here!"

She nodded numbly and started for the door. There she halted. "Wait. We need money!" She turned back to the reception desk and searched the drawers until she found the petty cash box. Twenty-two dollars was all it contained. "Always keep just enough for decent coffee beans," Hickey used to say. She pocketed the money. Then she reached up and yanked one of Hickey's old raincoats from the door hook. He wouldn't miss it. And she might need it for concealment. "Okay," she said, slipping on the coat. "Let's go."

They paused only a second to check the corridor. From another suite came the faint echo of laughter. Somewhere above, high heels clicked across a wooden floor. With Victor in the lead, they darted down the hall and out the front door.

The midday sun seemed to glare down on them like an accusing eye. Quickly they fell into step with the rest of the lunch crowd, the businessmen and artists, the Union Street chic. No one glanced their way. But even with people all around her, Cathy felt conspicuous. As though, in this bright cityscape of crowds and concrete, she was the focus of the painter's eye.

She huddled deeper into the raincoat, wishing it were a mantle of invisibility. Victor had quickened his pace, and she had to run to keep up.

"Where do we go now?" she whispered.

"We've got the film. Now I say we head for the bus station."

"And then?"

"Anywhere." He kept his gaze straight ahead. "As long as it's out of this city."

Chapter Seven

That pesky FBI agent was ringing his doorbell again.

Sighing, Jack opened the front door. "Back already?"

"Damn right I'm back." Polowski stamped in and shoved the door closed behind him. "I want to know where to find 'em next."

"I told you, Mr. Polowski. Over on Union Street there's a studio owned by Mr. Hickman—"

"I've been to Von Whats-his-name's studio."

Jack swallowed. "You didn't find them?"

"You knew I wouldn't. You warned 'em, didn't you?"

"Really, I don't know why you're harrassing me. I've tried to be—"

"They left in a hurry. The door was wide open. Food was still lying around. They left the empty cash box just sitting on the desk."

Jack drew himself up in outrage. "Are you calling my ex-wife a petty thief?"

"I'm calling her a desperate woman. And I'm calling you an imbecile for screwing things up. Now where is she?"

"I don't know."

"Who would she turn to?"

"No one I know."

"Think harder."

Jack stared down at Polowski's turgid face and marveled

that any human being could be so unattractive. Surely the process of natural selection would have dictated against such unacceptable genes?

Jack shook his head. "I honestly don't know."

It was the truth, and Polowski must have sensed it. After a moment of silent confrontation, he backed off. "Then maybe you can tell me this. Why did you warn them?"

"It—it was—" Jack shrugged helplessly. "Oh, I don't know! After you left, I wasn't sure I'd done the right thing. I wasn't sure whether to trust you. *He* doesn't trust you."

"Who?"

"Victor Holland. He thinks you're in on some conspiracy. Frankly, the man struck me as just the slightest bit paranoid."

"He has a right to be. Considering what's happened to him so far." Polowski turned for the door.

"Now what happens?"

"I keep looking for them."

"Where?"

"You think I'd tell *you*?" He stalked out. "Don't leave town, Zuckerman," he snapped over his shoulder. "I'll be back to see you later."

"I don't think so," Jack muttered softly as he watched the other man lumber back to his car. He looked up and saw there wasn't a cloud in the sky. Smiling to himself, he shut the door.

It would be sunny in Mexico, as well.

SOMEONE HAD LEFT in a hurry.

Savitch strolled through the rooms of the photo studio, which had been left unlocked. He noted the scraps of a meal on the four-poster bed: crumbs of sourdough bread, part of a salami, an empty pickle jar. He also took note of the coffee cups: there were two of them. Interesting, since Savitch had spotted only one person leaving the studio, a squat little man in a polyester suit. The man hadn't been there long. Savitch had observed him climb into a dark green Ford parked at a fifteen-minute meter. The meter still had three minutes remaining.

Savitch continued his tour of the studio, eyeing the tawdry photos, wondering if this wasn't another waste of his time. After all, every other address he'd pulled from the woman's black book had turned up no sign of her. Why should Hickman Von Trapp's address be any different?

Still, he couldn't shake the instinct that he was getting close. Clues were everywhere. He read them, put them together. Today, this studio had been visited by two hungry people. They'd entered through a broken window in the dressing room. They'd eaten scraps taken from the refrigerator. They (or the man in the polyester suit) had emptied the petty cash box.

Savitch completed his tour and returned to the front room. That's when he noticed the telephone message machine blinking on and off.

He pressed the play button. The string of messages seemed endless. The calls were for someone named Hickey—no doubt the Hickman Von Trapp of the address book. Savitch lazily circled the room, half listening to the succession of voices. Business calls for the most part, inquiring about appointments, asking when proofs would be ready and would he like to do the shoot for *Snoop* magazine? Near the door, Savitch halted and stooped down to sift through the pile of mail. It was boring stuff, all addressed to Von Trapp. Then he noticed, off to the side, a loose slip of paper. It was a note, addressed to Hickey.

"Feel awful about this, but someone stole all those rolls of film from my car. This was the only one left. Thought

I'd get it to you before it's lost, as well. Hope it's enough to save your shoot from being a complete waste—"

It was signed "Cathy."

He stood up straight. Catherine Weaver? It had to be! The roll of film—where the hell was the roll of film?

He rifled through the mail, searching, searching. He turned up only a torn envelope with Cathy Weaver's return address. The film was gone. In frustration, he began to fling magazines across the room. Then, in mid-toss, he froze.

A new message was playing on the recorder.

"Hello? Hello, Cathy? If you're there, answer me, will you? There's an FBI agent looking for you—some guy named Polowski. I couldn't help it—he made me tell him about Hickey. Get out of there now!"

Savitch stalked over to the answering machine and stared down as the mechanism automatically whirred back to the beginning. He replayed it.

Get out of there now!

There was now no doubt. Catherine Weaver had been here, and Victor Holland was with her. But who was this agent Polowski and why was he searching for Holland? Savitch had been assured that the Bureau was off the case. He would have to check into the matter.

He crossed over to the window and stared out at the bright sunshine, the crowded sidewalks. So many faces, so many strangers. Where, in this city, would two terrified fugitives hide? Finding them would be difficult, but not impossible.

He left the suite and went outside to a pay phone. There he dialed a Washington, D.C., number. He wasn't fond of asking the Cowboy for help, but now he had no choice. Victor Holland had his hands on the evidence, and the stakes had shot sky-high.

It was time to step up the pursuit.

THE CLERK YELLED, "Next window, please!" and closed the grate.

"Wait!" cried Cathy, tapping at the pane. "My bus is leaving right now!"

"Which one?"

"Number 23 to Palo Alto—"

"There's another at seven o'clock."

"But—"

"I'm on my dinner break."

Cathy stared helplessly as the clerk walked away. Over the PA system came the last call for the Palo Alto express. Cathy glanced around just in time to see the Number 23 roar away from the curb.

"Service just ain't what it used to be," an old man muttered behind her. "Get there faster usin' yer damn thumb."

Sighing, Cathy shifted to the next line, which was eight-deep and slow as molasses. The woman at the front was trying to convince the clerk that her social security card was an acceptable ID for a check.

Okay, Cathy thought. *So we leave at seven o'clock. That puts us in Palo Alto at eight. Then what? Camp in a park? Beg a few scraps from a restaurant? What does Victor have in mind...?*

She glanced around and spotted his broad back hunched inside one of the phone booths. Whom could he possibly be calling? She saw him hang up and run his hand wearily through his hair. Then he picked up the receiver and dialed another number.

"Next!" Someone tapped Cathy on the shoulder. "Go ahead, Miss."

Cathy turned and saw that the ticket clerk was waiting. She stepped to the window.

"Where to?" asked the clerk.

"I need two tickets to..." Cathy's voice suddenly faded.

"Where?"

Cathy didn't speak. Her gaze had frozen on a poster tacked right beside the ticket window. The words Have You seen This Man? appeared above an unsmiling photo of Victor Holland. And at the bottom were listed the charges: Industrial espionage and murder. If you have any information about this man, please contact your local police or the FBI.

"Lady, you wanna go somewhere or not?"

"What?" Cathy's gaze jerked back to the clerk, who was watching her with obvious annoyance. "Oh. Yes, I'm—I'd like two tickets. To Palo Alto." Numbly she handed over a fistful of cash. "One way."

"Two to Palo Alto. That bus will depart at 7:00, Gate 11."

"Yes. Thank you..." Cathy took the tickets and turned to leave the line. That's when she spotted the two policemen, standing just inside the front entrance. They seemed to be scanning the terminal, searching—for what?

In a panic, her gaze shot to the phone booth. It was empty. She stared at it with a sense of abandonment. *You left me! You left me with two tickets to Palo Alto and five bucks in my pocket!*

Where are you, Victor?

She couldn't stand here like an idiot. She had to do something, had to move. She pulled the raincoat tightly around her shoulders and forced herself to stroll across the terminal. *Don't let them notice me,* she prayed. *Please. I'm nobody. Nothing.* She paused at a chair and picked up a discarded *San Francisco Chronicle.* Then, thumbing through the Want Ads, she sauntered right past the two policemen. They didn't even glance at her as she went out the front entrance.

Now what? she wondered, pausing amidst the confusion of a busy sidewalk. Automatically she started to walk and had taken only half a dozen steps down the street when she was wrenched sideways, into an alley.

She reeled back against the trash cans and almost sobbed with relief. "Victor!"

"Did they see you?"

"No. I mean, yes, but they didn't seem to care—"

"Are you sure?" She nodded. He turned and slapped the wall in frustration. "What the hell do we do now?"

"I have the tickets."

"We can't use them."

"How are we going to get out of town? Hitchhike? Victor, we're down to our last five dollars!"

"They'll be watching every bus that leaves. And they've got my face plastered all over the damn terminal!" He slumped back against the wall and groaned. "*Have you seen this man?* God, I looked like some two-bit gangster."

"It wasn't the most flattering photo."

He managed to laugh. "Have you *ever* seen a flattering wanted poster?"

She leaned back beside him, against the wall. "We've got to get out of this city, Victor."

"Amend that. *You've* got to get out."

"What's that supposed to mean?"

"The police aren't looking for you. So *you* take that bus to Palo Alto. I'll put you in touch with some old friends. They'll see you make it somewhere safe."

"No."

"Cathy, they've probably got my mug posted in every airport and car rental agency in town! We've spent almost all our money for those bus tickets. I say you use them!"

"I'm not leaving you."

"You don't have a choice."

"Yes I do. I choose to stick to you like glue. Because you're the only one I feel safe with. The only one I can count on!"

"I can move faster on my own. Without you slowing me

down." He looked off, toward the street. "Hell, I don't even *want* you around."

"I don't believe that."

"Why should I care what you believe?"

"Look at me! Look at me and say that!" She grabbed his arm, willing him to face her. "Say you don't want me around!"

He started to speak, to repeat the lie. She knew then that it *was* a lie; she could see it in his eyes. And she saw something else in that gaze, something that took her breath away.

He said, "I don't—I won't have you—"

She just stood there, looking up at him, waiting for the truth to come.

What she didn't expect was the kiss. She never remembered how it happened. She only knew that all at once his arms were around her and she was being swept up into some warm and safe and wonderful place. It started as an embrace more of desperation than passion, a coming together of two terrified people. But the instant their lips met, it became something much more. This went beyond fear, beyond need. This was a souls' joining, one that wouldn't be broken, even after this embrace was over, even if they never touched again.

When at last they drew apart and stared at each other, the taste of him was still fresh on her lips.

"You see?" she whispered. "I was right. You do want me around. You do."

He smiled and touched her cheek. "I'm not a very good liar."

"And I'm not leaving you. You need me. You can't show your face, but I can! I can buy bus tickets, run errands—"

"What I really need," he sighed, "is a new face." He glanced out at the street. "Since there's no plastic surgeon handy, I suggest we hoof it over to the BART station. It'll be crowded at this hour. We might make it to the East Bay—"

"God, I'm such an *idiot!*" she groaned. "A new face is exactly what you need!" She turned toward the street. "Come on. There isn't much time...."

"Cathy?" He followed her up the alley. They both paused, scanning the street for policemen. There were none in sight. "Where are we going?" he whispered.

"To find a phone booth."

"Oh. And who are we calling?"

She turned and the look she gave him was distinctly pained. "Someone we both know and love."

JACK WAS PACKING his suitcase when the phone rang. He considered not answering it, but something about the sound, an urgency that could only have been imagined, made him pick up the receiver. He was instantly sorry he had.

"Jack?"

He sighed. "Tell me I'm hearing things."

"Jack, I'm going to talk fast because your phone might be tapped—"

"You don't say."

"I need my kit. The whole shebang. And some cash. I swear I'll pay it all back. Get it for me right now. Then drop it off where we shot the last scene of *Cretinoid*. You know the spot."

"Cathy, you wait a minute! I'm in trouble enough as it is!"

"One hour. That's all I can wait."

"It's rush hour! I can't—"

"It's the last favor I'll ask of you." There was a pause. Then, softly, she added, "Please."

He let out a breath. "This is the absolute last time, right?"

"One hour, Jack. I'll be waiting."

Jack hung up and stared at his suitcase. It was only half packed, but it would have to do. He sure as hell wasn't coming back *here* tonight.

He closed the suitcase and carried it out to the Jaguar. As he drove away it suddenly occurred to him that he'd forgotten to cancel his date with Lulu tonight.

No time now, he thought. I've got more important things on my mind—like getting out of town.

Lulu would be mad as a hornet, but he'd make it up to her. Maybe a pair of diamond ear studs. Yeah, that would do the trick.

Good old Lulu, so easy to please. Now there was a woman he could understand.

THE CORNER OF Fifth and Mission was a hunker-down, chew-the-fat sort of gathering place for the street folk. At five forty-five it was even busier than usual. Rumor had it the soup kitchen down the block was fixing to serve beef Bourguignonne, which, as those who remembered better days and better meals could tell you, was made with red wine. No one passed up the chance for a taste of the grape, even if every drop of alcohol was simmered clean out of it. And so they stood around on the corner, talking of other meals they'd had, of the weather, of the long lines at the unemployment office.

No one noticed the two wretched souls huddled in the doorway of the pawnshop.

Lucky for us, thought Cathy, burying herself in the folds of the raincoat. The sad truth was, they were both beginning to fit right into this crowd. Just a moment earlier she'd caught sight of her own reflection in the pawnshop window and had almost failed to recognize the disheveled image staring back. *Has it been that long since I've combed my hair? That long since I've had a meal or a decent night's sleep?*

Victor looked no better. A torn shirt and two days' worth of stubble on his jaw only emphasized that unmistakable look of exhaustion. He could walk into that soup kitchen down the block and no one would look twice.

He's going to look a hell of a lot worse when I get through with him, she thought with a grim sense of humor.

If Jack ever showed up with the kit.

"It's 6:05," Victor muttered. "He's had an hour."

"Give him time."

"We're running out of time."

"We can still make the bus." She peered up the street, as though by force of will she could conjure up her ex-husband. But only a city bus barreled into view. *Come on, Jack, come on! Don't let me down this time....*

"Will ya lookit that!" came a low growl, followed by general murmurs of admiration from the crowd.

"Hey, pretty boy!" someone called as the group gathered on the corner to stare. "What'd you have to push to get yerself wheels like that?"

Through the gathering of men, Cathy spied the bright gleam of chrome and burgundy. "Get away from my car!" demanded a querulous voice. "I just had her waxed!"

"Looks like Pretty Boy got hisself lost. Turned down the wrong damn street, did ya?"

Cathy leaped to her feet. "He's here!"

She and Victor pushed through the crowd to find Jack standing guard over the Jaguar's gleaming finish.

"Don't—don't touch her!" he snapped as one man ran a grimy finger across the hood. "Why can't you people go find yourselves a job or something?"

"A job?" someone yelled. "What's that?"

"Jack!" called Cathy.

Jack let out a sigh of relief when he spotted her. "This is the last favor. The absolute *last* favor—"

"Where is it?" she asked.

Jack walked around to the trunk, where he slapped away another hand as it stroked the Jaguar's burgundy flank. "It's right here. The whole kit and kaboodle." He swung out the makeup case and handed it over. "Delivered as promised. Now I gotta run."

"Where are you going?" she called.

"I don't know." He climbed back into the car. "Somewhere. Anywhere!"

"Sounds like we're headed in the same direction."

"God, I hope not." He started the engine and revved it up a few times.

Someone yelled: "So long, Pretty Boy!"

Jack gazed out dryly at Cathy. "You know, you really should do something about the company you keep. Ciao, sweetcakes."

The Jaguar lurched away. With a screech of tires, it spun around the corner and vanished into traffic.

Cathy turned and saw that every eye was watching her. Automatically, Victor moved close beside her, one tired and hungry man facing a tired and hungry crowd.

Someone called out: "So who's the jerk in the Jag?"

"My ex-husband," said Cathy.

"Doin' a lot better than you are, honey."

"No kidding." She held up the makeup case and managed a careless laugh. "I ask the creep for my clothes, he throws me a change of underwear."

"Babe, now ain't that just the way it works?"

Already, the men were wandering away, regrouping in doorways, or over by the corner newsstands. The Jaguar was gone, and so was their interest.

Only one man stood before Cathy and Victor, and the

look he gave them was distinctly sympathetic. "That's all he left you, huh? Him with that nice, fancy car?" He turned to leave, then glanced back at them. "Say, you two need a place to stay or somethin'? I got a lot of friends. And I hate to see a lady out in the cold."

"Thanks for the offer," said Victor, taking Cathy's hand. "But we've got a bus to catch."

The man nodded and shuffled away, a kind but unfortunate soul whom the streets had not robbed of decency.

"We have a half hour to get on that bus," said Victor, hurrying Cathy along. "Better get to work."

They were headed up the street, toward the cover of an alley, when Cathy suddenly halted. "Victor—"

"What's the matter?"

"Look." She pointed at the newsstand, her hand shaking.

Beneath the plastic cover was the afternoon edition of the *San Francisco Examiner.* The headline read: "Two Victims, Same Name. Police Probe Coincidence." Beside it was a photo of a young blond woman. The caption was hidden by the fold, but Cathy didn't need to read it. She could already guess the woman's name.

"Two of them," she whispered. "Victor, you were right...."

"All the more reason for us to get out of town." He pulled on her arm. "Hurry."

She let him lead her away. But even as they headed down the street, even as they left the newsstand behind them, she carried that image in her mind: the photograph of a blond woman, the second victim.

The second Catherine Weaver.

PATROLMAN O'HANLEY WAS a helpful soul. Unlike too many of his colleagues, O'Hanley had joined the force out of a true desire to serve and protect. The "Boy Scout" was what the other men called him behind his back. The epithet both annoyed and pleased him. It told him he didn't fit in with the rough-and-tumble gang on the force. It also told him he was above it all, above the petty bribe-taking and backbiting and maneuverings for promotion. He wasn't out to glorify the badge on his chest. What he wanted was the chance to pat a kid on the head, rescue an old granny from a mugging.

That's why he found this particular assignment so frustrating. All this standing around in the bus depot, watching for a man some witness *might* have spotted a few hours ago. O'Hanley hadn't noticed any such character. He'd eyeballed every person who'd walked in the door. A sorry lot, most of them. Not surprising since, these days, anyone with the cash to spare took a plane. By the looks of these folks, none of 'em could spare much more than pennies. Take that pair over there, huddled together in the waiting area. A father and daughter, he figured, and both of 'em down on their luck. The daughter was bundled up in an old raincoat, the collar pulled up to reveal only a mop of windblown hair. The father was an even sorrier sight, gaunt-faced, white-whiskered, about as old as Methuselah. Still, there was a remnant of pride in the old codger—O'Hanley could see it in the way the man held himself, stiff and straight. Must've been an impressive fellow in his younger years since he was still well over six feet tall.

The public speaker announced final boarding for number fourteen to Palo Alto.

The old man and his daughter rose to their feet.

O'Hanley watched with concern as the pair shuffled across the terminal toward the departure gate. The woman was carrying only one small case, but it appeared to be a heavy one. And she already had her hands full, trying to guide the old man in the right direction. But they were making progress, and O'Hanley figured they'd make it to the bus okay.

That is, until the kid ran into them.

He was about six, the kind of kid no mother wants to admit she produced, the kind of kid who gives all six-year-olds a bad name. For the last half hour the boy had been tearing around the terminal, scattering ashtray sand, tipping over suitcases, banging locker doors. Now he was running. Only this kid was doing it *backward.*

O'Hanley saw it coming. The old man and his daughter were crossing slowly toward the departure gate. The kid was scuttling toward them. Intersecting paths, inevitable collision. The kid slammed into the woman's knees; the case flew out of her grasp. She stumbled against her companion. O'Hanley, paralyzed, expected the codger to keel over. To his surprise, the old man simply caught the woman in his arms and handily set her back on her feet.

By now O'Hanley was hurrying to their aid. He got to the woman just as she'd regained her footing. "You folks okay?" he asked.

The woman reacted as though he'd slapped her. She stared up at him with the eyes of a terrified animal. "What?" she said.

"Are you okay? Looked to me like he hit you pretty hard."

She nodded.

"How 'bout you, Gramps?"

The woman glanced at her companion. It seemed to O'Hanley that there was a lot being said in that glance, a lot he wasn't privy to.

"We're both fine," the woman said quickly. "Come on, Pop. We'll miss our bus."

"Can I give you a hand with him?"

"That's mighty kind of you, officer, but we'll do fine."

The woman smiled at O'Hanley. Something about that smile wasn't right. As he watched the pair shuffle off toward bus number fourteen, O'Hanley kept trying to figure it out. Kept trying to put his finger on what was wrong with that pair of travelers.

He turned away and almost tripped over the fallen case. The woman had forgotten it. He snatched it up and started to run for the bus. Too late; the number fourteen to Palo Alto was already pulling away. O'Hanley stood helplessly on the curb, watching the taillights vanish around the corner.

Oh, well.

He turned in the makeup case at Lost and Found. Then he stationed himself once again at the entrance. Seven o'clock already and still no sighting of the suspect Victor Holland.

O'Hanley sighed. What a waste of a policeman's time.

FIVE MINUTES OUT of San Francisco, aboard the number fourteen bus, the old man turned to the woman in the raincoat and said, "This beard is killing me."

Laughing, Cathy reached up and gave the fake whiskers a tug. "It did the trick, didn't it?"

"No kidding. We practically got a police escort to the getaway bus." He scratched furiously at his chin. "Geez, how do those actors stand this stuff, anyway? The itch is driving me up a wall."

"Want me to take it off?"

"Better not. Not till we get to Palo Alto."

Another hour, she thought. She sat back and gazed out at the highway gliding past the bus window. "Then what?" she asked softly.

"I'll knock on a few doors. See if I can dig up an old friend or two. It's been a long time, but I think there are still a few in town."

"You used to live there?"

"Years ago. Back when I was in college."

"Oh." She sat up straight. "A *Stanford* man."

"Why do you make it sound just a tad disreputable?"

"I rooted for the Bears, myself."

"I'm consorting with the arch enemy?"

Giggling, she burrowed against his chest and inhaled the warm, familiar scent of his body. "It seems like another lifetime. Berkeley and blue jeans."

"Football. Wild parties."

"Wild parties?" she asked. "You?"

"Well, *rumors* of wild parties."

"Frisbee. Classes on the lawn…"

"Innocence," he said softly.

They both fell silent.

"Victor?" she asked. "What if your friends aren't there any longer? Or what if they won't take us in?"

"One step at a time. That's how we have to take it. Otherwise it'll all seem too overwhelming."

"It already does."

He squeezed her tightly against him. "Hey, we're doing okay. We made it out of the city. In fact, we waltzed out right under the nose of a cop. I'd call that pretty damn impressive."

Cathy couldn't help grinning at the memory of the earnest young Patrolman O'Hanley. "All policemen should be so helpful."

"Or blind," Victor snorted. "I can't believe he called me *Gramps*."

"When I set out to change a face, I do it right."

"Apparently."

She looped her arm through his and pressed a kiss to one scowling, bewhiskered cheek. "Can I tell you a secret?"

"What's that?"

"I'm crazy about older men."

The scowl melted away, slowly reformed into a dubious smile. "How much older are we talking about?"

She kissed him again, this time full on the lips. "Much older."

"Hm. Maybe these whiskers aren't so bad, after all." He took her face in his hands. This time he was the one kissing her, long and deeply, with no thought of where they were or where they were going. Cathy felt herself sliding back against the seat, into a space that was inescapable and infinitely safe.

Someone behind them hooted: "Way to go, Gramps!"

Reluctantly, they pulled apart. Through the flickering shadows of the bus, Cathy could see the twinkle in Victor's eyes, the gleam of a wry smile.

She smiled back and whispered, "Way to go, Gramps."

THE POSTERS WITH Victor Holland's face were plastered all over the bus station.

Polowski couldn't help a snort of irritation as he gazed at that unflattering visage of what he knew in his gut was an innocent man. A damn witchhunt, that's what this'd turned into. If Holland wasn't already scared enough, this public stalking would surely send him diving for cover, beyond the reach of those who could help him. Polowski only hoped it'd also be beyond the reach of those with less benign intentions.

With all these posters staring him in the face, Holland would've been a fool to stroll through this bus depot. Still, Polowski had an instinct about these things, a sense of how people behaved when they were desperate. If he were in Holland's shoes, a killer on his trail and a woman companion to worry about, he knew what *he'd* do—get the hell out of San Francisco. A plane was unlikely. According to Jack Zuckerman, Holland was operating on a thin wallet.

A credit card would've been out of the question. That also knocked out a rental car. What was left? It was either hitchhike or take the bus.

Polowski was betting on the bus.

His last piece of info supported that hunch. The tap on Zuckerman's phone had picked up a call from Cathy Weaver. She'd arranged some sort of drop-off at a site Polowski couldn't identify at first. He'd spent a frustrating hour asking around the office, trying to locate someone who'd not only seen Zuckerman's forgettable film, *Cretinoid,* but could also pinpoint where the last scene was filmed. The Mission District, some movie nut file clerk had finally told him. Yeah, she was sure of it. The monster came up through the manhole cover right at the corner of Fifth and Mission and slurped down a derelict or two just before the hero smashed him with a crated piano. Polowski hadn't stayed to hear the rest; he'd made a run for his car.

By that time, it was too late. Holland and the woman were gone, and Zuckerman had vanished. Polowski found himself cruising down Mission, his doors locked, his windows rolled up, wondering when the local police were going to clean up the damn streets.

That's when he remembered the bus depot was only a few blocks away.

Now, standing among the tired and slack-jawed travelers at the bus station, he was beginning to think he'd wasted his time. All those wanted posters staring him in the face. And there was a cop standing over by the coffee machine, taking furtive sips from a foam cup.

Polowski strolled over to the cop. "FBI," he said, flashing his badge.

The cop—he was scarcely more than a boy—instantly straightened. "Patrolman O'Hanley, sir."

"Seeing much action?"

"Uh—you mean today?"

"Yeah. Here."

"No, sir." O'Hanley sighed. "Pretty much a bust. I mean, I could be out on patrol. Instead they got me hanging around here eyeballing faces."

"Surveillance?"

"Yes, sir." He nodded at the poster of Holland. "That guy. Everyone's hot to find him. They say he's a spy."

"Do they, now?" Polowski took a lazy glance around the room. "Seen anyone around here who looks like him?"

"Not a one. I been watching every minute."

Polowski didn't doubt it. O'Hanley was the kind of kid who, if you asked him to, would scrub the Captain's boots with a toothbrush. He'd do a good job of it, too.

Obviously Holland hadn't come through here. Polowski turned to leave. Then another thought came to mind, and he turned back to O'Hanley. "The suspect may be traveling with a woman," he said. He pulled out a photo of Cathy Weaver, one Jack Zuckerman had been persuaded to donate to the FBI. "Have you seen her come through here?"

O'Hanley frowned. "Gee. She sure does look like… Naw. That can't be her."

"Who?"

"Well, there was this woman in here 'bout an hour ago. Kind of a down and outer. Some little brat ran smack into her. I sort've brushed her off and sent her on her way. She looked a lot like this gal, only in a lot worse shape."

"Was she traveling alone?"

"She had an old guy with her. Her pop, I think."

Suddenly Polowski was all ears. That instinct again—it was telling him something. "What did this old man look like?"

"Real old. Maybe seventy. Had this bushy beard, lot of white hair."

"How tall?"

"Pretty tall. Over six feet…" O'Hanley's voice trailed off as his gaze focused on the wanted poster. Victor Holland was six foot three. O'Hanley's face went white. "Oh, God…"

"Was it him?"

"I—I can't be sure—"

"Come on, come on!"

"I just don't know… Wait. The woman, she dropped a makeup case! I turned it in at that window there—"

It took only a flash of an FBI badge for the clerk in Lost and Found to hand over the case. The instant Polowski opened the thing, he knew he'd hit pay dirt. It was filled with theatrical makeup supplies. Stenciled inside the lid was: Property of Jack Zuckerman Productions.

He slammed the lid shut. "Where did they go?" he snapped at O'Hanley.

"They—uh, they boarded a bus right over there. That gate. Around seven o'clock."

Polowski glanced up at the departure schedule. At seven o'clock, the number fourteen had departed for Palo Alto.

It took him ten minutes to get hold of the Palo Alto depot manager, another five minutes to convince the man this wasn't just another Prince-Albert-in-the-can phone call.

"The number fourteen from San Francisco?" came the answer. "Arrived twenty minutes ago."

"What about the passengers?" pressed Polowski. "You see any of 'em still around?"

The manager only laughed. "Hey, man. If you had a choice, would *you* hang around a stinking bus station?"

Muttering an oath, Polowski hung up.

"Sir?" It was O'Hanley. He looked sick. "I messed up, didn't I? I let him walk right past me. I can't believe—"

"Forget it."

"But—"

Polowski headed for the exit. "You're just a rookie," he called over his shoulder. "Chalk it up to experience."

"Should I call this in?"

"I'll take care of it. I'm headed there, anyway."

"Where?"

Polowski shoved open the station door. "Palo Alto."

Chapter Eight

The front door was answered by an elderly oriental woman whose command of English was limited.

"Mrs. Lum? Remember me? Victor Holland. I used to know your son."

"Yes, yes!"

"Is he here?"

"Yes." Her gaze shifted to Cathy now, as though the woman didn't want her second visitor to feel left out of the conversation.

"I need to see him," said Victor. "Is Milo here?"

"Milo?" At last here was a word she seemed to know. She turned and called out loudly in Chinese.

Somewhere a door squealed open and footsteps stamped up the stairs. A fortyish oriental man in blue jeans and chambray shirt came to the front door. He was a dumpling of a fellow, and he brought with him the vague odor of chemicals, something sharp and acidic. He was wiping his hands on a rag.

"What can I do for you?" he asked.

Victor grinned. "Milo Lum! Are you still skulking around in your mother's basement?"

"Excuse me?" Milo inquired politely. "Am I supposed to know you, sir?"

"Don't recognize an old horn player from the Out of Tuners?"

Milo stared in disbelief. "Gershwin? That can't be *you?*"

"Yeah, I know," Victor said with a laugh. "The years haven't been kind."

"I didn't want to say anything, but…"

"I won't take it personally. Since—" Victor peeled off his false beard "—the face isn't all mine."

Milo gazed down at the lump of fake whispers, hanging like a dead animal in Victor's grasp. Then he stared up at Victor's jaw, still blotchy with spirit gum. "This is some kind of joke on old Milo, right?" He stuck his head out the door, glancing past Victor at the sidewalk. "And the other guys are hiding out there somewhere, waiting to yell *surprise!* Aren't they? Some big practical joke."

"I wish it were a joke," said Victor.

Milo instantly caught the undertone of urgency in Victor's voice. He looked at Cathy, then back at Victor. Nodding, he stepped aside. "Come in, Gersh. Sounds like I have some catching up to do."

Over a late supper of duck noodle soup and jasmine tea, Milo heard the story. He said little; he seemed more intent on slurping down the last of his noodles. Only when the ever-smiling Mrs. Lum had bowed good-night and creaked off to bed did Milo offer his comment.

"When you get in trouble, man, you sure as hell do it right."

"Astute as always, Milo," sighed Victor.

"Too bad we can't say the same for the cops," Milo snorted. "If they'd just bothered to ask around, they would've learned you're harmless. Far as I know, you're guilty of only one serious crime."

Cathy looked up, startled. "What crime?"

"Assaulting the ears of victims unlucky enough to hear his saxophone."

"This from a piccolo player who practises with earplugs," observed Victor.

"That's to drown out extraneous noise."

"Yeah. Mainly your own."

Cathy grinned. "I'm beginning to understand why you called yourselves the Out of Tuners."

"Just some healthy self-deprecating humor," said Milo. "Something we needed after we failed to make the Stanford band." Milo rose, shoving away from the kitchen table. "Well, come on. Let's see what's on that mysterious roll of film."

He led them along the hall and down a rickety set of steps to the basement. The chemical tang of the air, the row of trays lined up on a stainless-steel countertop and the slow drip, drip of water from the faucet told Cathy she was standing in an enormous darkroom. Tacked on the walls was a jumble of photos. Faces, mostly, apparently snapped around the world. Here and there she spotted a newsworthy shot: soldiers storming an airport, protestors unfurling a banner.

"Is this your job, Milo?" she asked.

"I wish," said Milo, agitating the developing canister. "No, I just work in the ol' family business."

"Which is?"

"Shoes. Italian, Brazilian, leather, alligator, you name it, we import it." He cocked his head at the photos. "That's how I get my exotic faces. Shoe-buying trips. I'm an expert on the female arch."

"For that," said Victor, "he spent four years at Stanford."

"Why not? Good a place as any to study the fine feet of the fair sex." A timer rang. Milo poured out the developer, removed the roll of film, and hung it up to dry. "Actually," he said, squinting at the negatives, "it was my dad's dying request. He wanted a son with a Stanford degree. I wanted four years of nonstop partying. We both got our wishes." He paused and gazed off wistfully at his photos. "Too bad I can't say the same of the years since then."

"What do you mean?" asked Cathy.

"I mean the partying's long since over. Gotta earn those profits, keep up those sales. Never thought life'd come down to the bottom line. Whatever happened to all that rabble-rousing potential, hey, Gersh? We sort of lost it along the way. All of us, Bach and Ollie and Roger. The Out of Tuners finally stepped into line. Now we're all marching to the beat of the same boring drummer." He sighed and glanced at Victor. "You make out anything on those negatives?"

Victor shook his head. "We need prints."

Milo flipped off the lights, leaving only the red glow of the darkroom lamp. "Coming up."

As Milo laid out the photographic paper, Victor asked, "What happened to the other guys? They still around?"

Milo flipped the exposure switch. "Roger's VP at some multinational bank in Tokyo. Into silk suits and ties, the whole nine yards. Bach's got an electronics firm in San José."

"And Ollie?"

"What can I say about Ollie?" Milo slipped the first print into the bath. "He's still lurking around in that lab over at Stanford Med. I doubt he ever sees the light of day. I figure he's got some secret chamber in the basement where he keeps his assistant Igor chained to the wall."

"This guy I have to meet," said Cathy.

"Oh, he'd love you." Victor laughed and gave her arm a squeeze. "Seeing as he's probably forgotten what the female of the species looks like."

Milo slid the print into the next tray. "Yeah, Ollie's the

one who never changed. Still the night owl. Still plays a mean clarinet." He glanced at Victor. "How's the sax, Gersh? You keeping it up?"

"Haven't played in months."

"Lucky neighbors."

"How did you ever get that name?" asked Cathy. "Gersh?"

"Because," said Milo, wielding tongs as he transferred another batch of prints between trays, "he's a firm believer in the power of George Gershwin to win a lady's heart. 'Someone to Watch Over Me,' wasn't that the tune that made Lily say..." Milo's voice suddenly faded. He looked at his friend with regret.

"You're right," said Victor quietly. "That was the tune. And Lily said yes."

Milo shook his head. "Sorry. Guess I still have a hard time remembering she's gone."

"Well, she is," said Victor, his voice matter-of-fact. Cathy knew there was pain buried in the undertones. But he hid it well. "And right now," Victor said, "we've got other things to think about."

"Yeah." Milo, chastened, turned his attention back to the prints he'd just developed. He fished them out and clipped the first few sheets on the line to dry. "Okay, Gersh. Tell us what's on this roll that's worth killing for."

Milo switched on the lights.

Victor stood in silence for a moment, frowning at the first five dripping prints. To Cathy, the data was meaningless, only a set of numbers and codes, recorded in an almost illegible hand.

"Well," grunted Milo. "That sure tells me a lot."

Victor's gaze shifted quickly from one page to the next. He paused at the fifth photo, where a column ran down the length of the page. It contained a series of twenty-seven entries, each one a date followed by the same three letters: EXP.

"Victor?" asked Cathy. "What does it mean?"

He turned to them. It was the look in his eyes that worried her. The stillness. Quietly he said, "We need to call Ollie."

"You mean tonight?" asked Milo. "Why?"

"This isn't just some experiment in test tubes and petri dishes. They've gone beyond that, to clinical trials." Victor pointed to the last page. "These are monkeys. Each one was infected with a new virus. A manmade virus. And in every case the results were the same."

"You mean this?" Milo pointed to the last column. "EXP?"

"It stands for expired," said Victor. "They all died."

SAM POLOWSKI SAT on a bench in the Palo Alto bus terminal and wondered: If I wanted to disappear, where would I go next? He watched a dozen or so passengers straggle off to board the 210 from San José, noting they were by and large the Birkenstock and backpack set. Probably Stanford students heading off for Christmas break. He wondered why it was that students who could afford such a pricey university couldn't seem to scrape up enough to buy a decent pair of jeans. Or even a decent haircut, for that matter.

At last Polowski rose and automatically dusted off his coat, a habit he'd picked up from his early years of hanging around the seamier side of town. Even if the grime wasn't actually visible, he'd always *felt* it was there, coating any surface he happened to brush against, ready to cling to him like wet paint.

He made one phone call—to Dafoe's answering machine, to tell him Victor Holland had moved on to Palo Alto. It was, after all, his responsibility to keep his supervisor informed. He was glad he only had to talk to a recording and not to the man himself.

He left the bus station and strolled down the street, heading Lord knew where, in search of a spark, a hunch. It was a nice-enough neighborhood, a nice-enough town. Palo Alto had its old professors' houses, its bookshops and coffee houses where university types, the ones with the beards and wire-rim glasses, liked to sit and argue the meaning of Proust and Brecht and Goethe. Polowski remembered his own university days, when, after being subjected to an hour of such crap from the students at the next table, he had finally stormed over to them and yelled, "Maybe Brecht meant it that way, maybe not. But can you guys answer this? *What the hell difference does it make?*"

This did not, needless to say, enhance his reputation as a serious scholar.

Now, as he paced along the street, no doubt in the footsteps of more serious philosophers, Polowski turned over in his head the question of Victor Holland. More specifically the question of where such a man, in his desperation, would hide. He stalked past the lit windows, the glow of TVs, the cars spilling from garages. Where in this warren of suburbia was the man hiding?

Holland was a scientist, a musician, a man of few but lasting friendships. He had a Ph.D. from MIT, a B.S. from Stanford. The university was right up the road. The man must know his way around here. Maybe he still had friends in the neighborhood, people who'd take him in, keep his secrets.

Polowski decided to take another look at Holland's file. Somewhere in the Viratek records, there had to be some employment reference, some recommendation from a Stanford contact. A friend Holland might turn to.

Sooner or later, he would have to turn to *someone*.

IT WAS AFTER midnight when Dafoe and his wife returned home. He was in an excellent mood, his head pleasantly abuzz with champagne, his ears still ringing with the heart-wrenching aria from *Samson and Delilah*. Opera was a passion for him, a brilliant staging of courage and conflict and *amore,* a vision of life so much grander than the petty little world in which he found himself. It launched him to a plane of such thrilling intensity that even his own wife took on exciting new aspects. He watched her peel off her coat and kick off her shoes. Forty pounds overweight, hair streaked with silver, yet she had her attractions. *It's been three weeks. Surely she'll let me tonight....*

But his wife ignored his amorous looks and wandered off to the kitchen. A moment later, the rumble of the automatic dishwasher announced another of her fits of housecleaning.

In frustration, Dafoe turned and stabbed the blinking button on his answering machine. The message from Polowski completely destroyed any amorous intentions he had left.

"...Reason to believe Holland is in, or has just left, the Palo Alto area. Following leads. Will keep you informed...."

Polowski, you half-wit. Is following orders so damn difficult?

It was 3:00 a.m. Washington time. An ungodly hour, but he made the phone call.

The voice that answered was raspy with sleep. "Tyrone here."

"Cowboy, this is Dafoe. Sorry to wake you."

The voice became instantly alert, all sleep shaken from it. "What's up?"

"New lead on Holland. I don't know the particulars, but he's headed south, to Palo Alto. May still be there."

"The university?"

"It is the Stanford area."

"That may be a very big help."

"Anything for an old buddy. I'll keep you posted."

"One thing, Dafoe."

"Yeah?"

"I can't have any interference. Pull all your people out. We'll take it from here."

Dafoe paused. "I might…have a problem."

"A problem?" The voice, though quiet, took on a razor's edge.

"It's, uh, one of my men. Sort of a wild card. Sam Polowski. He's got this Holland case under his skin, wants to go after him."

"There's such a thing as a direct order."

"At the moment, Polowski's unreachable. He's in Palo Alto, digging around in God knows what."

"Loose cannons. I don't like them."

"I'll pull him back as soon as I can."

"Do that. And keep it quiet. It's a matter of utmost security."

After Dafoe hung up, his gaze shifted automatically to the photo on the mantelpiece. It was a '68 snapshot of him and the Cowboy: two young marines, both of them grinning, their rifles slung over their shoulders as they stood ankle-deep in a rice paddy. It was a crazy time, when one's very life depended on the loyalty of buddies. When Semper Fi applied not only to the corps in general but to each other in particular. Matt Tyrone was a hero then, and he was a hero now. Dafoe stared at that smiling face in the photo, disturbed by the threads of envy that had woven into his admiration for the man. Though Dafoe had much to be proud of—a solid eighteen years in the FBI, maybe even a shot at assistant director somewhere in his stars, he couldn't match the heady climb of Matt Tyrone in the NSA. Though Dafoe wasn't clear as to exactly what position the

Cowboy held in the NSA, he had heard that Tyrone regularly attended cabinet meetings, that he held the trust of the president, that he dealt in secrets and shadows and security. He was the sort of man the country needed, a man for whom patriotism was more than mere flag-waving and rhetoric; it was a way of life. Matt Tyrone would do more than die for his country; he'd live for it.

Dafoe couldn't let such a man, such a friend, down.

He dialed Sam Polowski's home phone and left a message on the recorder.

This is a direct order. You are to withdraw from the Holland case immediately. Until further notice you are on suspension.

He was tempted to add, *by special request from my friends in Washington,* but thought better of it. No room for vanity here. The Cowboy had said national security was at stake.

Dafoe had no doubt it truly was. He'd gotten the word from Matt Tyrone. And Matt Tyrone's authority came direct from the President himself.

"THIS DOES NOT look good. This does not look good at all."

Ollie Wozniak squinted through his wire-rim glasses at the twenty-four photographs strewn across Milo's dining table. He held one up for a closer look. Through the bottle-glass lens, one pale blue eye stared out, enormous. One only saw Ollie's eyes; everything else, hollow cheeks, pencil lips and baby-fine hair, seemed to recede into the background pallor. He shook his head and picked up another photo.

"You're right, of course," he said. "Some of these I can't interpret. I'd like to study 'em later. But these here are definitely raw mortality data. Rhesus monkeys, I suspect." He paused and added quietly, "I hope."

"Surely they wouldn't use people for this sort of thing," said Cathy.

"Not officially." Ollie put down the photo and looked at her. "But it's been done."

"Maybe in Nazi Germany."

"Here, too," said Victor.

"What?" Cathy looked at him in disbelief.

"Army studies in germ warfare. They released colonies of Serratia Marcescens over San Francisco and waited to see how far the organism spread. Infections popped up in a number of Bay Area hospitals. Some of the cases were fatal."

"I can't believe it," murmured Cathy.

"The damage was unintentional, of course. But people died just the same."

"Don't forget Tuskegee," said Ollie. "People died in those experiments, too. And then there was that case in New York. Mentally retarded kids in a state hospital who were deliberately exposed to hepatitis. No one died there, but the ethics were just as shaky. So it's been done. Sometimes in the name of humanity."

"Sometimes not," said Victor.

Ollie nodded. "As in this particular case."

"What exactly are we talking about here?" asked Cathy, nodding at the photos. "Is this medical research? Or weapons development?"

"Both." Ollie pointed to one of the photos on the table. "By all appearances, Viratek's engaged in biological weapons research. They've dubbed it Project Cerberus. From what I can tell, the organism they're working on is an RNA virus, extremely virulent, highly contagious, producing over eighty-percent mortality in its lab animal hosts. This photo here—" he tapped one of the pages "—shows the organism produces vesicular skin lesions on the infected subjects."

"Vesicular?"

"Blisterlike. That could be one route of transmission, the fluid in those lesions." He sifted through the pile and pulled out another page. "This shows the time course of the illness. The viral counts, periods of infectiousness. In almost every case the course is the same. The subject's exposed here." He pointed to Day One on the time graph. "Minor signs of illness here at Day Seven. Full-blown pox on Day Twelve. And here—" he tapped the graph at Day Fourteen "—the deaths begin. The time varies, but the result's the same. They all die."

"You used the word *pox,*" said Cathy.

Ollie turned to her, his eyes like blue glass. "Because that's what it is."

"You mean like chickenpox?"

"I wish it was. Then it wouldn't be so deadly. Almost everyone gets exposed to chickenpox as a kid, so most of us are immune. But this one's a different story."

"Is it a new virus?" asked Milo.

"Yes and no." He reached for an electron micrograph. "When I saw this I thought there was something weirdly familiar about all this. The appearance of the organism, the skin lesions, the course of illness. The whole damn picture. It reminded me of something I haven't read about in decades. Something I never dreamed I'd see again."

"You're saying it's an old virus?" said Milo.

"Ancient. But they've made some modifications. Made it more infectious. And deadlier. Which turns this into a real humdinger of a weapon, considering the millions of folks it's already killed."

"Millions?" Cathy stared at him. "What are we talking about?"

"A killer we've known for centuries. Smallpox."

"That's impossible!" said Cathy. "From what I've read, we conquered smallpox. It's supposed to be extinct."

"It was," said Victor. "For all practical purposes. World-wide vaccination wiped it out. Smallpox hasn't been reported in decades. I'm not even sure they still make the vaccine. Ollie?"

"Not available. No need for it since the virus has vanished."

"So where did *this* virus come from?" asked Cathy.

Ollie shrugged. "Probably someone's closet."

"Come on."

"I'm serious. After smallpox was eradicated, a few samples of virus were kept alive in government labs, just in case someone needed it for future research. It's the scientific skeleton in the closet, so to speak. I'd assume those labs are top security. Because if any of the virus got out, there could be a major epidemic." He looked at the stack of photos. "Looks like security's already been breached. Someone obviously got hold of the virus."

"Or had it handed to them," said Victor. "Courtesy of the U.S. government."

"I find that incredible, Gersh," said Ollie. "This is a powderkeg experiment you're talking about. No committee would approve this sort of project."

"Right. That's why I think this is a maverick operation. It's easy to come up with a scenario. Bunch of hardliners cooking this up over at NSA. Or joint chiefs of staff. Or even the Oval Office. Someone says: 'World politics have changed. We can't get away with nuking the enemy. We need a new weapons option, one that'll work well against a Third World army. Let's find one.' And some guy in that room, some red, white and blue robot, will take that as the go-ahead. International law be damned."

"And since it's unofficial," said Cathy, "it'd be completely deniable."

"Right. The administration could claim it knew nothing."

"Sounds like Iran-Contra all over again."

"With one big difference," said Ollie. "When Iran-Contra fell apart, all you had were a few ruined political careers. If Project Cerberus goes awry, what you'll have is a few million dead people."

"But Ollie," said Milo. "I got vaccinated for smallpox when I was a kid. Doesn't that mean I'm safe?"

"Probably. Assuming the virus hasn't been altered too much. In fact, everyone over 35 is probably okay. But remember, there's a whole generation after us that never got the vaccine. Young adults and kids. By the time you could manufacture enough vaccine for them all, we'd have a raging epidemic."

"I'm beginning to see the logic of this weapon," said Victor. "In any war, who makes up the bulk of combat soldiers? Young adults."

Ollie nodded. "They'd be hit bad. As would the kids."

"A whole generation," Cathy murmured. "And only the old would be spared." She glanced at Victor and saw, mirrored in his eyes, the horror she felt.

"They chose an appropriate name," said Milo.

Ollie frowned. "What?"

"Cerberus. The three-headed dog of Hades." Milo looked up, visibly shaken. "Guardian of the dead."

IT WASN'T UNTIL Cathy was fast asleep and Milo had retired upstairs that Victor finally broached the subject to Ollie. It had troubled him all evening, had shadowed his every moment since they'd arrived at Milo's house. He couldn't look at Cathy, couldn't listen to the sound of her voice or inhale the scent of her hair without thinking of the terrible possibilities. And in the deepest hours of night, when it seemed all the world was asleep except for him and Ollie, he made the decision.

"I need to ask you a favor," he said.

Ollie gazed at him across the dining table, steam wafting up from his fourth cup of coffee. "What sort of favor?"

"It has to do with Cathy."

Ollie's gaze shifted to the woman lying asleep on the living room floor. She looked very small, very defenseless, curled up beneath the comforter. Ollie said, "She's a nice woman, Gersh."

"I know."

"There hasn't really been anyone since Lily. Has there?"

Victor shook his head. "I guess I haven't felt ready for it. There were always other things to think about...."

Ollie smiled. "There are always excuses. I should know. People keep telling me there's a glut of unattached female baby boomers. I haven't noticed."

"And I never bothered to notice." Victor looked at Cathy. "Until now."

"What're you gonna do with her, Gersh?"

"That's what I need you for. I'm not the safest guy to hang around with these days. A woman could get hurt."

Ollie laughed. "Hell, a *guy* could get hurt."

"I feel responsible for her. And if something happened to her, I'm not sure I could ever..." He let out a long sigh and rubbed his bloodshot eyes. "Anyway, I think it's best if she leaves."

"For where?"

"She has an ex-husband. He'll be working down in Mexico for a few months. I think she'd be pretty safe."

"You're sending her to her ex-husband?"

"I've met him. He's a jerk, but at least she won't be alone down there."

"Does Cathy agree to this?"

"I didn't ask her."

"Maybe you should."

"I'm not giving her a choice."

"What if she wants the choice?"

"I'm not in the mood to take any crap, Okay? I'm doing this for her own good."

Ollie took off his glasses and cleaned them on the table-cloth. "Excuse me for saying this, Gersh, but if it was me, I'd want her nearby, where I could sort of keep an eye on her."

"You mean where I can watch her get killed?" Victor shook his head. "Lily was enough. I won't go through it with Cathy."

Ollie thought it over for a moment, then he nodded. "What do you want me to do?"

"Tomorrow I want you to take her to the airport. Buy her a ticket to Mexico. Let her use your name. Mrs. Woz-niak. Make sure she gets safely off the ground. I'll pay you back when I can."

"What if she won't get on the plane? Do I just shove her aboard?"

"Do whatever it takes, Ollie. I'm counting on you."

Ollie sighed. "I guess I can do it. I'll call in sick tomor-row. That'll free up my day." He looked at Victor. "I just hope you know what you're doing."

So do I, thought Victor.

Ollie rose to his feet and tucked the envelope with the photos under his arm. "I'll get back to you in the morning. After I show these last two photos to Bach. Maybe he can identify what those grids are."

"If it's anything electronic, Bach'll figure it out."

Together they walked to the door. There they paused and regarded each other, two old friends who'd grown a little grayer and, Victor hoped, a little wiser.

"Somehow it'll all work out," said Ollie. "Remember. The system's there to be beaten."

"Sounds like the old Stanford radical again."

"It's been a long time." Grinning, Ollie gave Victor a clap on the back. "But we're still not too old to raise a little hell, hey, Gersh? See you in the morning."

Victor waved as Ollie walked away into the darkness. Then he closed the door and turned off all the lights.

In the living room he sat beside Cathy and watched her sleep. The glow of a streetlight spilled in through the window onto her tumbled hair. *Ordinary,* she had called herself. Perhaps, if she'd been a stranger he'd merely passed on the street, he might have thought so, too. A chance meeting on a rainy highway in Garberville had made it impossible for him to ever consider this woman ordinary. In her gentleness, her kindness, she was very much like Lily.

In other ways, she was very different.

Though he'd cared about his wife, though they'd never stopped being good friends, he'd found Lily strangely passionless, a pristine, spiritual being trapped by human flesh. Lily had never been comfortable with her own body. She'd undress in the dark, make love—the rare times they did— in the dark. And then, the illness had robbed her of what little desire she had left.

Gazing at Cathy, he couldn't help wondering what passions might lie harbored in her still form.

He cut short the speculation. What did it matter now? Tomorrow, he'd send her away. *Get rid of her,* he thought brutally. It was necessary. He couldn't think straight while she was around. He couldn't stay focused on the business at hand: exposing Viratek. Jerry Martinique had counted on him. Thousands of potential victims counted on him. He was a scientist, a man who prided himself on logic. His attraction to this particular woman was, in the grand scheme of things, clearly unimportant.

That was what the scientist in him said.

That problem finally settled, he decided to get some rest while he could. He kicked off his shoes and stretched out beside her to sleep. The comforter was large enough—they could share it. He climbed beneath it and lay for a moment, not touching her, almost afraid to share her warmth.

She whimpered in her sleep and turned toward him, her silky hair tumbling against his face.

This was more than he could resist. Sighing, he wrapped his arms around her and felt her curl up against his chest. It was their last night together. They might as well spend it keeping each other warm.

That was how he fell asleep, with Cathy in his arms.

Only once during the night did he awaken. He had been dreaming of Lily. They were walking together, in a garden of pure white flowers. She said absolutely nothing. She simply looked at him with profound sadness, as if to say, *Here I am, Victor. I've come back to you. Why doesn't that make you happy?* He couldn't answer her. So he simply took her in his arms and held her.

He'd awakened to find he was holding Cathy, instead.

Joy instantly flooded his heart, warmed the darkest corners of his soul. It took him by surprise, that burst of happiness; it also made him feel guilty. But there it was. And the joy was all too short-lived. He remembered that today she'd be going away.

Cathy, Cathy. What a complication you've become.

He turned on his side, away from her, mentally building a wall between them.

He concentrated on the dream, trying to remember what had happened. He and Lily had been walking. He tried to picture Lily's face, her brown eyes, her curly black hair.

It was the face of the woman he'd been married to for ten years, a face he should know well.

But the only face he saw when he closed his eyes was that of Catherine Weaver.

IT TOOK NICHOLAS Savitch only two hours to pack his bags and drive down to Palo Alto. The word from Matt Tyrone was that Holland had slipped south to the Stanford area, perhaps to seek out old friends. Holland was, after all, a Stanford man. Maybe not the red-and-white rah-rah Cardinals type, but a Stanford man nonetheless. These old school ties could run deep. It was only a guess on Savitch's part; he'd never gone beyond high school. His education consisted of what a hungry and ambitious boy could pick up on Chicago's south side. Mainly a keen, almost uncanny knack for crawling into another man's head, for sensing what a particular man would think and do in a given situation. Call it advanced street psychology. Without spending a day in college, Savitch had earned his degree.

Now he was putting it to use.

The *finder,* they called him. He liked that name. He grinned as he drove, his leather-gloved hands expertly handling the wheel. Nicholas Savitch, diviner of human souls, the hunter who could ferret a man out of deepest hiding.

In most cases it was a simple matter of logic. Even while on the run, most people conformed to old patterns. It was the fear that did it. It made them seek out their old comforts, cling to their usual habits. In a strange town, the familiar was precious, even if it was only the sight of those ubiquitous golden arches.

Like every other fugitive, Victor Holland would seek the familiar.

Savitch turned his car onto Palm Drive and pulled up in front of the Stanford Arch. The campus was silent; it was

2:00 a.m. Savitch sat for a moment, regarding the silent buildings, Holland's alma mater. Here, in his former stomping grounds, Holland would turn to old friends, revisit old haunts. Savitch had already done his homework. He carried, in his briefcase, a list of names he'd culled from the man's file. In the morning he'd start in on those names, knock on neighbors' doors, flash his government ID, ask about new faces in the neighborhood.

The only possible complication was Sam Polowski. By last report, the FBI agent was also in town, also on Holland's trail. Polowski was a dogged operator. It'd be messy business, taking out a Bureau man. But then, Polowski was only a cog, the way the Weaver woman was only a cog, in a much bigger wheel.

Neither of them would be missed.

Chapter Nine

In the cold, clear hours before dawn, Cathy woke up shaking, still trapped in the threads of a nightmare. She had been walking in a world of concrete and shadow, where doorways gaped and silhouettes huddled on street corners. She drifted among them, one among the faceless, taking refuge in obscurity, instinctively avoiding the light. No one pursued her; no attacker lunged from the alleys. The real terror lay in the unending maze of concrete, the hard echoes of the streets, the frantic search for a safe place.

And the certainty that she would never find it.

For a moment she lay in the darkness, curled up beneath a down comforter on Milo's living room floor. She barely remembered having crawled under the covers; it must have been sometime after three when she'd fallen asleep. The last she remembered, Ollie and Victor were still huddled in the dining room, discussing the photographs. Now there was only silence. The dining room, like the rest of the house, lay in shadow.

She turned on her back, and her shoulder thumped against something warm and solid. Victor. He stirred, murmuring something she couldn't understand.

"Are you awake?" she whispered.

He turned toward her and in his drowsiness enfolded her in his arms. She knew it was only instinct that drew him to her, the yearning of one warm body for another. Or perhaps it was the memory of his wife sleeping beside him, in his mind always there, always waiting to be held. For the moment, she let him cling to the dream. *While he's still half asleep, let him believe I'm Lily,* she thought. *What harm can there be? He needs the memory. And I need the comfort.*

She burrowed into his arms, into the safe spot that once had belonged to another. She took it without regard for the consequences, willing to be swept up into the fantasy of being, for this moment, the one woman in the world he loved. How good it felt, how protected and cared for. From the soap-and-sweat smell of his chest to the coarse fabric of his shirt, it was sanctuary. He was breathing warmly into her hair now, whispering words she knew were for another, pressing kisses to the top of her head. Then he trapped her face in his hands and pressed his lips to hers in a kiss so undeniably needy it ignited within her a hunger of her own. Her response was instinctive and filled with all the yearning of a woman too long a stranger to love.

She met his kiss with one just as deep, just as needy.

At once she was lost, whirled away into some grand and glorious vortex. He stroked down her face, her neck. His hands moved to the buttons of her blouse. She arched against him, her breasts suddenly aching to be touched. It had been so long, so long.

She didn't know how the blouse fell open. She knew only that one moment his fingers were skimming the fabric, and the next moment, they were cupping her flesh. It was that unexpected contact of skin on forbidden skin, the magic torment of his fingers caressing her nipple, that made any last resistance fall away. How many chances were left to them? How many nights together? She longed for so many more, an eternity, but this might be all they had. She welcomed it, welcomed him, with all the passion of a woman granted one last taste of love.

With a knowing touch, she slid her hands down his shirt, undoing buttons, stroking her way through the dense hair of his chest, to the top of his trousers. There she paused, feeling his startled intake of breath, knowing that he too was past retreat.

Together they fumbled at buttons and zippers, both of them suddenly feverish to be free. It all fell away in a tumult of cotton and lace. And when the last scrap of clothing was shed, when nothing came between them but the velvet darkness, she reached up and pulled him to her, on her.

It was a joyful filling, as if, in that first deep thrust within her, he also reached some long-empty hollow in her soul.

"Please," she murmured, her voice breaking into a whimper.

He fell instantly still. "Cathy?" he asked, his hands anxiously cupping her face. "What—"

"Please. Don't stop...."

His soft laughter was all the reassurance she needed. "I have no intention of stopping," he whispered. "None whatsoever..."

And he didn't stop. Not until he had taken her with him all the way, higher and further than any man ever could, to a place beyond thought or reason. Only when release came, wave flooding upon wave, did she know how very high and far they had climbed.

A sweet exhaustion claimed them.

Outside, in the grayness of dawn, a bird sang. Inside, the silence was broken only by the sound of their breathing.

She sighed into the warmth of his shoulder. "Thank you."

He touched her face. "For what?"

"For making me feel...wanted again."

"Oh, Cathy."

"It's been such a long time. Jack and I, we—we stopped making love way before the divorce. It was me, actually. I couldn't bear having him..." She swallowed. "When you don't love someone anymore, when they don't love you, it's hard to let yourself be...touched."

He brushed his fingers down her cheek. "Is it still hard? Being touched?"

"Not by you. Being touched by you is like...being touched the very first time."

By the window's pale light she saw him smile. "I hope your very first time wasn't too awful."

Now she smiled. "I don't remember it very well. It was such a frantic, ridiculous thing on the floor of a college dorm room."

He reached out and patted the carpet. "I see you've come a long way."

"Haven't I?" she laughed. "But floors can be terribly romantic places."

"Goodness. A carpet connoisseur. How do dorm room and living room floors compare?"

"I couldn't tell you. It's been such a long time since I was eighteen." She paused, hovering on the edge of baring the truth. "In fact," she admitted, "it's been a long time since I've been with anyone."

Softly he said, "It's been a long time for both of us."

She let that revelation hang for a moment in the semi-darkness. "Not—not since Lily?" she finally asked.

"No." A single word, yet it revealed so much. The three years of loyalty to a dead woman. The grief, the loneliness. How she wanted to fill that womanless chasm for him! To be his savior, and he, hers. Could she make him forget? No, not forget; she couldn't expect him ever to forget Lily. But she wanted a space in his heart for herself, a very large space designed for a lifetime. A space to which no other woman, dead or alive, could ever lay claim.

"She must have been a very special woman," she said.

He ran a strand of her hair through his fingers. "She was very wise, very aware. And she was kind. That's something I don't always find in a person."

She's still part of you, isn't she? She's still the one you love.

"It's the same sort of kindness I find in you," he said.

His fingers had slid to her face and were now stroking her cheek. She closed her eyes, savoring his touch, his warmth. "You hardly know me," she whispered.

"But I do. That night, after the accident, I survived purely on the sound of your voice. And the touch of your hand. I'd know them both, anywhere."

She opened her eyes and gazed at him. "Would you really?"

He pressed his lips to her forehead. "Even in my sleep."

"But I'm not Lily. I could never be Lily."

"That's true. You can't be. No one can."

"I can't replace what you lost."

"What makes you think that's what I want? Some sort of replacement? She was my wife. And yes, I loved her." By the way he said it, his answer invited no exploration.

She didn't try.

From somewhere in the house came the jingle of a telephone. After two rings it stopped. Faintly they heard Milo's voice murmuring upstairs.

Cathy sat up and reached automatically for her clothes. She dressed in silence, her back turned to Victor. A new modesty had sprung up between them, the shyness of strangers.

"Cathy," he said. "People do move on."

"I know."

"You've gotten over Jack."

She laughed, a small, tired sound. "No woman ever really gets over Jack Zuckerman. Yes, I'm over the worst of it. But every time a woman falls in love, really falls in love, it takes something out of her. Something that can never be put back."

"It also gives her something."

"That depends on who you fall in love with, doesn't it?"

Footsteps thumped down the stairs, creaked across the dining room. A wide-awake Milo stood in the doorway, his uncombed hair standing out like a brush. "Hey, you two!" he hissed. "Get up! Hurry."

Cathy rose to her feet in alarm. "What is it?"

"That was Ollie on the phone. He called to say some guy's in the area, asking questions about you. He's already been down to Bach's neighborhood."

"What?" Now Victor was on his feet and hurriedly stuffing his legs into his trousers.

"Ollie figures the guy'll be knocking around here next. Guess they know who your friends are."

"Who was asking the questions?"

"Claimed he was FBI."

"Polowski," muttered Victor, pulling his shirt on. "Has to be."

"You know him?"

"The same guy who set me up. The guy who's been tailing us ever since."

"How did he know we're here?" said Cathy. "No one could've followed us—"

"No one had to. They have my profile. They know I have friends here." Victor glanced at Milo. "Sorry, buddy. Hope this doesn't get you into trouble."

Milo's laugh was distinctly tense. "Hey, I didn't do nothin' wrong. Just harbored a felon." The bravado suddenly melted away. He asked, "Exactly what kind of trouble should I expect?"

"Questions," said Victor, quickly buttoning his shirt. "Lots of 'em. Maybe they'll even take a look around. Just keep cool, tell 'em you haven't heard from me. Think you can do it?"

"Sure. But I don't know about Ma—"

"Your Ma's no problem. Just tell her to stick to Chinese." Victor grabbed the envelope of photos and glanced at Cathy. "Ready?"

"Let's get out of here. Please."

"Back door," Milo suggested.

They followed him through the kitchen. A glance told them the way was clear. As he opened the door, Milo added, "I almost forgot. Ollie wants to see you this afternoon. Something about those photos."

"Where?"

"The lake. Behind the boathouse. You know the place."

They stepped out into the chill dampness of morning. Fog-borne silence hung in the air. *Will we ever stop running?* thought Cathy. *Will we never stop listening for footsteps?*

Victor clapped his friend on the shoulder. "Thanks, Milo. I owe you a big one."

"And one of these days I plan to collect!" Milo hissed as they slipped away.

Victor held up his hand in farewell. "See you around."

"Yeah," Milo muttered into the mist. "Let's hope not in jail."

THE CHINESE MAN was lying. Though the man betrayed nothing in his voice, no hesitation, no guilty waver, still Savitch knew this Mr. Milo Lum was hiding something. His eyes betrayed him.

He was seated on the living room couch, across from Savitch. Off to the side sat Mrs. Lum in an easy chair, smiling uncomprehendingly. Savitch might be able to use the old biddy; for now, it was the son who held his interest.

"I can't see why you'd be after him," said Milo. "Victor's as clean as they come. At least, he was when I knew him. But that was a long time ago."

"How far back?" asked Savitch politely.

"Oh, years. Yeah. Haven't seen him since. No, sir."

Savitch raised an eyebrow. Milo shifted on the couch, shuffled his feet, glanced pointlessly around the room.

"You and your mother live here alone?" Savitch asked.

"Since my dad died."

"No tenants? No one else lives here?"

"No. Why?"

"There were reports of a man fitting Holland's description in the neighborhood."

"Believe me, if Victor was wanted by the police, he wouldn't hang around here. You think I'd let a murder suspect in the house? With just me and my old Ma?"

Savitch glanced at Mrs. Lum, who merely smiled. The old woman had sharp, all-seeing eyes. A survivor's eyes.

It was time for Savitch to confirm his hunch. "Excuse me," he said, rising to his feet. "I had a long drive from the city. May I use your restroom?"

"Uh, sure. Down that hall."

Savitch headed into the bathroom and closed the door. Within seconds he'd spotted the evidence he was looking for. It was lying on the tiled floor: a long strand of brown hair. Very silky, very fine.

Catherine Weaver's shade.

It was all the proof he needed to proceed. He reached under his jacket for the shoulder holster and pulled out the semiautomatic. Then he gave his crisp white shirt a regretful pat. Messy business, interrogation. He would have to watch the bloodstains.

He stepped out into the hall, casually holding his pistol at his side. He'd go for the old woman first. Hold the barrel to her head, threaten to pull the trigger. There was an uncommonly strong bond between this mother and son. They would protect each other at all costs.

Savitch was halfway down the hall when the doorbell rang. He halted. The front door was opened and a new voice said, "Mr. Milo Lum?"

"And who the hell are you?" came Milo's weary reply.

"The name's Sam Polowski. FBI."

Every muscle in Savitch's body snapped taut. No choice now; he had to take the man out.

He raised his pistol. Soundlessly, he made his way down the hall toward the living room.

"*Another* one?" came Milo's peevish voice. "Look, one of your guys is already here—"

"What?"

"Yeah, he's back in the—"

Savitch stepped out and was swinging his pistol toward the front doorway when Mrs. Lum shrieked.

Milo froze. Polowski didn't. He rolled sideways just as the bullet thudded into the door frame, splintering wood.

By the time Savitch got off a second shot, Polowski was crawling somewhere behind the couch and the bullet slammed uselessly into the stuffing. That was it for chances—Polowski was armed.

Savitch decided it was time to vanish.

He turned and darted back up the hall, into a far bedroom. It was the mother's room; it smelled of incense and old-lady perfume. The window slid open easily. Savitch kicked out the screen, scrambled over the sill and sank heel-deep into the muddy flower bed. Cursing, he slogged away, trailing clumps of mud across the lawn.

He heard, faintly, "Halt! FBI!" but continued running.

He nursed his rage all the way back to the car.

MILO STARED IN bewilderment at the trampled pansies. "What the hell was that all about?" he demanded. "Is this some sort of FBI practical joke?"

Sam Polowski didn't answer; he was too busy tracking the footprints across the grass. They led to the sidewalk, then faded into the road's pebbly asphalt.

"Hey!" yelled Milo. "What's going on?"

Polowski turned. "I didn't really see him. What did he look like?"

Milo shrugged. "I dunno. Efrem Zimbalist-type."

"Meaning?"

"Tall, clean-cut, great build. Typical FBI."

There was a silence as Milo regarded Polowski's sagging belly.

"Well," amended Milo, "maybe not *typical*..."

"What about his face?"

"Lemme think. Brown hair? Maybe brown eyes?"

"You're not sure."

"You know how it is. All you white guys look alike to me."

An eruption of rapid Chinese made them both turn. Mrs. Lum had followed them out onto the lawn and was jabbering and gesticulating.

"What's she saying?" asked Polowski.

"She says the man was about six foot one, had straight dark brown hair parted on the left, brown eyes, almost black, a high forehead, a narrow nose and thin lips, and a small tattoo on his inside left wrist."

"Uh—is that all?"

"The tattoo read PJX."

Polowski shook his head in amazement. "Is she always this observant?"

"She can't exactly converse in English. So she does a lot of watching."

"Obviously." Polowski took out a pen and began to jot the information in a notebook.

"So who was this guy?" prodded Milo.

"Not FBI."

"How do I know *you're* FBI."

"Do I look like it?"

"No."

"Only proves my point."

"What?"

"If I wanted to pretend I was an agent, wouldn't I at least try to *look* like one? Whereas, if I *am* one, I wouldn't bother to try and look like one."

"Oh."

"Now." Polowski slid the notebook in his pocket. "You're still going to insist you haven't seen, or heard from, Victor Holland?"

Milo straightened. "That's right."

"And you don't know how to get in touch with him?"

"I have no idea."

"That's too bad. Because I could be the one to save his life. I've already saved yours."

Milo said nothing.

"Just why the hell do you think that guy was here? To pay a social visit? No, he was after information." Polowski paused and added, ominously, "And believe me, he would've gotten it."

Milo shook his head. "I'm confused."

"So am I. That's why I need Holland. He has the answers.

But I need him alive. That means I need to find him before the other guy does. Tell me where he is."

Polowski and Milo looked at each other long and hard.

"I don't know," said Milo. "I don't know what to do."

Mrs. Lum was chattering again. She pointed to Polowski and nodded.

"Now what's she saying?" asked Polowski.

"She says you have big ears."

"For that, I can look in the mirror."

"What she means is, the size of your ears indicates sagacity."

"Come again?"

"You're a smart dude. She thinks I should listen to you."

Polowski turned and grinned at Mrs. Lum. "Your mother is a great judge of character." He looked back at Milo. "I wouldn't want anything to happen to her. Or you. You both have to get out of town."

Milo nodded. "On that particular point, we both agree." He turned toward the house.

"What about Holland?" called Polowski. "Will you help me find him?"

Milo took his mother by the arm and guided her across the lawn. Without even a backward look he said, "I'm thinking about it."

"It was those two photos. I just couldn't figure them out," said Ollie.

They were standing on the boathouse pier, overlooking the bed of Lake Lagunita. The lake was dry now, as it was every winter, drained to a reedy marsh until spring. They were alone, the three of them, sharing the lake with only an occasional duck. In the spring, this would be an idyllic spot, the water lapping the banks, lovers drifting in rowboats, here and there a poet lolling under the trees. But today, under black clouds, with a cold mist rising from the reeds, it was a place of utter desolation.

"I knew they weren't biological data," said Ollie. "I kept thinking they looked like some sort of electrical grid. So this morning, right after I left Milo's, I took 'em over to Bach's, down in San José. Caught him at breakfast."

"Bach?" asked Cathy.

"Another member of the Out of Tuners. Great bassoon player. Started an electronics firm a few years back and now he's working with the big boys. Anyway, the first thing he says as I walk in the door is, 'Hey, did the FBI get to you yet?' And I said, 'What?' and he says, 'They just called. For some reason they're looking for Gershwin. They'll probably get around to you next.' And that's when I knew I had to get you two out of Milo's house, stat."

"So what did he say about those photos?"

"Oh, yeah." Ollie reached into his briefcase and pulled out the photos. "Okay. This one here, it's a circuit diagram. An electronic alarm system. Very sophisticated, very secure. Designed to be breached by use of a keypad code, punched in at this point here. Probably at an entryway. You seen anything like it at Viratek?"

Victor nodded. "Building C-2. Where Jerry worked. The keypad's in the hall, right by the Special Projects door."

"Ever been inside that door?"

"No. Only those with top clearance can get through. Like Jerry."

"Then we'll have to visualize what comes next. Going by the diagram, there's another security point here, probably another keypad. Right inside the first door, they've stationed a camera system."

"You mean like a bank camera?" asked Cathy.

"Similar. Only I'd guess this one's being monitored twenty-four hours a day."

"They went first class, didn't they?" said Victor. "Two secured doors, plus inspection by a guard. Not to mention the guard at the outside gate."

"Don't forget the laser lattice."

"What?"

"This inner room here." Ollie pointed to the diagram's core. "Laser beams, directed at various angles. They'll detect movement of just about anything bigger than a rat."

"How do the lasers get switched off?"

"Has to be done by the security guard. The controls are on his panel."

"You can tell all this from the diagram?" asked Cathy. "I'm impressed."

"No problem." Ollie grinned. "Bach's firm designs security systems."

Victor shook his head. "This looks impossible. We can't get through all that."

Cathy frowned at him. "Wait a minute. What are you talking about? You aren't considering going into that building, are you?"

"We discussed it last night," said Victor. "It may be the only way—"

"Are you crazy? Viratek's out to kill us and you want to break *in?*"

"It's the proof we need," said Ollie. "You try going to the newspapers or the Justice Department and they'll demand evidence. You can bet Viratek's going to deny everything. Even if someone does launch an investigation, all Viratek has to do is toss the virus and, *poof!* your evidence is gone. No one can prove a thing."

"You have photos—"

"Sure. A few pages of animal data. The virus is never identified. And all that evidence could've been fabricated by, say, some disgruntled ex-employee."

"So what *is* proof? What do you need, another dead body? Victor's, for instance?"

"What we need is the virus—a virus that's supposed to be extinct. Just a single vial and the case against them is nailed shut."

"Just a single vial. Right." Cathy shook her head. "I don't know what I'm worried about. No one can get through those doors. Not without the keypad codes."

"Ah, but those we have!" Ollie flipped to the second photo. "The mysterious numbers. See, they finally make sense. Two sets of seven digits. Not phone numbers at all! Jerry was pointing the way through Viratek's top security."

"What about the lasers?" she pointed out, her agitation growing. They couldn't be serious! Surely they could see the futility of this mission. She didn't care if her fear showed; she had to be their voice of reason. "And then there's the guards," she said. "Two of them. Do you have a way past them? Or did Jerry also leave you the formula for invisibility?"

Ollie glanced uneasily at Victor. "Uh, maybe I should let you two discuss this first. Before we make any other plans."

"I thought I was part of all this," said Cathy. "Part of every decision. I guess I was wrong."

Neither man said a thing. Their silence only fueled Cathy's anger. She thought: *So you left me out of this. You didn't respect my opinion enough to ask me what I think, what I want.*

Without a word she turned and walked away.

Moments later, Victor caught up with her. She was standing on the dirt path, hugging herself against the cold. She heard his approach, sensed his uncertainty, his struggle to find the right words. For a moment he simply stood beside her, not speaking.

"I think we should run," she said. She gazed over the

dry lake bed and shivered. The wind that swept across the reeds was raw and biting; it sliced right through her sweater. "I want to get away," she said. "I want to go somewhere warm. Some place where the sun's shining, where I can lie on a beach and not worry about who's watching me from the bushes...." Suddenly reminded of the terrible possibilities, she turned and glanced at the oaks hulking behind them. She saw only the fluttering of dead leaves.

"I agree with you," said Victor quietly.

"You do?" She turned to him, relieved. "Let's go, Victor! Let's leave now. Forget this crazy idea. We can catch the next bus south—"

"This very afternoon. You'll be on your way."

"*I* will?" She stared at him, at first not willing to accept what she'd heard. Then the meaning of his words sank in. "You're not coming."

Slowly he shook his head. "I can't."

"You mean you won't."

"Don't you see?" He took her by the shoulders, as though to shake some sense into her. "We're backed into a corner. Unless we do something—I do something—we'll always be running."

"Then let's *run!*" She reached for him, her fingers clutching at his windbreaker. She wanted to scream at him, to tear away his cool mask of reason and get to the raw emotions beneath. They had to be there, buried deep in that logical brain of his. "We could go to Mexico," she said. "I know a place on the coast—in Baja. A little hotel near the beach. We could stay there a few months, wait until things are safer—"

"It'll never be safer."

"Yes, it will! They'll forget about us—"

"You're not thinking straight."

"I am. I'm thinking I want to stay alive."

"And that's exactly why I have to do this." He took her face in his hands, trapping it so she could look nowhere but at him. No longer was he the lover, the friend—his voice now held the cold, steady note of authority and she hated the sound of it. "I'm trying to keep you alive," he said. "With a future ahead of you. And the only way I can do that is to blow this thing wide open so the world knows about it. I owe it to you. And I owe it to Jerry."

She wanted to argue with him, to plead with him to go with her, but she knew it was useless. What he said was true. Running would only be a temporary solution, one that would give them a few sweet months of safety, but a temporary one just the same.

"I'm sorry, Cathy," he said softly. "I can't think of any other way—"

"—But to get rid of me," she finished for him.

He released her. She stepped back, and the sudden gulf between them left her aching. She couldn't bear to look at him, knowing that the pain she felt wouldn't be reflected in his eyes. "So how does it work?" she said dully. "Do I leave tonight? Will it be plane, train or automobile?"

"Ollie will drive you to the airport. I've asked him to buy you the ticket under his name—Mrs. Wozniak. He'll have to be the one to see you off. We thought it'd be safer if I didn't come along to the airport."

"Of course."

"That'll get you to Mexico. Ollie'll give you enough cash to keep you going for a while. Enough to get you anywhere you want to go from there. Baja. Acapulco. Or just hang around with Jack if you think that's best."

"Jack." She turned away, unwilling to show her tears. "Right."

"Cathy." She felt his hand on her shoulder, as though he

wanted to turn her toward him, to pull her back one last time into his arms. She refused to move.

Footsteps approached. They both glanced around to see Ollie, standing a few feet away. "Ready to go?" he asked.

There was a long silence. Then Victor nodded. "She's ready."

"Uh, look," Ollie mumbled, suddenly aware that he'd stepped in at a bad time. "My car's over by the boathouse. If you want, I can, uh, wait for you there...."

Cathy furiously dashed away her tears. "No," she said with sudden determination. "I'm coming."

Victor stood watching her, his gaze veiled by some cool, impenetrable mist.

"Goodbye, Victor," she said.

He didn't answer. He just kept looking at her through that terrible mist.

"If I—if I don't see you again..." She stopped, struggling to be just as brave, just as invulnerable. "Take care of yourself," she finished. Then she turned and followed Ollie down the path.

Through the car window, she glimpsed Victor, still standing on the lake path, his hands jammed in his pockets, his shoulders hunched against the wind. He didn't wave goodbye; he merely watched them drive away.

It was an image she'd carry with her forever, that last, fading view of the man she loved. The man who'd sent her away.

As Ollie turned the car onto the road, she sat stiff and silent, her fists balled in her lap, the pain in her throat so terrible she could scarcely breathe. Now he was behind them. She couldn't see him, but she knew he was still standing there, as unmoving as the oaks that surrounded him. *I love you,* she thought. *And I will never see you again.*

She turned to look out. He was a distant figure now,

almost lost among the trees. In a gesture of farewell, she reached up and gently touched the window.

The glass was cold.

"I HAVE TO stop off at the lab," said Ollie, turning into the hospital parking lot. "I just remembered I left the checkbook in my desk. Can't get you a plane ticket without it."

Cathy nodded dully. She was still in a state of shock, still trying to accept the fact that she was now on her own. That Victor had sent her away.

Ollie pulled into a stall marked Reserved, Wozniak. "This'll only take a sec."

"Shall I come in with you?"

"You'd better wait in the car. I work with a very nosy bunch. They see me with a woman and they want to know everything. Not that there's ever anything to know." He climbed out and shut the door. "Be right back."

Cathy watched him stride away and vanish into a side entrance. She had to smile at the thought of Ollie Wozniak squiring around a woman—any woman. Unless it was someone with a Ph.D. who could sit through his scientific monologues.

A minute passed.

Outside, a bird screeched. Cathy glanced out at the trees lining the hospital driveway and spotted the jay, perched among the lower branches. Nothing else moved, not even the leaves.

She leaned back and closed her eyes.

Too little sleep, too much running, had taken its toll. Exhaustion settled over her, so profound she thought she would never again be able to move her limbs. *A beach,* she thought. *Warm sand. Waves washing at my feet...*

The jay's cry cut off in mid-screech. Only vaguely did Cathy register the sudden silence. Then, even through her half sleep, she sensed the shadowing of the window, like a cloud passing before the sun.

She opened her eyes. A face was staring at her through the glass.

Panic sent her lunging for the lock button. Before she could jam it down, the door was wrenched open. A badge was thrust up to her face.

"FBI!" the man barked. "Out of the car, please."

Slowly Cathy emerged, to stand weak-kneed against the door. *Ollie,* she thought, her gaze darting toward the hospital entrance. *Where are you?* If he appeared, she had to be ready to bolt, to flee across the parking lot and into the woods. She doubted the man with the badge would be able to keep up; his stubby legs and thick waist didn't go along with a star athlete.

But he must have a gun. If I bolt, would he shoot me in the back?

"Don't even think about it, Miss Weaver," the man said. He took her arm and gave her a nudge toward the hospital entrance. "Go on. Inside."

"But—"

"Dr. Wozniak's waiting for us in the lab."

Waiting didn't exactly describe Ollie's predicament. Bound and trussed would have been a better description. She found Ollie bent over double in his office, handcuffed to the foot of his desk, while three of his lab colleagues stood by gaping in amazement.

"Back to work, folks," said the agent as he herded the onlookers out of the office. "Just a routine matter." He shut the door and locked it. Then he turned to Cathy and Ollie. "I have to find Victor Holland," he said. "And I have to find him fast."

"Man," Ollie muttered into his chest. "This guy sounds like a broken record."

"Who are you?" demanded Cathy.

"The name's Sam Polowski. I work out of the San Francisco office." He pulled out his badge and slapped it on the desk. "Take a closer look if you want. It's official."

"Uh, excuse me?" called Ollie. "Could I maybe, possibly, get into a more comfortable position?"

Polowski ignored him. His attention was focused on Cathy. "I don't think I need to spell it out for you, Miss Weaver. Holland's in trouble."

"And you're one of his biggest problems," she retorted.

"That's where you're wrong." Polowski moved closer, his gaze unflinching, his voice absolutely steady. "I'm one of his hopes. Maybe his only hope."

"You're trying to kill him."

"Not me. Someone else, someone who's going to succeed. Unless I can stop it."

She shook her head. "I'm not stupid! I know about you. What you've been trying to—"

"Not me. The other guy." He reached for the telephone on the desk. "Here," he said, holding the receiver out to her. "Call Milo Lum. Ask him what happened at his house this morning. Maybe he'll convince you I'm on your side."

Cathy stared at the man, wondering what sort of game he was playing. Wondering why she was falling for it. *Because I want so much to believe him.*

"He's alone out there," said Polowski. "One man trying to buck the U.S. government. He's new to the game. Sooner or later he's going to slip, do something stupid. And that'll be it." He dialed the phone for her and again held out the receiver. "Go on. Talk to Lum."

She heard the phone ring three times, followed by Milo's answer "Hello? Hello?"

Slowly she took the receiver. "Milo?"

"Is that you? Cathy? God, I was hoping you'd call—"

"Listen, Milo. I need to ask you something. It's about a man named Polowski."

"I've met him."

"You *have?*" She looked up and saw Polowski nodding.

"Lucky for me," said Milo. "The guy's got the charm of an old shoe but he saved my life. I don't know what Gersh was talking about. Is Gersh around? I have to—"

"Thanks, Milo," she murmured. "Thanks a lot." She hung up.

Polowski was still looking at her.

"Okay," she said. "I want your side of it. From the beginning."

"You gonna help me out?"

"I haven't decided." She crossed her arms. "Convince me."

Polowski nodded. "That's just what I plan to do."

Chapter Ten

For Victor it was a long and miserable afternoon. After leaving the lake, he wandered around the campus for a while, ending up at last in the main quad. There in the courtyard, standing among the buildings of sandstone and red tile, Victor struggled to keep his mind on the business at hand: exposing Viratek. But his thoughts kept shifting back to Cathy, to that look she'd given him, full of hurt abandonment.

As if I'd betrayed her.

If she could just see the good sense in his actions. He was a scientist, a man whose life and work was ruled by logic. Sending her away was the logical thing to do. The authorities were closing in, the noose was growing ever tighter. He could accept the danger to himself. After all, he'd chosen to take on Jerry's battle, to see this through to the end.

What he hadn't chosen was to put Cathy in danger. *Now she's out of the mess and on her way to a safe place. One less thing to worry about. Time to put her out of my mind.*

As if I could.

He stared up at one of the courtyard's Romanesque arches and reminded himself, once again, of the wisdom of his actions. Still, the uneasiness remained. Where was she? Was she safe? She'd been gone only an hour and he missed her already.

He gave a shrug, as though by that gesture, he could

somehow cast off the fears. Still they remained, constant and gnawing. He found a place under the eaves and huddled on the steps to wait for Ollie's return.

At dusk he was still waiting. By the last feeble light of day, he paced the stone courtyard. He counted and re-counted the number of hours it should've taken Ollie to drive to San José Airport and return. He added in traffic time, red lights, ticket-counter delays. Surely three hours was enough. Cathy had to be on a plane by now, jetting for warmer climes.

Where was Ollie?

At the sound of the first footstep, he spun around. For a moment he couldn't believe what he was seeing, couldn't understand how she could be standing there, silhouetted beneath the sandstone archway. "Cathy?" he said in amaze-ment.

She stepped out, into the courtyard. "Victor," she said softly. She started toward him, slowly at first, and then, in a jubilant burst of flight, ran toward his waiting arms. He swept her up, swung her around, kissed her hair, her face. He didn't understand why she was here but he rejoiced that she was.

"I don't know if I've done the right thing," she mur-mured. "I hope to God I have."

"Why did you come back?"

"I wasn't sure—I'm still not sure—"

"Cathy, what are you doing here?"

"You can't fight this alone! And he can help you—"

"Who can?"

From out of the twilight came another voice, gruff and startling. "*I* can."

At once Victor stiffened. His gaze shifted back to the arch behind Cathy. A man emerged and walked slowly to-ward him. Not a tall man, he had the sort of body that, in a weight-loss ad, would've been labeled Before. He came up to Victor and planted himself squarely on the court-yard stones.

"Hello, Holland," he said. "I'm glad we've finally met. The name is Sam Polowski."

Victor turned and looked in disbelief at Cathy. "Why?" he asked in quiet fury. "Just tell me that. *Why?*"

She reacted as though he'd delivered a physical blow. Tentatively she reached for his arm; he pulled away from her at once.

"He wants to help," she said, her voice wretched with pain. "*Listen* to him!"

"I'm not sure there's any point to listening. Not now." He felt his whole body go slack in defeat. He didn't understand it, would never understand it. It was over, the running, the scraping along on fear and hope. All because Cathy had betrayed him. He turned matter-of-factly to Polowski. "I take it I'm under arrest," he said.

"Hardly," said Polowski, nodding toward the archway. "Seeing as he's got my gun."

"What?"

"Hey, Gersh! Over here!" Ollie yelled. "See, I got him covered!"

Polowski winced. "Geez, do ya have to wave the damn thing?"

"Sorry," said Ollie.

"Now, does that convince you, Holland?" asked Polow-ski. "You think I'd hand my piece over to an idiot like him if I didn't want to talk to you?"

"He's telling the truth," insisted Cathy. "He gave the gun to Ollie. He was willing to take the risk, just to meet you face-to-face."

"Bad move, Polowski," said Victor bitterly. "I'm wanted

for murder, remember? Industrial espionage? How do you know I won't just blow you away?"

"'Cause I know you're innocent."

"That makes a difference, does it?"

"It does to me."

"Why?"

"You're caught up in something big, Holland. Something that's going to eat you up alive. Something that's got my supervisor doing backflips to keep me off the case. I don't like being pulled off a case. It hurts my delicate ego."

The two men gazed at each other through the gathering darkness, each sizing up the other.

At last Victor nodded. He looked at Cathy, a quiet plea for forgiveness, for not believing in her. When at last she came into his arms, he felt the world had suddenly gone right again.

He heard a deliberate clearing of a throat. Turning, he saw Polowski hold out his hand. Victor took it in a handshake that could very well be his doom—or his salvation.

"You've led me on a long, hard chase," said Polowski. "I think it's time we worked together."

"BASICALLY," SAID OLLIE, "What we have here is just your simple, everyday mission impossible."

They were assembled in Polowski's hotel room, a five-member team that Milo had just dubbed the "Older, Crazier Out of Tuners," or Old COOTS for short. On the table in the center of the room lay potato chips, beer and the photos detailing Viratek's security system. There was also a map of the Viratek compound, forty acres of buildings and wooded grounds, all of it surrounded by an electrified fence. They had been studying the photos for an hour now, and the job that lay before them looked hopeless.

"No easy way in," said Ollie, shaking his head. "Even

if those keypad codes are still valid, you're faced with the human element of recognition. Two guards, two positions. No way they're gonna let you pass."

"There has to be a way," said Polowski. "Come on, Holland. You're the egghead. Use that creative brain of yours."

Cathy looked at Victor. While the others had tossed ideas back and forth, he had said very little. *And he's the one with the most at stake—his life,* she thought. It took incredible courage—or foolhardiness—even to consider such a desperate move. Yet here he was, calmly scanning the map as though he were planning nothing more dangerous than a Sunday drive.

He must have felt her gaze, for he slung his arm around her and tugged her close. Now that they were reunited, she savored every moment they shared, committed to memory every look, every caress. Soon he could be wrenched away from her. Even now he was making plans to enter what looked like a death trap.

He pressed a kiss to the top of her head. Then, reluctantly, he turned his attention back to the map.

"The electronics I'm not worried about," he said. "It's the human element. The guards."

Milo cocked his head toward Polowski. "I still say ol' J. Edgar here should get a warrant and raid the place."

"Right," snorted Polowski. "By the time that order gets through the judge and Dafoe and your Aunt Minnie's cousin, Viratek'll have that lab turned into a baby-milk factory. No, we need to get in on our own. Without anyone getting word of it." He looked at Ollie. "And you're sure this is the only evidence we'll need?"

Ollie nodded. "One vial should do it. Then we take it to a reputable lab, have them confirm it's smallpox, and your case is airtight."

"They'll have no way around it?"

"None. The virus is officially extinct. Any company caught playing with a live sample is, ipso facto, dead meat."

"I like that," said Polowski. "That ipso facto stuff. No fancy Viratek attorney can argue that one away."

"But first you gotta get hold of a vial," said Ollie. "And from where I'm standing, it looks impossible. Unless we're willing to try armed robbery."

For one frightening moment, Polowski actually seemed to give that thought serious consideration. "Naw," he conceded. "Wouldn't go over well in court."

"Besides which," said Ollie, "I refuse to shoot another human being. It's against my principles."

"Mine, too," said Milo.

"But theft," said Ollie, "that's acceptable."

Polowski looked at Victor. "A group with high moral standards."

Victor grinned. "Holdovers from the sixties."

"Sounds like we're back to the first option," said Cathy. "We have to steal the virus." She focused on the map of the compound, noting the electrified fence that circled the entire complex. The main road led straight to the front gate. Except for an unpaved fire road, labeled *not maintained,* no other approaches were apparent.

"All right," she said. "Assume you do get through the front gate. You still have to get past two locked doors, two separate guards and a laser grid. Come on."

"The doors are no problem," said Victor. "It's the two guards."

"Maybe a diversion?" suggested Milo. "How about we set a fire?"

"And bring in the town fire department?" said Victor. "Not a good idea. Besides, I've dealt with this night guard at the front gate. I know him. And he goes strictly by the book. Never leaves the booth. At the first hint of anything suspicious, he'll hit the alarm button."

"Maybe Milo could whip up a fake security pass," said Ollie. "You know, the way he used to fix us up with those fake drivers' licenses."

"He falsified IDs?" said Polowski.

"Hey, I just changed the age to twenty-one!" protested Milo.

"Made great passports, too," said Ollie. "I had one from the kingdom of Booga Booga. It got me right past the customs official in Athens."

"Yeah?" Polowski looked impressed. "So what about it, Holland? Would it work?"

"Not a chance. The guard has a master list of top-security employees. If he doesn't know the face, he'll do a double check."

"But he does let some people through automatically?"

"Sure. The bigwigs. The ones he recognizes on—" Victor suddenly paused and turned to stare at Cathy "—on sight. Lord. It just might work."

Cathy took one look at his face and immediately read his mind. "No," she said. "It's not that easy! I need to see the subject! I need molds of his face. Detailed photos from every angle—"

"But you *could* do it. You do it all the time."

"On film it works! But this is face-to-face!"

"It's at night, through a car window. Or through a video camera. If you could just make me pass for one of the exec's—"

"What are you talking about?" demanded Polowski.

"Cathy's a makeup artist. You know, horror films, special effects."

"This is different!" Cathy said. The difference being it was Victor's life on the line. No, he couldn't ask her to do this. If anything went wrong, she would be responsible. Having his death on her conscience would be more than she could live with.

She shook her head, praying he'd read the deadly earnestness in her gaze. "There's too much at stake," she insisted. "It's not as simple as—as filming *Slimelords!*"

"You did *Slimelords*?" asked Milo. "Terrific flick!"

"Besides," said Cathy, "it's not that easy, copying a face. I have to cast a mold, to get the features just right. For that I need a model."

"You mean the real guy?" asked Polowski.

"Right. The real guy. And I hardly think you're going to get some Viratek executive to sit down and let me slap plaster all over his face."

There was a long silence.

"That does present a problem," said Milo.

"Not necessarily."

They all turned and looked at Ollie.

"What are you thinking?" asked Victor.

"About this guy who works with me once in a while. Down in the lab…" Ollie looked up, and the grin on his face was distinctly smug. "He's a veterinarian."

THE EVENTS OF the past few weeks had weighed heavily on Archibald Black, so heavily, in fact, that he found it difficult to carry on with those everyday tasks of life. Just driving to and from his office at Viratek was an ordeal. And then, to sit down at his desk and face his secretary and pretend that nothing, absolutely nothing, was wrong—that was almost more than he could manage. He was a scientist, not an actor.

Not a criminal.

But that's what they would call him, if the experiments in C wing ever came to light. His instinct was to shut the lab down, to destroy the contents of those incubators. But Matthew Tyrone insisted the work continue. They were so close to completion. After all, Defense had underwritten the project, and Defense expected a product. This matter of Victor Holland was only a minor glitch, soon to be solved. The thing to do was carry on.

Easy for Tyrone to say, thought Black. *Tyrone had no conscience to bother him.*

These thoughts had plagued him all day. Now, as Black packed up his briefcase, he felt desperate to flee forever this teak-and-leather office, to take refuge in some safe and anonymous job. It was with a sigh of relief that he walked out the door.

It was dark when he pulled into his gravel driveway. The house, a saltbox of cedar and glass tucked among the trees, looked cold and empty and in need of a woman. Perhaps he should call his neighbor Muriel. She always seemed to appreciate an impromptu dinner together. Her snappy wit and green Jell-O salad almost made up for the fact she was 75. What a shame his generation didn't produce many Muriels.

He stepped out of his car and started up the path to the front door. Halfway there, he heard a soft *whht!* and almost simultaneously, a sharp pain stung his neck. Reflexively he slapped at it; something came away in his hands. In wonderment, he stared down at the dart, trying to understand where it had come from and how such a thing had managed to lodge in his neck. But he found he couldn't think straight. And then he found he was having trouble seeing, that the night had suddenly darkened to a dense blackness, that his legs were being sucked into some sort of quagmire. His briefcase slipped from his grasp and thudded to the ground.

I'm dying, he thought. And then, *Will anyone find me here?*

It was his last conscious thought before he collapsed onto the leaf-strewn path.

"IS HE DEAD?"

Ollie bent forward and listened for Archibald Black's breathing. "He's definitely alive. But out cold." He looked up at Polowski and Victor. "Okay, let's move it. He'll be out for only an hour or so."

Victor grabbed the legs, Ollie and Polowski, the arms. Together they carried the unconscious man a few dozen yards through the woods, toward the clearing where the van was parked.

"You—you sure we got an hour?" gasped Polowski.

"Plus or minus," said Ollie. "The tranquilizer's designed for large animals, so the dose was only an estimate. And this guy's heavier than I expected." Ollie was panting now. "Hey, Polowski, he's slipping. Pull your weight, will ya?"

"I am! I think his right arm's heavier than his left."

The van's side door was already open for them. They rolled Black inside and slid the door closed. A bright light suddenly glared, but the unconscious man didn't even twitch.

Cathy knelt down at his side and critically examined the man's face.

"Can you do it?" asked Victor.

"Oh, I can do it," she said. "The question is, will you pass for him?" She glanced up and down the man's length, then back at Victor. "Looks about your size and build. We'll have to darken your hair, give you a widow's peak. I think you'll pass." She turned and glanced at Milo, who was already poised with his camera. "Take your photos. A few shots from every angle. I need lots of hair detail."

As Milo's strobe flashed again and again, Cathy donned gloves and an apron. She pointed to a sheet. "Drape him for me," she directed. "Everything but his face. I don't want him to wake up with plaster all over his clothes."

"Assuming he wakes up at all," said Milo, frowning down at Black's inert form.

"Oh, he'll wake up," said Ollie. "Right where we found him. And if we do the job right, Mr. Archibald Black will never know what hit him."

It was the rain that awakened him. The cold droplets pelted his face and dribbled into his open mouth. Groaning, Black turned over and felt gravel bite into his shoulder. Even in his groggy state it occurred to him that this did not make sense. Slowly he took stock of all the things that were not as they should be: the rain falling from the ceiling, the gravel in his bed, the fact he was still wearing his shoes...

At last he managed to shake himself fully awake. He found to his puzzlement that he was sitting in his driveway, and that his briefcase was lying right beside him. By now the rain had swelled to a downpour—he had to get out of the storm. Half crawling, half walking, Black managed to make it up the porch steps and into the house.

An hour later, huddled in his kitchen, a cup of coffee in hand, he tried to piece together what had happened. He remembered parking his car. He'd taken out his briefcase and apparently had managed to make it halfway up the path. And then... what?

A vague ache worried its way into his awareness. He rubbed his neck. That's when he remembered something strange had happened, just before he blacked out. Something associated with that ache in his neck.

He went to a mirror and looked. There it was, a small puncture in the skin. An absurd thought popped into his head: *Vampires.* Right. *Damn it, Archibald. You are a scientist. Come up with a rational explanation.*

He went to the laundry hamper and fished out his damp shirt. To his alarm he spotted a droplet of blood on the lapel. Then he saw what had caused it: a common, everyday tailor's pin. It was still lodged in the collar, no doubt left there by the dry cleaners. There was his rational explanation. He'd been pricked by a collar pin and the pain had sent him into a faint.

In disgust, he threw the shirt down. First thing in the morning, he was going to complain to the Tidy Girl cleaners and demand they do his suit for free.

Vampires, indeed.

"EVEN WITH BAD lighting, you'll be lucky if you pass," said Cathy.

She stood back and gave Victor a long, critical look. Slowly she walked around him, eyeing the newly darkened hair, the resculpted face, the new eye color. It was as close as she could make it, but it wasn't good enough. It would never be good enough, not when Victor's life was at stake.

"I think he's the spitting image," said Polowski. "What's the problem now?"

"The problem is, I suddenly realize it's a crazy idea. I say we call it off."

"You've been working on him all afternoon. You got it right down to the damn freckles on his nose. What else can you improve on?"

"I don't know. I just don't feel *good* about this!"

There was a silence as she confronted the four men.

Ollie shook his head. "Women's intuition. That's a dangerous thing to disregard."

"Well, here's *my* intuition," said Polowski. "I think it'll work. And I think it's our best option. Our chance to nail the case."

Cathy turned to Victor. "You're the one who'll get hurt. It's your decision." What she really wanted to say was, *Please. Don't do it. Stay with me. Stay alive and safe and mine.* But she knew, looking into his eyes, that he'd already made his decision, and no matter how much she might wish for it, he would never really be hers.

"Cathy," he said. "It'll work. You have to believe that."

"The only thing I believe," she said, "is that you're going to get killed. And I don't want to be around to watch it."

Without another word, she turned and walked out the door.

Outside, in the parking lot of the Rockabye Motel, she stood in the darkness and hugged herself. She heard the door shut, and then his footsteps moved toward her across the blacktop.

"You don't have to stay," he said. "There's still that beach in Mexico. You could fly there tonight, be out of this mess."

"Do you want me to go?"

A pause, then, "Yes."

She shrugged, a poor attempt at nonchalance. "All right. I suppose it all makes perfect sense. I've done my part."

"You saved my life. At the very least, I owe you a measure of safety."

She turned to him. "Is that what weighs most on your mind, Victor? The fact that you *owe* me?"

"What weighs most on my mind is that you might get caught in the crossfire. I'm prepared to walk through those doors at Viratek. I'm prepared to do a lot of stupid things. But I'm not prepared to watch you get hurt. Does that make any sense?" He pulled her against him, into a place that felt infinitely warm and safe. "Cathy, Cathy. I'm not crazy. I don't want to die. But I don't see any way around this…."

She pressed her face against his chest, felt his heartbeat, so steady, so regular. She was afraid to think of that heart not beating, of those arms no longer alive to hold her. He was brave enough to go through with this crazy scheme; couldn't she somehow dredge up the same courage? She thought, *I've come this far with you. How could I dream of walking away? Now that I know I love you?*

The motel door opened, and light arced across the parking lot. "Gersh?" said Ollie. "It's getting late. If we want to go ahead, we'll have to leave now."

Victor was still looking at her. "Well?" he said. "Do you want Ollie to take you to the airport?"

"No." She squared her shoulders. "I'm coming with you."

"Are you sure that's what you want to do?"

"I'm never sure of anything these days. But on this I've decided. I'll stick it out." She managed a smile. "Besides, you might need me on the set. In case your face falls off."

"I need you for a hell of a lot more than that."

"Gersh?"

Victor reached out for Cathy's hand. She let him take it. "We're coming," he said. "Both of us."

"I'M APPROACHING THE front gate. One guard in the booth. No one else around. Copy?"

"Loud and clear," said Polowski.

"Okay. Here I go. Wish me luck."

"We'll be tuned in. Break a leg." Polowski clicked off the microphone and glanced at the others. "Well, folks, he's on his way."

To what? Cathy wondered. She glanced around at the other faces. There were four of them huddled in the van. They'd parked a half mile from Viratek's front gate. Close enough to hear Victor's transmissions, but too far away to do him much good. With the microphone link, they could mark his progress.

They could also mark his death.

In silence, they waited for the first hurdle.

"EVENING," SAID VICTOR, pulling up at the gate.

The guard peered out through the booth window. He was in his twenties, cap on straight, collar button fastened. This was Pete Zahn, Mr. By-the-book Extraordinaire. If anyone was to cut the operation short, it would be this man. Victor made a brave attempt at a smile and prayed his mask wouldn't crack. It seemed an eternity, that exchange of looks. Then, to Victor's relief, the man smiled back.

"Working late, Dr. Black?"

"Forgot something at the lab."

"Must be important, huh? To make a special trip at midnight."

"These government contracts. Gotta be done on time."

"Yeah." The guard waved him through. "Have a nice night."

Heart pounding, Victor pulled through the gate. Only when he'd rounded the curve into the empty parking lot did he manage a sigh of relief. "First base," he said into the microphone. "Come on, guys. Talk to me."

"We're here," came the response. It was Polowski.

"I'm heading into the building—can't be sure the signal will get through those walls. So if you don't hear from me—"

"We'll be listening."

"I've got a message for Cathy. Put her on."

There was a pause, then he heard, "I'm here, Victor."

"I just wanted to tell you this. I'm coming back. I promise. Copy?"

He wasn't sure if it was just the signal's waiver, but

he thought he heard the beginning of tears in her reply. "I copy."

"I'm going in now. Don't leave without me."

IT TOOK PETE Zahn only a minute to look up Archibald Black's license plate number. He kept a Rolodex in the booth, though he seldom referred to it as he had a good memory for numbers. He knew every executive's license by heart. It was his own little mind game, a test of his cleverness. And the plate on Dr. Black's car just didn't seem right.

He found the file card. The auto matched up okay: a gray 1991 Lincoln sedan. And he was fairly certain that *was* Dr. Black sitting in the driver's seat. But the license number was all wrong.

He sat back and thought about it for a while, trying to come up with all the possible explanations. That Black was simply driving a different auto. That Black was playing a joke on him, testing him.

That it hadn't been Archibald Black, at all.

Pete reached for the telephone. The way to find out was to call Black's home. It was after midnight, but it had to be done. If Black didn't answer the phone, then that must be him in the Lincoln. And if he *did* answer, then something was terribly wrong and Black would want to know about it.

Two rings. That's all it took before a groggy voice answered, "Hello?"

"This is Pete Zahn, night man at Viratek. Is this—is this Dr. Black?"

"Yes."

"Dr. *Archibald* Black?"

"Look, it's late! What is it?"

"I don't know how to tell you this, Dr. Black, but…" Pete cleared his throat. "Your double just drove through the gate…."

"I'M THROUGH THE front door. Heading up the hall to the security wing. In case anyone's listening." Victor didn't expect a reply, and he heard none. The building was a concrete monstrosity, designed to last forever. He doubted a radio signal would make it through these walls. Though he'd been on his own from the moment he'd entered the front gate, at least he'd had the comfort of knowing his friends were listening in on the progress. Now he was truly alone.

He moved at a casual pace to the locked door marked Authorized Personnel Only. A camera hung from the ceiling, its lens pointed straight at him. He pointedly ignored it and turned his attention to the security keypad mounted on the wall. The numbers Jerry had given him had gotten him through the front door; would the second combination get him through this one? His hands were sweating as he punched in the seven digits. He felt a dart of panic as a beep sounded and a message flashed on the screen: *Incorrect security code. Access denied.*

He could feel the sweat building up beneath the mask. Were the numbers wrong? Had he simply transposed two digits? He knew someone was watching him through the camera, wondering why he was taking so long. He took a deep breath and tried again. This time, he entered the digits slowly, deliberately. He braced himself for the warning beep. To his relief, it didn't go off.

Instead, a new message appeared. *Security code accepted. Please enter.*

He stepped through, into the next room.

Third hurdle, he thought in relief as the door closed behind him. Now for the home run.

Another camera, mounted in a corner, was pointed at him. Acutely conscious of that lens, he made his way across the room to the inner lab door. He turned the knob and a warning bell sounded.

Now what? he thought. Only then did he notice the red light glowing over the door, and the warning *Laser grid activated.* He needed a key to shut it off. He saw no other way to deactivate it, no way to get past it, into the room beyond.

It was time for desperate measures, time for a little chutzpah. He patted his pockets, then turned and faced the camera. "Hello?" He waved.

A voice answered over an intercom. "Is there a problem, Dr. Black?"

"Yes. I can't seem to find my keys. I must have left them at home…."

"I can cut the lasers from here."

"Thanks. Gee, I don't know how this happened."

"No problem."

At once the red warning light shut off. Cautiously Victor tried the door; it swung open. He gave the camera a goodbye wave and entered the last room.

Inside, to his relief, there were no cameras anywhere—at least, none that he could spot. A bit of breathing space, he thought. He moved into the lab and took a quick survey of his surroundings. What he saw was a mind-numbing display of space-age equipment—not just the expected centrifuges and microscopes, but instruments he'd never seen before, all of them brand-new and gleaming. He headed through the decontamination chamber, past the laminar flow unit, and went straight to the incubators. He opened the door.

Glass vials tinkled in their compartments. He took one out. Pink fluid glistened within. The label read Lot #341. Active.

This must be it, he thought. This was what Ollie had told him to look for. Here was the stuff of nightmares, the grim reaper distilled to sub-microscopic elements.

He removed two vials, fitted them into a specially

padded cigarette case, and slipped it into his pocket. *Mission accomplished,* he thought in triumph as he headed back through the lab. All that lay before him was a casual stroll back to his car. Then the champagne…

He was halfway across the room when the alarm bell went off.

He froze, the harsh ring echoing in his ears.

"Dr. Black?" said the guard's voice over some hidden intercom. "Please don't leave. Stay right where you are."

Victor spun around wildly, trying to locate the speaker. "What's going on?"

"I've just been asked to detain you. If you'll hold on, I'll find out what—"

Victor didn't wait to hear the reason—he bolted for the door. Even as he reached it, he heard the whine of the lasers powering on, felt something slash his arm. He shoved through the first door, dashed across the anteroom and out the security door, into the hallway.

Everywhere, alarms were going off. The whole damn building had turned into an echo chamber of ringing bells. His gaze shot right, to the front entrance. No, not that way— the guard was stationed there.

He sprinted left, toward what he hoped was a fire exit. Somewhere behind him a voice yelled, "Halt!" He ignored it and kept running. At the end of the hall he slammed against the opening bar and found himself in a stairwell. No exit, only steps leading up and down. He wasn't about to be trapped like a rat in the basement. He headed up the stairs.

One flight into his climb, he heard the stairwell door slam open on the first floor. Again a voice commanded, "Halt or I'll shoot!"

A bluff, he thought.

A pistol shot exploded, echoing up the concrete stairwell.

Not a bluff. With new desperation, he pushed through the landing door, into the second-floor hallway. A line of closed doors stretched before him. Which one, which one? There was no time to think. He ducked into the third room and softly shut the door behind him.

In the semidarkness, he spotted the gleam of stainless steel and glass beakers. Another lab. Only this one had a large window, now shimmering with moonlight, looming over the far countertop.

From down the hall came the slam of a door being kicked open and the guard's shouted command: "Freeze!"

He was down to one last escape route. Victor grabbed a chair, raised it over his head, and flung it at the window. The glass shattered, raining moonlight-silvered shards into the darkness below. He scarcely bothered to look before he leapt. Bracing himself for the impact, he jumped from the window and landed in a tangle of shrubbery.

"Halt!" came a shout from above.

That was enough to jar Victor back to his feet. He sprinted off across a lawn, into the cover of trees. Glancing back, he saw no pursuing shadow. The guard wasn't about to risk his neck leaping out any window.

Got to make it out the gate...

Victor circled around the building, burrowing his way through bushes and trees to a stand of oaks. From there he could view the front gate, way off in the distance. What he saw made his heart sink.

Floodlights illuminated the entrance, glaring down on the four security cars blocking the driveway. Now a panel truck pulled up. The driver went around to the back and opened the doors. At his command two German shepherds leaped out and danced around, barking at his feet.

Victor backed away, stumbling deeper into the grove of oaks. *No way out,* he thought, glancing behind him at the fence, topped with coils of barbed wire. Already, the dogs' barking was moving closer. *Unless I can sprout wings and fly, I'm a dead man....*

Chapter Eleven

"Something's wrong!" Cathy cried as the first security car drove past.

Polowski touched her arm. "Easy. It could be just a routine patrol."

"No. Look!" Through the trees, they spotted three more cars, all roaring down the road at top speed toward Viratek.

Ollie muttered a surprisingly coarse oath and reached for the microphone.

"Wait!" Polowski grabbed his hand. "We can't risk a transmission. Let him contact us first."

"If he's in trouble—"

"Then he already knows it. Give him a chance to make it out on his own."

"What if he's trapped?" said Cathy. "Are we just going to sit here?"

"We don't have a choice. Not if they've blockaded the front gate—"

"We *do* have a choice!" said Cathy, scrambling forward into the driver's seat.

"What the hell are you doing?" demanded Polowski.

"Giving him a fighting chance. If we don't—"

They all fell instantly silent as a transmission suddenly hissed over the receiver. "Looks like I got myself in a bind, guys. Don't see a way out. You copy?"

Ollie snatched up the microphone. "Copy, Gersh. What's your situation?"

"Bad."

"Specify."

"Front gate's blocked and lit up like a football field. Big time alarms going off. They just brought in the dogs—"

"Can you get over the fence?"

"Negative. It's electrified. Low voltage, but more than I can handle. You guys better hit the road without me."

Polowski grabbed the microphone and barked, "Did you get the stuff?"

Cathy turned and snapped: "Forget that! Ask him where he is. *Ask him!*"

"Holland?" said Polowski. "Where are you?"

"At the northeast perimeter. Fence goes all the way around. Look, get moving. I'll manage—"

"Tell him to head for the east fence!" Cathy said. "Near the midpoint!"

"What?"

"Just tell him!"

"Go to the east fence," Polowski said into the microphone. "Midpoint."

"I copy."

Polowski looked up at Cathy in puzzlement. "What the hell are you thinking of?"

"This is a getaway car, right?" she muttered as she turned on the engine. "I say we put it to its intended use!" She threw the van into gear and spun it around, onto the road.

"Hey, you're going the wrong way!" yelled Milo.

"No, I'm not. There's a fire road, just off to the left somewhere. There it is." She made a sharp turn, onto what was little more than a dirt track. They bounced along, crashing through tree branches and shrubs, a ride so violently spine-shaking it was all they could do to hang on.

"How did you find this *wonderful* road?" Polowski managed to ask.

"It was on the map. I saw it when we were studying the plans for Viratek."

"Is this a scenic route? Or does it go somewhere?"

"The east fence. Used to be the construction entrance for the compound. I'm hoping it's still clear enough to get through…."

"And then what happens?"

Ollie sighed. "Don't ask."

Cathy steered around a bush that had sprung up in her path and ran head-on into a sapling. Her passengers tumbled to the floor. "Sorry," she muttered. Reversing gear, she spun them back on the road. "It should be just ahead…."

A barrier of chain link suddenly loomed before them. Instantly she cut the lights. Through the darkness, they could hear dogs barking, moving in. Where was he?

Then they saw him, flitting through the moonlight. He was running. Somewhere off to the side, a man shouted and gunfire spat the ground.

"Brace yourselves!" yelled Cathy. She snapped on her seatbelt and gripped the steering wheel. Then she stepped on the gas.

The van jerked forward like a bronco, barreled through the underbrush, and slammed into the fence. The chain link sagged; electrical sparks hissed in the night. Cathy threw the gears into reverse, backed up, and hit the gas again.

The fence toppled; barbed wire scraped across the windshield.

"We're through!" said Ollie. He yanked open the sliding door and yelled: "Come on, Gersh! Come on!"

The running figure zigzagged across the grass. All around him, gunfire exploded. He made a last flying leap across the coil of barbed wire and stumbled.

"Come on, Gersh!"

Gunfire spattered the van.

Victor struggled back to his feet. They heard the rip of clothing, then he was reaching up to them, being dragged inside, to safety.

The door slammed shut. Cathy backed up, wheeled the van around and slammed on the gas pedal.

They leaped forward, bouncing through the bushes and across ruts. Another round of bullets pinged the van. Cathy was oblivious to it. She focused only on getting them back to the main road. The sound of gunfire receded. At last the trees gave way to a familiar band of blacktop. She turned left and gunned the engine, anxious to put as many miles as possible between them and Viratek.

Off in the distance, a siren wailed.

"We got company!" said Polowski.

"Which way now?" Cathy cried. Viratek lay behind them; the sirens were approaching from ahead.

"I don't know! Just get the hell out of here!"

As yet her view of the police cars was blocked by trees, but she could hear the sirens moving rapidly closer. *Will they let us pass? Or will they pull us over?*

Almost too late she spotted a clearing, off to the side. On sudden impulse she veered off the pavement, and the van bounced onto a stubbly field.

"Don't tell me," groaned Polowski. "Another fire road?"

"Shut up!" she snapped and steered straight for a clump of bushes. With a quick turn of the wheel, she circled behind the shrubbery and cut her lights.

It was just in time. Seconds later, two patrol cars, lights flashing, sped right past the concealing bushes. She sat frozen, listening as the sirens faded in the distance. Then, in the darkness, she heard Milo say softly, "Her name is Bond. Jane Bond."

Half laughing, half crying, Cathy turned as Victor scrambled beside her, onto the front seat. At once she was in his arms, her tears wetting his shirt, her sobs muffled in the depths of his embrace. He kissed her damp cheeks, her mouth. The touch of his lips stilled her tremors.

From the back came the sound of a throat being cleared. "Uh, Gersh?" inquired Ollie politely. "Don't you think we ought to get moving?"

Victor's mouth was still pressed against Cathy's. Reluctantly he broke contact but his gaze never left her face. "Sure," he murmured, just before he pulled her back for another kiss. "But would somebody else mind driving...?"

"HERE'S WHERE THINGS get dangerous," said Polowski. He was at the wheel now, as they headed south toward San Francisco. Cathy and Victor sat in front with Polowski; in the back of the van, Milo and Ollie lay curled up asleep like two exhausted puppies. From the radio came the soft strains of a country western song. The dials glowed a vivid green in the darkness.

"We've finally got the evidence," said Polowski. "All we need to hang 'em. They'll be desperate. Ready to try anything. From here on out, folks, it's going to be a game of cat and mouse."

As if it wasn't already, thought Cathy as she huddled closer to Victor. She longed for a chance to be alone with him. There had been no time for tearful reunions, no time for any confessions of love. They'd spent the last two hours on a harrowing journey down backroads, always avoiding the police. By now the break-in at Viratek would have been reported to the authorities. The state police would be on the lookout for a van with frontal damage.

Polowski was right. Things were only getting more dangerous.

"Soon as we hit the city," said Polowski, "we'll get those vials off to separate labs. Independent confirmation. That should wipe any doubts away. You know names we can trust, Holland?"

"Fellow alum back in New Haven. Runs the hospital lab. I can trust him."

"Yale? Great. That'll have clout."

"Ollie has a pal at UCSF. They'll take care of the second vial."

"And when those reports get back, I know a certain journalist who loves to have a little birdie chirp in his ear." Polowski gave the steering wheel a satisfied slap. "Viratek, you are dead meat."

"You enjoy this, don't you?" said Cathy.

"Workin' the right side of the law? I say it's good for the soul. It keeps your mind sharp and your feet on their toes. It helps you stay young."

"Or die young," said Cathy.

Polowski laughed. "Women. They just never understand the game."

"I don't understand it, at all."

"I bet Holland here does. He just had the adrenaline high of his life. Didn't you?"

Victor didn't answer. He was gazing ahead at the blacktop stretching before their headlights.

"Well, wasn't it a high?" asked Polowski. "To claw your way to hell and back again? To know you made it through on nothing much more than your wits?"

"No," said Victor quietly. "Because it's not over yet."

Polowski's grin faded. He turned his attention back to the road. "Almost," he said. "It's almost over."

They passed a sign: San Francisco: 12 Miles.

FOUR IN THE morning. The stars were mere pinpricks in a sky washed out by streetlights. In a North Beach doughnut shop, five weary souls had gathered around steaming coffee and cheese Danish. Only one other table was occupied, by a man with bloodshot eyes and shaking hands. The girl behind the counter sat with her nose buried in a paperback. Behind her, the coffee machine hissed out a fresh brew.

"To the Old Coots," said Milo, raising his cup. "Still the best ensemble around."

They all raised their cups. "To the Old Coots!"

"And to our newest and fairest member," said Milo. "The beautiful—the intrepid—"

"Oh, *please,*" said Cathy.

Victor wrapped his arm around her shoulder. "Relax and be honored. Not everyone gets into this highly selective group."

"The only requirement," said Ollie, "is that you have to play a musical instrument badly."

"But I don't play anything."

"No problem." Ollie fished out a piece of waxed paper from the pile of Danishes and wrapped it around his pocket comb. "Kazoo."

"Fitting," said Milo. "Since that was Lily's instrument."

"Oh." She took the comb. Lily's instrument. It always came back to *her,* the ghost who would forever be there. Suddenly the air of celebration was gone, as though swept away by the cold wind of dawn. She glanced at Victor. He was looking out the window, at the garishly lit streets. *What are you thinking? Are you wishing she was here? That it wasn't me being presented this silly kazoo, but her?*

She put the comb to her lips and hummed an appropriately out-of-tune version of "Yankee Doodle." Everyone laughed and clapped, even Victor. But when the applause was over, she saw the sad and weary look in his eyes. Quietly she set the kazoo down on the table.

Outside, a delivery truck roared past. It was 5:00 a.m.; the city was stirring.

"Well, folks," said Polowski, slapping down a dollar tip. "We got a hotshot reporter to roust outta bed. And then you and I—" he looked at Victor "—have a few deliveries to make. When's United leave for New Haven?"

"At ten-fifteen," said Victor.

"Okay. I'll buy you the plane tickets. In the meantime, you see if you can't grow yourself a new mustache or something." Polowski glanced at Cathy. "You're going with him, right?"

"No," she said, looking at Victor.

She was hoping for a reaction, any reaction. What she saw was a look of relief. And, strangely, resignation.

He didn't try to change her mind. He simply asked, "Where will you be going?"

She shrugged. "Maybe I should stick to our original plan. You know, head south. Hang out with Jack for a while. What do you think?"

It was his chance to stop her. His chance to say, *No, I want you around. I won't let you leave, not now, not ever.* If he really loved her, that's exactly what he would say.

Her heart sank when he simply nodded and said, "I think it's a good idea."

She blinked back the tears before anyone could see them. With an indifferent smile she looked at Ollie. "So I guess I'll need a ride. When are you and Milo heading home?"

"Right now, I guess," said Ollie, looking bewildered. "Seeing as our job's pretty much done."

"Can I hitch along? I'll catch the bus at Palo Alto."

"No problem. In fact, you can sit in the honored front seat."

"Long as you don't let her behind the wheel," grumbled Milo. "I want a nice, quiet drive home if you don't mind."

Polowski rose to his feet. "Then we're all set. Everyone's got a place to go. Let's do it."

Outside, on a street rumbling with early-morning traffic, with their friends standing only a few yards away, Cathy and Victor said their goodbyes. It wasn't the place for sentimental farewells. Perhaps that was all for the best. At least she could leave with some trace of dignity. At least she could avoid hearing, from his lips, the brutal truth. She would simply walk away and hold on to the fantasy that he loved her. That in their brief time together she'd managed to work her way, just a little, into his heart.

"You'll be all right?" he asked.

"I'll be fine. And you?"

"I'll manage." He thrust his hands in his pockets and looked off at a bus idling near the corner. "I'll miss you," he said. "But I know it doesn't make sense for us to be together. Not under the circumstances."

I would stay with you, she thought. *Under any circumstances. If I only knew you wanted me.*

"Anyway," he said with a sigh, "I'll let you know when things are safe again. When you can come home."

"And then?"

"And then we'll take it from there," he said softly.

They kissed, a clumsy, polite kiss, all the more hurried because they knew their friends were watching. There was no passion here, only the cool, dry lips of a man saying goodbye. As they pulled apart, she saw his face blur away through the tears.

"Take care of yourself, Victor," she said. Then, shoulders squared, she turned and walked toward Ollie and Milo.

"Is that it?" asked Ollie.

"That's it." Brusquely she rubbed her hand across her eyes. "I'm ready to go."

"TELL ME ABOUT Lily," she said.

The first light of dawn was already streaking the sky as they drove past the boxy row homes of Pacifica, past the cliffs where sea waves crashed and gulls swooped and dove.

Ollie, his gaze on the road, asked: "What do you want to know?"

"What kind of woman was she?"

"She was a nice person," said Ollie. "And brainy. Though she never went out of her way to impress people, she was probably the smartest one of all of us. Definitely brighter than Milo."

"And a lot better-looking than Ollie," piped a voice from the backseat.

"A real kind, real decent woman. When she and Gersh got married, I remember thinking, 'he's got himself a saint.'" He glanced at Cathy, suddenly noticing her silence. "Of course," he added quickly, "not every man *wants* a saint. I know I'd be happier with a lady who can be a little goofy." He flashed Cathy a grin. "Someone who might, say, crash a van through an electrified fence, just for kicks."

It was a sweet thing to say, a comment designed to lift her spirits. It couldn't take the edge off her pain.

She settled back and watched dawn lighten the sky. How she needed to get away! She thought about Mexico, about warm water and hot sand and the tang of fresh fish and lime. She would throw herself into working on that new film. Of course, Jack would be on the set, Jack with his latest sweetie pie in tow, but she could handle that now. Jack would never be able to hurt her again. She was beyond that now, beyond being hurt by any man.

The drive to Milo's house seemed endless.

When at last they pulled up in the driveway, the dawn had already blossomed into a bright, cold morning. Milo climbed out and stood blinking in the sunshine.

"So, guys," he said through the car window. "Guess here's where we go our separate ways." He looked at Cathy. "Mexico, right?"

She nodded. "Puerto Vallarta. What about you?"

"I'm gonna catch up with Ma in Florida. Maybe get a load of Disney World. Wanna come, Ollie?"

"Some other time. I'm going to go get some sleep."

"Don't know what you're missing. Well, it's been some adventure. I'm almost sorry it's over." Milo turned and headed up the walk to his house. On the front porch he waved and yelled, "See you around!" Then he vanished through the front door.

Ollie laughed. "Milo and his ma, together? Disney World'll never be the same." He reached for the ignition. "Next stop, the bus station. I've got just enough gas to get us there and—"

He didn't get a chance to turn the key.

A gun barrel was thrust in the open car window. It came to rest squarely against Ollie's temple.

"Get out, Dr. Wozniak," said a voice.

Ollie's reply came out in a bare croak. "What—what do you want?"

"Do it now." The click of the hammer being cocked was all the coaxing Ollie needed.

"Okay, okay! I'm getting out!" Ollie scrambled out and backed away, his hands raised in surrender.

Cathy, too, started to climb out, but the gunman snapped, "Not you! You stay inside."

"Look," said Ollie, "You can have the damn car! You don't need her—"

"But I do. Tell Mr. Holland I'll be in contact. Regarding Ms. Weaver's future." He went around and opened the passenger door. "You, into the driver's seat!" he commanded her.

"No. Please—"

The gun barrel dug into her neck. "Need I ask again?"

Trembling, she moved behind the wheel. Her knee brushed the car keys, still dangling from the ignition. The man slid in beside her. Though the gun barrel was still thrust against her neck, it was the man's eyes she focused on. They were black, fathomless. If any spark of humanity lurked in those depths, she couldn't see it.

"Start the engine," he said.

"Where—where are we going?"

"For a drive. Somewhere scenic."

Her thoughts were racing, seeking some means of escape, but she came up with nothing. That gun was insurmountable.

She turned on the ignition.

"Hey!" yelled Ollie, grabbing at the door. "You can't do this!"

Cathy screamed, "Ollie, no!"

The gunman had already shifted his aim out the window.

"Let her go!" yelled Ollie. "Let her—"

The gun went off.

Ollie staggered backward, his face a mask of astonishment.

Cathy lunged at the gunman. Pure animal rage, fueled by the instinct to survive, sent her clawing first for his eyes. At the last split second he flinched away. Her nails scraped down his cheek, drawing blood. Before he could shift his aim, she grabbed his wrist, wrenching desperately for control of the gun. He held fast. Not with all her strength could she keep the gun at bay, keep the barrel from turning toward her.

It was the last image she registered: that black hole, slowly turning until it was pointed straight at her face.

Something lashed at her from the side. Pain exploded

in her head, shattering the world into a thousand slivers of light.

They faded, one by one, into darkness.

Chapter Twelve

"Victor's here," said Milo.

It seemed to take Ollie forever to register their presence. Victor fought the urge to shake him to consciousness, to drag the words out of his friend's throat. He was forced to wait, the silence broken only by the hiss of oxygen, the gurgle of the suction tube. At last Ollie stirred and squinted through pain-glazed eyes at the three men standing beside his bed. "Gersh. I didn't—couldn't—" He stopped, exhausted by the effort just to talk.

"Easy, Ollie," said Milo. "Take it slow."

"Tried to stop him. Had a gun…" Ollie paused, gathering the strength to continue.

Victor listened fearfully for the next terrible words to come out. He was still in a state of disbelief, still hoping that what Milo had told him was one giant mistake, that Cathy was, at this very moment, on a bus somewhere to safety. Only two hours ago he'd been ready to board a plane for New Haven. Then he'd been handed a message at the United gate. It was addressed to passenger Sam Polowski, the name on his ticket. It had consisted of only three words: *Call Milo immediately.*

Passenger "Sam Polowski" never did board the plane.

Two hours, he thought in anguish. What have they done to her in those two long hours?

"This man—what did he look like?" asked Polowski.

"Didn't see him very well. Dark hair. Face sort of…thin."

"Tall? Short?"

"Tall."

"He drove off in your car?"

Ollie nodded.

"What about Cathy?" Victor blurted out, his control shattered. "He—didn't hurt her? She's all right?"

There was a pause that, to Victor, seemed like an eternity in hell. Ollie's gaze settled mournfully on Victor. "I don't know."

It was the best Victor could hope for. *I don't know.* It left open the possibility that she was still alive.

Suddenly agitated, he began to pace the floor. "I know what he wants," he said. "I know what I have to give him—"

"You can't be serious," said Polowski. "That's our evidence! You can't just hand it over—"

"That's exactly what I'm going to do."

"You don't even know how to contact him!"

"He'll contact *me*." He spun around and looked at Milo. "He must've been watching your house all this time. Waiting for one of us to turn up. That's where he'll call."

"If he calls," said Polowski.

"He will." Victor touched his jacket pocket, where the two vials from Viratek still rested. "I have what he wants. He has what I want. I think we're both ready to make a trade."

THE SUN, GLARING and relentless, was shining in her eyes. She tried to escape it, tried to close her lids tighter, to stop those rays from piercing through to her brain, but the light followed her.

"Wake up. *Wake up!*"

Icy water slapped her face. Cathy gasped awake, coughing, rivulets of water trickling from her hair. She struggled to make out the face hovering above her. At first all she saw was a dark oval against the blinding circle of light. Then the man moved away and she saw eyes like black agate, a slash of a mouth. A scream formed in her throat, to be instantly frozen by the cold barrel of a gun against her cheek.

"Not a sound," he said. "Got that?"

In silent terror she nodded.

"Good." The gun slid away from her cheek and was tucked under his jacket. "Sit up."

She obeyed. Instantly the room began to spin. She sat clutching her aching head, the fear temporarily overshadowed by waves of pain and nausea. The spell lasted for only a few moments. Then, as the nausea faded, she became aware of a second man in the room, a large, broad-shouldered man she'd never before seen. He sat off in a corner, saying nothing, but watching her every move. The room itself was small and windowless. She couldn't tell if it was day or night. The only furniture was a chair, a card table and the cot she was sitting on. The floor was a bare slab of concrete. *We're in a basement,* she thought. She heard no other sounds, either outside or in the building. Were they still in Palo Alto? Or were they a hundred miles away?

The man in the chair crossed his arms and smiled. Under different circumstances, she might have considered that smile a charming one. Now it struck her as frighteningly inhuman. "She seems awake enough," he said. "Why don't you proceed, Mr. Savitch?"

The man called Savitch loomed over her. "Where is he?"

"Who?" she said.

Her answer was met by a ringing slap to her cheek. She sprawled backwards on the cot.

"Try again," he said, dragging her back up to a sitting position. "Where is Victor Holland?"

"I don't know."

"You were with him."

"We—we split up."

"Why?"

She touched her mouth. The sight of blood on her fingers shocked her temporarily into silence.

"Why?"

"He—" She bowed her head. Softly she said, "He didn't want me around."

Savitch let out a snort. "Got tired of you pretty quick, did he?"

"Yes," she whispered. "I guess he did."

"I don't know why."

She shuddered as the man ran his finger down her cheek, her throat. He stopped at the top button of her blouse. *No,* she thought. *Not that.*

To her relief, the man in the chair suddenly cut in. "This is getting us nowhere."

Savitch turned to the other man. "You have another suggestion, Mr. Tyrone?"

"Yes. Let's try using her in a different way." Fearfully Cathy watched as Tyrone moved to the card table and opened a satchel. "Since we can't go to him," he said, "we'll have Holland come to us." He turned and smiled at her. "With your help, of course."

She stared at the cellular telephone he was holding. "I told you. I don't know where he is."

"I'm sure one of his friends will track him down."

"He's not stupid. He wouldn't come for me—"

"You're right. He's not stupid." Tyrone began to punch in a phone number. "But he's a man of conscience. And that's a flaw that's every bit as fatal." He paused, then said into the telephone, "Hello? Mr. Milo Lum? I want you to pass this message to Victor Holland for me. Tell him I have something of his. Something that won't be around much longer..."

"IT'S HIM!" HISSED Milo. "He wants to make a deal."

Victor shot to his feet. "Let me talk to him—"

"Wait!" Polowski grabbed his arm. "We have to take this slow. Think about what we're—"

Victor pulled his arm free and snatched the receiver from Milo. "This is Holland," he barked into the phone. "Where is she?"

The voice on the other end paused, a silence designed to emphasize just who held the upper hand. "She's with me. She's alive."

"How do I know that?"

"You'll have to take my word for it."

"Word, hell! I want proof!"

Again there was a silence. Then, through the crackle of the line, came another voice, so tremulous, so afraid, it almost broke his heart. "Victor, it's me."

"Cathy?" He almost shouted with relief. "Cathy, are you all right?"

"I'm…fine."

"Where are you?"

"I don't know—I think—" She stopped. The silence was agonizing. "I can't be sure."

"He hasn't hurt you?"

A pause. "No."

She's not telling me the truth, he thought. *He's done something to her…*

"Cathy, I promise. You'll be all right. I swear to you I'll—"

"Let's talk business." The man was back on the line.

Victor gripped the receiver in fury. "If you hurt her, if you just touch her, I swear I'll—"

"You're hardly in a position to bargain."

Victor felt a hand grasp his arm. He turned and met Polowski's gaze. *Keep your head* was the message he saw.

Go along with him. Make a bargain. It's the only way to buy time.

Nodding, Victor fought to regain control. When he spoke again, his voice was calm. "Okay. You want the vials, they're yours."

"Not good enough."

"Then I'll throw myself into the bargain. A trade. Is that acceptable?"

"Acceptable. You and the vials in exchange for her life."

An anguished cry of *"No!"* pierced the dialogue. It was Cathy, somewhere in the background, shouting, "Don't, Victor! They're going to—"

Through the receiver, Victor heard the thud of a blow, followed by soft moans of pain. All his control shattered. He was screaming now, cursing, begging, anything to make the man stop hurting her. The words ran together, making no sense. He couldn't see straight, couldn't think straight.

Again, Polowski took his arm, gave it a shake. Victor, breathing hard, stared at him through a gaze blurred by tears. Polowski's eyes advised: *Make the deal. Go on.*

Victor swallowed and closed his eyes. *Give me strength,* he thought. He managed to ask, "When do we make the exchange?"

"Tonight. At 2:00 a.m."

"Where?"

"East Palo Alto. The old Saracen Theater."

"But it's closed. It's been closed for—"

"It'll be open. Just you, Holland. I spot anyone else and the first bullet has her name on it. Clear?"

"I want a guarantee! I want to know she'll be—"

He was answered by silence. And then, seconds later, he heard a dial tone.

Slowly he hung up.

"Well? What's the deal?" demanded Polowski.

"At 2:00 a.m. Saracen Theater."

"Half an hour. That barely gives us time to set up a—"

"I'm going alone."

Milo and Polowski stared at him. "Like hell," said Polowski.

Victor grabbed his jacket from out of the closet. He gave the pocket a quick pat; the cigarette case was right where he'd left it. He turned and reached for the door.

"But Gersh!" said Milo. "He's gonna kill you!"

Victor paused in the doorway. "Probably," he said softly. "But it's Cathy's only chance. And it's a chance I have to take."

"HE WON'T COME," said Cathy.

"Shut up," Matt Tyrone snapped and shoved her forward.

As they moved down the glass-strewn alley behind the Saracen Theater, Cathy frantically searched her mind for some way to sabotage this fatal meeting. It *would* be fatal, not just for Victor, but for her, as well. The two men now escorting her through the darkness had no intention of letting her live. The best she could hope for was that Victor would survive. She had to do what she could to better his chances.

"He's already got his evidence," she said. "You think he'd give that up just for me?"

Tyrone glanced at Savitch. "What if she's right?"

"Holland's coming," said Savitch. "I know how he thinks. He's not going to leave the little woman behind." Savitch gave Cathy's cheek a deceptively gentle caress. "Not when he knows exactly what we'll do to her."

Cathy flinched away, repelled by his touch. *What if he really doesn't come?* she thought. *What if he does the sensible thing and leaves me to die?*

She wouldn't blame him.

Tyrone gave her a push up the steps and into the building. "Inside. Move."

"I can't see," she protested, feeling her way along a pitch-black passage. She stumbled over boxes, brushed past what felt like heavy drapes. "It's too dark—"

"Then let there be light," said a new voice.

The lights suddenly sprang on, so bright she was temporarily blinded. She raised her hand to shield her eyes. Through the glare she could make out a third man, looming before her. Beyond him, the floor seemed to drop away into a vast blackness.

They were standing on a theater stage. It was obvious no performer had trod these boards in years. Ragged curtains hung like cobwebs from the rafters. Panels of an old set, the ivy-hung battlements of a medieval castle, still leaned at a crazy tilt against the back wall, framed by a pair of mops.

Tyrone said, "Any problems, Dafoe?"

"None," said the new man. "I've reconned the building. One door at the front, one backstage. The emergency side doors are padlocked. If we block both exits, he's trapped."

"I see the FBI deserves its fine reputation."

Dafoe grinned and dipped his head. "I knew the Cowboy would want the very best."

"Okay, Ms. Weaver." Tyrone shoved Cathy forward, toward a chair placed directly under the spotlight. "Let's put you right where he can see you. Center stage."

It was Savitch who tied her to the chair. He knew exactly what he was doing. She had no hope of working her hands free from such tight, professional knots.

He stepped back, satisfied with his job. "She's not going anywhere," he said. Then, as an afterthought, he ripped off a strip of cloth tape and slapped it over her mouth. "So we don't have any surprises," he said.

Tyrone glanced at his watch. "Zero minus fifteen. Positions, gentlemen."

The three men slipped away into the shadows, leaving Cathy alone on the empty stage. The spotlight beating down on her face was hot as the midday sun. Already she could feel beads of sweat forming on her forehead. Though she couldn't see them, by their voices she could guess the positions of the three men. Tyrone was close by. Savitch was at the back of the theater, near the building's front entrance. And the man named Dafoe had stationed himself somewhere above, in one of the box seats. Three different lines of fire. No route of escape.

Victor, don't be a fool, she thought. *Stay away...*

And if he doesn't come? She couldn't bear to consider that possibility, either, for it meant he was abandoning her. It meant he didn't care enough even to make the effort to save her.

She closed her eyes against the spotlight, against the tears. *I love you. I could take anything, even this, if I only knew you loved me.*

Her hands were numb from the ropes. She tried to wriggle the bonds looser, but only succeeded in rubbing her wrists raw. She fought to remain calm, but with every minute that passed, her heart seemed to pound harder. A drop of sweat trickled down her temple.

Somewhere in the shadows ahead, a door squealed open and closed. Footsteps approached, their pace slow and deliberate. She strained to see against the spotlight's glare, but could make out only the hint of shadow moving through shadow.

The stage floorboards creaked behind her as Tyrone strolled out from the wings. "Stop right where you are, Mr. Holland," he said.

Chapter Thirteen

Another spotlight suddenly sprang on, catching Victor in its glare. He stood halfway up the aisle, a lone figure trapped in a circle of brilliance.

You came for me! she thought. *I knew, somehow I knew, that you would....*

If only she could shout to him, warn him about the other two men. But the tape had been applied so tightly that the only sound she could produce was a whimper.

"Let her go," said Victor.

"You have something we want first."

"I said, *let her go!*"

"You're hardly in a position to bargain." Tyrone strolled out of the wings, onto the stage. Cathy flinched as the icy barrel of a gun pressed against her temple. "Let's see it, Holland," said Tyrone.

"Untie her first."

"I could shoot you both and be done with it."

"Is this what it's come to?" yelled Victor. "Federal dollars for the murder of civilians?"

"It's all a matter of cost and benefit. A few civilians may have to die now. But if this country goes to war, think of all the millions of Americans who'll be saved!"

"I'm thinking of the Americans you've already killed."

"Necessary deaths. But you don't understand that.

You've never seen a fellow soldier die, have you, Holland? You don't know what a helpless feeling it is, to watch good boys from good American towns get cut to pieces. With this weapon, they won't have to. It'll be the enemy dying, not us."

"Who gave you the authority?"

"I gave myself the authority."

"And who the hell are *you?*"

"A patriot, Mr. Holland! I do the jobs no one else in the Administration'll touch. Someone says, 'Too bad our weapons don't have a higher kill ratio.' That's my cue to get one developed. They don't even have to ask me. They can claim total ignorance."

"So you're the fall guy."

Tyrone shrugged. "It's part of being a good soldier. The willingness to fall on one's sword. But I'm not ready to do that yet."

Cathy tensed as Tyrone clicked back the gun hammer. The barrel was still poised against her skull.

"As you can see," said Tyrone, "the cards aren't exactly stacked in her favor."

"On the other hand," Victor said calmly, "how do you know I've brought the vials? What if they're stashed somewhere, a publicity time bomb ticking away? Kill her now and you'll never find out."

Deadlock. Tyrone lowered the pistol. He and Victor faced each other for a moment. Then Tyrone reached into his pocket, and Cathy heard the click of a switchblade. "This round goes to you, Holland," he said as he cut the bindings. The sudden rush of circulation back into Cathy's hands was almost painful. Tyrone ripped the tape off her mouth and yanked her out of the chair. "She's all yours!"

Cathy scrambled off the stage. On unsteady legs, she moved up the aisle, toward the circle of the spotlight, toward Victor. He pulled her into his arms. Only by the thud of his racing heart did she know how close he was to panic.

"Your turn, Holland," called Tyrone.

"Go," Victor whispered to her. "Get out of here."

"Victor, he has two other men—"

"Let's have it!" yelled Tyrone.

Victor hesitated. Then he reached into his jacket and pulled out a cigarette case. "They'll be watching me," he whispered. "You move for the door. Go on. *Do it.*"

She stood paralyzed by indecision. She couldn't leave him to die. And she knew the other two gunmen were somewhere in the darkness, watching their every move.

"She stays where she is!" said Tyrone. "Come on, Holland. The vials!"

Victor took a step further, then another.

"No further!" commanded Tyrone.

Victor halted. "You want it, don't you?"

"Put it down on the floor."

Slowly Victor set the cigarette case down by his feet.

"Now slide it to me."

Victor gave the case a shove. It skimmed down the aisle and came to a rest in the orchestra pit.

Tyrone dropped from the stage.

Victor began to back away. Taking Cathy's hand, he edged her slowly up the aisle, toward the exit.

As if on cue, the click of pistol hammers being snapped back echoed through the theater. Reflexively, Victor spun around, trying to sight the other gunmen. It was impossible to see anything clearly against the glare of the spotlight.

"You're not leaving yet," said Tyrone, reaching down for the case. Gingerly he removed the lid. In silence he stared at the contents.

This is it, thought Cathy. *He has no reason to keep us alive, now that he has what he wants....*

Tyrone's head shot up. "Double cross," he said. Then, in a roar, *"Double cross! Kill them!"*

His voice was still reverberating through the far reaches of the theater when, all at once, the lights went out. Blackness fell, so impenetrable that Cathy had to reach out to get her bearings.

That's when Victor pulled her sideways, down a row of theater seats.

"Stop them!" screamed Tyrone in the darkness.

Gunfire seemed to erupt from everywhere at once. As Cathy and Victor scurried on hands and knees along the floor, they could hear bullets thudding into the velvet-backed seats. The gunfire quickly became random, a blind spraying of the theater.

"Hold your fire!" yelled Tyrone. "Listen for them!"

The gunfire stopped. Cathy and Victor froze in the darkness, afraid to give away their position. Except for the pounding of her own pulse, Cathy heard absolute silence. *We're trapped. We make a single move and they'll know where we are.*

Scarcely daring to breathe, she reached back and pulled off her shoe. With a mighty heave, she threw it blindly across the theater. The clatter of the shoe's landing instantly drew a new round of gunfire. In the din of ricocheting bullets, Victor and Cathy scurried along the remainder of the row and emerged in the side aisle.

Again, the gunfire stopped.

"No way out, Holland!" yelled Tyrone. "Both doors are covered! It's just a matter of time...."

Somewhere above, in a theater balcony, a light suddenly flickered on. It was Dafoe, holding aloft a cigarette lighter. As the flame leapt brightly, casting its terrible light against the shadows, Victor shoved Cathy to the floor behind a seat.

"I know they're here!" shouted Tyrone. "See 'em, Dafoe?"

As Dafoe moved the flame, the shadows shifted, revealing new forms, new secrets. "I'll spot 'em any second. Wait. I think I see—"

Dafoe suddenly jerked sideways as a shot rang out. The flame's light danced crazily on his face as he wobbled for a moment on the edge of the balcony. He reached out for the railing, but the rotten wood gave way under his weight. He pitched forward, his body tumbling into a row of seats.

"Dafoe!" screamed Tyrone. "Who the hell—"

A tongue of flame suddenly slithered up from the floor. Dafoe's lighter had set fire to the drapes! The flames spread quickly, dancing their way along the heavy velvet fabric, toward the rafters. As the first flames touched wood, the fire whooshed into a roar.

By the light of the inferno, all was revealed: Victor and Cathy, cowering in the aisle. Savitch, standing near the entrance, semiautomatic at the ready. And onstage, Tyrone, his expression demonic in the fire's glow.

"They're yours, Savitch!" ordered Tyrone.

Savitch aimed. This time there was no place for them to hide, no shadows to scurry off to. Cathy felt Victor's arm encircle her in a last protective embrace.

The gun's explosion made them both flinch. Another shot; still she felt no pain. She glanced at Victor. He was staring at her, as though unable to believe they were both alive.

They looked up to see Savitch, his shirt stained in a spreading abstract of blood, drop to his knees.

"Now's your chance!" yelled a voice. *"Move, Holland!"*

They whirled around to see a familiar figure silhouetted against the flames. Somehow, Sam Polowski had magically appeared from behind the drapes. Now he pivoted, pistol clutched in both hands, and aimed at Tyrone.

He never got a chance to squeeze off the shot.

Tyrone fired first. The bullet knocked Polowski backward and sent him sprawling against the smoldering velvet seats.

"Get out of here!" barked Victor, giving Cathy a push toward the exit. "I'm going back for him—"

"Victor, you can't!"

But he was on his way. Through the swirling smoke she could see him moving at a half crouch between rows of seats. *He needs help. And time's running out....*

Already the air was so hot it seemed to sear its way into her throat. Coughing, she dropped to the floor and took in a few breaths of relatively smoke-free air. She still had time to escape. All she had to do was crawl up the aisle and out the theater door. Every instinct told her to flee now, while she had the chance.

Instead, she turned from the exit and followed Victor into the maelstrom.

She could just make out his figure, scrambling before a solid wall of fire. She raised her arm to shield her face against the heat. Squinting into the smoke, she crawled forward, moving ever closer to the flames. "Victor!" she screamed.

She was answered only by the fire's roar, and by a sound even more ominous: the creak of wood. She glanced up. To her horror she saw that the rafters were sagging and on the verge of collapse.

Panicked, she scurried blindly forward, toward where she'd last spotted Victor. He was no longer visible. In his place was a whirlwind of smoke and flame. Had he already escaped? Was she alone, trapped in this blazing tinderbox?

Something slapped against her cheek. She stared, at first uncomprehending, at the human hand dangling before her face. Slowly she followed it up, along the bloodied arm, to the lifeless eyes of Dafoe. Her cry of terror seemed to funnel into the fiery cyclone.

"Cathy?"

She turned at the sound of Victor's shout. That's when she saw him, crouching in the aisle just a few feet away. He had Polowski under the arms and was struggling to drag him toward the exit. But the heat and smoke had taken its toll; he was on the verge of collapse.

"The roof's about to fall!" she screamed.

"Get out!"

"Not without you!" She scrambled forward and grabbed Polowski's feet. Together they hauled their burden up the aisle, across carpet that was already alight with sparks. Step by step they neared the top of the aisle. Only a few yards to go!

"I've got him," gasped Victor. "Go—open the door—"

She rose to a half crouch and turned.

Matt Tyrone stood before her.

"Victor!" she sobbed.

Victor, his face a mask of soot and sweat, turned to meet Tyrone's gaze. Neither man said a word. They both knew the game had been played out. Now the time had come to finish it.

Tyrone raised his gun.

Just as he did, they heard the loud crack of splintering wood. Tyrone glanced up as one of the rafters sagged, spilling a shower of burning tinder.

That brief distraction was all the time Cathy needed. In an act of sheer desperation she lunged at Tyrone's legs, knocking him backward. The gun flew from his grasp and slid off beneath a row of seats.

At once Tyrone was back on his feet. He aimed a savage kick at her. The blow hit her in the ribs, an impact so agonizing she hadn't the breath to cry out. She simply sprawled in the aisle, stunned and utterly helpless to ward off any other blows.

Through the darkness gathering before her eyes, she saw two figures struggling. Victor and Tyrone. Framed against a sea of fire, they grappled for each other's throats. Tyrone threw a punch; Victor staggered back a few paces. Tyrone charged him like a bull. At the last instant Victor side-stepped him and Tyrone met only empty air. He stumbled and sprawled forward, onto the smoldering carpet. Enraged, he rose to his knees, ready to charge again.

The crack of collapsing timber made him glance sky-ward.

He was still staring up in astonishment as the beam crashed down on his head.

Cathy tried to cry out Victor's name but no sound escaped. The smoke had left her throat too parched and swollen. She struggled to her knees. Polowski was lying beside her, groaning. Flames were everywhere, shooting up from the floor, clambering up the last untouched drapes.

Then she saw him, stumbling toward her through that vision of hellfire. He grabbed her arm and shoved her toward the exit.

Somehow, they managed to tumble out the door, dragging Polowski behind them. Coughing, choking, they pulled him across the street to the far sidewalk. There they collapsed.

The night sky suddenly lit up as an explosion ripped through the theater. The roof collapsed, sending up a whoosh of flames so brilliant they seemed to reach to the very heavens. Victor threw his body over Cathy's as the windows in the building above shattered, raining splinters onto the sidewalk.

For a moment there was only the sound of the flames,

crackling across the street. Then, somewhere in the distance, a siren wailed.

Polowski stirred and groaned.

"Sam!" Victor turned his attention to the wounded man. "How you doing, buddy?"

"Got...got one helluva stitch in my side...."

"You'll be fine." Victor flashed him a tense grin. "Listen! Hear those sirens? Help's on the way."

"Yeah." Polowski, eyes narrowed in pain, stared up at the flame-washed sky.

"Thanks, Sam," said Victor softly.

"Had to. You...too damn stupid to listen..."

"We got her back, didn't we?"

Polowski's gaze shifted to Cathy. "We—we did okay."

Victor rubbed a hand across his smudged and weary face. "But we're back to square one. I've lost the evidence—"

"Milo..."

"It's all in there." Victor stared across at the flames now engulfing the old theater.

"Milo has it," whispered Sam.

"What?"

"You weren't looking. Gave it to Milo."

Victor sat back in bewilderment. "You mean you *took* them? You took the vials?"

Polowski nodded.

"You—you stupid son of a—"

"Victor!" said Cathy.

"He stole my bargaining chip!"

"He saved our lives!"

Victor stared down at Polowski.

Polowski returned a pained grin. "Dame's got a head on her shoulders," he murmured. "Listen to her."

The sirens, which had risen to a scream, suddenly cut off. Men's shouts at once sliced through the hiss and roar of the flames. A burly fireman loped over from the truck and knelt beside Polowski.

"What've we got here?"

"Gunshot wound," said Victor. "And a wise-ass patient."

The fireman nodded. "No problem, sir. We can handle both."

By the time they'd loaded Polowski into an ambulance, the Saracen Theater had been reduced to little more than a dying bonfire. Victor and Cathy watched the taillights of the ambulance vanish, heard the fading wail of the siren, the hiss of water on the flames.

He turned to her. Without a word he pulled her into his arms and held her long and hard, two silent figures framed against a sea of smoldering flames and chaos. They were both so weary neither knew which was holding the other up. Yet even through her exhaustion, Cathy felt the magic of that moment. It was eerily beautiful, that last sputtering glow, the reflections dancing off the nearby buildings. Beautiful and frightening and final.

"You came for me," she murmured. "Oh, Victor, I was so afraid you wouldn't...."

"Cathy, you knew I would!"

"I *didn't* know. You had your evidence. You could have left me—"

"No, I couldn't." He buried a kiss in her singed hair. "Thank God I wasn't already on that plane. They'd have had you, and I'd have been two thousand miles away."

Footsteps crunched toward them across the glass-littered pavement. "Excuse me," a voice said. "Are you Victor Holland?"

They turned to see a man in a rumpled parka, a camera slung over his shoulder, watching them.

"Who are you?" asked Victor.

The man held out his hand. "Jay Wallace. *San Francisco*

Chronicle. Sam Polowski called me, said there'd be some fireworks in case I wanted to check it out." He gazed at the last remains of the Saracen Theater and shook his head. "Looks like I got here a little too late."

"Wait. *Sam* called you? When?"

"Maybe two hours ago. If he wasn't my ex-brother-in-law, I'd a hung up on him. For days he's been dropping hints he had a story to spill. Never followed through, not once. I almost didn't come tonight. You know, it's a helluva long drive down here from the city."

"He told you about me?"

"He said you had a story to tell."

"Don't we all?"

"Some stories are better than others." The reporter glanced around, searching. "So where is Sam, anyway? Or didn't the Bozo show up?"

"That Bozo," said Victor, his voice tight with anger, "is a goddamn hero. Stick *that* in your article."

More footsteps approached. This time it was two police officers. Cathy felt Victor's muscles go taut as he turned to face them.

The senior officer spoke. "We've just been informed that a gunshot victim was taken to the ER. And that you were found on the scene."

Victor nodded. His look of tension suddenly gave way to one of overwhelming exhaustion. And resignation. He said, quietly, "I was present. And if you search that building, you'll find three more bodies."

"Three?" The two cops glanced at each other.

"Musta been some fireworks," muttered the reporter.

The senior officer said, "Maybe you'd better give us your name, sir."

"My name…" Victor looked at Cathy. She read the message in those weary eyes: *We've reached the end. I have to tell them. Now they'll take me away from you, and God knows when we'll see each other again....*

She felt his hand tighten around hers. She held on, knowing with every second that passed that he would soon be wrenched from her grasp.

His gaze still focused on her face, he said, "My name is Victor Holland."

"Holland... Victor Holland?" said the officer. "Isn't that..."

And still Victor was looking at her. Until they'd clapped on the handcuffs, until he'd been pulled away, toward a waiting squad car, his gaze was locked on her.

She was left anchorless, shivering among the dying embers.

"Ma'am, you'll have to come with us."

She looked up, dazed, at the policeman. "What?"

"Hey, she doesn't have to!" cut in Jay Wallace. "You haven't charged her with anything!"

"Shut up, Wallace."

"I've had the court beat. I know her rights!"

Quietly Cathy said, "It doesn't matter. I'll come with you, officer."

"Wait!" said Wallace. "I wanna talk to you first! I got just a few questions—"

"She can talk to you later," snapped the policeman, taking Cathy by the arm. "*After* she talks to us."

The policemen were polite, even kind. Perhaps it was her docile acceptance of the situation, perhaps they could sense she was operating on her last meager reserves of strength. She answered all their questions. She let them examine the rope burns on her wrists. She told them about Ollie and Sarah and the other Catherine Weavers. And the whole time, as she sat in that room in the Palo Alto police station, she kept hoping she'd catch a glimpse of Victor. She knew he had to be close by. Were they, at that very moment, asking him these same questions?

At dawn, they released her.

Jay Wallace was waiting outside near the front steps. "I have to talk to you," he said as she walked out.

"Please. Not now. I'm tired...."

"Just a few questions."

"I can't. I need to—to—" She stopped. And there, standing on that cold and empty street, she burst into tears. "I don't know what to do," she sobbed. "I don't know how to help him. How to reach him."

"You mean Holland? They've already taken him to San Francisco."

"What?" She raised her startled gaze to Wallace.

"An hour ago. The big boys from the Justice Department came down as an escort. I hear tell they're flying him straight to Washington. First-class treatment all the way."

She shook her head in bewilderment. "Then he's all right—he's not under arrest—"

"Hell, lady," said Wallace, laughing. "The man is now a genuine hero."

A hero. But she didn't care what they called him, as long as he was safe.

She took a deep breath of bitingly chill air. "Do you have a car, Mr. Wallace?" she asked.

"It's parked right around the corner."

"Then you can give me a ride."

"Where to?"

"To..." She paused, wondering where to go, where Victor would look for her. Of course. Milo's. "To a friend's house," she said. "I want to be there when Victor calls."

Wallace pointed the way to the car. "I hope it's a long drive," he said. "I got a lot of gaps to fill in before this story goes to press."

VICTOR DIDN'T CALL.

For four days she sat waiting near the phone, expecting to hear his voice. For four days, Milo and his mother brought her tea and cookies, smiles and sympathy. On the fifth day, when she still hadn't heard from him, those terrible doubts began to haunt her. She remembered that day by the lake bed, when he'd tried to send her away with Ollie. She thought of all the words he could have said, but never had. True, he'd come back for her. He'd knowingly walked straight into a trap at the Saracen Theater. But wouldn't he have done that for any of his friends? That was the kind of man he was. She'd saved his life once. He remembered his debts, and he paid them back. It had to do with honor.

It might have nothing to do with love.

She stopped waiting by the phone. She returned to her flat in San Francisco, cleaned up the glass, had the windows replaced, the walls replastered. She took long walks and paid frequent visits to Ollie and Polowski in the hospital. Anything to stay away from that silent telephone.

She got a call from Jack. "We're shooting next week," he whined. "And the monster's in terrible shape. All this humidity! Its face keeps melting into green goo. Get down here and do something about it, will you?"

She told him she'd think about it.

A week later she decided. Work was what she needed. Green goo and cranky actors—it was better than waiting for a call that would never come.

She reserved a one-way flight from San José to Puerto Vallarta. Then she packed, throwing in her entire wardrobe. A long stay, that's what she planned, a long vacation.

But before she left, she would drive down to Palo Alto. She had promised to pay Sam Polowski one last visit.

Chapter Fourteen

(AP) Washington.

Administration spokesman Richard Jungkuntz repeated today that neither the President nor any of his staff had any knowledge of biological weapons research being conducted at Viratek Industries in California. Viratek's Project Cerberus, which involved development of genetically altered viruses, was clearly in violation of international law. Recent evidence, gathered by reporter Jay Wallace of the *San Francisco Chronicle,* has revealed that the project received funds directly authorized by the late Matthew Tyrone, a senior aide to the Secretary of Defense.

In today's Justice Department hearings, delayed four hours because of heavy snowstorms, Viratek president Archibald Black testified for the first time, promising to reveal, to the best of his knowledge, the direct links between the Administration and Project Cerberus. Yesterday's testimony, by former Viratek employee Dr. Victor Holland, has already outlined a disturbing tale of deception, cover-ups and possibly murder.

The Attorney General's office continues to resist demands by Congressman Leo D. Fanelli that a special prosecutor be appointed...

Cathy put down the newspaper and smiled across the hospital solarium at her three friends. "Well, guys. Aren't you lucky to be here in sunny California and not freezing your you-know-what's off in Washington."

"Are you kidding?" groused Polowski. "I'd give anything to be in on those hearings right now. Instead of hooked up to all these—these *doohickeys*." He gave his intravenous line a tug, clanging a bottle against the pole.

"Patience, Sam," said Milo. "You'll get to Washington."

"Ha! Holland's already told 'em the good stuff. By the time they get around to hearing my testimony, it'll be back-page news."

"I don't think so," said Cathy. "I think it'll be front-page news for a long time to come." She turned and looked out the window at the sunshine glistening on the grass. *A long time to come.* That's how long it would be before she'd see Victor again. If ever. Three weeks had already passed since she'd last laid eyes on him. Via Jay Wallace in Washington, she'd heard that it was like a shark-feeding whenever Victor appeared in public, mobs of reporters and federal attorneys and Justice Department officials. No one could get near him.

Not even me, she thought.

It had been a comfort, having these three new friends to talk to. Ollie had bounced back quickly and was discharged—or kicked out, as Milo put it—a mere eight days after being shot. Polowski had had a rougher time of it. Post-operative infections, plus a bad case of smoke inhalation, had prolonged his stay to the point that every day was another trial of frustration for him. He wanted out. He wanted back on the beat.

He wanted a real, honest-to-God cheeseburger and a cigarette.

One more week, the doctors said.

At least there's an end to his waiting in sight, Cathy thought. *I don't know when I'll see or hear from Victor again.*

The silence was to be expected, Polowski had told her. Sequestration of witnesses. Protective custody. The Justice Department wanted an airtight case, and for that it would keep its star witness incommunicado. For the rest of them, depositions had been sufficient. Cathy had given her testimony two weeks before. Afterward, they'd told her she was free to leave town any time she wished.

Now she had a plane ticket to Mexico in her purse.

She was through with waiting for telephone calls, through with wondering whether he loved her or missed her. She'd been through this before with Jack, the doubts, the fears, the slow but inevitable realization that something was wrong. She knew enough not to be hurt again, not this way.

At least, out of all this pain, I've discovered three new friends. Ollie and Polowski and Milo, the most unlikely trio on the face of the earth.

"Look, Sam," said Milo, reaching into his backpack. "We brought ya something."

"No more hula-girl boxer shorts, okay? Caught hell from the nurses for that one."

"Naw. It's something for your lungs. To remind you to breathe deep."

"Cigarettes?" Polowski asked hopefully.

Milo grinned and held up his gift. "A kazoo!"

"I really needed one."

"You really do need it," said Ollie, opening up his clarinet case. "Seeing as we brought our instruments today and we weren't about to leave you out of this particular gig."

"You're not serious."

"What better place to perform?" said Milo, giving his piccolo a quick and loving rubdown. "All these sick, depressed patients lying around, in need of a bit of cheering up. Some good music."

"Some peace and quiet!" Polowski turned pleading eyes to Cathy. "They're not serious."

She looked him in the eye and took out her kazoo. "Dead serious."

"Okay, guys," said Ollie. "Hit it!"

Never before had the world heard such a rendering of "California, Here I Come!" And, if the world was lucky, never again. By the time they'd played the last note, nurses and patients had spilled into the solarium to check on the source of that terrible screeching.

"Mr. Polowski!" said the head nurse. "If your visitors can't behave—"

"You'll throw 'em out?" asked Polowski hopefully.

"No need," said Ollie. "We're packing up the pipes. By the way, folks, we're available for private parties, birthdays, cocktail hours. Just get in touch with our business manager—" at this, Milo smiled and waved "—to set up your own special performance."

Polowski groaned, "I want to go back to bed."

"Not yet," said the nurse. "You need the extra stimulation." Then, with a sly wink at Ollie, she turned and whisked out of the room.

"Well," said Cathy. "I think I've done my part to cheer you up. Now it's time I hit the road."

Polowski looked at her in astonishment. "You're leaving me with these lunatics?"

"Have to. I have a plane to catch."

"Where you going?"

"Mexico. Jack called to say they're shooting already. So I thought I'd get on down there and whip up a few monsters."

"What about Victor?"

"What about him?"

"I thought—that is—" Polowski looked at Ollie and Milo. Both men merely shrugged. "He's going to miss you."

"I don't think so." She turned once again to gaze out the window. Below, in the walkway, an old woman sat in a wheelchair, her wan face turned gratefully to the sun. Soon Cathy would be enjoying that very sunshine, somewhere on a Mexican beach.

By their silence, she knew the three men didn't know what to say. After all, Victor was their friend, as well. They couldn't defend or condemn him. Neither could she. She simply loved him, in ways that made her decision to leave all the more right. She'd been in love before, she knew that the very worst thing a woman can sense in a man is indifference.

She didn't want to be around to see it in Victor's eyes.

Gathering up her purse, she said, "Guys, I guess this is it."

Ollie shook his head. "I really wish you'd hang around. He'll be back any day. Besides, you can't break up our great little quartet."

"Sam can take my place on the kazoo."

"No way," said Polowski.

She planted a kiss on his balding head. "Get better. The country needs you."

Polowski sighed. "I'm glad somebody does."

"I'll write you from Mexico!" She slung her purse over her shoulder and turned. One step was all she managed before she halted in astonishment.

Victor was standing in the doorway, a suitcase in hand. He cocked his head. "What's this about Mexico?"

She couldn't answer. She just kept staring at him, thinking how unfair it was that the man she was trying so hard to escape should look so heartbreakingly wonderful.

"You got back just in time," said Ollie. "She's leaving."

"What?" Victor dropped his suitcase and stared at her in dismay. Only then did she notice his wrinkled clothes, the day-old growth of beard shadowing his face. The toe of a sock poked out from a corner of the closed suitcase.

"You can't be leaving," he said.

She cleared her throat. "It was unexpected. Jack needs me."

"Did something happen? Is there some emergency?"

"No, it's just that they're filming and, oh, things are a royal mess on the set...." She glanced at her watch, a gesture designed to speed her escape. "Look, I'll miss my plane. I promise I'll give you a call when I get to—"

"You're not his only makeup artist."

"No, but—"

"He can do the movie without you."

"Yes, but—"

"Do you *want* to leave? Is that it?"

She didn't answer. She could only look at him mutely, the anguish showing plainly in her eyes.

Gently, firmly, he took her hand. "Excuse us, guys," he said to the others. "The lady and I are going for a walk."

Outside, leaves blew across the brown winter lawn. They walked beneath a row of oak trees, through patches of sun and shadow. Suddenly he stopped and pulled her around to face him.

"Tell me now," he said. "What gave you this crazy idea of leaving?"

She looked down. "I didn't think it made much difference to you."

"Wouldn't make a *difference?* Cathy, I was climbing the walls! Thinking of ways to get out of that hotel room and back to you! You have no idea how I worried. I wondered if you were safe—if this whole crazy mess was really over. The lawyers wouldn't let me call out, not until the hearings were finished. I did manage to sneak out and call Milo's house. No one answered."

"We were probably here, visiting Sam."

"And I was going crazy. They had me answering the same damn questions over and over again. And all I could think of was how much I missed you." He shook his head. "First chance I got, I flew the coop. And got snowed in for hours in Chicago. But I made it. I'm here. Just in time, it seems." Gently he took her by the shoulders. "Now. Tell me. Are you still flying off to Jack?"

"I'm not leaving for Jack. I'm leaving for *myself.* Because I know this won't work."

"Cathy, after what we've been through together, we can make *anything* work."

"Not—not this."

Slowly he let his hands drop, but his gaze remained on her face. "That night we made love," he said softly. "That didn't tell you something?"

"But it wasn't *me* you were making love to! You were thinking of Lily—"

"Lily?" He shook his head in bewilderment. "Where does she come in?"

"You loved her so much—"

"And you loved Jack once. Remember?"

"I fell out of love. You never did. No matter how much I try, I'll never measure up to her. I won't be smart enough or kind enough—"

"Cathy, stop."

"I won't be *her.*"

"I don't want you to be her! I want the woman who'll hang off fire escapes with me and—and drag me off the side of the road. I want the woman who saved my life. The woman who calls herself average. The woman who doesn't know just how extraordinary she really is." He took her face in his hands and tilted it up to his. "Yes, Lily was a wonderful woman. She was wise and kind and caring. But she wasn't you. And she and I—we weren't the perfect couple. I used to think it was my fault, that if I were just a better lover—"

"You're a wonderful lover, Victor."

"No. Don't you see, it's *you*. You bring it out in me. All the want and need." He pulled her face close to his and his voice dropped to a whisper. "When you and I made love that night, it was like the very first time for me. No, it was even better. Because I loved you."

"And I loved you," she whispered.

He pulled her into his arms and kissed her, his fingers burrowing deep into her hair. "Cathy, Cathy," he murmured. "We've been so busy trying to stay alive we haven't had time to say all the things we should have…."

His arms suddenly stiffened as a startling round of applause erupted above them. They looked up. Three grinning faces peered down at them from a hospital balcony.

"Hit it, boys!" yelled Ollie.

A clarinet, piccolo and kazoo screeched into concert. The melody was doubtful. Still, Cathy thought she recognized the familiar strains of George Gershwin. "Someone to Watch Over Me."

Victor groaned. "I say we try this again, but with a different band. And no audience."

She laughed. "Mexico?"

"Definitely." He grabbed her hand and pulled her toward a taxi idling at the curb.

"But, Victor!" she protested. "What about our luggage? All my clothes—"

He cut her off with another kiss, one that left her dizzy and breathless and starved for more.

"Forget the luggage," she whispered. "Forget everything. "Let's just go...."

They climbed into the taxi. That's when the band on the hospital balcony abruptly switched to a new melody, one Cathy didn't at first recognize. Then, out of the muddy strains, the kazoo screeched out a solo that, for a few notes, was perfectly in tune. They were playing *Tannhäuser*. Wedding music!

"What the hell's that terrible noise?" asked the taxi driver.

"Music," said Victor, grinning down at Cathy. "The most beautiful music in the world."

She fell into his arms, and he held her there.

The taxi pulled away from the curb. But even as they drove away, even as they left the hospital far behind them, they thought they could hear it in the distance: the sound of Sam Polowski's kazoo, playing one last fading note of farewell.

* * * * *

A ringing phone in the middle of the night...

Trying to stay one heartbeat ahead of a dangerous killer might prove fatal...

Guilty until proven innocent

When you're investigating secrets that people would kill to protect, knowing who to trust can be far from clear cut...

www.mirabooks.co.uk

In a world where trust is a double-edged sword...

...friends become enemies and enemies become killers

'FANS OF *GONE GIRL* WILL EMBRACE THIS' —LISA GARDNER

Mia Dennett can't resist a one-night stand with
the enigmatic stranger she meets in a bar.

But going home with him will turn out to be
the worst mistake of her life.

An addictively suspenseful and tautly written thriller,
The Good Girl reveals how, even in the perfect
family, nothing is as it seems.

HARLEQUIN®MIRA®
www.mirabooks.co.uk

Loved this book?
Let us know!

Find us on **Twitter @Mira_BooksUK**
where you can share your thoughts, stay up
to date on all the news about our upcoming
releases and even be in with the chance of
winning copies of our wonderful books!

Bringing you the best voices in fiction